ANG[...]

Winner of the Black [...]

"Thanks to Haulsey's [...] and beautiful woman [...] leaps off the page, engaging the reader with the tears, anger, love, and laughter of a triumphant spirit."
—*Black Issues Book Review*

"Haulsey's prose is suffused with quiet poetry. . . . This is an extraordinary life rendered in extraordinarily poetic prose. May Edward Chinn's eyes remained on the prize, and the world is better for it."
—*The Washington Post Book World*

"The novel is faithful to the known details of Chinn's life, and the vibrancy of 1920s Harlem shines through in Chinn's fictitious encounters with prominent historical figures of the time, from Zora Neale Hurston and Langston Hughes to Jean Toomer, Fats Waller, and Wallace Thurman. Haulsey's respectful homage to Chinn and her accomplishments will bring overdue attention to this notable figure in African American history."
—*Publishers Weekly*

"Haulsey manages to convey the human dimensions of a young woman struggling with self-doubt, family conflicts, and societal limitations."
—*Booklist*

"[Haulsey's] clean, clear prose works in a similar fashion to the young May Chinn at the piano in her premed days, accompanying the great Paul Robeson in a concert. . . . Thanks to Kuwana Haulsey, we get to hear the powerful music, high notes and low, of this extraordinary life."
—Alan Cheuse, NPR's All Things Considered

"Kuwana Haulsey magically recreates Chinn's world."
—*Port of Harlem*

"There's more than a whiff of talent in *Angel of Harlem*, which confirms the promise Haulsey showed in her debut novel. A richly dramatized take on a profoundly accomplished life, *Angel* ultimately supplies the very thing that [Langston] Hughes's poem describes: a triumphant song for a genius child."
—*The Crisis*

"A lyrical, intoxicating, and timeless novel."
—MEL WATKINS, author of *Dancing with Strangers: A Memoir*
and *On the Real Side: A History of African American Humor*

"With keen vision, careful research, and nuanced sensibility, Kuwana Haulsey captures in this novel the triumphant spirit and amazing accomplishments of Dr. May Chinn. . . . Haulsey's characters faithfully evoke the era's immense promise and stark contradictions."
—A'LELIA BUNDLES, author of
On Her Own Ground: The Life and Times of Madam C. J. Walker

"Kuwana Haulsey is an awe-inspiring artist with a rare willingness to high-dive into the abyss, not troubled by such mere trifles as where she'll land. This beautiful, expressive novel displays her unique gift for delving straight to the heart of the human condition. With *Angel of Harlem*, Haulsey has once again managed to take my breath away."
—NICK CHILES, author of *Love Don't Live Here Anymore*

Praise for

THE RED MOON

2002 Hurston/Wright Award Finalist for Debut Fiction
2001 Washington Post Book World Rave

"This is a novel that should be read by everyone who wants insight into modern Africa and the women who mother and daughter it."
—NIKKI GIOVANNI

"Writing in a stark but delicate style that seems to mimic the terrain, Haulsey unsparingly depicts the miseries of East African tribal life: routine domestic violence, alcoholism and disease, as well as the complications of polygamy and ritual circumcision. . . . This unflinching tale marks Haulsey as a promising young writer." —*Publishers Weekly*

"Haulsey deftly plays tangled personal and cultural differences against one another [in her] smoothly written, engrossing novel."
— *The Washington Post Book World*

"*The Red Moon* is an impressive first novel [that is] moving, shocking, and unforgettable."
— *Essence*

"Haulsey very effectively handles the colliding themes of tradition and modernity in the lives of a Kenyan family . . . [she] does an excellent job of mapping the intricacies of a shifting world and a people striving to manipulate what they know and what is to come."
— *Mosaic*

"Chronicling the yearning of a brave woman and depicting a nation searching for a truthful and lasting spiritual independence, Haulsey produces *The Red Moon* with vitality."
— *Sunday Oklahoman*

"This vivid, first novel portrays the 'Dark Continent's' kaleidoscopic nature, its subtle cultural patterns and dynamic history. [It's] varied narratives reveal the many facets of African experience."
— *The Seattle Times*

"A touching coming-of-age story . . . written in a tone both lyrical and sweeping . . . [Haulsey] is a gifted and promising writer."
— New Orleans *Data News Weekly*

"*The Red Moon* is a lyrical account, awash in lush language."
— *Home News Tribune*

"Kuwana Haulsey crafts an emotive coming-of-age story. . . . [She] will encourage readers to rethink notions of African identity and understand the challenges that individuals, particularly young women, face in creating a sense of themselves."
— *Black Issues Book Review*

ALSO BY KUWANA HAULSEY

The Red Moon

ANGEL OF HARLEM

A Novel

ONE WORLD • BALLANTINE BOOKS • NEW YORK

ANGEL OF HARLEM

Kuwana Haulsey

Angel of Harlem is a work of fiction. All incidents and dialogue, and all characters with the exception of some well-known historical and public figures, are products of the author's imagination and are not to be construed as real. Where real-life historical or public figures appear, the situations, incidents, and dialogues concerning those persons are entirely fictional and are not intended to depict actual events or to change the entirely fictional nature of the work. In all other respects, any resemblance to persons living or dead is entirely coincidental.

2006 One World Books Trade Paperback Edition

Copyright © 2004 by Kuwana Haulsey
Reader's Guide copyright © 2006 by Random House, Inc.
Excerpt of *The Red Moon* copyright © 2001 by Kuwana Haulsey

Published in the United States by One World Books, an imprint of The Random House Publishing Group, a division of Random House, Inc., New York.

ONE WORLD is a registered trademark and the One World colophon is a trademark of Random House, Inc.

Originally published in hardcover in the United States by Striver's Row/One World Books, an imprint of The Random House Publishing Group, a division of Random House, Inc., in 2004.

Owing to limitations of space, permissions acknowledgments can be found on p. 355, which constitutes an extension of this copyright page.

Library of Congress Cataloging-in-Publication Data

Haulsey, Kuwana.
    Angel of Harlem : a novel / by Kuwana Haulsey.
    p.   cm.
    ISBN 0-375-76133-0
    1. Chinn, May Edward, 1896—Fiction.   2. African American women physicians—Fiction.   3. Harlem (New York, N.Y.)—Fiction.   4. Women physicians—Fiction.   I. Title.
PS3558.A7576A54 2004
813'.6—dc22
                             2004049284

Printed in the United States of America

www.oneworldbooks.net

2   4   6   8   9   7   5   3   1

Text design by Casandra J. Pappa

For my mother, Janis Dansby,
whose love makes all things possible.

Wait a minute.

I have too much love flowing through my life to confine it to just one dedication page. So . . .

For Michael Harris—my light, my truth, my East Coast best friend.

and

For Michael Bernard Beckwith—my teacher, my muse, my West Coast best friend.

I thank God for you both.

PART ONE

Chapter 1

I t took seventy-three years for my father to die.

He held on, cloaked beneath a broad quilt of memories, peering out his window onto the wide basin of winter below. Memory had creased his face with fresh gullies and markers that ran east, toward the river. When memory escaped him, he searched it out, skating his eyes along the sagging white rooftops outside until he found what he was looking for. Papa refused to wade into the drifts of his understanding, though, to get thick into it like he could have, deep enough to allow for release.

So stubborn, that old man. Just tiring.

And I am nothing but his daughter.

My papa managed to make it all the way to the outskirts of spring in 1936. February and March had been humbling throughout the city, but especially in Harlem. Gutters hardened into icy spillboxes. Streets drained of color and smell, except the heavy, spoiled odor of snow.

Months before, when it still sparkled, I'd plunged into the snow stacks with the neighborhood children, flinging it at little pecan-colored boys with wild hair and hatless heads. They'd scatter and re-form, creeping up like bright-eyed kittens, wiggling and ready to pounce. The children all wore patched sackcloth coats; some had mufflers, some had gloves, but none had both. If I'd taken off their shoes, I'd have found soles tattooed with newspaper ink and tiny, ashy toes wrinkled from adventure.

I adored those children, had birthed two or three, the ones who called me Mama May instead of Dr. May or Ma'am.

On those late afternoons, when the sun deepened and lay like sheaves of wheat or, sometimes, like thick cream over the covered roads, those babies reminded me of truth. They taught me that play created gulfs of unintended joy, then unmasked circumstance—not as an adversary, but a coconspirator in the game. I needed with all my heart to remember the wisdom born inside innocence, to see myself in their eyes and maybe find worth in that unspoiled vision.

So I squealed like a young girl when they yelled, "*Git her!*" and stuffed snowballs down my cotton shirtwaist. I pretended to run so they could foil my escape, sneaking more snow into the pockets of my covert-cloth coat, the first good, new brown coat I'd had in three years. It didn't matter. I giggled anyway, licking snow off my rose-colored palms before the flakes could melt, while they were still glassy and protruding and round.

But by March, things had changed.

The streets were blackened by spitting trucks and feet and mules and human waste in areas where sewer pipes routinely bal-looned with cold and then burst. Weals of mud sprouted through the ice and concrete, snaking along the roads all the way out to the river, which itself was hoary and stiff, poised with frost.

By March, the children had long since trudged home. Now the streets stayed empty unless some kind of work refused to wait. So, things being the way they were, no one came to stand watch at my father's feet. No old-time friend whispered cures or condolences into my mother's ear. No nieces or cousins dropped by, donating heaping pans of simmered greens and crisp fried rabbit as a love offering.

Not even his lost daughters returned to see him off. I'd written Irene the month before and she'd written back, *"Can't quite make it. Much to do here. But I'll pass the word. Tell the old man I said good luck."*

Such carelessness offended Papa in a way that death never could have.

His intention had been to make it back home to Chinn Ridge in Virginia, where all parts of his death would be warm and dusty with road songs, and sweet. He had memories secreted away there, stashed in the swollen, ocher hills like treasure. He had people in those hills too. Most of them were years dead, but some still lingered, telling stories only he could rightly remember and pass judgment on. True or false was his alone to say. My papa yearned to be with people who allowed him his place. In the end, though, he was too weak to make the trip.

Despite his sincere efforts to wait out the last whispers of winter and escape, my papa died cold. He died shivering like the wind in his bed, while my mother, who was the sun, stood by his pillow playing "Pennies from Heaven" over and over again on the phonograph to warm him. She used burned rum and music on his fever chills because the Depression was so unyielding that year that we hadn't any extra blankets. Without thinking, I'd given them all away to my patients, every last one. I hadn't been a good enough daughter to save even one warm, gray blanket on which my father could die.

My selfishness and lack of forethought embarrassed me. To make up for it, I waited on him, trying to get him things he didn't need—an out-of-season apricot, a bit of soft, sky-blue calico, pinecones to rub against his whiskers and his round, red cheeks and then toss onto the coal in the stove. Then the house would smell of woods, like when he was a boy. He smiled and let me do these things because he loved me more than I'd thought I loved him. All I knew for sure was that I let him down. I'd been distracted by my work, by my own thoughts, hunkered down and birthing other things. I hadn't stayed aware.

Each time my mother passed his bed, Papa mouthed her name . . . *Lulu*. His gaze followed her, sucking up what he could— her black eyes, her butternut skin, her silence.

His spirit lingered around just to be near her, long past his physical endurance. Papa's flesh was bloated by then, fat and ripe with decay. But still he stayed. After a while my mother began to fear, not for the comfort of his body, but for the direction of his soul. Finally, late one evening, she sat on the edge of his bed and took his hand. Leaning in to kiss his eyelids, she whispered, "It's all right, William. Go 'head now. Go on."

She released him.

Just like that, after all that waiting, he went.

No more words passed between them, just a look of simple wonder that crossed my father's face as he let go, a look of gratitude that said he hadn't known dying could be so easy.

My mother didn't speak again until we'd laid Papa out in the church. Hair parted, tie straightened, she smoothed him over, readied him for all the hardness of the earth. Even then, the only thing she managed to say was "When shadows fly, they cover the stones below. Remember, May."

Then the Negro seeped out of her face, and she became a Chickahominy again, so silent that I lost track of her breath, so ancient and wide that her presence suddenly felt as inescapable, as untouchable, as the dusky, violet sky. When she was a black woman, my mother railed and sang and cut her eyes. As a Chickahominy, she was free. Lulu became a Chickahominy every time she got mad at my father. So when she stood at the foot of his coffin with her arms akimbo and got free, that's how I knew for sure that she missed him, too.

After a while I asked, "What did you mean by that, Mama?"

It's not so much that I needed to know, but the incredible length of her solitude was too much for me. I wanted to put it away for her, to roll it up like a bolt of cloth over my arms. I wanted to hear its dusty "clap" as it turned and turned, hitting the floor at my feet. But I couldn't. The space that she held was too vast, too dense, much more like the rolling of river water than some dry piece of cloth.

Standing next to my mother felt like wading through the sand at the bottom of a stream. Her solitude rose, filling the ripening red of the carpet, the velvety creases in the drapes, even the gray lapels of Papa's suit. The undercurrent of her grief ruffled the waves in his hair. She sighed so soft and, for once, I knew that her memories of my father had nothing whatsoever to do with me.

"I s'ppose," she replied slowly, "I just meant that you can't untie the past from its present, that's all." She reached behind her, stretched vigorously, and sighed again. "Well, at least his love was good, and it lasted. You can't ask for much more."

I disagreed, but didn't bother to say so. Didn't have to—she already knew what I was thinking. She always knew. She'd spent the past forty years knowing.

Just to prove the point, Mama coughed politely into the back of her hand, raised the long, woolen hem of her mourning dress and limped toward the back door. As she swung the door open, I felt a breeze shift through the funeral parlor. It roused the heavy curtains and antique lace draped over the mahogany tables in the corner, twisting through the worn pews—a breeze with enough April floating through it to catch butterflies. Despite the cold, my father had managed to produce an unseasonably beautiful afternoon for his burial. I had to smile.

"I'ma check on that carriage right quick. Be back shortly, Ladybug."

The carriage was already out back, waiting to take us out of Harlem and up to Woodlawn Cemetery in the Bronx. We both knew that. This was just her way of giving me some privacy to do my grieving.

I stared down at my father William and touched his smooth, firm, pale skin. My heart refused to see the blotted veins congealed in whirlpools around his nose and across his cheeks. In my mind, I stared into his shining hazel eyes, and I took some time to love the way they danced.

It was his eyes. That's what did it. When I finally stopped pretending and looked down at his eyes. The sunken lids, rutted with veins, so fragile looking, like paper, like if I pressed even slightly, my finger would go straight through. It dawned on me then that my father would never get to see me again. It was over. He was gone.

For a moment, I thought I'd died. Blackness snatched me up— no light, no sound, no breath, no skin. No heartbeat, no pain. Through the absence of everything, one thought rose up, not from within me, but from somewhere off to the side, a child's toy floating by in the ocean: *This is wonderful.*

Grief erupted inside my body. It exploded in a sickening physical blow that crumpled me like I'd been kicked in the chest, harder than Papa had ever had the courage to hit. The pain left me doubled over, my nails digging into the grooves on the side of the coffin, unsteady and shaking with regret. I wanted to cry out for my mother, but I didn't. I couldn't. Instead, I opened myself to the sorrow. I let it come in and shower me, wash me clean.

My father had been a slave, his father a master. Which master, he never knew, but a master nonetheless. The question of it, the uncertainty, had dogged him his entire life. He'd always believed his father to be his Master Benjamin but Grammy Susan refused to tell him one way or the other when he was a child. The question of his lineage had been roundly considered to be grown-folks' business and, therefore, none of his concern.

"Shoo, little fly, don't bother me," she'd sing, and sweep him away with her broom or dust him out the door with a crisp cotton rag.

"But, ma'am . . ."

"Boy, I *know* you ain't tryin' to work my nerves with this foolishness. Not today. Now get on outside *and stay out grown-folks' business.*"

That was always the end of it. By the time he grew old enough to know, he'd been alone and on his own for many years, Grammy Susan long since gone. To this day, I believe that my father's confusion over the matter was the real reason he himself never learned to master without controlling, to control without descending into tyranny, or to recognize the wisdom in releasing that which had never belonged to him in the first place.

Proud and brilliant as he was, white people often mistook William Chinn as white. Other Negroes, however, never made that mistake. His carriage and the fierceness of his dignity gave him away as one of them, even though his skin color did not. Still, no matter how he tried, he'd never been able to find any forgiveness for his old life, nor a suitable, painless place in the present. Unmet expectation had chained him to his past because the past was the only thing he had to blame.

As a child, of course, I hadn't understood these things. I didn't know what his feelings were or how to name them. But when I felt the sadness come down on him, thick and clinging to his feet like mud, I'd crawl behind my mother's ancient potbellied stove and cry.

As an adult, I tried my best to ignore his moods, just as he'd sworn to ignore me for the rest of his life after learning I intended to disgrace him by going to college. When Mama told him I'd decided to continue on to medical school, he'd fled the house and hadn't returned for more than three months. When he finally did slink on home, he'd begged my mother to stop my foolishness. If it was all right for a Colored woman to become a doctor, he reasoned, then why hadn't they heard of anyone here in the city who'd done it before? Because it wasn't for anyone else to do, she'd explained. The job had been waiting on me.

Papa disavowed me. Again. In spite of the fact that we lived in the same house, he refused to utter a single word to me. He would rage about me to my mother, to the neighbors across the air shaft or off into the sky, ranting that *a cackling rooster and a crowing hen don't never come to no good end!* In fact, he claimed, there were two things he flat out didn't believe in: God and doctors. Somehow, he'd managed to get hooked up with a daughter who thought she was both. Mama would continue to sew velvet or wash the kettle or dust the piano. I'd read my anatomy books in silence. Eventually, he'd skulk out the door with nothing but the price of a bottle in his pocket.

For nearly a decade, I was a ghost to my father. Then one night about eight years before, he nearly died. In the midst of that first false death, he slipped and said the word, the one word that made everything else in my life begin to make sense.

I STAGGERED HOME during the time of morning so early that you can smell the sunrise long before you see it. The soft, grassy scent of dawn edged up over the river as I crossed the trolley tracks on Lenox Avenue and turned onto 138th Street. As impossible as it seemed, it was only a two-block walk to my flat from Harlem General Hospital, where I interned. My calves clenched and unclenched in spasms, like a heartbeat, and I stumbled over the curb, nearly falling into the corner lamppost. Under my breath I murmured a song, something to distract myself from the fire in my back that came from hefting and heaving a grown man's weight.

Epiphany! Light of lights that shineth ere the world began. Draw thou near, and lighten the heart of every man.

Railroad ties and twisted nails had shredded my long white skirt and then the skin on my knees beneath. My face was blackened and slick with grease. But I had such a wide, free feeling bubbling through me, something even stronger than the tiredness, so strong that I had to sing it out.

I'd saved someone that night. And though I could barely move, though no one else would ever know, there was joy dancing through my fingers and toes. I knew. That was enough.

Moonlight shivered through the branches of the maple trees. It slid, mirrorlike, across the windows of the fifty-year-old brownstones and tenements that lined both sides of our street. I was the only person up and about, but I knew that in another twenty or thirty minutes, the street would flex and stretch and come alive for the day. Throngs of people would swarm onto the avenue, crowded together almost shoulder to shoulder, in a teeming brown-and-black wave. I smiled, knowing that I would be warm and lazy in my sleep well before then.

Walking with my eyes half-closed, I retraced my steps from memory, stepping high in front of 165 to avoid the oak roots that raised a hump in the sidewalk, to the left around the Wilsons' trash barrel in front of 167. I never even saw the heap sprawled at the bottom of our stoop until I fell over him. In midthought, my feet flew out from underneath me and I landed hard on the concrete

step. The shadow on the ground cringed a little, trying to shield his
head with one of his hands. He moaned. When I heard the raspy
breath, I knew. I didn't have to turn him over or call his name. I
just knew. Shame cut across my body, cool and smooth and bright
as the morning moon.

Papa lay on the ground, curled up on his side, smelling old and
sharp, funky with cheap liquor. He'd vomited on himself. I could
smell that too. The odor of it wafted onto me, bitterness nestled in
my own breath.

Look, Papa,

*"Look," I whisper, "look at the horse." The horse bolts from the stable, just
past us on the lawn. Its gray muzzle is streaked with long handles of spit and
foam. The other men dive for cover while the little blond girl on the saddle
struggles not to fly off, screaming, crying, pulling the horse's mane instead of
taking the reins.*

*Papa leaps from our blanket and, as the horse comes round again, he tack-
les it by the neck and scissors his way onto its back. The horse whinnies and
bucks and the girl begins to tumble. But before she can fall under the hooves,
Papa's arm snaps out and catches her. A jubilant cry goes up from the crowd.
He holds her by the silk of her little blue dress until he's talked the horse still.*

*Instantly, a huge crowd appears around him, white men helping them
down, clapping his back, white women weeping at the heroism, the daring of it
all. He's sweating and shaking, so beautiful that I fall out against my mother
and begin to cry too. I stretch out my arms but he can't find me. The crowd is
too thick, too radiant with his goodness for him to notice me. I'm three years old,
so small I can't be seen.*

*"Come on, fellow, let's us go inside and buy you some drinks. Lord God!
Did you see what he did?"*

*Papa stops. Papa stares. He cannot go inside. The 126th Street Riding
Club refuses Colored. That is why we picnic, each weekend, on the grass outside. The men don't understand this. They look at his face, at his bright eyes*

and the strands of hair plastered to his forehead with sweat, and they want to embrace him.

"*Oh, what is it, fellow? Your family out here somewhere? Well, bring them too!*"

"*Yes, please,*" says the little blond girl's father. "*Please, I must tell your wife what you did. You are a hero, sir. You saved—*" He can't go on. He breaks down in tears. The women surround him and applaud softly.

"*Where are your people, man? Let's go inside and celebrate!*"

Slowly my father turns to face Mother and me, still sitting on our shabby cotton blanket. He does not look at us directly, but over our heads. He's wilted. Papa's sad now, and I don't know why.

Though we are the only two sitting on this part of the lawn, the men still don't understand. There is good-natured, confused silence for a moment. Then one of the men's faces goes blank. Like when I erase anthills in the sandy dirt with my hand. One minute there is life, the next minute everything is smooth. It makes you think maybe nothing was ever there at all.

"*He's Colored.*" The man grimaces. "*He's a nigger.*"

"*What?*" "*Yeah. Look.*" "*No.*" "*Yeah. Look, dammit, look.*" "*Lord God. He is, isn't he? Hey, boy, look at me. Hey. I'm talking to you. Yeah, look at him. I bet he is.*" "*Jesus, that nigger had his hands all over your daughter.*"

The crowd is unraveling, some moving away from Papa, some approaching slowly, with rigid steps. They're deciding something. Before they can conclude, Papa breaks away, strides over to us and sweeps us up. I hear voices, louder and louder. But I don't understand. I confuse anger with gratitude, joy with splintering rage. Mama's clutching me too tight, squeezing me. Papa's got our blanket, our liverwurst sandwiches dashed into the basket, his fiddle jammed down in the basket too, getting nasty with meat and jelly. We're flying, flying. We're gone. We'll picnic somewhere else from now on.

Look at you, Papa.

For a moment I watched him struggling to raise his head. Then I stood and turned to continue on up the stairs without him.

But I couldn't move. Tears gathered at the back of my throat and sprouted up in my chest, bursting open like seeds. My father's dignity was a sham. He was nothing but a filthy heap in a doorway.

But if he's nothing, how can I be more?

I looked again and saw that his jacket was open. He'd worn his green wool vest, but no scarf. He never remembered his scarf. Without thinking, I reached for him, ready to cover that soft place at the hollow of his throat with my hands. But then I stopped and glanced around quick. The idea of touching him scared me to where I couldn't think, couldn't see straight. What if I put my hands on him and he didn't move?

She's so smart she's stupid. Always walkin' crooked to go straight. Lulu, can't you see?

My father had so many cutting ways about him, so many awkward, tilting truths. He used his silence as a blade for so long that my heart became clear water and my purpose, a whetstone—edgeless, heavy, but unbreaking.

This is what he wanted. So let the old man lie in the bed he made.

Literally.

I turned again to walk away. But I didn't know where to go. Surely not upstairs to my mother, who, at that moment, was probably scowling over her coffee because the two of us were still out of doors, somewhere on the street. It seemed better just to sit down in the dark and disappear. That made much more sense. I'd relax myself, ease and sink into nothingness. Like him. Struggle accomplished nothing.

All I'd ever wanted was for him to recognize me, for him to stand up as tall as I stood and hold my face and say *yes*! And then nothing else would matter.

I turned back, knelt beside him and shook him.

"Papa? Papa get up. Come on."

When he didn't respond, I checked his wrist. His pulse gently fluttered under the pressure of my thumb and his breath came in short, shallow gasps. I pulled down his lower lids. His eyes were bloody with broken vessels, rolled up into his head.

Grabbing one arm, I hauled him to his knees. Then I wrapped his arm around my shoulder and stood slowly, leveraging myself against his dangling weight as it threatened to drag me back down. Step by step, we climbed the stoop, pushed through the heavy door and started on our way up to the fifth floor. Each time we rounded the corner on a landing, my legs cramped, refusing to go any farther. It didn't matter. We climbed beyond my legs, past the thoughts in my mind and the burning in my chest. If I stopped, I'd just lie where I was until someone found us and called out "Ho!" to my mother, but by then it would be too late.

"Papa? Can you hear me? Come on, stay with me, Papa. Talk to me."

My father's eyes flickered open and his head bobbed as he tried to turn toward the sound of my voice.

"That's it, Papa! Do you know where you are? Tell me who I am, Papa. Can you do that? Who am I?"

"*Fanny?*"

My body slumped forward and we collapsed in a heap on the landing in front of our apartment. Papa's body landed on top of me. He reeked of pot liquor and ashes and I pushed him off because I couldn't breathe with him so close. My hair hung in my face, dragging on the floor as I crawled to the door, calling for my mother.

Then the door opened and Lulu was there and suddenly we were inside. She carted Papa to his bedroom and plopped me on the sofa in the sitting room. Flying out the door, she yelled over her shoulder something about getting another doctor, someone other than me, because we both knew that's what my father would insist on if he could talk.

It seemed as though the door had just closed when it opened again and I heard Dr. Jackson's high voice and long stride move past me toward the bedroom. Then he was back, out into the hall, banging on doors, calling the men on the floor to help him carry Papa downstairs. Rolling him up in a plaid blanket, they rushed my father across the street to Harlem General. When I moved to follow, Mama said, "No. You stay here," and snapped the door shut behind them.

An hour or so later, she was back. Alone.

"Dr. Crump took him into surgery. Said his appendix ruptured."

She eased herself down at the foot of the sofa.

"You better go see about him. Say what you need to say, even if you don't get to say it to his face."

"It's like that?"

"They wasn't sure. Could be. Dr. Crump said if he makes it through surgery, that'd be a good sign. Come on, Sweetness, sit up. You OK. Let me rub you with some oil and put a little gauze over those cuts on your legs. Then you can go on over. Don't stay too long though. You need to sleep."

"Who's Fanny?"

Mama looked at me so blankly that anyone else would have thought her ignorant.

"You need to wash your face," she said. "Let me help you. You got work again tonight."

I didn't answer, so she said, "You know, when my father used to do things that were bad or that I didn't understand and I asked about it, my grandfather would say: 'Truth tells vivid tales that linger in the mouth of time and can never be unspoken, can never be hushed.' Maybe it loses a little somethin' in translation, but that's the gist. Point is, I knew not to ask again."

"Who is she?"

Mama huffed at me and cut her eyes. "What part of 'mind your business' got you confused?"

"Mama—"

"Those are things for him to talk, not me."

"What if he can't?"

"Look, May, let's let it rest until tonight or maybe morning. We'll talk if you get home early enough in the morning. How's that sound?"

She asked it as a question, so it was mine to answer as though I were rolling around some choices and making a decision. But in reality, the subject was closed. So I said, "Sounds fine," to save face, and let her run out the door.

The sun had risen. She was late.

Chapter 2

Emmaline Miller was sixteen and grimy with crusted-over sweat. She heaved her body out of bed, scratching her back against the leaning bureau in the corner, like a cat. When that brought no relief, the girl howled in frustration and tried to ram her spine against the edge of the bureau. I lunged just in time to wedge my hand in between. The back of my hand caught the pointed edge of the wood, right on the bone, and instantly flared white with pain.

"Me can' do it," she sobbed.

"Yes, you can, Emmy. You're already doing it."

I whispered to her, low and steady, my hands clasping her head so she had no choice but to look into my eyes. Her schoolgirl braids unraveled and wilted against my fingers, contracting with her sweat. She had blood in her hair, massaged into her scalp like dots of oil. It was the bright and streaky rouge flaking from her cheeks.

Emmy cried out again, long and loud. She cried until the door crept open and a brown, frightened face appeared in the crack. I held up a hand, the bruised one, and the door shut quickly, with a quiet click.

"Shh, shh, shh, little one. It'll be over soon. I promise."

Crouched over, curling the mountain of her body into my body, she sniffled and hiccuped. I sang to her, inventing songs without words because words would be jarring and intrusive, and wiped strings of snot that dangled from her lip like a baby's. I held her like my father used to hold me when I was a little girl, safe from knowing.

"Promise?" she asked.

"I do."

Emmy cupped both of my hands in hers and laid them at the base of her belly.

"Take it out now," she whispered.

"Not yet," I told her. "But soon."

We walked over to the narrow bed in the middle of the room and I pressed her down onto the wet, flattened mattress. She didn't resist me, didn't have the energy, but the tears came fresh as her body rubbed against the rough blanket draped across the bed. It was raw wool, itchy and crude, and it hurt her. Everything hurt her just then.

"When you're scared," I said, "it hurts more. Don't be afraid. There's nothing to be afraid of. This is only part of you reaching out to yourself. Remember? Breathe, baby. You feel it? This is how you contribute to God."

I impressed myself with how much I sounded like my mother. I didn't necessarily understand it all, but so what. It worked. My young daughter's eyes softened and stilled. She took my hand and pressed it to her heart.

Emmaline's thin cotton dress had once been a cheerful robin's-egg blue. She'd soiled it, overwhelmed the fabric in blood. Useless.

I lifted it over her head, dropped it on the floor, and wrapped a clean blanket over her shoulders. I'd brought the blanket from home, especially for her, soft and fresh smelling. She immediately took the edge between her puffy, oval lips and began to chew. For some reason, this made me laugh. She tried to smile in return, but another pain hit and the smile turned into a wince and then a scream.

So fragile, this child. So delicate. Emmaline didn't belong here, in this room, in all this pain. She belonged in the sun, maybe back in Kingston where she was born, somewhere down by the sea.

I massaged her stomach in almond oil steeped with sage. Up near the top where the ribs converged and vaulted like wings, right in the center under her parted breasts, I touched the crown of another, tiny head.

As I rubbed wide circles across her belly, I thought about a dream I'd had the night before. Early in the evening, just before I woke, I'd dreamt of Emmaline, standing before me, naked and swollen and brown, like sun-baked clay. She smiled and without a trace of accent, said, "You are the mist on the ocean, the smoke rising from the sea. Thank you." Then she vanished.

It was a small dream, which, under other circumstances, might have been insignificant. Maybe I wouldn't even have remembered. But I woke up knowing that she'd be calling me, even though it was five weeks too soon, and I knew that, no matter how it looked, I wouldn't let her or her child die. I didn't know exactly what I'd have to do, but that part didn't matter. It would come to me.

I polished Emmy's skin until it was warm and glowing. Then I put a hot compress over the rise of her stomach and reached down to spread her legs. Dipping my fingers in oil, I slid two of them inside her and pressed against the wall of her vagina. This part, too, I rubbed and stroked, pushing it down, making it wider, more pliable, more supple. She opened like a flower in my hand, dripping with fluid, flushed and engorged.

"It's time, sweetheart. I want you to get on the floor."

Emmaline sat up, with me prodding her from behind, and slid off the bed. Her mother had woven her a birth mat, had seeded within it a pattern of roots and the flush, coral bloom of an island flame tree. Climbing from the trunk was a large-breasted black woman with branches of living hair, wide arms and a spread-open mouth, her chant laced into the thread. Down on her hands and knees, on this rough-knotted mat that her mother had woven, Emmaline started to push.

When the knee came through her opening, Emmy let out a piercing shriek and tried to crawl away. But the pain followed her, stopped her, and left her trembling at the edge of the bed with her forehead pressed against the cool metal of the frame, crying.

When she cried out, the four women outside the door began to moan, softly at first, voices cracking and splitting open as the body split open, and then louder, in time with the body's widening and release. Wordless low and high tones blended to form a gentle river's base and foam, giving the child a safe conduit on which to enter the world.

"Listen to me, Emmy. Are you listening? Don't push again. Not until I tell you to. No matter what. Don't push yet. Do you understand?"

I thought she said yes but I couldn't tell for sure. With one hand underneath cradling her stomach, I took the other hand and pushed the baby's knee back inside. Emmy bucked and screamed as I felt for the baby's foot and popped it out. Then I reached up inside her again, uncrossed the baby's other leg and slid that foot out.

"OK, push, Emmy! Push!"

With her back arched and her head buried in the edge of the

bed, Emmaline expelled her child's legs and pelvis. The voices in the hall soared.

"Good girl! You have a little boy on the way. I'm so proud of you!"

The baby began sliding out and I let him dangle between her legs, brushing against her thighs, as his weight pulled him farther down. Then, caught on his own arms, he stopped.

"Me wan' push. It's comin'."

"Wait! Not yet."

Gently, I lifted his tiny body by the waist and began to rotate it back and forth.

"OK. Now!"

Emmaline pushed as I turned him, working loose first one arm, and then the other.

Grunting, she pushed again and the baby's shoulders slid out. Then the opening closed around his neck with his head still stuck inside. Letting him dangle again, I reached inside with my left hand and tried to find his chin. I couldn't.

Meanwhile, the umbilical cord had stopped pulsating, which meant that it wasn't pumping any more oxygen to his brain. In a minute, the child would suffocate in his own birth canal. I wedged my other hand inside Emmy and pushed down on the top of the baby's head. His chin grazed the tip of my left fingers and I took hold.

"Emmy push!"

"Me can'."

"Yes, baby. You have to push right now. Right now!"

But she was fading out. I couldn't tell if she even heard me.

"Emmaline!"

"Dr. May, me can' do it."

"You have to, please. Just once more. Ready?"

She was hoarse. She couldn't scream anymore so she panted

instead, panted and growled and pushed. As she pushed, I pulled. The women's song peaked at that instant, and then evaporated into silence as the little boy slipped out in a rush of fluid and blood.

He was tiny and gray, covered in birth residue that was slick like mucus. *My God how beautiful!* I thought. How beautifully alive and healthy.

It wasn't until I turned him over to clear his nose and mouth that I saw the caul. A thin web, like clear skin, stretched over his face. I'd heard of this before, had been told what it meant, but I'd never actually seen a child born with one. So then, not only was this boy beautiful and resourceful, but he would be able to see with the closed eye. Gently, I lifted the caul and set it aside, then tied the umbilical cord and cut it at the base.

He took three shallow gulps of air and opened his eyes.

"You did it, Emmy," I whispered.

"Me wan' see 'im." She turned her head toward the sound of her baby's whimpering, and I brought him around closer, so she wouldn't have to move so much. Emmy studied this new child of hers but didn't move to take him in her arms. She just stared, trying, it seemed, to recognize some part of him, or perhaps to figure out where she knew him from.

I had warm water in a basin waiting on a stool by the door. We walked over to the water, this child and I, to bathe. When he was clean, I wrapped him in a blanket and set him down in a basket on the floor. I brought more water over for Emmy, stood her up and sponged her body clean, washing her tenderly, like the child that she'd been, instead of the mother she'd become. Then I slipped a fresh cotton nightgown over her head and turned the mattress over, onto the dry side, so that she and her son could rest. The girl climbed into her bed and, for the first time, reached for her baby.

"What's his name?" I asked as I laid him in the crook of her arm.

"What you tink?"

"Well," I replied slowly. "He looks like a David to me. Or maybe a Michael."

"Michael. That's what Ma'dear said too. Michael for a boy. How 'bout Michael Anthony? What you tink?"

She said the name like An'tny, and it took me a minute to understand what she was saying. When I did, I told her, "Yes, that's a fine name. It's the name of a very strong man."

Emmy's face shone when I said that, and I knew that I'd said the right thing.

The baby was already rooting for her breast. When he couldn't find it through the nightgown, he began to cry for the first time.

"Wha's wrong, man? What a likkle ting like you be makin' that big fuss for?"

She wrapped baby Michael in her arms and surrendered her worn-out child's body over to his searching. They found each other that simply. These two, mother and son, became entrenched in a love that materialized as naturally, as instinctively, as his first breath.

My throat tightened as I watched them together and my mouth filled with a sour taste that I recognized as longing. Longing for the past. Longing to feel the fullness, the weight and the richness of my own scent, like roots and breath embedded in the soil. This is what I needed, but would never have.

Part of me couldn't believe that it still hurt so much, after so many years. A living grief that old struck me as incredible. It didn't seem right. I should be more powerful, able to rebuke and forget a pain so old that it had become brittle. But how? Especially when it could part and slip and drain, like water from an opened hand. The best I could do was distance myself, let the sadness belong to someone else. I gave it to another girl, one much younger than myself, who didn't appear to know better.

I moved toward the tiny window and looked out, down onto the alley behind the building. A zigzag of clotheslines crowded with waistcoats and skirts and linens hung suspended from pegs above the wooden windowsills. White things fluttered in the dark, puffed up by the wind as though they already had people in them. By dawn, the clothes would be taken inside, pressed flat and folded, and the women off to work.

Carefully avoiding Emmy's eyes, I turned my attention back to the room and went to work myself. Although I didn't have to clean up, I wanted to. It was my job to present this special, second-sight child in a proper way. But I also wanted to distract myself from the tightening that had moved down into my chest and settled there.

I pressed the lonely feeling, the sense of separation, way down into my hands, rinsing it out as I scrubbed the floor. The jealousy also got scoured away as I cleaned, sopping up the blood and the afterbirth and the sadness, making sure to get underneath the bed and in the corners. I put the birthing mat and Emmy's old dress in a sack for burning. I saved the caul for tea and further examination.

Emmy was having trouble with Michael. The pain had started as she tried to feed him. It was time to call the other women in; I wanted to reach over and help her, but that was for her mother to do. I opened the door and said, "Come in. He's here."

Ruth Miller and her three sisters sprinted into the room and descended on the child before I could get the door open good.

"Look 'dere," said the oldest sister, Rose. "Look a dat big man 'dere."

They were in love. Michael Anthony, the only man in the house.

" 'Im somethin', ain't dat so?" Miss Ruth said.

"Dat baby look jus' like my Henry before 'im pass, God bless his heart," said Aunt Lucy.

Annie, the youngest, stoutest sister, leaned in and wrinkled up her nose.

"Oh, what is it now, Annie?" Rose snapped. "What you scrunch yo' face up fo' jus so?"

"Somethin' wrong wit dat baby," Annie said.

The other women immediately began cussing her out in patois, most of which I didn't understand. But Annie wouldn't back down.

"Naw," she insisted. " 'Im smell bad—bad I'm tellin' you. But me can' figure out what kinda smell dat is."

"Annie—" Miss Ruth started toward her.

"I'm tellin' you sure, 'im smell." Then Annie's face lit up. "I got it! I know what 'im smell like."

"What?" Aunt Lucy asked.

" 'Im smell like *pussy*!"

All the women shrieked with laughter, fell out against the wall, across the bed, on top of the bureau with laughter, danced a cake-walk and twirled in laughter. This baby was a party. He made the women giddy.

I, however, was scandalized to hear such language from respectable women. My father had never even allowed me to say the word d-a-m-n. If I ever got mad enough to cuss, I had put my hand over my heart and say "Oh, my dear!"

Of course, the redder my face got, the harder they laughed.

"Stop it!" Lucy cried. "Look what you did. You scared our doctor."

"Not so! Lady Doctor's got one jus' like—"

"*No!*" the other women hollered, tears streaming from their eyes.

Then Aunt Rose came to my defense. Sort of.

"Good lady doctors don' speak such tings," she informed them. "Isn't it so, Dr. May? An' anyway, Miss Landry down at the hair shop on Lenox say Dr. May ain' never had no man no way, so she be extra ticklish 'bout such tings."

At that, the women gasped and threw up their hands. Then they started talking, one over the other, so fast that I could barely keep up.

"No man! How you live wit' no man, girl?" (Aunt Lucy)

"Is not so." (Aunt Annie)

"Can' be so." (Miss Ruth)

"Not at your age, dearie." (Aunt Rose)

"She look so young." (Miss Ruth)

"Like a baby." (Aunt Lucy)

"She ain' dat young." (That big-mouth Annie)

Then Aunt Lucy said, "Tell the truth, girl. What man you got?" and the room fell instantly silent.

After a moment's pause, Annie sucked her teeth. "She ain' gwan answer."

"That's what *she* tink," said Aunt Lucy.

There was nothing else I could do under the circumstances—I took the coward's way out and held up the caul.

The women clapped their hands over their mouths (*silent at last*) and backed up all the way to the wall.

"You'll want to keep this," I told them. "He came out that way, with it over his face."

"Yes, Dr. May," Miss Ruth said softly. She reached out to take it from me, but stopped short and drew back her hand. She seemed afraid of the thing.

I felt like a heel. I'd sucked all the happiness right out of the room, just like that. Births were supposed to be joyous. Now these women looked solemn and overawed. Miss Ruth stood there staring at the caul, wringing her hands in front of her like she didn't want to touch it. I walked over to the bureau, set it down and wrapped it in a soft piece of cloth lying next to my medical bag.

"Ma'dear, 'is name is Michael Anthony."

Gentle, fully exposed, the hope in Emmy's voice stopped us all. Miss Ruth turned her attention back to her child and grandchild. The women seemed to see him all over again, with brand-new eyes. Then the baby yawned and stretched, letting his sheer perfectness break the tension.

"Look at dat lazy likkle ting," Aunt Rose cooed.

"Yes, ma'am. I ain' give 'im a bit a work to do yet an' already 'im feignin' sleep," said Miss Ruth.

Once again, there was laughter in the room.

IT WAS WELL AFTER four in the morning before I turned onto Lenox Avenue, headed back toward the hospital. I had no watch, but I could feel the time drop off just the same. So used to the night, I knew how the silence of 2:45 AM differed from the silence of 3:30 AM. There's a distinct smell, a new taste in the air as the stars start to shift and settle. It's a hard thing to explain, but the later the night gets, the freer it becomes. And then by dawn, there are hardly any constraints on it at all.

I passed Rudy's Recovery Room Bar & Grill across from the hospital and thought about peeking in. The place should have been closed hours before, but quite often old Rudy and his cronies, which sometimes included Papa, would stick around, shouting each other down until the sun came up.

What would the low men and late-night drinkers think if they saw me stroll on in for a taste? *Scandal!* Word would be syndicated all across Central Harlem before lunch. The low men would become pious and indignant in the telling; the late-nighters would only be able to shake their heads, *umm-umm-umm.*

"Dr. May? Lil' Bit May from round the corner? In Rudy's? Naw, man. You lyin'."

"If I'm lyin' I'm flyin'. I know what I seen. She come on up in there, crack a dawn, just as bold as brass. I do believe she had a little somethin'-somethin' beforehand, too."

The thought made me laugh, quick and devilish, wicked laughter. When I laughed like that, I could breathe. Standing at the curb, tapping my toes, I let a mule-drawn cart meander by first, essentially out of courtesy since it was the only other moving thing on the street.

The main entrance of the hospital stood directly in front of me on the other side of the avenue. On the third floor, in the north-west wing, my father lay in bed, recuperating. He'd survived the surgery and, though no one was quite sure, they hoped he'd make it through the night.

Just as I was about to cross the street and head in, I stopped. It dawned on me that I didn't want to be there, possibly to see my father die. I couldn't do it. If his dying had to happen, then it was going to happen without me leaning over him, faking equanimity. We had too many things unresolved between us. It wasn't in me to shoulder that kind of lie for the rest of my life.

I felt the wind kick up and brush by my face—a good-smelling wind, sweet and delicious. Thankful for the distraction, I followed it away from the hospital, around the corner and back across 137th Street toward Eighth.

Sometimes Harlem would just do that, you understand. It would open up and reveal itself in a rigorous display of scents, various and commanding, floating its sounds around and above you, where they swirled generously, like autumn colors. In a while, you couldn't tell what was what, really, or where the sensations came from.

Most people don't realize, but it's in that nebulous place of mixed senses that songs are born, first laid out as stories in two-four time. Eventually, the stories become truths, strewn into more complex patterns, held as rhythm because rhythm cannot be lost. It is indestructible and it is ours, boldly immortal and free.

There were eighth notes on the downslope of Sugar Hill, and because they called to me, smiling, I forgot about the hospital and followed them. It was the only thing to do—answer and follow.

I needed to get away from the feeling of being caged inside my body, of being subject to so many other people's demands. I needed to think, and it was hard for me to do that inside the hospital. By then, everyone surely knew that Dr. Crump had offered to pay for Papa's surgery and recovery bed. The others would be incensed and hostile, wanting to know why. In a hospital that served more than 200,000 people with only 273 beds, what made William Chinn so deserving? There would be loud grumbling and angry talk about "special treatment." Reprisals.

Too many people already watched me all the time, although they pretended not to. Even worse, they fully expected me to pretend that I was unaware of their pretending. That kind of theater had quickly become burdensome and trying. It was the real reason I convinced my advisor to let me go out on ambulance duty.

Over the last few years only a select handful of women (every one of them white) had completed the internship program. None were allowed to do ambulance duty. All the men were required to do it, but Harlem was too dangerous, too sullen and unpredictable to chance a woman's safety. It made no sense to the other doctors why I'd kept insisting and badgering. But they didn't have to tolerate the eyes. They didn't have to un-know all that they knew, yet still remember everything that every one of them had been asked to learn simply to satisfy those eyes.

Most of them wanted me out, doctors and interns alike, but I had nowhere else to go. Where else was I needed except at this place, with my patients? They were anchors, strategically placed to ground me, pinions holding me down to my life. Otherwise, I could float away at any time, become a new and perhaps unrecognizable thing. Then what would I do?

I rounded the corner and crossed the street, where the sidewalk still smelled of peppered oil and pork even though Pig Foot Mary wouldn't be back, serving gossip, buttered yams, and entrails out of her pushcart, until at least ten in the morning. Then back uptown, no turned around and farther downtown, past the brownstones with their falling-down brick face, past the red-and-tan tenements that boiled and stank in the summer, no matter how much the women cleaned. Past the unpainted, ramshackle houses that breathed hard in the winter, stretching and cracking their bones and their windows, so that the heat couldn't stay in and the cold wouldn't stay out.

This was where I lived, where it felt like I'd always lived.

I wondered if baby Michael was asleep yet, and if Emmy had remembered to put a warm compress over her breasts, like I'd told her. I needed to go back and check on her in the next day or so, just to know that she was all right. I'd go before I went on duty for the evening. The other women were still up, I was sure, toasting new life. Mama wasn't awake yet, but she would be soon, though, in just a few more minutes. Then she and I would be up and thinking about each other at the same time, which made me feel much better.

Thinking of Mama, I realized I needed to sign out for the night. We still had to talk.

Part of me resisted the idea of conversation, the sudden urgency that lit up inside me. I shouldn't need other people's answers just to feel right inside my own skin. On the other hand, I was tired of feeling alone, like I'd taken many things, many people, inside my heart, as part of me, though they seemed to feel no need to return the favor.

What if he really does die?

The thought came on its own, whispering into my ear on the right side, the side closest to the cobblestone street. What if he died with nothing solved between us? How much harder would it be then?

I turned back toward Harlem. Almost angry at my sudden urge to rush, I hustled down the empty, quiet street just the same, just short of running.

I could still make it.

I SWUNG THE DOOR open just as Mama sat down at the kitchen table in the living room. She blew waves into her coffee, letting the steam rise through her plaited hair, where it tilted for a second, like a snappy little hat, before evaporating. A second cup of coffee sat across from her, waiting.

I slipped in quietly but forgot to lock the door—again. Mama reminded me with her lowered eyes. She was right, of course. I'd been followed home and robbed twice already, once at gunpoint, for the codeine powder and morphine pills in my bag. Somehow, though, such things didn't set with me. After locking the door, I walked over to the table and scooted my chair as close to her as I could without crowding.

"Mornin', Sweetness." She smiled like she hadn't expected me. "You home early."

"Mornin'."

"How's your father?"

"Same. His condition hasn't changed since this evening."

"How was work?"

"Good," I said. "Miller baby came early."

"But you knew that already. Baby all right?"

"Yes, ma'am. He and the mother are fine." I blew on the cinnamon swirls in my coffee and took a sip.

"Praise God."

"He had a caul, too."

"You don't say?" Mama sighed and closed her eyes. Lightly, absently, with her eyes still closed, she grazed her fingertips across my cheek. "You really want to know who Fanny is?"

"Yes, ma'am."

"Why? Why you need to know?"

I shrugged, even though she wasn't looking. "I can't explain it, really. It just feels important."

That was only half-true, but now wasn't the time to discuss it. I wrapped my fingers around the heavy, metal coffee cup so she wouldn't see my hands shaking.

"All right," she said.

It took my mother another good long while to speak again. When she finally opened her black eyes and began to talk, she was already somewhere else.

Chapter 3

Susan kept the name Chinn because her Mama Patty and Papa John kept the name Chinn. All were the property of a man called Gibson, but still, they held on with eyeteeth to the Chinn name, even after long years devoted to the buying and selling of men had made the association confusing.

Papa John steadily insisted the name belonged just as much to them as any white man. So little William and his twin sister Fanny, along with all eight of Susan's other children, their aunts, uncles and cousins, were swaddled with the name Chinn and left to roam the hills and cornfields of the Fleetwood plantation.

Fleetwood sat on some of the finest, darkest soil in Prince William County. Mama Patty and Papa John, their children and their grandchildren worked John Gibson's land like it was their own. They tilled and sowed burgundy fields where the earth smelled so rain-and-honey sweet that the children would get lost in it, wallowing in soil that was soft and delicious like clay, soil that lent itself straightaway to dreaming.

William and Fanny were always the first ones lost. They would be caught, eventually, rustling the cornstalks as they buried peach pits by the roots. That way, in the spring, the corn would burst open with fuzzy white ears and deliriously sweet, dripping flesh. Or they would be discovered slinking through the barn, their cheeks smeared in butter and big with filched biscuits. William would be down on the floor in Fat Sally's stall, his mouth open and Fanny trying to aim one of the cow's udders in his direction. Sometimes, though, they would just disappear.

No one ever chastised the twins too vigorously. Miss Frances, for whom Fanny was named, never raised a hand to them; neither did their mother Susan. Likewise, the black overseers turned a blind eye when it came to the twins. The job of discipline had been left to Mama Patty, but by the twins' tenth summer, Mama Patty had passed on, and Papa John rarely did any more than swat in their general direction.

By and large, it was understood that the twins were left alone because the grown folks felt sorry for Fanny, who was born with a clubfoot. She had such a severe limp that no one ever asked any hard labor from her, just a little ironing, maybe, or some cake baking. Because William never left her side unless forced to, he also learned to bake and sew and iron a collar that knew how to stand at attention. The other children mocked him, called him Wilhelmina and sashayed past the kitchen, swinging their hips. William would shrug and shove another biscuit in his mouth.

The non-Chinn children taunted him, calling out "hey, white boy!" and "look—young massa' Will," because he, like the rest of his straight-haired, hazel-and-blue-eyed siblings, could pass for white. William endured the teasing with shy smiles and silence. But sometimes the other boys went too far, and when that happened, it was Fanny who would blaze up.

"Ya'll big-headed roughnecks bet' not mess with him or you gon' catch it, you hear!"

Then the children would quickly disperse. They knew that, though William would never lift a finger for himself, if anyone even looked sideways at Fanny, he'd fly at them swinging and biting and screaming until two or three grown folks managed to pull him off. He was her protector and she was his heart, these two who understood the specifics of the world with no words attached. When he was hungry, she had bread. When she was thirsty, he brought water all the way from the stream instead of getting it from the brick well out front because Fanny liked her water to be different from one day to the next.

In March, the green walnut pods were budding on the trees, hard as tiny marbles and just right for throwing—the perfect ammunition to worry a lazy cow or a pack of roughneck boys. The air, warm and poised, held the first glimpse of summer.

It was 1862 and war thundered around them. However the children had little thought for it. Nothing about their daily life had changed. But then one evening Master Benjamin Chinn of the Lancaster Chinns came to Fleetwood to talk to John Gibson. William and Fanny knew Benjamin Chinn well, the younger of two Chinn sons. He'd known their mother Susan since she was born because Mama Patty and Papa John had originally belonged to his father, Master John Chinn. There was always much whispering and hand talking when Benjamin Chinn visited Fleetwood. The man had such a light and breezy way of sauntering down to the slave quarters, like he wasn't after anything in particular besides a stroll. But here he was at Fleetwood and this time he talked of nothing but war.

The Federals had landed on the Peninsula, about a hundred miles southeast of Richmond. All men of fighting age were packing their rifles and heading to Richmond to defend the capital.

Manassas had been stripped bare of men and the niggers were on the run, bolting at every opportunity across the woods and swamps toward the Union lines. It was chaos. The Union cry of "booty and beauty!" had sounded and seemed to ring continuously, as eager flames swallowed their precious Southern cities and towns.

He, himself, had had to shoot two of his best niggers at the beginning of last week—on the Lord's Day, no less. What kind of brute takes up and gets himself shot on the Lord's Day? Stupid things. They'd run off sometime Saturday night. He'd tracked them fairly easy, intending to save them, net them and bring them back home. But after his party treed them, one pulled out a pistol and fired. At that point, there was nothing else for him to do. He'd buried them well, though, almost like proper men, before riding home to count his losses. Since then, he'd sent most of his slaves down to Lancaster, where it would be harder for them to escape. What he hadn't figured, though, was that the work would be so rough on him. Could John spare one or two slaves until things settled down? He could sure use an extra hand on the farm. They chose William because everyone knew he'd never run without Fanny, and Fanny couldn't run. William was safe.

Master Benjamin lived with his family out at the Chinn House on Hazel Plain. All throughout the spring, William and Fanny cleaned for his wife, Miss Edmonia, picked corn, peaches and walnuts, and trained Master Benjamin's horses. There was rarely a chore that was assigned to one of them alone; it was always "William and Fanny, I need you to store these potatoes under the house for me," or "William and Fanny, its time to milk those cows 'round back, you know." Sometimes it was "William and Fanny, how many times do I have to show you how to iron a shirt without leaving cat faces on it? *I swear!*" While it was easier for everyone involved simply to acknowledge the eleven-year-old twins as one person, Master Benjamin sometimes forgot—or chose not—to do this, which usually ended up with William getting a beating. When Benjamin told William to do something that Fanny couldn't do, like run past Warrenton Turnpike to the Cushing farm, drop off a message and be back before dark, William simply wouldn't do it.

"Willie, just go," Fanny would plead. "I'm fine here with Miss Edmonia."

"You think I'ma leave you here and let that white man look at you any which way he please? You a natural fool."

"You got nerve to be callin' somebody else fool when you the one always gettin' beat."

"Whatever you say. I still ain't got to do nothin'."

"You know what? That's why I'm gonna let Raw Head and Bloody Bones get you when you go sleep tonight. I ain't singin' them away no more."

"Gal, please. That's just stories. That's Edmonia tryin' to keep us inside at night so we don't clean the peaches off her precious tree. I don't believe in that old stuff. I was just fakin' so *you* wouldn't be scared. Shoot. I'll throw Raw Head *and* Bloody Bones in a pot for stew. What now?"

And William would turn away and pretend not to hear his sister no matter what she said after that.

By the middle of August, Master Benjamin packed up his family and his slaves and moved into a Confederate encampment. The fighting had moved steadily closer to Manassas and the Federals had taken control of the town. In retaliation for being forced off their land, the Confederate soldiers surrounded all the shops, sheds, warehouses, supply depots and anything else that might have had some value and burned them to the ground before marching south. The Federals would have nothing, *nothing*, to use against the Confederate army when the time came to fight.

And that time was coming. Brave men watched their towns,

their homes, be overrun by ghosts in blue Highlander coats with colt revolvers and sabers dangling at their sides. They stomped their feet and shook their fists and swore that they'd run those godless sons of bitches out of their country just like before. But William overheard Master Benjamin and some other white men whispering about the Indian summer just past and how the rains had brought rivulets of blood bubbling up from the foot of Matthew's Hill. A thousand men lay buried under that soft, dusty soil, buried where they fell in the last battle a year ago. Could the earth hold any more?

William and Fanny heard other rumors, too, hushed, lonely murmurs that Negro men and women were gathering in the forests and the fields outside Manassas waiting for the opportune moment that would bring freedom. If they could make it to the Union base in town, they could be free. Free. Not just for an hour or for a day, but free forever.

William heard the word *free* rattling around in black men's mouths, and for the first time, the word made him thirsty. It made him cry for a place where children couldn't be separated from their mothers and brothers and sisters and cousins at another man's whim. He felt unsteady and furious with desire. He slapped horses and broke broomsticks. He slept in the fields, praying for rain. Fanny told him that his freedom wishes were making him crazy.

"You better run, Willie," Fanny nagged. "You better go now while you can. You don't know what could happen tomorrow. They could drive the Yankees away and then you be lost for sure. You never be free."

"Fanny, yo' foot ain't no good. You won't make it."

"I ain't said me, *fool*, I said you. Go without me!"

"Girl, if you don't shut your big mouth, I don't know what I'll do. If you can't go, I can't go. Now, if you wanna do somethin' right, find a way for both of us to get to the line. Otherwise, shut up."

"I just can't stand you! You the most stupidest, most mule-faced nigger ever!"

"I know, Fanny. I know. But ask me do I care . . ."

Every day the complaint was the same and every day it brought the same response. Staying or leaving was the only thing besides corn bread cakes and the "William-chores" that the twins ever argued about.

Late one afternoon, when the sky had already dusked down to a velvety charcoal, Master Benjamin called them in. "William, let's hurry up and go. You got to come with me to Camp Pickens. I need some help loading supplies."

William lifted Fanny into the back of the wagon and then climbed up himself. By the time they got to Camp Pickens, it was almost totally dark. Master Benjamin jumped down from his leather buckboard seat and headed toward the large supply tent that sold grain and feed. William hopped down and reached back to grab Fanny by the waist as she scooted to the edge of the wagon.

"Here now, son, let me help the little lady."

A wide-hipped white man with a thick blond beard nudged William aside and grabbed Fanny by the waist. William blanched at the sight of the callused, pinkish hands wrapped around his sister, and his fingers curled into fists. He lowered his head, ready to fling himself onto the man's broad back, but before William could move, Master Benjamin called over, "Don't bother, man. Those children ain't white. They just niggers."

The brawny man jumped back off Fanny like she'd burned him. Glaring as if the twins had tricked him on purpose, just for spite, he spit in the dirt and strode away. William watched the stranger disappear into the crowd and didn't know which to hate him for—helping his sister or refusing to help his sister.

They stayed the night at Camp Pickens, the children sleeping in the back of the open wagon, Master Benjamin in a tent. At dawn, William and Fanny awoke to victory cries and jubilant men dancing through the narrow, dusty streets, shouting "Hoo-rah!" and drinking toasts to the sunrise. Stonewall had seized Pope's supply depot at Manassas and run the Yankees out. Manassas was free! Master Benjamin sank to his knees, lifted his arms in the air and shouted, "Praise Jesus!"

Fanny looked at William in tears, and William sensed he was powerless to do anything bold or meaningful to soothe her. He felt weak and worthless. So the little boy did what little boys do: He shoved his fists to his ears and kicked dirt at her shins and screamed, "I don't hear you! I don't care!" and ran off to hide behind one of the ammunition tents. By the time Fanny made her way around the rear of the tent, William was desperate to make up. She eased down next to him. He handed her his favorite red-painted pinecone and a peppermint ball covered in lint from the inside of his pocket. She put her hand over his, rested her head on his shoulder, and that was the end of it.

They didn't leave the smoke and swearing and laughter of Camp Pickens until late the following morning. Master Benjamin was hungover, constantly rubbing the bristly red whiskers that had sprouted across his cheeks, as though his jaw ached from the effort of opening and closing all night with the drink. His aches seemed to make him full of fire. There wasn't a thing William could do right. When he sat silently in the back of the wagon next to Fanny or put his head in her lap and watched the sky, he wasn't being helpful enough. If he climbed onto the buckboard with Master Benjamin, he was too damn close and he better get the hell back before he got his damn nigger face busted open.

William was still sitting in the back figuring on what he could do, when Master Benjamin yelled, "Whoa!" and edged the sweating bay gelding off the side of the road. The children peered over the side of the wagon and saw Teacher Brice waving and hobbling toward them from the cover of a dense pine grove. Teacher Brice walked with a wicked limp just like Fanny's, but his was not from a clubfoot—just an old man's busted hip.

"Don't go that way!" he was yelling. "Turn back!"

"What's going on, Jerrod?" Master Benjamin asked. Suddenly the slur evaporated from his voice, and his sleepy, red eyes narrowed.

The old man reached the edge of the wagon, panting and groaning. Sweat popped up on the top of his bald head and leaked down his face and neck. Teacher Brice slapped at his bad hip in frustration, contorted in pain.

"You can't get up to the Ridge or to the camp," he wheezed. "It's started."

"Tell me what's goin' on, old man. What's started? Be clear."

"Stonewall's men attacking the Federals at Warrenton. Fightin's everywhere."

"Where's our people? The Gaskins, the Monroes, the Dogons?"

"Everybody, the women, children, everybody took off for Catlett. Been down there since yesterday. What men we got is gatherin' up by Groveton."

Master Benjamin unsheathed his whip and, with a fierce crack, drove it into the horse's flank. The horse reared back and bolted, hurling the children onto the piled-up sacks of flour and grain. William looked behind them for Teacher Brice, but all he could see was a wavering figure trapped in a screen of dust. To just leave the old man by himself in the middle of the road, maybe even to die there, seemed cruel. But Master Benjamin didn't stop. He whipped the horse, riding her faster down Old Alexandria Road, racing over ruts and crevices.

William threw his body over Fanny to keep her from flying out of the back of the wagon. When they got to the turnoff for Lewis

Lane, Master Benjamin pulled over to the side of the road. He turned around and stared at William, who immediately dropped his eyes and bowed his shoulders, softening his angles like his mother had taught him.

"Look here, boy," Master Benjamin said. "I need you to do somethin'. Somethin' big. Now, I been knowin' you since you were born. You understand that? Your family is almost like . . . kin to me. I got to count on you now, boy. I want to trust you, William. Can I trust you to do what I say?"

"Yes, sir," William mumbled.

By then they could hear cannon fire in the distance and see smoke wafting like mist through the willow trees to the north.

"I want you to take these supplies back to Catlett. Leave 'em with the first person you see and tell whoever it is that you come for me. Leave Fanny and the wagon in Catlett. You hear me, boy? I mean it. It's too dangerous for Fanny to follow you. She'll die, and it'll be your fault. You understand that? Leave Fanny, unhitch the bay and take her for yourself. Then see if you can find my horse. If not, take any good horse they got and meet me at Grove-ton. Bring both my rifles, the pistols and any extra rounds you can get hold of. Can you do that, William?"

"Yes, sir."

"Good boy. Now go."

Master Benjamin jumped from the cab and darted across the road into a stand of moss-and-ivy-covered cedars. He waved once and was gone, running through the woods alongside the lane.

"What you gon' do, Willie? You goin' to Catlett?"

"Aw, *hell* naw, girl. What you think? I ain't goin' to no damn Catlett."

"Well what then?"

"We goin' to Pennsylvania. Then I'ma come back and fight with the Yankees."

"Nigger, you crazy? We can't make it to Pennsylvania. Besides that, the Yankees don't take nigger soldiers anyway. And even if they did, how you gon' pass for sixteen? You ain't but a minute old. Think for real, boy. This ain't no game."

"So what you suggest then, Miss Big Mouth?"

"Run, Willie. Unhitch this horse and run. Can't nobody catch you on a horse. I can make it back to Catlett on my own. I'll tell 'em anything. I'll tell 'em the Yankees got you."

"That's stupid."

"Willie—"

"No! I ain't leavin' nobody."

"Willie, why can't you listen even once? Please. If you fool around with me, they'll catch you, and Master Benjamin'll kill you too."

"I don't care," William grumbled.

"That so?"

"Uh-huh. It is."

"Well fine! If you don't care, I don't care too! Ole Ben gonna kill you dead and it'll be good for you."

"We got to get off this road. Soldiers could be comin' 'round anytime."

Fanny began to sniffle and cry, but William ignored her, pretending not to see. He pulled the wagon off the road behind a stout group of pin oaks on a steep grade. Then he unhitched the horse and, taking Fanny's hand, walked east into the woods toward Chinn House.

The woods were overrun with towering, skinny trees whose branches bridged out to block the sun, coloring the air cool and green. The children's feet slipped through the warm moss peat and dead leaves that carpeted the ground, while from unseen places all around them, the earth bellowed and belched smoke. William tried to hurry Fanny along, bending back the reedy saplings so that she could pass without being slapped and stung. No deer shifted softly behind the bushy ferns; no birds rustled the leaves as they took flight. The creatures had fled long before.

The farther the children trekked through the woods, the louder and fiercer the noises ahead of them became. The bark of rough, panicked shouts broke through the trees, coming steadily closer. Fanny shrank against William's chest when they heard the *tat-tat-tat-tat-tat-tat* of artillery fire and the rumble of cannons exploding in the distance. She squeezed his hand until it was numb, and William squeezed back, striding forward, trying to look as though he was sure of where he was taking them. But it was habit that led him east, not any real plan for their safety. In his heart, he was lost and wondering if they were going to die like he was sure that Teacher Brice had already died.

They hurried along Chinn Branch, a small creek that ran just east of Chinn House. William looked to his right and saw something bobbing in the water. The knot between his ribs began to throb, and he suddenly felt a vicious burning in his belly that made him think that he was about to wet himself. But he let go of Fanny's hand, gave her the horse's reins, and walked over to the water's edge to face down whatever it was.

A Union man was caught in the current on some brambles. When William saw the blue, he scrambled over to help the man out of the water. But he stopped at the bank when he realized that the man's chest was opened wide, his heart caught on a shiny brass button. The soldier was sodden, already starting to bloat, with his mouth stretched open, gulping swirls of bloody water.

William stumbled back and turned to tell Fanny to run. But before he could speak, he heard the whistling and splintering of branches, and he knew it was too late.

The cannonball exploded just beyond them, and the force of the blast knocked him back into the stream, into the arms of the

Union man. William flailed in the water, punching and scratching the dead soldier, ripping loose sinew, heart, and buttons, struggling to get free. His bare feet touched bottom and he lunged forward, flinging himself onto the muddy bank. Then he dropped down to his knees and vomited the copper taste of the water up out of his throat.

"*Fanny!*"

William dashed back over to the spot where she'd been standing. About five yards away, he saw the old blond horse lying on its side. Its midsection had been ripped open by shrapnel and its steaming intestines oozed out onto the cooling forest floor.

William felt the life drain from the soles of his feet. His body wavered, just as he'd seen Teacher Brice waver through the cover of orange dust, and he thought *I'm full of dust too, that's all, just dust.* Then he turned back toward the water thinking to wet himself for substance, thinking to climb into the current, make his bed and lie down.

Then he heard the ragged sound of his sister breathing, and he knew that she was alive and trying to call his name. Panic flared through his body and he turned from the water, screaming Fanny's name without a care that someone would hear him. He ran around the horse's body and found her curled against the trunk of a ruined pine.

"Fanny," William cried, "you a'right? Please be a'right."

He pushed her hair out of her face and leaned in so close that their noses touched.

"William?"

"Yeah. I'm here. I ain't goin' nowhere. I'm right here with you."

He tried to get Fanny to look at him, but her eyes wouldn't focus. She was dazed and incoherent. He could barely make out her words when she muttered, "Willie, I think my leg's mess up."

William lifted the blue-checkered hem of her dress and saw the shinbone of her right leg, the bad one, peeking out through a hole in her flesh. He could see down to the dark, stormy gray of the marrow and it made him think of their mother who, when she killed and cooked a chicken, liked to suck that part of the bone because she said it made you strong.

She'll die and it'll be your fault. You understand that?

The voice he heard was so strong that William looked around before he realized that it was in his head.

"Get up, Fanny," he pleaded.

"Uh-uh. I can't."

"Then I'll carry you."

She tried to say something but the words wouldn't come out. William pulled her by the arm and then ducked underneath so that when she stood, her arm was over his shoulder and he was supporting her weight. William half carried, half dragged Fanny through the woods, crouching low when they heard gunfire at close range and ducking behind bushes or brambles or anything that would give shelter when they saw gray-clad shadows dodging through the trees.

The white clapboards of the Chinn House appeared through the trees on William's left side.

"Fanny? You a'right? Talk to me, Fanny. Say something, 'kay?"

She didn't answer, and William was too terrified to look over into her eyes or even slow down. He kept moving toward the house. The redbrick chimney at the side of the house stood directly in front of them. Smoke spiraled from both stacks of the double chimney on the far side of the house. From his viewpoint, the white smoke seemed to be curling up from the shaggy crown of the walnut tree in the yard. William stopped.

Smoke. Someone was inside.

He didn't know what to do. William was bent, breaking slowly to his right under Fanny's weight, ready to snap to splinters and disappear. But he couldn't. If he did, Fanny would die, and it would be all his fault. A volley of rapid fire from a group of thirty-pound Parrott rifles exploded in the distance, but William had no idea how close or far the fighting was. He was hearing the screams of men he couldn't see.

And someone was in the house.

Across the field to the right, glinting light shot from the metal shafts of bayonets. The light drew William's eye toward the marching gray ghosts heading away from them, wading northwards through the wheat-colored, thigh-high prairie grass. The yard was empty and so he decided to take a chance.

William led Fanny out from beneath a curtain of green shadows into a brilliant cast of hazy, gold light. Putting his head down to his chest, he tightened his grip around Fanny's waist and started across the yard toward the cellar of the Chinn House. Fanny's face and lips had gone stark white, but William couldn't stop to see if she was all right or even still awake. He put one foot in front of the other, dragging her, waiting for the *crack* of a Mississippi rifle or a .54 at their backs. Dense blue smoke began rolling in through the trees and across the yard, creeping along the ground like fog. In seconds it blanketed the children and they were invisible. William was suddenly a ghost too, like the men he envisioned hounding and trapping them.

They reached the house and William gently laid Fanny in the dirt beside one of the cellar windows. The cellar of the Chinn House was ground level. The foundation of the house had been carved from red sandstone blocks that reached almost to William's waist. The three feet of space between the ground and the wooden frame of the house, which rested on top of the stone foundation, was the cellar. Master Benjamin stored his grain, potatoes and fruit in that part of the house because it was the coolest. It could be reached through a trapdoor in the floor of the sitting room or through one of the four windows carved into the foundation.

William slid back the wooden window screen, lay on his belly and wriggled feetfirst in through the window. When he was halfway in, he grabbed Fanny and tried to drag her through behind him. She was unconscious, and William had to turn himself around and brace his feet against either side of the window in order to get enough leverage to pull her deadweight. Once Fanny was inside, he slid the wooden screen back into place and latched it from the inside.

The cellar was black like oil, or like water reflecting the haze of a turbulent night sky. There *was no* reflection, no self peering back for him to recognize and touch. There was only smothered breath, the tart smell of apples, and stinging smoke that seeped through every chink and crack in the stone. The blackness was like a live, breathing thing with smooth wings that fluttered against his cheeks. It kept the dirt cool and hard as the marble wedded to Miss Edmonia's fireplace. He crawled through the dark, begging its pardon, trying to remember where things were, and when he couldn't, trying not to curse and cry because he was sure the mad flapping in his head was the sound of the darkness laughing at him.

Behind a stack of burlap sacks filled with what he thought were oats, he found a space to hide. There wasn't enough room for standing straight up so William crouched and crawled over to where he'd left his sister and, sliding backward on his knees through the loose earth, dragged her behind their wall of grain. He put his ear to her mouth and swore that if there was no sound, he'd lift the trapdoor and let the light in. There would be no reason for him to hide, no reason to run.

When he heard her gasp and murmur, "Git up off me, fool. Whatchu doin'?" William was beside himself with joy.

"Shut up, stupid girl," he whispered and almost immediately passed out against her shoulder into an exhausted sleep.

THE CREAK OF THE trapdoor opening woke them. Yellow candle-light seeped across the ground and peered over bags and crates.

"What's down there, man?"

William's hand clapped down over Fanny's mouth. *Don't move.* He breathed the words into her ear and though her body tensed and trembled, she made no sound.

"There's nothing here but rations, Dr. Wheeler. I can check through it in the morning to see what all is down here if you want, sir."

"Fine. But make sure you do it before Colonel Corse comes through."

"Yes, sir," the young voice said, and pushed the door shut.

There was darkness snaking through William's head, cutting the soles of his bare feet and laughing. Always laughing. Only the pressure of Fanny's body pinned against his kept him from coiling up against the stones and screaming.

"Fanny, get up. We got to get outta here."

"Willie, I can't move. I swear to God I can't."

William felt through the dark for her leg and found it hard and swollen to more than twice its size. He could feel her body heaving as she tried to cry with no sound.

"Oh please, God, please. Willie don't touch it. Please don't."

"Fanny, I don't know what to do."

"Run, Willie," she hissed. "You got to get outta here. You can't stay. They'll kill you."

"Stop it, Fanny!"

"Willie, what I'm gonna do without you? At least if you run,

you can come back and get me later and we could go north together. If you dead, I ain't goin' nowhere."

That made William stop and think. But still, he shook his head
no and because it was too dark for Fanny to see, he said again out
loud, "No."

Fanny didn't say anything else. William could hear her panting
beside him, and he knew that she was quiet not because she
agreed, but because of the pain. He also knew that if he touched
her cheeks, they would be wet. He rubbed her shoulder with his
palm and laid his head against her neck, where he could hear the
whoosh of blood under her skin. The sound of it eventually lulled
him into a fitful sleep.

In his sleep, he dreamt of many-eyed creatures with crimson
lips and wings over their hearts and Fanny was there and she was
one of them. He heard her calling to him, "William, William get
up" and when he woke, he was already screaming.

Fanny was screaming too, in such pain that his arms couldn't
hold her, and at first William couldn't tell either of their screams
from the violent howling and shrieking coming from above.

Men. There were men all around them, prowling the floors
above their head. William could smell blood and dirt, and he
couldn't stop screaming because he thought he could smell their
sweat too, and it smelled like it was coming from him. He didn't
know where he was. The dark was crowing and pecking at him
and he tried to stand, tried to run, but he couldn't. There wasn't
enough room. His head hit the floorboards above him and that's
when he remembered where he was. In the cellar. He knelt back
down and felt through the dark for Fanny and grasped her hand.
But she was crying, calling for their mother and Miss Frances. She
didn't even know he was there.

William shook her hand off and crawled away because he

couldn't stand to hear her suffering like that, knowing that Master Benjamin would blame him. His fault. Everything was always his fault. William crouched under the trapdoor with his fists pressed against the hollow place in the center of his chest, rocking back and forth, hearing voices, hearing words and names being called, but not making any sense of them. The only things that filtered clearly through his head were the screams and the very audible sound of a saw raking across what William could only imagine to be bone.

They hid in that cellar all through the day and another night. Fanny had a fever now and it was getting harder and harder to wake her. When William couldn't get her to stir, he just let her be, checking her breath every time his heart got scared and wiping the sweat from her face. He preferred that she not wake up too much because the screaming and cursing men above their heads terrified her. The stench of blood and wounded, rotting flesh made her retch. Each time a boot fell hard across the trapdoor, making it shudder, she'd bang her head against the sandstone and wail. William had to get her out.

He tried to listen through the cracks in the floor to hear any news that might help him figure out what to do. But there wasn't much he could make out in all the shouting and the chaos above them.

The Federals had hit Groveton (where Master Benjamin was) and men were dying in rivers and woods, splayed across wheat-fields and curled up in ditches without faces, without hearts, without legs. There was no time to take the wounded ones to the Stone House doctor off Sudley Road. Too much death over there anyway. They had enough. The doctor here at the Chinn House had to do.

Soft lead shatters hard bone every time, and the doctor almost always had to cut. *What's to be done with the arms and legs, sir?* William never heard the doctor's answer.

Then the rumbling came, sounding like the house was wrapped in thunder, and William could hear the Confederate army amassing right outside. He knew they had to be Confederates on the march from the way the men inside the house whooped and hollered. The marching soldiers woke Fanny, and William held her to him, huddling close. They weren't sure anymore whether it was day or night outside, if the Federals were winning or losing. All they knew was that they were trapped. Master Benjamin could be standing outside the window for all William knew, waiting. He couldn't stand not knowing.

"What we gon' do, Willie?"

"I think I'ma see what's goin' on out there, that's what."

"No, Willie. You can't go out there. Those men kill you. Don't do it!"

"I ain't goin' out nowhere. I'ma just peek."

When Fanny began whimpering, William hugged her neck and said, "Sissy, we been waitin' too long. I gotta know what's happenin' or else we could be trapped down here forever."

Fanny didn't answer, but she loosened her grip on William's neck, and he crawled over to the window that faced out on the front of the house. William undid the latch and slid the wood back an inch. Smoke and heat and light flooded through the crack, blinding him so that he ducked away from the window, cursing. But then he was right back, tears coursing from his burning eye, with his face pressed against the wood.

He heard the hoofbeats of horses off to the left. But the soldiers blocked his view.

Gray-clad soldiers had descended on the house. They were everywhere. There was no space in his limited line of vision that they did not fill. The sky was gray and so was the air and the leaves on the trees. The soldiers stood poised, their muskets and rifles with the winking bayonets at the ready. William heard a man's voice give a command.

Then, as one body, one mind, the soldiers began to march. They were thunder, pregnant in the air, skimming and rocking the earth. Unconquerable. Northward they moved, toward the falling-down worm fence that marked the edge of Benjamin Chinn's yard. The first line of Confederate soldiers had marched about one hundred yards, just at the line of the fence, when the air around them ripped open and men began to fall. The Federals rose through the cover of smoke and, from behind the fence, opened fire.

It lasted perhaps a quarter of an hour. Perhaps less. But William watched, transfixed, as though there were gods at war, gods who had no thought for day or night, gods who crunched forever between their teeth and spit out the bones of the less fortunate, men not lucky enough to know eternity.

Blue smoke rolled across the fields, cushioning the men as they fell. Gunfire roared, blasting through bodies, shredding men and horses. The dead lay contorted in heaps, while the ones who were still dying cried out and writhed like earthworms through the high grass. How many? Hundreds, surely. Hundreds of men dead in an instant. William couldn't breathe for watching. He didn't hear Fanny pleading with him to shut the window and come back. He opened the window wider and didn't cough when the smoke and dust pierced his lungs.

There was a lull in the fighting. William could see them. The Federals. They were coming for him and Fanny. The two of them would be free!

But then William heard a rallying cry go up, urging the infantry men of the Seventh and the Eleventh on into the fray. Suddenly the booming of cannons answered the soldiers' cries, and the Federals were being pushed back. Yards from the house, close enough so that William could see beards and blood on their faces, and they were being pushed back. He waited, watching men turn to animals, screaming, slashing, stabbing and shooting. An officer galloped into the tangle of bodies with his musician's sword raised and sliced off a man's arm at the shoulder. When the man fell to the ground, the officer's horse trampled him. But still William wouldn't look away. Even as he saw the Federals begin to retreat, he waited at the window knowing that the soldiers would come back for them. They had to.

In another hour or so, the battle cries began receding over the ridge. When he heard the gray ghosts shout "On to Henry Hill!" he finally admitted to himself that the Federals weren't coming back. The Confederates were about to rout them out at their camp. It was over.

William left the window, put his head on Fanny's shoulder and sobbed.

"What more do you need to see, Willie? You know you got to go."

He tried to say no but it came out just a weak, squeaking sound.

"You got to get behind the lines before they run those Federals out, Willie. If you go, I can make my way out of here and get help for my leg."

He couldn't fight her. She was right and he knew it. But how could he tell her that he was terrified at the thought of leaving her, of being alone in the world without anyone that loved him?

"If I go," he whispered, "I'ma come back and get you. I ain't gonna leave you here alone for long. When I'm free, I'ma come back and you be free too. You believe me, Fanny?"

"I believe you, Willie."

He touched the soft curls at the top of her head. There was nothing else to say or do. Somehow he managed to turn away.

"Don't go out the front," she called. "Go out the back and slip into the woods so they don't shoot at you."

"I'm comin' back."

"I know, Willie."

William slid the wooden slat back from one of the rear windows and found the opening blocked by a mound of amputated arms and legs. The men must have thrown the useless limbs out of the first-floor window. A wall of flies had gathered and lit on the soft, rotting flesh. William held his breath and knocked the severed limbs out of his way. He shimmied on his belly out of the window and took off running.

All around him, bodies littered the ground. He ran through the tawny prairie grass that slapped his thighs and through raging clouds of gnats and flies that had come to feast. With his head down and heart racing, William ran through smoke and leapt over prone bodies. Dazed men wandered the fields and searched the sky. They didn't react to the sound of artillery fire and cannons in the distance. William swooped past those men. He didn't care about them. He didn't care who saw him or heard him or tried to stop him. He ran on, daring the sniper's bullet, ready to fight and die like those men had fought and died because no one who wasn't prepared to kill him was going to stop him from reaching Henry Hill. He ran down through the poplars, shrouded in smoke, and leapt over tree roots that drank from streams of blood. William ran until the trees became a blur and the high grass flew under his feet. He ran until he saw blue.

He never saw his sister again.

Chapter 4

I am wrought with understanding that surpasses the sand and the sea. It says that my love has often been a shower through a sieve, and not a coursing stream. This is why I have never felt full.

My mind wrapped itself around this thought long before I woke, so that when I opened my eyes, it already felt old to me, a reprise of someone else's revelation. In my sleep I'd begun to see how certain pains always seek to be validated by more pain. And what happened to me when I let them.

These were my first thoughts after waking from a procession of vivid but colorless dreams the second night after I found my father unconscious on the stoop. So much to consider. Never enough time.

I stretched out on the bed a little while longer, letting the dusk drape me in broad shadows. Then I stumbled over the cold floor to the kitchen to heat some water for my bath. Mama wasn't home from work yet, and Papa was still in the hospital, so I had the flat to myself. Free to rub my father's past, his sister, his pain, from my back and the flesh over my womb. Free to stretch my legs, watch the water bead up and slide across my bones. I wanted to run to my papa and hold him and tell him that I understood. At least a little. I could help if he'd let me. And he could begin to allow himself to protect me without fear. Love that came from fear tended to be big and strident and empty. It would be a hard thing for us, to love in prayers and whispers again. But we could do it.

My father had lived with the emptiness of fear in greater and lesser degrees all his life. A different kind of slave brand. If that hadn't been so, he and his sister could have walked out of that house and taken another road straight over the ridge. By Papa's own admission, all the white people who might have known him were far away, in places like Groveton or Catlett. To those unfamiliar soldiers, he and his sister would have been poor little lost white children. If they'd been bold enough, they probably could've gotten another horse and directions. But in their minds, they were marked. They wore their black slave skin inside out. How could there ever be freedom in that?

I poured water along the brown and purple tracks on my legs and pushed down on the new scabs softening in the heat of the bath. If I picked them, they'd bleed. There was no skin yet underneath.

THE AMBULANCE ROARED down St. Nicholas Avenue, bells clanging, as we raced through the darkness toward Jungle Alley. The crowd in front of the building at the corner of 133rd Street gestured and pointed to one of the top floors. I snatched up my medical bag and jumped from the ambulance before it fully stopped.

"What number?" I called over my shoulder.

Neither of my drivers answered me. It was the small concession they made to try to keep me from going alone into this building, one of the many places in Harlem where policemen refused to enter in groups of less than four. We'd been ordered (specifically me—*I'd* been ordered) not to step foot inside buildings like 454 St. Nicholas Avenue until a police escort arrived.

Robert O'Neill and Andrew Fabiano, the two drivers who assisted me, always waited patiently outside for the escort to come. Both men were at least ten years older than I. They made it clear that they had no intention of getting their heads cracked open because of my childish, feminine foolishness. There'd been times when I'd had to have uncles and little brothers and even grandmothers help me carry patients outside to the ambulance because the police hadn't arrived and the drivers wouldn't budge without them. Robert and Andrew always felt quite comfortable scolding me after the fact. They insisted—sometimes over the heads of my patients—that this was *exactly* why women had no business being doctors. We were reckless, all emotions with no good sense to temper our feelings, not even the fear for our own safety.

I didn't bother looking back for them. Instead, I asked one of the women standing on the sidewalk, "The man that was stabbed—where is he?"

She shifted the whole dark moon of her body toward me, cocked her head to the side and frowned. "Fourth floor. On the F line."

At my back I heard someone say, "That Colored woman a nurse or somethin'?" A number of people stopped pointing at the building and began pointing at me instead.

I pushed open the metal door and headed in. A cluster of light fixtures hung from the ceiling in the entranceway. The bulbs in each one had been smashed. Lingering shards of glass crunched under my feet. I raised my skirt to keep it from sweeping up glass but also because the wood paneling near the floor and the tiles reeked of fresh urine. As I felt my way through the dark, doors creaked open and lit the hall with bars of dull yellow light. Each door banged shut as I approached, then edged slowly open again as I passed. Everyone was curious about things they didn't want to know.

It wasn't until I'd almost reached the staircase that I realized I might be in trouble.

There were people under the stairs.

I could hear them breathing. At such close range, I smelled them, too. Wine-hot and musky and sour. They were the reason that the white men wouldn't follow me into this place. They'd been waiting. I thought of the small plastic pouches of codeine powder in my medical bag and lifted it up, clutching it against my chest. One of them crept out from under the stairs and sidled toward me, mumbling.

". . . don't you move. You hear? Stand there. Right there. Don't make me come get you . . ."

I sprinted past him up the staircase. The man grabbed for me. His hand swiped the back of my coat but he couldn't catch hold. Hiking up my skirt, I took the stairs three at a time without looking back.

On the landing between the third and the fourth floors, I yelled out, "Doctor's here!"

A man heard me calling and opened the corner door.

"Man's been stabbed in here, ma'am. Where the doctor at?"

"I'm the doctor," I said, and brushed past without even looking at him. It would take him a minute or so to believe me. Eventually, when no one else came up the stairs, he'd follow.

I glanced around the sitting room, trying to catch my breath, while I figured out what to do. A row of wooden high-backed chairs had been overturned. Broken glasses lay scattered across the floor where people had dropped their highballs in the panic to escape. Someone tracked footprints through a path of smeared blood that led from the sofa to a man's body slumped in a kitchen corner next to the fat, cast-iron stove. Kneeling in a wide circle of blood, a brown-skinned woman wearing a tan frock coat kissed the man's hand. She sobbed in broken, hitching moans. Two men and two other women stood in front of her, staring off at the wall or down at their feet. None of them met her eyes.

"I'm Dr. Chinn," I said to the room. "Ma'am, you'll have to move back now."

"Who are you?" the woman asked.

"Dr. Chinn," I repeated, looking directly into her face. She nodded at me but didn't move.

Meanwhile, I scanned the room, searching for a place to peel off the man's clothes and examine him. The kitchen had only the black stove, a bathtub with no cover, a slop sink, some shelving and an ironing board standing in the corner.

The ironing board would have to do.

"Ma'am, what's your name?" I asked the slender woman behind me.

"Elena Chiefs, Miss . . . ma'am."

"Miss Chiefs, raise that ironing board for me over here in the middle of the room under the light. If there are any other lights or lamps in this apartment, I need them in here now. Ma'am? Yes, you in the blue dress. Yes, you. Put some water on to boil for me and then take your friend"—I motioned to the lady in tan—"into the sitting room. Make sure she stays there. Gentlemen, on my count I want you to help me lift this man here—"

"Oliver," said the bloodied woman. "He has a name. It's Oliver Joseph."

"All right, Mr. Joseph. In the meantime, you have to wait in the other room. Now on my count, help me lift Mr. Joseph onto the ironing board and then brace the ends. Everyone clear?"

Nobody moved.

Again and again this happened. The thought of having to fight my way out of this same cage, every day, for the rest of my life made me want to scream.

When I spoke again I used my father's voice, low and cold and sharp, so soft that it could barely be heard.

"This man is bleeding to death on your floor," I said. "If that's all right with you, I'll pick up my bag and go. You all can explain to the police what happened, whenever they get here. If you want to at least try to save him, I suggest you move—right now."

It took a second for the words to sink in, but then the women bolted to their tasks. The men followed suit, snapping into action, and together we heaved Oliver Joseph up onto the wooden ironing board. The first two men held the board steady while the third man, who had finally stopped waiting in the hall for help to arrive, held my leather bag open and within reach. I stripped Mr. Joseph naked in the middle of that kitchen and began counting his wounds.

My God.

"What happened to this man?"

A good doctor has a studied impartiality. There's an infallible tone of assurance that becomes second nature. That is what I had learned. But as I stared down at the broken body in front of me, I forgot all that. My question quivered and shrunk in the air, making me sound, even to my own ears, like a cowed child.

"Party was goin' on," said the freckled man at Mr. Joseph's feet. "Man come up in here with a bunch of friends talkin' loud and startin' mess. He grabbed hold of Jay's woman and when Jay tried to make him quit, he pulled out his blade."

Ten, fifteen, twenty. I stopped counting. Oliver Joseph's chest was opened full of red eyes, eyes winking with the labor of breath, eyes welling with tears that dripped down the wood and stained it like rust. Here a snatch of lung, there a running vein that I had to press on to keep quiet. Eyes in his groin, blinded by a slick mat of pubic hair, peeking down toward emptied testicles.

What had happened to this man? Several veins and arteries had been severed. I made Elena Chiefs wash her hands in antiseptic soap and then press together the slit-open ends of an artery in his leg.

Apply pressure to the flesh wounds to stop the bleeding. Slice the skin even more, reaching deeper with a scalpel the size of my ring finger, the blade like a nail, to find the alpha point of the gash in a cleaved organ.

Oliver Joseph shivered on the table, and Elena screamed, flinging herself back against the wall. Freed of pressure, the broken artery began to surge and run.

Oliver was growing cold in my hands. Shock. I pumped his chest to stimulate the heart. But it faltered and slowed. Too weak. No blood left to feed it.

A burly, red-haired police officer kicked in the door with his gun drawn. Four more officers charged in behind him, with Robert and Andrew carrying a canvas litter at the rear. "Police!" he shouted.

No one answered. No one moved until I took my hands out of Oliver Joseph's chest and turned my back to the officers to reach the sink.

"Good," I said over my shoulder. "You're just in time to call ahead to the morgue."

BY THE TIME WE turned onto 103rd Street, I was tired. I ticked off the new address in my ledger as the fifteenth answered call in the past eight hours. We had four more hours to go.

Thank God for a short night.

The ambulance passed under the brick archway of the Park Avenue El and headed straight toward Lexington. Mt. Sinai was much closer, only two or three blocks away. But the address on the call said Spanish Harlem, a neighborhood not (under any circumstances) in the jurisdiction of Mt. Sinai. If it had been a block east, where the Italians lived, another doctor would have been summoned. But it wasn't, so I went.

The ambulance stopped in front of a narrow, soot-streaked tenement. The building stank, even from the curb, of smoke damage from a recent fire. Robert and Andrew followed at a distance as I wove past the early-morning men clustered on the stoop and into the doorway. A kerosene lamp lit the vestibule, hanging from a hook in the wall. But still the gloom persisted, swallowing mouthfuls of light in the crevices, unrolling shadows underfoot to carpet the dingy tiles. Burlap cloth had been glued to the walls and painted white. Likewise, the tin roofing had been painted white. But, even in the dark, one could see the paint chipping and shredding, floating down like ash from the spout of an incinerator.

"*Medico,*" I called. "Doctor's here."

On the second floor I passed an empty toilet, which was always shared among at least four families in buildings like this. A door on the left swung open and a boy of about eight or nine popped his head out and then ducked back inside.

"*¡Mami,*" he cried, "*la doctora es una mujer! Una mujer negra. ¡Papi se va a morir!*"

"*¡Callate!*"

The woman threw the door open so hard that it slammed into the wall behind and rattled some plaster loose. The plaster fell lightly, dotting the woman's head with powder. Shining in the lamplight, her thick, wiry hair looked like it was covered in spiderwebs. The woman's eyes widened when she saw my face, and she immediately looked around me, over my head. When Robert and Andrew came trudging up the stairs she smiled in naked gratitude, sagging with relief against the doorframe. As they neared, she pushed past me and began gesturing inside the house and rambling feverishly in Spanish.

"No." Robert wouldn't even look at her. "No. Go to her. She's doctor. Not me. She."

Andrew pointed my way and made a *scoot scoot* gesture with his hands like he was pushing water. The woman turned back to me and covered her trembling lips with her hand. I turned away when she began to cry and went into the apartment to find my patient.

The wide wooden planks in the floor were warped and buckled into slanted bowl shapes. Behind the bed, a massive hulk of a man writhed against the splintering wood, wedged into the largest of the distorted sinks. I couldn't guess the age, but his height seemed to be anywhere from five foot seven to five foot ten. His weight must have been at least eight hundred pounds. He wore nothing but frayed gray underwear and dress socks. Sweat congealed in the rolls and puckers of his flesh.

"*Dios,*" he cried over and over and then growled low in his throat as another wave of pain shook him.

"Does anyone here speak English? *¿Un poquito ingles?*"

The little boy idled up beside me and shook his head no.

I knelt down beside the man. "Can you understand me, sir? What's your name? Uh . . . *¿se llama?*"

"Raphael DeLeon." The woman stood in the doorway, still weeping.

"Senor DeLeon, *me llama* Dr. Chinn. You're going to have to straighten out so I can examine you and find out what's wrong."

But he either didn't understand or couldn't comply because of the pain. There was obviously something wrong with his stomach from the way he clutched it. When I slid my hands across the slippery mound of his abdomen and tried to palpate it, he screamed and lashed out with his fists, nearly cracking me in the nose.

"Should we restrain him for you, Chinn?" Andrew asked.

"No. I'd rather find some way to get him to the hospital for a closer look. I can't make heads or tails of anything here. Do you think he can fit through the door?"

Robert looked at Andrew, who scratched his head and glanced

dubiously over at me. Then all three of us looked down at the slim canvas litter that they held between them.

"We're gonna need some backup."

We grabbed the men from the stoop, who were more than happy to help because it gave them some good work to do, something heavy for their hands to maneuver. We called the hospital and four more attendants came with litters. Robert flagged down a man driving past in a flatbed truck and paid him, from his own pockets, for use of the vehicle. All told, it took thirteen people, an ax, and an empty coal truck to get Raphael DeLeon to the emergency room at Harlem Hospital.

I rang the night bell at the back door and after a few minutes my advisor, Dr. Sterling Fields, opened it. As the head of the medical program, all nineteen interns, including me, answered to him. Fields was a booming, cherry-faced man with an opulent stomach and frameless glasses angled on top of his thinning, silver head. When he wasn't careful, or when he thought no one could see, he'd rest his various clipboards and files on the rise of his paunch and sigh like a broken old man. He was old. Broken too. However, I believe what made him so angry—angry with himself, his patients, his staff and, most especially, with me—wasn't the fact that he lived in this state of brokenness, but that he was too small a man to hide it effectively.

Dr. Fields hated me. He looked for chances to be cruel. If I were impeccable on a particular day and he couldn't find even a phony reason, he settled for ignoring me.

As our crew wheeled Mr. DeLeon into the examining room, I braced myself. A group of interns gathered 'round, some of them already smirking.

"What have we got here, Dr. Chinn?"

"This is, uh, Mr. Ralph, I mean Raphael DeLeon. Hispanic male, I'm not sure of the age, approximately eight hundred pounds. He's having severe stomach pains."

"Very good, Doctor. Now tell me something that we can't guess by feeling around in the dark."

The others tittered and nudged each other.

"This should be good," said an intern named Edwards. The two men on either side of him grinned.

"Well, sir," I began, "the truth is I couldn't find what was wrong with Mr. DeLeon. The conditions in the home . . . were not . . . conducive . . . for conducting a thorough examination. His heart rate is somewhat accelerated, he's feverish but there's . . . a language barrier—"

"What? A language barrier? Come on, Dr. Chinn. I thought all you people spoke the same language."

Outright laughter now. Raphael DeLeon stared at me in panic. His eyes never left my face.

"Let's see. Did you check his appendix, Dr. Chinn?"

His appendix! Was I purposely trying not to think of that? Oh my God. What an idiot.

"Well, no, sir."

"No? What do you mean, no? A man is writhing around in agony holding his abdomen and you forget to check his appendix?"

"Well, sir I—"

"I don't believe you. What have you been doing here for two years? Maybe if I took away your privileges and made you clean some toilets you'd feel more at home."

All the laughing stopped. No one dared to move. It was like they all evaporated.

I was alone.

Dr. Fields lifted the folds of flesh and reached underneath toward the man's right side, just above his groin. When the doctor touched that spot, Mr. DeLeon roared and arched his back, trying to swing himself off the table. Four of the interns leapt to Dr. Fields's side and pinned Raphael down. Fields kept prodding and was about to flip the man over onto his side when he noticed something. He dug into Raphael's enormous belly. The giant man shrieked and began to pray.

Dr. Fields slipped off his plastic glove and said to one of the nurses stationed inside the door, "Prepare this man for surgery, Dolores. Right now."

To me he turned and said, "Well, Dr. Chinn, it looks like it's not appendicitis after all."

"What is it?" I asked. I hated my tiny little voice. The childish way it cracked in front of those men.

"It seems that Mr. DeLeon has a very small, very delicate gunshot wound about eight inches down and three inches to the right of his navel."

He let the weight, the magnitude of my mistake get comfortably nestled inside the mind of every man in the room. As he strolled from the room with his back turned to me, he took a moment to wonder aloud:

"How, may I ask, Dr. Chinn, does one misdiagnose a bullet hole?"

THE TEARS WOULDN'T wait until I got home. The best I could do was hold them in my head until I heard the metal door slam and smelled the rush of river water on the wind behind me. My father was swirling in that wind. He'd been abiding with me all night—in the whoosh of my skirt on the staircase, in the shadow of the candle's flare, and the frightened eyes that saw in me a brand-new thing. He shifted as well, deep inside those eyes that saw nothing at all.

My mother was in that wind also. Her voice walked me home.

I'd humiliated myself in front of Fields, knowing that he already wanted me thrown out of the program. A part of me, the part that grew larger with each slight, each exclusion, each "practical joke" at my expense, told me to say *fine* and just walk away. But there was also another part of me that saw mistakes and indecision and said, Well, what do you expect? I didn't know what to say to that part. I wanted to argue with myself on my own behalf. It shouldn't have been such a hard case to make.

I trudged home and stood silently outside our apartment door for a moment, securing my tired-face. I had to make sure that I'd snapped my mask tightly into place so my mother couldn't pull it off and peek behind it. How could I tell her that maybe I just didn't deserve to be a doctor? Maybe Papa had been right and we'd both been wrong.

"May? That you?" Mama called through the door. "Girl, what you doin'?"

At the same time, she pulled and I pushed, making us nearly smack heads. Mama laughed and swooped me inside. Luckily, she was in a rush that morning. She barely even looked at me.

"I got to get in early today since I missed so much time. Mrs. Dawson havin' a party and you know what that means."

Guilt fanned through my chest. On top of everything else, Mama had a heart condition. Dr. Jackson had ordered her to stop working altogether because it put too much stress on her heart. The pressure could kill her. She threw him out of the house and told him to stop tellin' tales before she really got on his case. And if she had to do that, it wouldn't be pretty.

Mama worked from dawn to five, six days a week to support me. My father hadn't put a scrap of food in my mouth in ten years. She did. And she did it because she had dreams for me. I was going to be the first Negro woman doctor in New York City. Now, to be fair, there'd been a couple of others, women who, back in the 1800s, had practiced on Long Island and in Brooklyn County. But here in the city, where we lived, it had never happened before. Until me.

Mama, I nearly killed a man today. I watched one man die and then, be-

cause I didn't want him to be lonely, I guess, I tried to send him along some company. I don't know if I can really do this anymore.

What I said was: "I'll see you when you get in then, Mama."

"Papa's coming home this evening. They said he'll be all right, but he'll have to rest for a long time. You know, you gonna have to shave him every morning, May."

"*Why?* What did I do?"

Mama shot me a sharp look. "Well, I'm not doin' it. That man is swingin' from my last nerve. Doctor said he must've been in horrible pain for some time now. But did he tell anybody? 'Course not. That would be simple. And Lord knows William Chinn can't do nothin' simple. I swear I just can't look at that man right now. You gon' have to shave and dress him till he's well enough to do it himself. You know how proud he is. If one of us don't do it, he'll hurt himself tryin' to get it done. And I ain't gon' do it, so that leaves you."

She kissed my forehead and rushed out the door before I could set up an argument. What else could I do?

I groomed and dressed my papa every day for the next six weeks, until he was well enough to stand and walk on his own two legs. The only thing he ever said to me in all that time was *mornin'*. I always answered his greeting politely and worked hard not to stare into his eyes too long or nick him with the straight-edge. It was the most time that we had spent together in years and in a way, I began to enjoy it.

In a way.

In another way, it was tiring. I constantly had to be on guard because the frustration, the bitterness, was always there, ready and waiting to creep in.

I had to keep reminding myself that things hadn't always been this way between us.

There was a time, years ago, when all three of us had been greatly in love.

Chapter 5

On a mountainside at dusk I was conceived and thought of, and the first sound my mother heard when she knew that I was listening was the trickling of water that turned moss to sponge and rain to midsummer song. There were lightning bugs and wildcats in those mountains. There were bears and white men hunting in those mountains. And there was Lulu and William tucked into the pines listening to the rasp of my breath, which sounded, at the time, more like wind.

My mother told me the stories of their courtship and my birth so many times that I can call them up, one by one, to see and taste at will. Sometimes the stories are swirling and bitter with fragrance, like strong tea. Sometimes they melt like snow or sugar on the heat of my tongue. I make up what I don't know because in my heart, I believe that my rendering is the only one that could possibly be right.

My father was an old man of forty back then, and he already had a wife and three children. My mother was a girl of sixteen, round and fertile and dark like oak, with hair swinging wild across her shoulders, but very rarely smiling. She was new to the mountains of Massachusetts and not afraid to show her displeasure in this place where good Colored people couldn't stand around on a street corner and say how-do to the passersby for fear of being called common.

The first few times she'd seen Papa in town, she hadn't been sure that he was even Colored. He never wore a sack coat, not even while working the counter at the drugstore. Each time she'd seen him, he'd been wearing a new-looking Prince Albert cutaway like the finest of white men. Then one day, when she was just too curious, when she couldn't stay out of the drugstore a minute longer, she finally allowed him to catch her glance. That's when he smiled at her. Lulu understood who he was then, plain as day, and she saw that there was a good, long journey in his eyes. Right then, she decided that he was for her. Satisfied with her mischief, she turned and strode from the drugstore without having purchased a thing.

For months they danced around one another with sly glances and whispered conversations, which, at heart, never had anything to do with the subjects at hand. Then, on a hazy afternoon in August, William sent word to her that he wouldn't wait a minute longer. Lulu wondered what had taken him so long, but what she said was "Tell me, and I'll be where you want me to be."

The summer sky was ginger-colored, already full of early-evening stars, when the time was made for coming together on the rising side of the mountain.

They lay atop the summit of this mountain, which the whites called "Monument" but that my mother and the others who looked like her referred to as "A Nest Standing Up." He won her there, with a story.

"There was a maid, the fairest of Indian maids, Bright-eyed, with wealth of raven tresses, a light form, and a gay heart. About her cabin door the wide old woods resounded with her song and fairy laughter all the summer day. She loved her cousin; such a love was deemed, by the morality of those stern tribes, incestuous, and she struggled hard and long against her love, and reasoned with her heart, as a simple Indian maiden might. In vain."

My mother listened, enraptured, as the maiden wasted from want of love. William's voice soared and dipped, rose again, then sank like the steepest mountain cliffs as he recounted the young girl's pain. His sleepy green eyes went wide and glowed like sunset as Lulu sat transfixed, trying to see what he saw.

"She went to weep where no eyes saw and was not found. She said, 'I am sick of life. All night I weep in darkness, and the morn glares on me, as upon a thing accursed, that has no business upon the earth. I cannot from my heart root out the love that wrings it so, and I must die.' "

Lulu was awestruck. This man indeed carried many journeys inside him and spilled them from his lips like sweetmilk. And yet, it was not the poem that she loved. In fact, she thought the sentiments expressed were dry and hateful and false. She'd never heard of an Indian woman who could turn that kind of pain inward on herself. The ones she knew turned it loose where they found it; released it outward to the moon and river, to the tracks of woolly leaves underfoot or, perhaps, out over the apple orchards to the south.

No, the poem could not impress her because it did not know. What moved her, what made her get to humming deep inside her chest, was his remembrance of it and his telling. It was rich and cloaked in strident color. For the rest of her life, she remembered his telling as a lively dancing thing, draped in green and gold, and scented with almonds (almond because the smell sat on his breath after he ate a whole brown bagful of them without offering any to share). Everything about the tale was hers from then on; the way his voice rose at the ends of the lines and how the blackbirds circled overhead, soaring higher and higher the closer the maiden came to death. The certainty in his tone made her ease her head down into his old man's lap. It kept her mouth closed as he slowly began to scratch her scalp with his long, oval nails.

William finished the poem and waited in silence until the sun had slipped down the chests of the trees, snagging shadows in the crevices and knolls of the skinny oaks.

Finally Lulu whispered, "You was a slave."

William nodded.

"So how'd you learn to recite such things? You read?"

"I do," he replied proudly.

"Your white people teach you?" she asked.

"Aw, no. Boy up here taught me back when I was probl'y eighteen or nineteen years old. It was William DuBois, in fact. He was just a youngster, no more than eight or nine himself at the time, but smart like a grown man. 'Cause of him, now I can read and write good as any white man in this town."

They sat in silence for a long time while Lulu digested this. William broke the silence when he asked her gently, "Do you read?"

Lulu had never in her life felt a need for any part of school learning. But when he asked and she realized she would have to say no, she became fiercely and vociferously ashamed.

Heat swept across her face and arms until she had to hide her anguish in a kiss that lasted long past the ripening and bloom of night.

Of course, William let the topic drop and got on to other things. But he wasn't fooled. And the last thing he said to her that evening before they left each other was "Don't worry, Lu. I'll teach you what I know."

Then William went home to his wife and children, and Lulu came home with me.

Six months later, with his wagon wheels reeling and engorged from the ice lodged inside the spokes, my father rode through Great Barrington proper, over the Housatonic River and down slightly south to Butternut Basin. My mother was waiting outside her room in the servants' quarters behind Sheffield Manor. She clutched a carpetbag full of cooking utensils against her bulging belly and an old tweed coat that belonged to her employer, Mr. Martin Sheffield. As she stepped into the wagon, she handed the coat to my father, who stared at it hungrily, but was too proud to put it on just then. Instead, he laid it casually on the boards behind him. So my mother shrugged and pretended not to notice that he was still wearing the Prince Albert coat that she'd met him in, the one made for summertime, over a bundle of frayed work shirts and an itchy-looking woolen muffler. William flicked the reins, and Lulu also turned her face from his shivering hands with their bone-white knuckles chapped bloody from cold. Silently, they started back across the river.

He'd rented two rooms in Mrs. Bessie Cullen's boardinghouse down toward the end of Rossiter Street. William's old wife, Martha, and his three other daughters lived across the backyard on Elm Street at the end of the crooked alley that connected it to Rossiter. If he looked hard enough through the brittle brown web of morning glory vines behind Mrs. Cullen's house, he would see his old family sitting down to supper through their window. If the air were clear enough, he would smell the food, too. An unfortunate and embarrassing situation to say the least, but it couldn't be avoided.

Great Barrington had only two streets where a Negro family could settle in without risking some other family's hostility.

When William and Lulu pulled up in front of Mrs. Cullen's place, Martha and her girls were waiting. The oldest child (that would be Irene) was only about five years younger than Lulu, and she looked tall enough and fired up enough to beat her. Taking in the older girl out of the corner of her eye, Lulu instinctively cupped her arms around her hefty stomach. She glanced at the younger ones, holding hands and huddling against the cold with snot drying across their cheeks, and dropped her eyes to her shoes. Realizing that there was no way to get around them, Lulu took a breath, stepped down from the wagon and plodded through the icy mud up the porch stairs.

Martha Chinn, who was blue-eyed and had prize hair that hung to her hips, stared incredulously at my mother. Mama gazed back at her, sadly, almost painfully, but with no offer of apology. Martha's eyes welled and she raised her fingers to her throat to block the wind.

"Just wanted to have a look at you," she whispered. "Won't be back, though."

She nodded at my mother but Mama didn't move. Then Martha and her children were gone back into the house to cut across the yard and take the short way home through the garden path.

Mrs. Cullen sat judge in her parlor window, Bible in her lap and a stovepipe for a gavel, reading lips because it was too cold to lift the beveled panes. But she saw enough to suit her. Old Culley passed the word around quick—in time for it to be dished up with supper—that William Chinn had gotten himself mixed up with a half-Indian conjure woman (who by the by wasn't even half as pretty as high-yellow Martha) without any heart or shame to speak of.

My mother knew what was going on and later that night begged my father to take her far away from Rossiter Street.

He licked the slender edges of his mustache and told her, "Don't be a child, Lulu. Niggers talk. That's just what they do. Sometimes that's all they do. If you not used to that by now, you never will be."

Then he reached for his hat and he left.

FOR THREE YEARS, my mother, my father and I lived in Mrs. Cullen's two back rooms. Very few people were friendly with us, but after a while it didn't matter. As I recall (even though it's more of a feeling than a recollection), we were happy. Outside our rooms, we shared the face of silence, used it as a shield, a high gray wall that was hard on the outside and hollow within. But inside, alone with ourselves, we unfurled great dramas of love and laughter. And in those dramas, my father was the narrator, mother a dancer and scribe. I was a creamy-colored cherub, warm and sleepy with love.

Papa had stayed good to his word and taught Mama how to read. She was a swift and greedy pupil, devouring entire sections of the Bible, which she insisted on learning from but that my father, the atheist, hated to crack open. They'd finally compromised on Song of Solomon, and with those words they played, nearly every night together.

I can remember Mama saying to me, "Learn this. You're going to learn this, May. You're going to tell these stories like your papa does, in a way that I can't. You will."

Then she would leave my ear and begin twirling around my father, who always seemed to breathe her in with great swallows before speaking.

On those nights he would recite, " 'How fair is thy love, my sister, my spouse! How much better is thy love than wine! Thy lips, O my spouse, drop as the honeycomb: honey and milk are under thy tongue; and the smell of thy garments is like the smell of Lebanon. A garden enclosed is my sister, my spouse; a spring shut up, a fountain sealed . . . a well of living waters and streams . . .' "

And, as I watched, my mother would grow tall. She became *Amana* then—the purple mountain of birth and redemption in Solomon's song, the womb of the desert river Abana around which ancient tribes drew breath and villages prayed.

And she responded to him with the words that he'd given her. Her voice would stand up to meet his, stiffly at first, much like one pictured Lazarus stumbling up out of his death. Then, when she was sufficiently large and free, she'd speak.

" 'The voice of my beloved!' " she'd say. " 'Behold, he cometh leaping upon the mountains, skipping upon the hills. My beloved spake and said unto me, Rise up, my love, my fair one, and come away. For, lo, the winter is past, the rain is over and gone. The flowers appear on the earth; the time of the singing birds is come. My beloved is mine and I am his: he feedeth among the lilies . . .' "

That was our fountainhead, our church, in which my father, the keeper of the words, taught my mother and me to pray.

Having been so young, I only remember scraps of fact, like faded photographs. But the heat, the truth of love, is what I remember deeply, even now as I grow old.

This was how we lived, in a private world of poetry and song, until the one evening when my father didn't come home at the usual time.

That night, I don't remember much at all. I know that my mother left me in our bed to search the streets for him. I know that she dragged him in, and I smelled, for the first time in my life that I can recall, the heavy odor of liquor on his clothes. She stood silently while he beat the walls, and that caused Old Culley to come storming up to our door, cursing like the worst kind of sinner and threatening eviction. They tossed around some heated words about Martha. Then, after a great commotion, my mother retrieved her carpetbag from beneath our bed and threw all three of her dresses into it.

I don't know what happened next. I only know that, shortly after, the three of us boarded a train bound for New York City and I never saw Great Barrington again.

WHEN WE ARRIVED IN New York, my father found us a one-room, cold-water flat on Sixteeth Street and First Avenue in the middle of a row of dilapidated tenements. The surrounding apartment houses unfailingly intercepted any traces of sunlight or fresh air so that our building stood in a haze of perpetual shadow. In the musty courtyard that connected the rear of our tenement to three others, stray cats, dogs and derelicts fought for sleeping space.

Inside, the rooms were in a horrendous state of disrepair. State law said that every room had to have a window. So the landlords carved out a square high in the wall of each interior room and shoved a pane of glass into it. But most of these "windows" were already cracked or broken. Shards and splinters and rat droppings littered the hallway floor. Mama carried me inside that first day. She never set me down once while she inspected the room that was supposed to be her new home.

Compared to the other rooms in the building, the one that Papa managed to get for us was spacious. It had once been the living room of a four-room apartment. In the corner near the door was a bathtub. When no one was bathing, my mother placed two long pieces of plywood across it and used it as a table. On the other side of the door, a small sink with a rusted spigot leaned from the wall. Next to the sink stood a potbellied stove that burned wood and coal. Papa pushed two small beds with wrought-iron frames into the remaining two corners of the room. To get to the toilet, we had to walk through the Johnsons' room. The Wilsons next door had to walk through both our flat and the Johnsons'.

I fretted every time I had to use the toilet. The dank, tiny box of a room reeked of waste. At night, the pipes froze. During the day, after thawing out, they often spewed a thick soup of feces and urine across the floor and down the hall.

Over these and other indignities, my mother grew withdrawn and anxious. Papa held her, crooning promises softly into her hair as they lay on their bed. I listened to him from my bed, the warm one directly across from the stove, while he pledged freedom and security as soon as the streets thawed and the work came.

The months passed and the promises remained the same, but the work never materialized. Mama got a job as a maid a few weeks after arriving in New York. But for Papa, there were no jobs to be had. Mama begged him to pass, just during the day, just at work, so he could get a good construction job like the Poles and the Irish and the Italians were getting. He refused. Before long my parents began to fight. The first blowout that I remember started because I was four years old and hungry.

There was no bread in the house and no milk, no flour for biscuits, nor wood for the stove. No sugar for sugar water. So I cried. I cried until my own crying frightened me and I started kicking the rotted wood on the wall in the corner near my bed. Mama stood behind me and let me kick and scream until I tired myself out and eventually fell asleep in her arms.

I woke up in the middle of the night when I heard, "Where you been at, William?"

Then the door creaked shut and Papa's voice whispered, "The

foreman over at the construction site on Fifth and Thirty-third asked me to wait—"

"Nigger, where have I heard *that* before?"

"Lulu, I'm doing the best I can. You know that. Why you got to start this—"

"Just tell me where you been. You ain't been with no foreman this long."

"Look, I just want to get off my feet—"

"You been drinking, William."

Papa sucked in a deep breath. "Naw, Lulu. That's not how it is."

"Don't lie, William. Please."

"How I'm gonna be out drinkin', Lu? I ain't got money for drinkin'."

"Yes you do," she whispered. "I put my only dollar in your jacket pocket last night so you wouldn't come beggin' me this morning. Don't talk to me like I'm stupid."

Mama's voice wilted under the weight of her words. The angrier she got, the quieter she got. "You promised, William. You promised to bring something in tonight. But here you come with your hands empty. Again. You know May hasn't eaten since last evening. What you gonna tell her?"

"Lulu, that's not fair—"

"Don't talk to me about fair. You don't know nothin' about fair. Just like you don't know nothin' about pride. Seems to me like a real man that's got some dignity and some worth to him takes care of his own. Don't you think? But then again, you don't have the best record at doing that anyway, do you? Looks like I should've figured that out way back in the beginning."

Papa flung his cane across the room. "I am a grown man," he muttered. "I'm out there every day scrappin', trying to box groceries or dig ditches or anything so I can bring something back here into this house. I ain't gonna take this mess off you."

"So what you want to do? Huh? Leave?"

Papa was silent.

"Answer up, *man*. What you gon' do? You wanna leave? Do you? 'Cause if you wanna leave, go ahead. It don't make no difference. Matter of fact, I want you to leave."

Mama went to the door and threw it open. "Go on. Go 'head and get out. Go."

"Lulu, you just angry. Talkin' loud. You don't mean it."

"*Nigger, don't tell me what I mean. Now I said get out.*"

"Baby, why you want to fuss with me like this? Why you want to wake up Ladybug and spread our business for all these other people to hear us? Come on, now. Close the door. Come on, let's us get in the bed. We both tired."

"Naw, man. You ain't tired. *I'm* the one tired 'cause *I'm* the one been at work all day."

Papa's voice was small, so small I almost didn't hear it. He said softly, "I don't want to go, Lulu."

"What?"

"I said I don't want to go. I don't want to leave you. I don't."

Mama sighed. "You mean you ain't got nowhere else to go," she said, and closed the door.

Mama slept with me that night and for quite a while after. Papa tried hard to make up with her. He was up with her at dawn every day. After a quick breakfast of coffee and bread, Papa put on his gray three-piece suit and bowler hat, took his cane from behind the door and went out to the construction sites, liveries and notions shops making inquiries. He talked on his plans to move every day.

"You wait," he'd say. "There's going to be three, no *four* rooms with a proper kitchen like Mrs. Cullen had so you can fix those casseroles like you used to. I know I promised Ladybug a hobby-horse at Christmas, so as soon as we move I'm gonna make one. I know where I can get good wood for it, too. And it won't be too expensive. Our place is gonna be on a good street, in the Bronx, and it'll be so good that Ladybug can sit outside on her hobbyhorse all afternoon and you won't even worry about her."

If he hadn't stumbled in after hours the night before, Mama would listen and encourage him. She'd tell him that he was bound to find work. They were going to have to open the tunnel construction to qualified Negro drillers soon. And they were practically snatching men off the boats and flinging them into the subway stations to complete the underground West Side line up to 145th Street. Sooner or later they'd have to start picking from the lines of Negro men haunting the construction sites, watching and waiting, looking for a break. If they picked anyone, surely it would be him. In the meanwhile, the twenty-five-dollar-a-month rent wasn't too much for her. She could do it and still put a little aside for furniture for the apartment when it came.

Chapter 6

The summer I turned five, Mama decided that she'd had enough of the Lower East Side. At least for me. She hadn't told Papa, or anyone, but she'd been saving money since before we came to New York. And she'd never touched it, not for food or fuel or clothes. That money was mine.

Without consulting my father, she took the money she'd saved, paid off a full year of tuition and bought a train ticket for me to Bordentown Manual Training and Industrial School. The Bordentown School was the top Negro Primary School in the East, tucked away into sleepy Bordentown, New Jersey, about one hundred miles south of New York.

Housed on an old estate, the school had once been owned by Commodore Charles Stewart. Stewart's fierce fighting in the War of 1812 prompted his fellow soldiers to give him the nickname "Old Ironside." The townspeople continued to call his mansion Old Ironside, even after the Colored children moved into it and took it over. It was my first time away from home, the first time in my life that I was to spend even a night separated from my mother. I cried bitterly for the entire trip. But when I arrived at the school gates, almost immediately, all of my little-girl fears evaporated.

A gorgeous chocolate-skinned woman named Miss Morrison showed me up to the second-floor dormitory. There I saw the most amazing thing: an entire roomful of fidgeting, giggling, pouncing little girls just like me. I had never been around children my own age, and they seemed to me to be almost fantastic, like the little elves and fairies that my father made up stories about. I believed then, in my truest heart, that they'd been made and set down in this place specifically for me.

Those days at Bordentown were some of the best of my childhood. Being the youngest children at the school, my class of five-year-olds weren't as strictly monitored as the rest. So we spent much of our time in devilish pursuits, wandering the fields and gardens surrounding the school, searching for the spark of creation we used to mold the ordinary into the magical. On the grounds, we unearthed wild artichokes and ate them raw, while they were still wet from the morning dew. We dug up stalks of wild asparagus, which we ferried to the kitchen to be cooked. We little girls lay in the dirt on our bellies and ate raspberries and black-berries and strawberries off the vine until our faces dripped purple with juice.

In the woods along the railroad tracks that ran beside the river, there had once been a vineyard. It had long since grown over with thickets. We waded in among the brambles to pick grapes, fat like marbles and big as an eyeball, so dense and juicy they looked nearly black. We steadily ignored the snakes, beetles, and all other manner of creatures that were supposed to send our little-girl selves off screaming—but never did.

The townspeople, black and white, had gathered together and built us a tall red barn where we kept cows. The headmaster assigned the older boys and girls to milk the cows in shifts, but some-how I got put on the case too. An apple-headed fifth grader named Wilford, otherwise known as Pee-De-Bed Will, who I loved, whose job I was doing, told me that if you milked a cow the wrong way, she'd kick over your bucket. Well, my skinny white cow Eartha never kicked over my bucket, but she never gave me any milk either. I pulled and pulled on those teats for what seemed like hours, but not one drop of milk fell. My biggest concern that autumn in Bordentown was how to get the milk to fall.

Of the academics, I don't recall much except that I got a copy of a book by Charles Kingsley called *Water Babies* as a reward for high scholarship. That delicious woman Miss Morrison handed me the book and said, "May, you know you're smart. We know you're smart. We're not going to let you back away from that." And then I was dismissed, left alone with a pride swelling in my chest so big and so tight that I couldn't speak. I just sat with my book, with my feeling, and coddled it silently, dreaming of growing up so that I could be a teacher, too, and stay at school with Miss Morrison forever.

In this way I began to discover my self, to understand the fact that I existed apart from mother, father, teacher. It dawned within me that I was more than a thought that smiled when someone else smiled and walked with an outstretched hand. I wouldn't ever vanish because my mother had turned out a light and walked away a long distance, off by herself.

Upon learning this about myself, mirrors became attractive to me for the first time in my life. Reflecting pools, the headmaster's tea service, a warm, full milk pail with the foam scraped away—anything that showed me my face. The lamp beside my bed stayed on during the night because the glimmering light dropped a curtain at the window, erasing fields, oak branches, the flight and full circle of the moon. Only my face remained.

I found that I could make mirrors out of anything. Inside, outside, anywhere. It gave me magic. And, as it's in the nature of children to draw as close to magic as possible and adore it, the other children began to love me. Little girls followed me and fought over who could hold my hand next. Little boys got quiet when I passed and made small circles in the dirt with their toes. The teachers hugged and cuddled me, engulfing me in scents of cinnamon and lavender. And I don't think they even knew why. But I did. I understood exactly why. Because shortly after Miss Morrison gave me *Water Babies*, I'd taken it under my bed and, with a large quill pen, wrote on the inside cover:

This is May's.

DURING THAT FIRST WINTER, I got a toothache. Eventually, the dull pain passed and I thought no more of it. But suddenly I felt tired all the time and nauseous. I had fevers that made me sweat, but at the same time, I was wracked with chills down to the bone.

A girl named Ruby, who slept in the bed next to mine, first noticed the small sore on the right side of my face, near the area where I'd had the bad tooth.

"I don't know what that is comin' out your face, May, but it sure is nasty."

All us girls ran to the end of the corridor where there was an oval mirror low enough for us to see in. I looked, and sure enough, saw a dime-sized lesion on my face dripping pus.

The teachers called in the doctor from town, a tall, lanky white fellow named Dr. Jordan. Dr. Jordan had four long, vertical scars on his face. Each time he turned to the left to retrieve something, I stared at them. I couldn't help it. He looked like a roustabout with those scars, like a drunkard or one of those just-off-the-boat

Irishmen that Papa complained about all the time. I'd never seen a gentleman with a mashed-up face like that before.

"You know, May," he said when he caught me staring, "you can touch my face if you want. You don't have to be frightened. You might not believe this, but when I was a little boy, I had the same sickness that you have. It's something called osteomyelitis. When I was about your age, I fell off my bicycle and fractured my cheekbone. The bone got infected just like your tooth got infected. I had operations just like you're going to have. But I tell you what. I'm going to do a much better job with you than I got. You're much too beautiful to have a hangdog face like mine when you grow up."

He laughed and smiled, and I tried to smile back but couldn't quite manage it.

For months, I struggled with a sickness that my teachers did their best to help me understand but that still made no sense to me. Explanations meant nothing. I lived in excruciating pain with a disease that had eaten a hole clear through the side of my face.

Each week for nine weeks, Dr. Jordan scraped the infected tissue from the interior of the lower right side of my jaw. At least twice a week, the area had to be packed with a yellowish, crystalline compound made from iodine. This was held in place by gauze and a large bandage that tied around my head.

I tried, as much as I could, to attend my classes so I could sit with my friends and watch Miss Morrison float around the bright yellow classroom. But it became too much. More and more often, I was confined to bed, unable to eat or speak properly and struck dumb with pain. Eventually, they called Mama to come and take me home.

She arrived a day later and packed me onto a train bound for Irvington-on-the-Hudson. When I realized that we weren't going back to the city, I knew that, wherever we ended up, my father wouldn't be there.

Eventually I got up the courage to ask, "Mama, where do we live now?"

"With the people that I work for."

"Oh," I mumbled. And then, because I was still curious, I asked, "Where does Papa live?"

"Back in Manhattan. Somewhere on the west side of town, I think. Why?"

"Just wondering, that's all," I muttered. For the rest of the trip, I stared at the cover of my *Water Babies*, silently mouthing the words. I didn't need to open it. I had long since memorized all the words and could call the pictures up in my mind clearer than the landscape flashing past my window.

My mother took me to a grand estate at the end of Millionaire Row in Irvington-on-the-Hudson. It was the home of Charles Tiffany, the founder of Tiffany & Company in New York. Mama hustled me around the house, introducing me to the family and the other servants. I barely glanced at any of them. The house captured me. The polished marble floors, the velvet drapes brushing against the pale silk wallpaper, the crystal dangling from the ceilings and fixed to the walls—I'd never even imagined that anything could look so fine.

The only things that I didn't like about the house were the mirrors. Gilded, minutely engraved mirrors everywhere. Mirrors that reminded me what everyone else saw now when they looked at me. Why, instead of smiling with approval and pleasure, people held their hands in front of their mouths and looked away, far above my head. No one wanted to look at a bent-over, pale-skinned child whose hair had fallen out in patches; a child that shuffled around with a sticky red-, yellow-, and brown-streaked bandage wrapped under her chin and tied in a knot at the crown of her head.

I hated my face now, all slashed with scars. In the places on my right cheek where the skin was still intact, maps of crusty scabs emerged. If I moved or smiled too quickly they cracked and oozed pus.

My friends had disappeared to where I would never find them again. My father had vanished too. And, once again, I knew why.

When Mama showed me to our small basement room, I tucked my *Water Babies* under the farthest corner of the bed and left it there.

EACH MORNING, Mama served the young Mrs. Tiffany breakfast in her suite—croissants, peeled fruits, chilled juice that smelled fresh and strong as the coffee. Then, as I watched, Mama would help Mrs. Tiffany into a corset that took her tiny frame and squeezed it unnaturally thin. Next, she would don one of her many tea gowns, sometimes plum satin, at other times, perhaps, a beaded silk crepe with a long lace train. I lusted after those gowns, imagining Mama wrapped in chiffon and standing before the long mirror, laughing softly at some clever thing I'd said as I dressed her.

At night, I slept with Mama in her room in the servants' quarters. During the day, I stayed with the Tiffany children. We ate together, played together and took our lessons from the governess. We learned French, German and art history along with our other basic studies. On Saturday mornings, Mrs. Tiffany would take us into the city to places like the Hippodrome Society Circus or to see plays like *Peter Pan* with Maude Adams. The Walter Damrosch Children's Concerts were my favorites. It was the first time that I'd ever heard classical music. When Rachmaninoff's Piano Concerto Number 2 played, it awoke in me an almost painful desire to run my finger along the flickering edges of those sounds, to taste the notes. If I could eat them, they would taste clear like rain, I thought. Or sometimes, when the music stretched and swelled wide, I knew that the sound would drip like yellow honey from my chin.

Sometimes, on weekend evenings, Papa came to visit. He was always very quiet and polite, always sober, and he made sure to take his bowler hat off at the front gate, lest the other staffers call my mother common. He brought small presents, whatever he could afford—toilet water for Mama, a top or some marbles for me. And they would sit and talk politely in her room for an hour or two while I played on the floor. Papa never left without begging Mama to come back to him. He'd plead softly, whispering into her hair while she stared down at me as I pretended to be tiny and invisible. I pretended that I didn't have ears.

When she wouldn't answer, he'd say, "Well, you just think about it. How about that?" And then I'd walk him out to the front gate.

Papa and I had a ritual. He'd lean down and kiss my good cheek. Then he'd move to the right side of my face and kiss above and below the puckered, scarred skin underneath my cheekbone. Then he'd kiss right in the middle of the scar, in the place where all the flesh was gone, where the skin sagged dryly against my jawbone, and he'd say, "My goodness. You sure are lovelier and lovelier every time I see you, Ladybug. I swear you are."

And then he'd be gone.

During the winter, the Tiffanys lived down in the family mansion in Manhattan. Only the servants stayed on premises. My mother and I, two other maids, a butler and the groundskeepers were all that remained in the house on Millionaire Row. The place seemed cavernous and cold. I could see my breath when I wandered up the spiral staircases, into the upper rooms, hiding in the corners where the feckless heat from the cook's kitchen fire never reached. I learned how to be alone in those rooms and on those snowy lawns. I learned how to open the silence like one of my books and read it, telling the stories of my life to come without words.

But Mama got worried at my silence. I don't think she liked the quality of it.

"You actin' just like this house, and I'll not stand for it," she said one day. She threw on my hat and coat and ushered me out the door with Grover, the gardener, who walked me a mile and a half to the Irvington Primary School.

But my time at the Irvington School didn't last very long. The other children constantly stared at my scars, sticking their fingers into the dented, creased trough on my face. The boys made much admiration over it. They punched me in the arm and said how I didn't look much tougher than the ordinary girl but *gosh*—I must be if I could have half my face scraped off and live to tell. The girls whispered and shook their heads. Two of them were Negro like me. They were two plump, butternut brown girls called Thelma and Amy. One afternoon, they walked up to me and firmly informed me (as though the question had been up for debate for quite some time) that they would not be me, not even with all that pale skin and long hair of mine, for nothin' in the world 'cause of my scarred face. If not for the scars, then maybe they would want to be me, but as it stood, uh-uh, no thank you. They would stay brown and unscarred forever.

I raced home in tears and refused to listen when my mother tried to tell me that the others didn't mean any particular harm. They were just being children, and it was in the nature of a child to be curious and forthright. Still, she stopped insisting that I go to school in town. Instead, she left me alone to read for long hours in her bed, while she and the others dawdled through the huge rooms or sat silently over coffee. Sometimes I joined them and got a small cup of coffee of my own that smelled like cinnamon and looked gold like the peels of bark from a eucalyptus tree. I never looked at my mother or the other women at these times because they never looked at me. Instead, I stared out the picture windows at the spines of the maple branches, which were dusted with ice, while thinking of spring and other human sounds.

A fresh layer of snow had appeared on the ground the morning that word came about Mr. Tiffany being dead and us having to move. His son, Louis Comfort, had taken over and divided up the estate. Mama's services were no longer needed.

Papa came up that weekend. As usual, he wrapped his arms around Mama's waist and whispered, "Lulu, I miss you awfully bad. I can't live no more without you and Ladybug. How long you going to make me beg before you come back to me?"

This time, Mama sighed and said, "All right, William. I'll get us packed."

Papa blanched. " 'Scuse me?" he sputtered. "Come again now?"

"I said we gon' come back to the city with you, William. You go on up and fix you a sandwich and some coffee, and we'll be ready in a few minutes."

Papa stood in the middle of the room with his mouth agape and his eyes fastened to his feet. Mama watched him. I watched him.

"What is it, William?"

"Well, I . . . I just . . . But Lulu, I didn't think . . . I mean I didn't know that . . . It's just that I need some . . . some time to . . . do things. I thought you were gonna be here for a while. Tomorrow there's a fellow that said he wants to see me—"

Mama sat at the foot of the bed next to me and put her head down.

"You ain't got a job yet, do you?"

Papa glanced at me and his face flamed.

"Where you livin' then, William?"

"Ladybug, please leave the room for your ma and me to talk."

"*Where?*"

"Ladybug, please—"

"You ain't got nowhere to live, do you? You still sleepin' in one of those nasty, pissy hot beds on somebody's kitchen floor. Same as last winter. Ain't you?"

"Lulu, you got to listen to me."

Mama hadn't raised her voice once. But now as she spoke, it shook, and the trembling instantly brought tears slipping down my face.

"You better tell me the truth, William. You better tell it fast and you better tell it right. I been livin' on premises scratching for these white people and you been comin' here this whole time with flowers and promises. And now, when we need you, you mean to tell me that you in the same exact place we left out of two years ago?"

Papa didn't answer. He didn't look at either of us.

"May," Mama said. "Go on. Get upstairs now."

I sped past my father toward the door and never even thought to close it behind me as I crashed up the stairs.

A WEEK LATER, Mama and I boarded a train that wound its way up the Hudson Valley toward Pawling, New York. Through one of the other servants, Mama got work with a Quaker family called the Wheelers. They were very severe, hardworking people who raised cattle for milk and slaughter. Their land stretched across the valley and up to the foot of the Berkshire Mountains, almost to the Connecticut border.

I don't remember much about the year and a half that we spent in Pawling. I know that my mother worked very hard for

Mrs. Wheeler. She rose before dawn every day to go up the farmhouse, and most nights she wouldn't finish until well after dark.

Every week when she got paid, she'd send me to town for supplies. When I returned, she'd take any change that I brought home and put it into glass jars labeled with tape and one of my red drawing pencils: 50¢, 25¢, 10¢ and 5¢. Even the pennies got stored in a cracked bric-a-brac container that she kept under the bed. The folding money went somewhere that only Mama knew about. I'd watched her do this all my life. But for the first time, in Pawling, I began to take note. I started to understand.

Mama sent me to a one-room schoolhouse in Quaker Hill, where I was the only Colored child in attendance. These children, at least, didn't pick at my scars and single me out. They didn't seem to have the imagination for it. For the most part, their imaginations had been strictly disciplined and honed into acceptable shape. And if variety got suppressed in them, spontaneity was expressly forbidden. It seemed as if my differences never occurred to them as different or in any other way remarkable. They seemed friendly enough, but wholly uninspired. This suited me perfectly.

On the farm, there were no other children for me to play with, except Olivia, the daughter of the town mailman. They lived relatively close, a couple miles south of the Wheelers, in a two-room cabin. She was a retarded girl, two years older than I. Though I played almost exclusively with Olivia for a year and a half, all I remember of her face is that it was open and adoring. The other things that I've kept back are sparse and disconnected. I know that she was born in December and that she had strong and wavy hair that looked like fire when it spread. I remember thinking at the time that she had hair that looked like it belonged on a much smarter girl.

Our routines never varied, never once, until the afternoon that my father drove up to the Wheelers' front door in a hired buggy and a charcoal three-piece suit to tell my mother that he'd gotten a job.

Mama seemed confused. I prayed for her face to open up and be happy. I prayed for her to smile at him. She looked tired, though. Too tired for smiling. But at least that meant that she was also too tired to argue. So I took out the carpetbag and started packing while Papa gently kissed her hair and wiped his cheeks with a new cotton handkerchief.

Within a week, we arrived back in New York City and moved into a two-room flat in San Juan Hill. I was heartbroken. It felt good to have my father back, but I missed Olivia terribly. I missed my school, where the children never pointed or stared or snickered. I loathed the tickle of roaches bold enough to crawl across my legs and feet as I slept. Eventually, I only slept in fits and starts. I couldn't eat, and if I spilled a glass of milk or couldn't answer a question quickly enough, I cried.

Mama was beside herself. I heard her at night, pacing the floor when she should have been sleeping. Eventually, she hit on the idea of music. She knew how I'd been fascinated by the Damrosch concerts that the Tiffanys had taken me to. So she dragged my father out one Saturday morning and came back, hours later, hauling a rickety upright piano to our third-floor flat.

To this day, I have no idea where or how she got that piano. But her inclination was dead-on. The music soothed me. In fact, it flooded me. Music became my joy, my spirit, the bulk and the width of my memories. The notes became integral to me in a breathing way, a way that only my mother's presence had ever occupied my soul.

Girdled in the quiet of that new peace, Lulu slept.

*   *   *

SEPTEMBER CAME AND Mama enrolled me in the nearest elementary school, a three-story brick building on West Sixty-third Street. A strictly Negro school. All of the children, like me, came from the tenements of San Juan Hill and down into Hell's Kitchen. After the first day of classes, I came home and Mama looked through my schoolbooks. Usually, she'd sit and read the beginnings of the stories with me and then guess how she thought they would end. But when she opened my new textbook, she gasped and covered her mouth like she did when spiders got in the house.

"May, come over here."

"Yes, ma'am."

"That teacher up there at the school—she give you this book looking like this?"

"Yes, ma'am."

"You sure? You sure you ain't done nothin' to this book, nothin' at all on your own?"

"No, ma'am. I just put it in my strap and carried it home," I mumbled.

"All right, baby. You go on into the other room now."

Mama put a pot of coffee on to boil. Then she sat down with her back to the stove and flipped through every ripped up, scribbled on, dog-eared, greasy page in that book. She made a study of each furrow, all the curse words scrawled in pencil in the margins, every comprehension story that had the ending torn out. Papa came home, but Mama never looked up from the book in her lap. He spoke to her but she didn't speak back. Eventually, he went to bed with no supper. If she noticed, neither of us could tell. Late in the night, she was still at that table. I came up beside her and called her name. When she looked up, I saw something that I'd never before seen in my life.

My mother was crying.

Silently, with her fist in her mouth, with her back to the door where I slept and that book still perched in her lap, she sat crying. Her tears horrified me. Suddenly, I couldn't breathe. I stretched open my mouth to cry too, but no sound came out. Mama scooped me up and instantly started crooning. *Hush, baby, nothin's wrong. Mama's fine. Hush yourself.* Back to bed I went and this time, she went with me. She lay next to me on the bed and let her hair down so that it covered my face. The coconut-oil smell of my mother's hair lulled me to sleep.

A month later, I came in from school to find Mama already at home and everything we owned packed up, waiting by the door. "We moving, May," she informed me. "There's a neighborhood opening up, and we got in."

"Opening up" meant that a few black families had managed to get into a white neighborhood. White flight instantly ensued. But in the interim, while the Negroes were still coming and the whites going, the schools would be kept in top form. The city never allowed the schools to get run-down until the last of the whites had gone—and that could take months or even years.

For the next ten years, my mother chased the white flight all across New York City. During that time, we lived at Columbus Circle, right across the street from Central Park, 101st Street, Ninety-third Street at Amsterdam Avenue and then all the way downtown to Sixteeth Street so that I could attend Washington Irving High School in the very first year that it opened. Every time we moved, Mama made Papa drag that battered, crazy-looking upright along with us. Papa agreed, as long as I swore on my life that I'd never play ragtime. Only sluts played syncopation and ragtime on the piano.

I said yes, of course, and took my music with me.

PART TWO

Chapter 7

The summer ended in flames.

Nations erupted and were purged in these fires, which blazed across fields and meadows and between borders, camouflaging a continent in drifting ash.

I'd just turned eighteen. Eighteen and beginning the tenth grade in a year when men started digging graves all across Europe and calling them trenches. Germany declared war on Russia and France, and then invaded Belgium. Britain, Serbia and Montenegro spit in the dirt and declared war on Germany. Austria, not to be left out, declared war on Russia too. Russia, France and Britain turned around and declared war on Turkey.

"They get what they deserve," Papa stated daily, and threw his paper in the trash. Then he'd fish it out moments later to reread some particularly frustrating bit.

"No need to get so upset at something ain't even your fight, William."

"Not yet," he'd say. "But we gon' be in it soon enough. And

who do you think they gon' send? When we go in, who you think gon' be doing most of the dying? Colored. Colored and these damned immigrants. White boys fight with words. Then they expect us to pick up the guns and the shovels. Mark my words. When that happens, we suddenly gon' be full-fledged citizens then. Believe it."

I wanted to be concerned in a way that felt suitably poignant. In my outrage, I might've signed up for patriot classes at school—mechanics and printing, that kind of thing. But, by and large, the fear, the atrocities of war escaped me.

I was in love.

Ferdinand and his wife were dead. And I was in love. General Zamon became president of Haiti. Which meant next to nothing to me because I was in love. Boston defeated Philadelphia 4–0 to win the World Series. And guess what?

Gabriel attended Morris High School, like me. Though he was a year ahead of me, I was a year older. We found each other in the most peculiar way—because he recognized Stravinsky's latest, *Le Rossignol*, and decided that he wanted to hear more.

Classes had just begun. I stayed late one afternoon in the music room practicing with my best girlfriend, Lila Laurie. Lila should have been singing the words to "Watch Your Step." But Irving Berlin was the farthest thing from her mind. Instead she lounged across the top of the piano, laughing at nothing and gorging herself on Mama's oatmeal cookies. I didn't mind. We left the classroom windows wide open so we could smell the nest of red hibiscus planted right outside and see ourselves lit up with sun. Lila liked specific notes particularly well—C sharp, D flat, A minor—so I made sure to add them into as many phrases as I could, even when they didn't belong. Beautiful, silly, sepia-skinned Lila. Big-boned Lila, who spoke three languages, including Latin, which

I hated. Lila, who made the white boys and the black boys drop their books when she passed. She could make me laugh at anything.

Since Lila wasn't concentrating, I decided to fiddle with something new. *Le Rossignol.* I stroked the keys gently, barely touching them, trying to tell her a corrupted story with more silence weaving through it than sound. But I wanted to tell it simply. Simple and true. That way I knew that she'd get it.

Eyes closed, I found a flow of notes like the words I remembered from my childhood. *How fair is thy love . . . how much better is thy love than wine . . . milk and honey are under thy tongue; and the smell of thy garments is like the smell of Lebanon . . .* Tones stretching into meaning that had never been intended, colors on the higher notes that sounded pulled apart and green, like an early sunset.

Somewhere in the middle, Gabriel peeked his head in. Our eyes met and he said one word: "*Rossignol?*"

That was it.

Lila vanished, but not before fluffing my hair and pinching my cheeks (*to make them rosy. Trust me*). Then, on her way out, she "accidentally" knocked my books off the back of the piano onto the floor. That was her test. If the boy was any class of gentleman, he'd stop and pick them up. When Gabriel bent down to retrieve my geometry and history texts, Lila grinned and flew out the door. Silly girl.

"I'm Gabriel Stevens," he said. I nodded as if his beautiful new face was the most ordinary sight of God.

"How did you learn to play like that?" Gabriel's voice made me blush. It sounded soft and sure, like a grown man who smiles and leans way in to you before he speaks.

"Been playing since I was about seven or eight," I told him. "The lady I study with, Miss Lee, only allows two things. Classics and hymns. So does my father. He hates ragtime like the plague. But I don't mind. I love the classics. I've loved this kind of music since before I can remember."

I had no earthly excuse for talking so much.

"Your playing is . . . well, I don't know what to call it. It's so different. How often do you have to practice to play like that?"

"Oh, I play some every day."

"Every day?" He whistled, impressed. "You have your own piano?"

I nodded.

"Oh boy. Your parents must have some money to buy you your own piano."

"No, it's nothing like that." I slipped my hands across the keys, gently plucking a chord in D minor. "They just . . . love me. They make sacrifices."

Gabriel edged a bit closer. He had quiet eyes, so dark that the irises had spilled over into the white parts. They looked cloudy.

"That must be nice," he said. "You're very lucky, May."

"How do you know my name?"

"Who doesn't know you?" He laughed deep in his throat until I blushed again and closed the lid over the keys.

"Can I walk you home?" he asked.

I shouldn't have said yes. But I did.

THE DIRECT ROUTE HOME from school circled nearly two miles around the outskirts of Crotona Park. On that day, though, we must have walked at least five.

Gabriel Stevens glowed. Ginger-skinned with thick thighs that tugged at the seams of his trousers, his beauty interrupted my thought.

His family was new to the States he told me, having moved

here from Halfway Tree in Jamaica about four years before. When he said that, I was able to place his accent, the crisp, precise King's English that moved so prominently in his voice. It was beautiful, just like him. Gabriel wore simple clothes: dark slacks, a tan shirt with a real collar, black oxfords and a derby pushed way back on his head, like a scamp. Honest. Respectable. Wonderful qualities that, unfortunately, would mean next to nothing to my father. Papa didn't tolerate beaus. To his way of thinking, a man shouldn't call on a young woman or expect to take her out alone unless he was prepared for marriage. That can be a hard thing to explain to an eleventh grader.

However, in those first bright moments of laughter and recognition between the two of us, I couldn't have cared less about my father.

We strolled through Mott Haven, past the stove factory on Third Avenue and East 134th Street. Past a squat, soot-smeared building where the wooden sign above the door read: JANES, KIRTLAND AND COMPANY. Inside they smelted iron, had constructed the dome for the Capitol in Washington. As we passed, we could smell the heat of the ore and the working men inside. Farther down and around the corner came the piano factories, which laced the sidewalk with wood and sawdust and varnish smells. I breathed deep. These scents made me happy.

Taking an unexpected turn, we wandered farther out of the way. Neither of us particularly cared where the streets led, only that they suddenly seemed wider, more fragrant and attractive. We headed down one of the quiet residential blocks lined with elegant row houses and bushy crab apple trees, still in bloom. The tree branches sagged under the weight of their flowers, some trees budding with pink blossoms, some white. Stacks of petals drifted onto the sidewalk and I waded through, kicking them up, letting them whirl around my skirt. My heart beat hard. Not fast, but hard and heavy, like a footstep. Gabriel's body took up my space. It seemed to fill the sidewalk.

"I've always wanted to play the piano like you play," he said.

"I'll teach you whatever I know. If you want."

We turned back onto Mott Avenue, strolling slow, brazenly taking up each other's time. Unchaperoned. He grabbed my hand at a crossing, and I felt a jolt in my chest that brought life springing to places that had never drawn breath before. I peeked up at Gabriel's proud head, his wide back, and saw in him the chance to take hold of a freedom that would leave my entire world changed.

That, it turned out, would be one of the absolute truths of my life.

Meet me in the gardens today at 3:30.—GS

I turned the tiny slip of paper over on the other side and wrote: *Can't. My father.—MC*

A year had passed since that first walk home.

In that year, Gabriel became my world. We manufactured every possible excuse to wring extra moments out of our day. He'd even taken a repeat of Civics just so that we could sit near each other for forty-five minutes each morning. But there was always so little time. Papa kept me on a strict schedule to make sure I wasn't out running the streets.

When Mr. Bennett turned to the chalkboard to write, I passed the note underneath the desk behind me and he grabbed it, letting his fingertips graze mine for two or three seconds longer than necessary. This was our ritual.

The teacher kept talking, about what I don't know. I creased my eyebrows and puckered my lips, trying to do a passable imitation of what listening looked like. But while Mr. Bennett's words aggravated my ears, they never actually penetrated my brain. Luckily, he never called on Colored students. So I never worried about getting embarrassed in front of the class.

Then I heard it: Gabriel's pencil gently tapping the edge of his desk. I reached my hands behind me and sighed as I felt his fingers clasp mine.

> *Please! I need to talk to you.—GS*
>
>> *Why?—MC*
>
> *I can't talk about it right now. But I will say that your last letter brought about a panoply of emotions within me. So many things have been happening lately. I feel that if I don't express myself to you, this dam that has welled within me will burst and I'll be helpless to stop it.*
>
> *Don't make me wait.—GS*

What else could I say to that?

> *Our usual spot. I'll be there.—MC*

THE SILENCE HAD weight in the forest. It had a deep, sweet tea-colored blush to it that gave the hemlock trees knowledge and watchful eyes. My mother's people would have called this forest texture Spirit breath. But the absence, the soundlessness, they'd say, was simply a trick. It was something that happened when certain spirits held their breath and pretended to disappear. The light that sifted through the trees and coaxed the saplings to rise, breathing on them, whispering "grow, grow" in their ears, like God, that would have been Spirit's fingers. The river, to the people's way of thinking, became the length and breadth of Spirit's wide mouth. The light flicking off It was Its teeth. *Many as one, all as every. Each of us a finger on the same hand.* So there was no need to be afraid of the silence when the forest suddenly shut its mouth and you could feel the deafening absence, pressing on your ears like palms, nothing moving but your own heart. *That's God speaking,* my mother's people would say. *Don't be afraid. Be quiet and listen. Wait until you hear.*

I waited in the silence for Gabriel to come. It was three forty-five. At least. I counted breaths to calm myself and wondered what I'd do if I had to wait all the way until the next morning to see him. The hours of my day ordered themselves around whether or not I'd be able to see him. What I had to do in the meantime to make the hours go. How much of something I could do and for how long until I looked up and there he'd be, smiling, waiting for me. He called me careless, heartless, sometimes. Like I didn't ache to see him the way he ached for me. *You could fool me,* he'd say, *the way you were into that book. The way you were playing that piano. The way you were grading Mrs. Simon's papers. I bet you forgot I was even coming. Admit it. Tell the truth.*

He didn't know.

I picked at the soft, stringy bark of a red cedar tree with my fingernail. Then I sat on the ground and played with the scaly needles, making one nest for the sparrows and one for the wrens. I prayed too. No matter what, I had to beat Papa home. Because Papa knew. I can't explain how. He didn't really know about Gabriel, but *he knew.* And it set him on edge. He picked fights and then dared Mama and me to do something.

But I couldn't leave without at least holding Gabriel's face in my hands, without letting him kiss me on the lips. Then I wouldn't feel so suffocated until the morning, when the school bell rang and I could begin my daily search for his face in the crowded hallway. He was never hard to spot. He was always the tallest, the most beautiful, the one scanning the hall just as anxiously, looking for me.

"May!"

I got up and turned, and he was there, his arms around me, breathing deeply into my hair.

We stood there, wrapped up tight, for a very long time. How long I don't know, but even when Gabriel whispered, "Come on, let's walk," and I said, "Yes," neither of us moved.

He kissed me and kissed me and kissed me. With his fingers dug into my hair, Gabriel scratched my scalp until the pins fell out. My hair unraveled and came tumbling down my back. Then he trailed his fingertips lightly along the back of my neck. His touch sent waves of heat through my legs and hips, making my hands numb and my face flush with a pleasure so sharp it hurt. I couldn't breathe. He pressed my head against his chest and grabbed another handful of hair. Then he pulled my lips back onto his and, instead of kissing me, whispered my name against my tongue.

A need deeper than anything I'd ever suspected exploded in my chest. Dizzy, disoriented, I tried to pull him even closer, desperate for another kiss. It was only when Gabriel moved toward the buttons on my blouse that I found, from somewhere, the presence of mind to let go of his lips and say no. We separated, both panting and shaking and blushing. That kind of greediness frightened me. But then Gabriel smiled and somehow, without any words, his smile made it all right. I trusted him. When I pulled myself away and looked around, I noticed that the sound returned to the hemlocks. It felt all right to move on.

Holding hands, we strolled across the uneven ground, laughing even though neither of us had said anything yet. I dug my face into his side, smelling his clean smell, slightly wet, slightly sharp, like he'd been running.

We passed through a grove where the trees were old and dead, the tops of them looking like the silver tines of a fork. I held Gabriel's hand tighter because the spirits spoke much louder in this copse, even though he didn't seem to hear them.

"Do you know what I read this weekend?" he asked.

"What?"

"That theorem by Albert Einstein that he just published this year. His theory of relativity. Absolutely incredible stuff. It just floored me. It made me look at everything, the entire world, differently, you know?"

I didn't know. But it didn't matter. I smiled and waited patiently for him to explain what this had to do with me. With us. I knew there had to be some kind of connection. Gabriel didn't waste words. He looked into my eyes and frowned. Then he got quiet again. I shrugged and continued to wait.

We walked in the direction that the forest had taken as it birthed itself, moving from the oldest, dead trees, to an area where the red cedars were wizened and crippled, but still alive. The twisted trunks had multiple growths of shaggy, gray-weathered crowns. Many were hundreds of years old. So beautiful, these trees, looking like old black men to me. Like elders who still overshadowed the youth, even with their warped bodies, because they'd survived so much longer than they were meant to. They had strong life and glowing beauty, and all because they'd finally given up on time.

Gabriel sighed. "My father wants me to go away after graduation, May. To Canada, I think. Then back home to Jamaica."

Gabriel had taught me that Western hemlocks have blunt-tipped needles, pale green or yellow on the top, white or gray underneath—soft, flat and shiny. I stood next to a tiny tree, no taller than me, with reddish brown and scaly bark that drooped off to one side. I tried hard to concentrate on the tree, only the tree, as I watched it shed a clump of needles. Slowly, a dry heat began to rise in the soft space between my ribs. It drifted up to my throat and clotted there. I started to feel suffocated again.

"I don't want to leave you," he was saying. "But I think my father's right. I don't think I can stay here. This place isn't what we thought it would be. There's so much I want to do, May. When I read Einstein's theory, I can't really explain what it did to me. All I know is he put words to things that I sensed but didn't have an explanation for. That's the kind of work that I'm supposed to be doing. But I can't do what he does here. It's not possible. I'd never be recognized. Maybe in Canada. If the war wasn't on, I could go to Europe. That's what my sister did. She went to Holland and now she's married to a Dutchman. They live in Antilles, on Sint Maarten. Who knows? Maybe I'll eventually go back home. But I can't stay here."

"That's not true," I said. But it was feeble. He didn't even bother answering me. A Negro scientist.

Hey. What do you call a Colored scientist?

What?

A janitor!

Loud, loud laughter. I'd heard those white boys in the science lab, the skinny, petulant ones who couldn't grasp even the rudimentary elements of what Gabriel could do. I saw Gabriel's face as he continued to work on the other side of the room. Passive, absorbed, like those boys had never spoken. When the teacher, Mr. Walker, started laughing too, it set me on fire. I stalked through the door and sat down on a stool behind him. Gabriel never looked at me and I never looked at him, but those boys got quiet in my presence. They didn't dare speak again.

What do you call a Colored scientist?

A dreamer.

"Why now? After college you could go. Why not then?"

"I . . . I . . . have opportunities . . . ," he whispered. "Some people have contacted my father already. I don't think I want to go to college here anyway. Maybe these four or five years have been enough."

When the tears stood out in my eyes again, he got very big and very paternal, stroking my hair, the scars on my face, cuddling me.

"Shh, beautiful girl. How can you cry? What could be wrong while I'm holding you? I love you, May. All of you. I don't want you to hide from me. I'll always be here with you. I'll always love you. No matter what happens. I promise. Hush now, likkle 'un. Come on. Hush."

That's the only time I ever heard the other kind of accent come out in his voice. When he called me "little one."

Gabriel held me so tight that I lost track of time. When we looked up, the sun was about to set. With a quick kiss good-bye, Gabriel rushed off one way and I the other.

I raced beside the slender stream on my left. Its waters had been dyed with tannins that'd spilled like nectar from the rings and furrows of dead trees, first into the moist ground, then into the lazy brook beside it. Gabriel had taught me about that too, about how the trees can bleed straight through a river's walls into its flow.

Flying alongside the tea-colored stream, I cut past the waterfall farther south and through a stand of silver fir. I flashed through the trees, dodging fuzzy yellow hives of Old Man's Beard that hung from the many branches. As late and as frightened as I was, I still noticed the fir trees. They were Gabriel's favorite. He thought they were beautiful.

On this winding trail, I made my way from the Botanical Gardens and out onto Fordham Road to catch the trolley home. I saw my trolley idling at the corner, so jammed with people that they hung out of the doorway—legs, skirt tails and bottoms. Elbows and hands jutted out of windows, packages dangling.

"Hold! Hold please!"

I ran as fast as I could go, my skirt hitched way up high. The trolley driver saw me. I know he did. His trolley had mirrors on the edges, by the doors. But he clanged his bell and pulled off anyway. And there wasn't another trolley in sight.

By the time I finally turned onto my block, I knew that Papa was already home. Waiting.

At the corner, a moon-faced, black-haired Polish woman stuck her head out of a second-floor window above me.

"*Kochanie*," she called, singsong, "*choć do domu.*"

As though they'd been waiting on her signal, the women of Mott Avenue began lifting their own windows and peeking out. Hanging out onto fire escapes, breasts and stomachs bulging against the sills, they searched up and down the block, calling their own children home. They called in Polish, Greek, Hungarian and Italian from the apartments above the shops.

Mott Haven wasn't at all like San Juan Hill, where we'd first moved after coming back home. In San Juan Hill, there'd been days when I had to run home from school, dodging bottles and bricks. In the cracks between Hell's Kitchen and the Hill, Irish and Negro boys clashed daily. They were never too much concerned with who got in the way. They waged fierce, pitched battles that cut up the streets and alleys with blood. They used bricks and bottles and bats and poles and rolling pins and socks filled with rocks and tied at the ends. Here, on Mott Avenue, people lived in peace. They mostly stuck to their own, but they looked after one another, too. We were the only Negro family in the neighborhood and so far, it hadn't made any difference.

"*Γειά σας!*—Hello there, Miss May. How you feel tonight?"

Mr. Karunos, the Greek greengrocer who owned the shop across the street from our apartment building, called to me from the entrance of his store.

"Hello, Mr. Karunos. How are you?"

"Good. So good. Now that I see you." He smiled. "How is Mama?"

"She's just fine. How are the children?" I asked.

"Just doing good. They miss you. Have not seen you in store for weeks."

Mr. Karunos was a baggy pants man. He'd moved to the Bronx from Athens to escape the memory of a five-years-dead wife. His two chubby children, Woodrow and Theresa, had both been born on the morning that their mother died. Such a nice old man, with a face darker than Papa's and a bushy mustache to hide his smile.

Behind him, ripe oranges, apples, pears, heads of cabbage, string-tied carrots and, my favorite, persimmons, vied for space. Mr. Karunos set his broom down and rubbed his hands clean on his apron. Then he picked up a soft, red persimmon and put it in my palm.

"You take. Is good. Best one."

"Thank you, sir."

"Not 'sir' for you. Vassiliki."

"All right, Mr. Karunos. I have to be getting inside now. See you soon."

I waved and smiled a bit and then hurried across the street to deal with my father.

He was waiting.

Chapter 8

Keep in mind that it wasn't me he hit. It was her.

As I walked through the door, before I could explain, before I could set my books on the floor in the corner and walk to him, he sprang. Mama leapt between us and said, "Now, William, wait a minute—"

He punched her. Hit her so hard that she lifted up into the air and crashed onto her back in front of the sofa. Legs splayed, apron torn loose, skirt way up across her thighs, Mama struggled to sit up or, failing that, at least close her legs. I stood there studying the triangle of her closed knees, calves and the floor, and then started to scream.

Something frightened him. My scream or maybe his own hands. But he held perfectly still for a moment with his head cocked back. Then he snatched his old gray coat from the hook and ran out the door.

Hours later, when she still couldn't move, Mama sent me running back downstairs to knock on Mr. Karunos's door. Could I get a bottle of Kilmer's Swamp Root? I didn't have the 79¢, but I'd have it by the end of the week. Mama was having some wicked back pains and a lot of swelling. Though I'd woken him from a sound sleep, he didn't ask any questions and threw in some Epsom salts and aspirins for free.

I laid Mama down in the bed with me. My bed was bigger than theirs anyway. It was nearly dawn by the time the pain had subsided enough for her to sleep.

Just before she drifted off, she whispered, "You wanna leave?"

I draped my arm over her, lightly, and patted her shoulder.

"No, ma'am. I'm not leaving. I'm staying."

"You sure?"

"Yes, ma'am."

"Well, I think I'm leaving."

"I wish you wouldn't. But I understand if you do."

"You gonna stay anyway?"

"Yes, ma'am."

"Well, all right. If you think it's best. We'll stay."

We did this periodically. When one wanted to go, the other decided to stay. Somehow, we never managed to get it together at the same time. My family stayed intact by default.

Even though I wanted to leave, I couldn't. The fight was my fault. So I'd have to make it right. I'd have to be much more careful in the future.

Mama slept, and I gazed out the window at the flood of mist and clouds hugging the hillside. Fog drained into the narrow basin that, on a clear night, would have been the Harlem River.

The next day, I stayed home from school to nurse my mother. I fed her chicken soup and Swamp Root and laid warm compresses over her back every half hour. Papa returned late that night but never apologized. Instead of speaking, he sat in the wing-backed rocker by the window sipping whiskey and reading from one of his twelve-volume set of books on the Spanish-American and Civil Wars. The only thing he said to me when I happened to look up and couldn't avoid his eyes was: "Maybe I should have been a soldier."

I never told Gabriel what happened, but he noticed and brooded when I cut back on our meetings. Refusing him felt like closing myself up in an airtight box. Especially after what he'd told me. In his mind, I was only proving him right. It broke my heart, but I had to do it. Gabriel and I saw each other only three times a week outside of school. On Tuesday and Friday Papa worked late. On Sunday, Gabriel came to my church, St. Phillips, where I taught Sunday school.

St. Phillips was the best Negro church in New York. For the most part, only established families went there. Papa always encouraged me to attend, not because he'd suddenly found religion, but because he wanted me to make a good match with one of the respectable St. Phillips boys. Parents with eligible sons were known to comb the pews for prospective mates. It was always best to have references if possible, but a comely young woman could do well with a bit of luck. Of course, having pale skin and hair nearly to my waist didn't hurt matters either.

Papa, who refused to even acknowledge God at any other time, would actually make the sign of the cross over my head before I left on Sunday mornings. He insisted on checking my dress, my complexion and my hair before I could go. If he thought I'd been in the sun too much that week, he'd make me wear Mama's wide-brimmed straw hat. If I tried to braid my hair or pin it up, he'd let it back down for me before I walked out the door, fanning it out over my shoulders so that the length and texture would be clearly noted. I would've laughed if there wasn't so much passion in his face. He had so much hope on Sundays.

The very next Sunday after our fight, Reverend Bishop asked

my teacher Miss Lee to put together a short program to be per-
formed after service in two weeks. She asked three of her other
students to perform and requested that I do the finale.

My first thought was of Gabriel. The thought of him seeing
me perform in front of all those people made my stomach weak
and fluttery. I saw myself, fingers flying over the keys, fixated on
the piano in front of a hushed audience. I'd finish and the people
would be in such rapt awe, that they wouldn't be able to applaud
at first. Finally, Gabriel would get to see who I really was. He'd
realize that he wanted more from me than he ever knew that he
wanted. Most importantly, he'd stop talking about leaving. At least
he wouldn't talk anymore about leaving alone.

I practiced all week, rushing home straight from school before
Mama and Papa got in from work. I didn't want them to see me
playing my selection, Bach. I was afraid that they would hear the
music and know. Mama, at least, would catch me. She noticed
things. She'd see the way I hunched over the keys, breathless and
miserable until the change of phrase. Then joy. Joy with no reason. I practiced early, so that by the time they got home I'd already
be passed out sleeping.

For those two weeks, Mama sewed every night. She wanted me
to have a decent dress for the recital. She wanted it so much that
she went down to Miss Ceil's Notions Store and traded her good
winter coat for a black cats-and-dogs wrap. Then she exchanged
her credit for four yards of garnet satin crepe. Each night she cut
and stitched and sewed well past midnight, even though she'd be
up again in four or five hours. I caught her, more than once, asleep
leaning over her broom or her mixing bowls in the evening. Slack-
jawed, chin to her chest, drooling a little, she slept at the table
while shelling peas, her fingers still working as she napped.

But the Sunday morning of the recital, I woke to find the dress hanging from the wardrobe at the foot of my bed. It was cinched at the waist with leg-o-mutton sleeves, trimmed in satin ribbons and lace. It looked almost too beautiful to wear. If I hadn't sat and watched Mama sew for two straight weeks, I'd have thought there was some mistake. It looked like one of the dresses that the other girls wore, the ones who mingled at the Frederick Douglass Social Club. Their fathers were professionals and business owners. Their mothers didn't work. My parents could never be in a league with people like that. Papa had assigned himself a distinctive air of importance, leaving the house every day in his three-piece suit with a timepiece fixed to his vest, carrying his bowler hat and cane, and a paper rolled under his arm. But he was still just what he was: the porter and general handyman at Gorham's Silversmith Shop down on Fifth Avenue. It was good work. Honest work. It allowed Papa to feel proud, like he'd kept his promises. But that's about all.

I washed and dressed slowly, hoping that Mama would get up before I left for service. But I didn't dare wake her on the only day that she got to sleep past dawn. It didn't seem fair to me that after all her hard work, she didn't have the energy to get up and come to the service to see me play. I'd tell her about it later, of course, tell her so that she could see and smell and hear everything in the sanctuary. But still.

I slipped out quietly, with my high-heeled boots in my hand. All the way across the bridge into Harlem, I wondered what it would be like if things were different.

St. Phillips was so packed the ushers had to turn people away at the door. I sat in the first row, squeezed between Reverend Bishop's wife and Miss Lee. The other girls scheduled to play sat in the second row. I searched the pews for Gabriel and finally found him sitting in one of the middle rows, right on the aisle. Watching me. Once I saw his face, I relaxed.

After the service, Miss Lee rushed us into an anteroom off to the left of the pulpit.

"Your audience mustn't see you before time," she warned us. "It spoils the ambiance."

So we waited quietly, hands folded, ankles crossed, while some of the boys decorated the pulpit and turned it into a concert stage. Then it was time.

One by one, Miss Lee led the girls out. I waited in that tiny room sitting on a hard mahogany bench fidgeting with the pages of my Bible for more than an hour and a half. Finally the last girl's piece came to a rattling end. I stood and walked over to the door, out of sight, but ready.

"Last of all," said Miss Lee, "it is my great pleasure to introduce a brilliant young lady that we all know and dearly love. I give you Miss May Edward Chinn."

I walked in from the side door and waved at the audience, which responded to me enthusiastically, whistling and calling out "Bravo!" My friends stomped their feet and the applause grew louder. Embarrassed, I ducked my head and moved toward center stage, where I knew that the piano would be. Walking quickly, grinning, staring intently at my feet, I climbed the four steps up onto the stage.

I should have looked up as I walked. I should have been more careful.

When I raised my head, all I saw was myself. My face. Surrounding me on all sides.

Three towering mirrors bordered the piano, the fourth wall open toward the audience. My face. My self. Everywhere. In front of me, to the side. Behind me. The audience watched my right side. My scars.

A terrible, oozing hole erupted in the center of my chest. It paralyzed me and rooted me to the floor. Sweat slipped down the back of my neck and behind my ears. I felt slick and nasty and exposed.

Gabriel. I turned and looked for him, but suddenly I couldn't find his face. *Gabriel, what's happening? Gabriel, where are you?*

I wanted to die.

I don't remember walking to the piano bench. But I must have. Because I collapsed on the seat and slumped over the keys. The women with the silk brocade fans and the ostrich feather hats in the front rows began murmuring. Their voices filtered in from behind me, up from underneath me, down from the stained-glass windows and the rafters on the roof. But I didn't understand what on earth they could be saying.

Miss Lee stood from her seat in the front row and announced for me, "Miss Chinn will now play a selection from Bach."

Relieved, the audience applauded once more. They were gentle this time, though. Trying to prop me up, I think, with their hands. Hold me tightly. Because I felt myself slipping. I looked up to anchor myself in the sheet music, only to catch my own eyes in the mirror in front of me. Then the back of my head reflected within that reflection from the mirror behind me.

My hands, so stiff and busy from holding off these walls, could not play, would not move. More sweat collected underneath my arms and between my thighs. Pinpricks of sweat dotted my nose and rolled down toward the corners of my mouth. My mouth. So full, so flush. I couldn't speak. A minute passed in silence. And then another.

My God, I wanted to die.

"Temperamental artist, indeed!"

Miss Lee laughed, crackling and high-pitched. The sound broke over a hump in her throat, too sharp to be natural. But everyone else laughed along just the same.

I stared hard at the keys and my rigid fingers poised just above.

They'd curled like witch fingers. It was actually kind of funny looking. If I'd been able to open my mouth, I might have made a joke about it.

The silence stretched. In my head, I heard the music coming out in streams. But the hall stayed silent except for a cough, a clearing of someone's throat, the rustling of skirts. Shoes tapped the wood floor from the crossing and uncrossing of legs. If I could just straighten my back enough to move, I'd walk directly down the center aisle, right out the doors, right on home. Just as the silence became absolutely unbearable, Miss Lee scurried up onto the makeshift stage and smiled as brightly as I'd ever seen her smile before.

"Stage fright," she clucked. "After such accomplishment, so many accolades, it appears that Miss Chinn has been struck with the fear of God."

People smiled. I could see them reflected in the mirror to my left. Some chuckled and applauded lightly. Sitting down next to me, Miss Lee rubbed my leg and then spread her fingers wide across the ivory panel. She struck a dramatic, rumbling chord and I found that if I looked nowhere else but her hands, I could follow. So this is what I did. I followed her pale, spidery fingers flickering across the keys, followed and then, eventually, led. I could do it as long as I didn't look up. When she stopped, I kept going. The chords sounded wooden and predictable to my ears, but at least I could play. I didn't have the wherewithal to mold the music myself, so I let it become what it wanted to be. It emerged with hardly any help from me at all.

I played well, possibly. I don't know. But when I was done, no one moved. Peeking over Miss Lee's shoulder, I saw that a few were in tears. I wanted to cry too. I was so ashamed of myself and embarrassed. When they sprang to their feet and began to applaud, I thought I really would die. I curtsied once to the audience

and once to Miss Lee, then walked slowly off the stage and out the
back door.

I CROSSED THE RIVER on foot. So when I got to our spot in the
Gardens—hot, sweating, sticky-faced—Gabriel was already there
waiting. He stood beneath a plug of blazing, seven-foot-tall azaleas with wide, purple blooms, erect and waving above my head.
Fall had come but the summer flowers wouldn't fade. The azaleas
stood radiant against nature's idea of time.

"Hello, Ladybug."

All around me, azalea petals fell into the clumps of step moss.

"What happened?"

Gabriel reached for me and wrapped his hands in my hair,
holding me against his chest. He held me until something relaxed
and uncurled inside my soul. Every time he touched me, I expanded a little more to meet him. When Gabriel looked down at
me, I saw another tree in bloom, sweet and pale and hard and
bright. Awake with the strong, salty smell of sunlight. I thought
that the sunlight in his face could sweep away the confusion. I
kissed him and then buried my face in his palms and kissed the
well in the center of his cupped hands.

He returned my kisses, bending down first to my neck then
lower.

I didn't stop him. I needed to be touched, to feel his body covering what had felt so horribly exposed.

Something that my mother once said about God ran through
my mind. *"You don't ask the sun rays if they'll please give you some sunshine,"* she said. *"You go on outside and turn your face up and stand in the
light."*

I reached up and sketched the light in the planes of his face
with my fingertips. The need inside overflowed.

He loved me.

I took his hand and led him from under the blossoms, toward the water. An ash tree jutted through a slit in a boulder on an outcropping of rock that fell away into the stream below. The granite had long given way to the breathing and the balance of the tree. The ash had been cramped, though. Confined. It had tried to rise from the tight, unyielding space and walk away. Some branches were draped arms, pushing steadily against the crooked rock. Corded root legs, bent at the knee, had stepped out of the gray slit into empty space. But the tree had moved impatiently, without looking, without consulting the river below. So it had nowhere to go. Its leg roots wrapped around, underneath the jetty of rock, and back into the wall of moist, dark earth overlooking the stream. I lay down on this rock looking out over the water and let him drape his body across mine.

He touched me softly, hesitantly, and I made up my mind not to stop him. He'd proved himself. He was there with me, the only one. And he knew enough not to ask me what was wrong more than once. Gabriel held me and let that be enough.

Chapter 9

I t grew cold.

Slowly, slowly, slowly, as I got tired, as my stomach got weak and my breasts began to swell and burn with the pain of their new weight, Gabriel stopped coming to see me. By the end of the semester, I hadn't heard from him in weeks. In school, he disappeared. Signed out of civics class. He hadn't needed it anyway. When I went to the Gardens now, I went alone.

I strolled alongside the heath and holly, watching the afternoon sun fade. Searching. But never for too long. Just long enough to crack the waxy, green holly leaves between my fingers, and breathe in their crisp, winter smell. Anything green smelled like Gabriel to me. I passed the hellebore with the white blooms and the green ones, always looking out for the ones with the purple flowers. Not too much like azaleas, but the color seemed true enough. So I picked purple Christmas roses and waited for him to come back, though he never did.

Gabriel. With his wide, wide hands smoothing my skin, breaking me open.

Through his hands, I'd seen myself as new again, erasing what
was small and stale; I'd traced the curve of my stomach and cuddled the astounded breasts, marveling and open to the sun.

"GOOD MORNING, Miss May." The grocer smiled.

"Morning, Mr. Karunos. Nice to see you today."

I really did like Mr. Karunos, who spoke English to all his
customers—including the other Greeks—and dispensed credit to
all when they needed it, regardless of color. He appreciated it when
I'd look after his children, take them for ice cream and carousel
rides. I appreciated the way he'd brought things for Mama while
her back healed, unasked and always before Papa got home.

"How are the children?"

"They miss a lady. You nice lady for them," he said. "God bless
you."

I waved good-bye and continued on to school. About a block
and a half before I reached the campus, Lila called my name.

"That confirms it," she said. "Carmen Jackson, Hellura, and
Willetta all said that Gabriel's planning to go to the Christmas
ball. You have to go now. When you show up there on Brandon's
arm, his heart is gonna fall right out of his chest."

"I just want to talk to him. That's all."

She shrugged. "Well, this is your chance."

Lila didn't understand. And I could never admit that I'd believed him when he said he wanted to look at my face forever.

The water and his lips, his hands on my back, had finally made
a mirror I could see into. I thought it was the only one. Things like
that would never make any sense to anyone but me.

* * *

MAMA TOLD PAPA THAT I'd be staying over at Lila's house to help her study for an English exam. We had to lie, otherwise he'd never let me out of the house alone for the whole evening. My garnet dress was too tight at that point. So I snuck into Mama's wardrobe while she was downstairs at the grocer's and took her one good silk dress. It was at least three inches too short on me. Ankle length, when the cut was clearly meant to be a street sweeper. But I had no choice. Nothing fit me right anymore.

I met Brandon, my date, outside the main doors of the school. We walked arm in arm into the gymnasium, decorated with red crepe paper and green paper lanterns. Brandon had barely taken off my coat when I saw *him* from across the room. Broad, smiling and golden, surrounded by a group of laughing boys and girls.

Gabriel. Holding hands with a bronze beauty in flowing, plum dress and thick curls that she'd piled high on top of her head. I think her name was Anna Rhodes. I know. I know it. That was her name. Anna Rhodes. Anna Rhodes snuggled up beneath Gabriel's arm.

It was almost like he felt me walk into the room. He turned his head and looked straight at me. And he kept smiling.

I am my father's daughter. Proud.

I smiled back.

There was a scream wedged into the back of my throat, hot and tight, agonizing. But I smiled, smiled at Brandon, smiled at Lila, who came rushing over and circled me, warily, waiting to see what I would do.

In the end, Lila saved me. She saw me smiling, smiling and trembling, smiling as my face got pale, then red and dark. Smiling even though I couldn't seem to focus my eyes. She pretended to be sick, like something she ate made her nauseous and begged me to ride home early with her. Brandon and her date, David, were understandably upset. We'd just gotten there. But they claimed they understood and agreed to stay behind when Lila insisted that she not spoil their good time. She got me outside just in time for me to stumble behind the bushes and vomit. After I wiped my mouth and caught my breath, we headed back toward the main road. I vomited twice more on the long walk home, but I never cried.

IT RAINED. For months. Soft rain, held carefully like a light cloth over the city. The rain was pale blue or misty pearl or sometimes white with fog depending on the time of day. With my window open, I watched it rain from winter right into spring. Smelling the humid air, sweet and fresh, settled my nerves.

I barely even played anymore and never during the day, too afraid that the neighbors would hear me and inquire from Mama whether I was ill. Most of the women worked longer hours than the men, but still, I wanted to be careful. So I sat in the window all day and waited, watching a muffled city veil and unveil itself across the river.

Curled up in the sitting room window, wrapped in Mama's old blue blanket, I composed music in my head and I ate. Biscuits, cold meat sandwiches, cookies, potatoes baked high till the skin was crisp and the inside flaked like tender fish. Anything at all.

"May, a young lady should be healthy, needs some weight to her," Mama told me shortly after Valentine's Day. "Lord knows don't no man want no skin-and-bones woman. But be careful, baby. You're getting kinda big. Don't you think?"

So I cut down after that. But I couldn't help it. I needed the food. It didn't matter what. After Mama talked to me, I stopped eating more regular food than normal and took to chewing on cornstarch and flour. It eased my stomach, but only slightly.

One warm day in March, Mama came home early. The clink of the lock turning woke me from a sound sleep by the window. There was a small, wooden clock with a glass face on a side table next to the sofa. It was noon.

Mama walked in carrying two sacks of groceries in one arm. The other hand was free, bandaged with three thin lines of blood soaking through the gauze. We both spoke at the same time.

"What happened to your hand?"

"What are you doing home?"

The answers to both questions were clear.

Mama's body collapsed from the inside. She didn't move, but her back, her limbs, her face, her chest folded up and got small. I'd never before in my life seen my mother so small.

"When?" she asked.

"I haven't been back since December. I'm not going back, either. I can't."

"No," she said, still at the door, still holding packages. "When?"

"Last fall. When it was warm."

"My God. Jesus. Jesus. *Jesus*. And I didn't see?"

I didn't have the answer to what she was really asking, so I stayed quiet.

"Oh my God Jesus."

It was over. All over. No more hiding. No more lies. I studied my nails, specifically the hangnail on my right thumb that I'd been worrying all morning. I chewed on it slow, deliberately, to give myself something to do. Something that held a little bit of pain. It shocked me that I didn't feel anything other than shame and relief. Shame for what I'd done. And relief that I could finally share some of the burden with someone else. I wouldn't have to keep it all to myself anymore.

She dropped the groceries, came into the sitting room, and pulled up a chair from the table. Sitting directly across from me at the window, she took my hand and kissed it and asked, "Who was it?"

"Just a boy."

"Stop crying, Sweetness. Stop crying and let me talk to you now. Do you love him?"

I nodded.

"Does he love you?"

"He never did. I thought he did, but I was so stupid. He lied to me the entire time."

"So he won't marry you then."

"I'd never marry him!" I blurted. "He's a liar. I hate him!"

Mama nodded and stared out the window at the river in the rain. She sat that way, nodding, until the color returned to her face and I could hear her breathing in deep, rhythmic breaths.

"That's the worst part of it for you, isn't it?" she asked gently. "You can't even grieve."

MAMA SENT ME AWAY to Albany two days later. She didn't tell Papa until I was already on the train, at my window, eating smothered chicken wrapped in hard bread on the Northeastern Express that cut straight through the center of the state. Mama waited until I was gone because she wasn't sure what Papa might do if he knew the truth and still had to wake up and look at me in the morning.

She sent me to a woman she knew up in Albany, Miss Annie Lewis, who ran a home for wayward girls. When I stepped off the train, Miss Annie was standing on the platform.

"Miss May? Mornin'. How you feeling today?"

I'd expected anger and scorn and judgment. I wasn't prepared for this thin, cinnamon-freckled woman who offered nothing but her smile and even reached to carry my bag. Stepping to the side, she waited for the white passengers to exit the platform first, humming a little tune. Miss Annie didn't shiver or turn her collar up against the freezing wind. She didn't frown or make her face go blank as the white people passed. With a kind of open-faced curiosity, she watched them walk and was content to be, for the moment, invisible. I liked her.

She took me to a three-story, whitewashed house with a rickety wraparound porch and dirt-brown shingles and shutters. Six girls in various stages of their pregnancies waited for us on the screened-in porch. Four of them were black, one was Spanish and one was white. The white girl, Elizabeth, had gotten pregnant by a Negro, I found out later. Her parents decided to let her stay where she was obviously more comfortable. She wasn't welcomed home again after the baby was born. The beautiful Spanish girl, Marita, and one of the Negro girls, Nora, had been forced. The others, like me, had just been naïve and careless. I never told any of them my story. When they asked who the father was, I looked off over my shoulder, like I had much more important things on my mind, and said, "Oh, just this pretentious boy I knew. No one, really." They laughed and said they could see how we got together.

One day, Nora asked me, "Didn't you ever love him?"

"I thought I did," I said. "Until he showed me who he really was."

That was the only truthful response I ever gave. Other than that, I simply listened to the girls, sympathizing when I could, and waiting to be done so I could go back home.

Curly hair on his chest, soft, sparse wool pressed against my heart. My fingers knead his scalp, his back, wet and shining, breathing in sweat and fascination and calling it love.

I contract and
weep with joy as thick as the hands that find my calves and trace lines of sun-
light all the way up my thighs. He places his palm there, where I am completely
untouched, and he holds it, holds utterly still.

I swell and then wait
as he swallows me whole with his stillness, pressing until I shiver and peak,
fearless, suddenly, without breath. Only then does he slide above me.

Only then, a beginning of release.

ON THE DAY THAT Gabriel graduated from high school, I gave
birth to a son.

I thought of him only once. Gabriel slipped in at a point when
the waves of pain had battered me senseless and left me vulnera-
ble to his face. Like a camera pulling back in a picture show, his
body appeared in increments before me, as real as he was the first
afternoon in the music room. He hovered there, in his brown suit
and his oxfords, smiling.

Miss Annie told me that I passed out, that she had to pull the
baby's legs out herself. She said I'd made her very, very scared for
a while there. But I don't remember any of that. I only remember
that Gabriel smiled at me and, for the first time since I held him in
me, I returned his love.

For the first time, I didn't care that he was a liar. I only cared
that I'd found truth.

MY BABY'S NAME WAS Peter.

My God, that child was so perfect. So complete. Peter had
butter-colored skin and pale eyes and a thin layer of smooth, downy
hair all over him. Miss Annie told me that he slid out of my body
already sucking his thumb and looking around. Peter never cried.

In fact, when I woke up and pulled him close to my face he smiled, even though newborns aren't supposed to be able to do that. I held him against my breast and stroked his cheek, and felt my heart break and break and break with love. Looking at my child, it seemed so clear that nothing on earth could be as important as to be waiting for him every time he opened his eyes. The strongest desire I'd ever known in my life rushed through me. It was the hunger for his skin and the sound of his breathing. The need simply to hold him. When Peter was born, so was I.

But then his new family came.

The woman was short and round, with lemony skin and careful curls that had been ironed stiff. She cooed over my son's hair because she could look at me and see that it would stay curly even after the sixth month, that his skin wouldn't darken too much. He could really be hers. Her name was Mrs. Robinson. She strode into my room wearing a purple peacock feather hat and silk stockings, like it was a special occasion. A celebration. The man was tall and deep brown. He wore a Stetson that Papa would have died to own cocked way back on his head. While the woman was busy cradling my baby, Mr. Robinson sat gently on the edge of my bed and took my hand. He looked into my eyes for a long time without saying anything at all. Because of that, I decided that I liked him. With him, maybe Peter would be all right.

Mama paced back and forth beside my bed and asked the gentleman to excuse himself so that she could lay a compress over my breasts to ease the pain. I'd only fed my baby a few times before they came rushing in. My breasts were hot and bursting. Watery milk spread across the front of my cotton nightdress.

"Don't cry any more," Mama whispered. "You'll get to see him from time to time. I promise. I know these people. Trust Mama."

So I handed my baby over to the man and his woman. The woman lifted my son to her face and rubbed her cheek against his and breathed in his perfect, heart-soft smell of milk and talcum powder. She actually laughed outright until she glanced over and remembered me; then she turned her back and faced the window.

"Come on, Phillip, my love," she whispered to my son. "Let's go on home now."

That was it. Only the man, Mr. Robinson, looked at me again. He took off his hat and put it over his heart for a moment before following his wife from the cramped attic room.

They took my son.

Mama had driven up with the Robinsons. So when they walked out, she turned to leave with them.

"I'll be back," she promised. "I'm coming by the end of the week and I'll bring you home."

I closed my eyes.

Don't leave. Mama, please don't go. Without moving, I called to her. I willed her to stop and stand. She would fling open her arms. She would see that I was bleeding. She'd know that if she walked out that door, she'd never see me again.

They were going. I heard the woman's heels clicking down the wooden stairs. If they got down to their car, I'd be lost.

I couldn't let them take my baby. I had to stop them. Desperate, I scanned the room with my eyes, looking for something to hold on to and pull myself up. I tried to swing my legs out of the bed but got tangled in the covers.

Mama.

She was gone too, closing the door behind them, murmuring something that I couldn't understand. I called her and I'm sure must have she heard me. She had to. I was screaming. I was dying. Everything in me had shriveled down to nothing. A husk. Cut off and left alone to live and relive the worthlessness holed up underneath my skin. It hurt to breathe. My arms and legs shook with the effort it took to pull myself to the edge of the bed. I tried to clear my mind and think, but the thoughts refused to gel. Incoherent, weak, useless, my brain wouldn't work. Jumbled-up thoughts fell down into the hole inside me that was my womb, scraped clean and raw. There were many things to be buried there now, in that empty space. Dying would be easier.

They leave, and I know it'll never end. I'll be buried with it.

Outside, a car engine turned over and a door closed.

"Mama!"

But she couldn't hear me. They took my child and left.

Chapter 10

When I got home, I went to work. Downtown. In a factory. Tying ribbons onto calendars.

The first time I walked through the door after all those months gone, Papa cried. He sat in his rocker by the window, the one that I'd curled up in for months, and stared out at the river. Wouldn't look at me, wouldn't move, wouldn't make a sound. He sat, tie straight, bowler hat still fixed on his head, mustache wet and slick with mucus, holding volume eight of *The Spanish-American–Civil War* set open on his lap.

I crept past him into my bedroom and found my blanket shredded, piled in a corner by the wardrobe, and the mattress gone. I slept on the floor until Mama somehow managed to get a new mattress. I don't know how and I didn't ask.

During that whole first week, I slept. The sleep came almost against my will. For some strange reason, I couldn't keep my eyes open more than a half an hour at a time. Too exhausting. Staying awake for an hour or more left me shaking and queasy, too weak to make a solid fist. To compensate, I slept on my left side so I could at least see out the window. I opened my eyes at intervals as the sky shifted from navy to sea green, to a crisp, sparkling turquoise, and then, finally, a tamer shade of daytime blue. In the afternoon, the heat drained the color from the sky, leaving the rest of the day pale, hazy with steam and the briny smell of the water.

I dreamt about my baby Peter (Phillip), trying, even within the dream, to shut my eyes to him. But my eyes wouldn't close, not even to blink. My dream self stood there, in blackness, seeing nothing but him like there was a lantern suspended somewhere over his head. In seconds, I watched him grow from wrinkled infancy to a toddler to a stout, dirty-kneed boy in knickers. I watched him, unblinking, suffocating, all the while knowing that, though he was staring straight at me, he couldn't see me. I was invisible to him. As soon as I realized that he didn't see me, would never see me, the dream started all over again.

These dreams haunted me. They sapped my energy. But no matter how hard I tried to stay awake so I wouldn't have to see his face (the dimple in his right cheek, the slanted hazel eyes, the heavy lips and scabs on his little-boy shins), sleep seemed to crush me. It deadened my mind, snatched me down and held me there, like a living thing with its own volition.

Mama spoon-fed me vegetable and chicken broth while Papa screamed at her.

"What do you expect? What did you think was going to happen?"

"William, please calm down," Mama would whisper. "The girl is ill."

"The girl is dead."

And the front door would slam.

After the second week, when they were having this same conversation at least three to four times a day, I forced myself up and into some clothes. This, too, overwhelmed me. I had to lie back down in my blue skirt and white lace blouse and go to sleep again. But after a few days, I could dress myself rather easily and make it down the stairs and outside, almost to the corner.

By the end of the fourth week, I'd made it all the way downtown to Thirty-third Street and applied for a job. The effort had me panting for breath and sweating through the lace blouse. But the foreman of this particular factory, a hunchbacked old Russian named Yusim, didn't appear to notice.

"You come Monday," he told me. "I have work for you. Don't be late, don't miss days, I don't fire you."

When I got home that night and told Mama what I'd done, she left her potatoes half cut on the table and sat down in Papa's rocker by the window. I wondered what the water meant to her as she watched it, turning her whole head to follow the path of a schooner shifting through the current. The river meant something new to each of us every time we settled in to look at it now. She studied the river. I studied her.

For the second time in my life, I saw my mother cry.

THAT WAS HOW I found myself working at the Madison-Haynes Calendar Factory. I arrived each morning at eight and walked up the seven flights of stairs to the top floor. The staircase was black. Not a shimmer of daylight to play against the concrete and the brick. The walls and the floor lay covered in cobwebs and grime and soot from some fire that I dared not think about. Even the thought was paralyzing. I'd been here in the city six years before. I'd walked by the holes in the ground outside the Triangle building, staring with my hand clapped over my mouth at the jagged rips where the pavement had literally been broken through by falling bodies. Burned bodies being hoisted up afterward like buckets from a well. Things really hadn't changed.

Hundreds of us trekked up the stairs each morning, feeling our way in the darkness like ants using antennae to sense the packed space around them. No one talked inside the staircase. Breathing was heavy and hard. The women coughed all the way up the stairs as their feet sifted through years of residue. It filtered inside us, into our throats and lungs and stomachs. Smoke clung to the walls. The fire there, inside the mortar, had apparently never died. The landings and the handrails and the steps and the hems of our skirts stayed covered in white ash. Some of the women coughed and spit blood as they climbed. They'd been there much too long.

The rumble and thud of the collating machine met me every day, sputtering to life somewhere around the fifth-floor landing. By the time I reached the gray double doors on the seventh floor, the press was already humming smoothly. The wheels on the collator screeched and whined like an ungreased engine. The machine would collate the calendar pages, shuffling together vibrant drawings of sunsets, wheatfields and red-cheeked, green-eyed babies according to month. And then I would be waiting, with a red satin ribbon that tied through the top and kept the pages neatly in place.

All morning I tied ribbons. At noon, we got a half hour break for lunch, usually an egg or cheese or peanut butter sandwich that Mama made before she left the house. Then at twelve thirty, back up the seven flights of stairs to my cramped, dingy table in front of the machine, sitting on a high stool or standing, to tie ribbons again until five thirty.

Summer thinned and faded this way, and winter came on, fat and boisterous. There was no autumn that year, so I had plenty of time to contemplate. And that is exactly what I did, living out the monotony as a small, everyday death.

I saw the Robinsons once, just before Christmas, walking with a brand-new, shining pram down 143rd Street. In my heart, I fell into the hard-packed street, spread all over the ground, wailing and pulling out my hair out like I'd seen the Irishwomen do when their men died. But in my body, I kept walking, talking myself home, just as my mother might: *one more step, one more step, one more, that's it . . .*

When I got in that evening, Mama was waiting for me.

"Put on your good dress, baby. We're having company tonight."

"Who?" I asked. But I didn't care though.

"I don't know," she said. "Strangest thing. Your papa just said set an extra place and look pretty. He's up to something, you know."

I went to change. It was nice to be able to fit into my clothes again. I'd lost more weight than I'd gained during my long sleep. It was a small but welcome pleasure to have my body back as my own again. To know that if I ever wanted to look, generally speaking, I'd be able to recognize what I saw.

An hour later, the chicken had been roasted and the table set with Mama's good ivory lace tablecloth. Papa paced by the window. Occasionally I caught his eyes darting in my direction. He never looked at me full on anymore. He almost seemed afraid. When the knock at the door came, Papa jumped from his seat.

"Get it, Lu," he ordered.

Mama politely obliged without acknowledging his tone.

"Oh, Mr. Karunos. How are you, sir? Come in, please."

Mr. Karunos appeared at the threshold of our door holding a bouquet of water lilies. Gone were the baggy pants and the apron that I'd gotten so used to seeing him in at the grocery store downstairs. This evening he wore a red-checkered, old-world kerchief tied at his neck and a blue suit. He'd slicked back his hair, revealing a much more ample forehead than I ever gave him credit for. Mr. Karunos glanced shyly at Mama. He pulled a tiny wooden box out of his jacket pocket and handed it to her.

"You take. Is for you, Missus." He pushed the little box into her hand and waved her off when she protested.

"Please," he said. "You must take this small thing. I cannot come in without bringing you something. Is not right."

"Well, thank you, sir." Mama smiled. "I do truly appreciate it. And to what do we owe the honor of this visit?"

"I would like to speak to your husband, Missus."

"I'm here, Mr. Karunos." Papa eased from the kitchen into the sitting room, eyeing the grocer through thick, lowered lashes and smiling. I couldn't remember him smiling at me for nearly a year. It used to be that I could make him smile just by walking into the room.

"Please come in and have a seat. What can I do for you, sir?"

"I speak now from my heart, Mr. Chinn. Hear me out, yes?"

"Yes, of course."

"I am very much loving your daughter, sir. I don't have words to say so. This English"—he laughed—"is not so good for me. I speak and hope you understand what is in my heart."

"What are you asking me, sir?"

"I would like to marry Miss May. I need your . . . permission . . . is right word? . . . permission to have your daughter."

Mama and I gasped at the same time. Papa and Mr. Karunos both swiveled their heads toward us as we stood frozen over the dinner platters. We looked away. They looked away. It was like a dance. Poor Mr. Karunos. He seemed so naked sitting there. So hopeful. So old. Papa, on the other hand, looked stricken. *Don't ruin this for me.* If I could read his eyes, that's what they would've said. *Don't say a word.*

"Why don't we have some dinner first, sir?" Papa clapped the old man gently on his back. "My wife is an excellent cook. And she's already taught little May everything she knows. Perhaps you and I can go downstairs to O'Hara's after dinner and discuss your proposal in more detail. How does that sound?"

"That is just fine, sir." Mr. Karunos smiled at my father, now the most charming man on earth.

A slow, torturous dinner followed. I kept my head buried in my plate. Mama reached down into her Indian bag and disappeared. So Papa and Mr. Karunos laughed extra hard and ate more than was necessary, or polite, to fill empty the space.

When the men rose to leave, Mama and I got up to clear the table. Before he walked out the door, Mr. Karunos edged over to me and took my hand in his.

"Miss May, good night to you. I will see you again very soon. I hope you enjoyed dinner."

He couldn't look me in the eye, poor man, so he bowed his head and rubbed his forehead against my knuckles before kissing my hand. Mama had to clear her throat from the kitchen to make him let go.

"*Ó αγαττώ μωρό,*" he told me. Then he let Papa steer him out the door and shut it softly behind them, gazing at my face one last time.

Mama and I stared at each other over the chicken bones and the potato skins.

"You know, that might be an acceptable match if you could just skip a few steps and make some grandbabies for him. Leave out the middle man entirely."

We both snorted and fell out. I dropped the chicken, laughing so hard it hurt. Down on the floor, sweeping up bones with our hands, Mama stopped and dabbed my eyes with the front of her skirt.

The laughter dwindled to some giggling and then to a few hiccups. Mama took my face in her hands and said, "Really, Sweetness. What you want to do?"

"*Mr. Karunos,* Mama?"

"You ain't heard me, girl. I said what you want to do? 'Cause if you intend to stay at that factory, you might as well go on and marry that old man. What else you got to wait on if that's the case?"

What could I tell her? That I barely felt strong enough to get out of bed in the morning? I hadn't thought as far as the next week, much less the next year or two. Or ten. I hadn't had a future since the last time I'd had an autumn.

"Lila dropped out, too," I said, like that meant something.

"Lila got married, and they already trying for they second child. What do *you* want to do, girl?"

"I'm not a girl."

Mama got up off the floor, brushed her hands across her skirt and started into the kitchen.

"A woman acts like it," she said as she stacked the dishes in the slop sink.

THAT WAS HOW AND when I died to my father for the first time. When he came home that evening and said, "May, we figuring on you getting married sometime before summer hits. How does that sound?"

And I said, "No."

Papa got still like an animal gets still before it strikes. Unblinking, arms slightly tensed away from his body, head low. He started toward me with tiny steps, circling me to cut off my exit to the bedroom. The kitchen had no door.

But I wasn't going to run. He was either going to kill me or leave me alone.

"You . . ."

"I won't do it, Papa. I can't."

"You won't do it? *You won't do it?* Now you gon' get up in my face and tell me what you will and won't do? You think you that grown?

Seems to me like the only thing you want to do is lay up in this house and be a whore."

"William, that's enough!" Mama jumped between us.

"This is *my* house, goddammit! I'll say when it's enough." Papa turned back to me. "That you want? You want to give your body away over and over again so every low-down nigger that takes a mind to can wipe his ass with your hair?"

"William!"

"I'm sorry, Papa . . . I can't . . ."

"You ass-backward heifer! What you think this is? You think life is some kinda game? What a Colored woman got in this world if she don't got no protection? That man is honest. He works hard."

"He's an old white man," Mama spit.

"Karunos ain't white! He's Greek. That's number one. And number two, there's the same age difference between him and May that there was between me and you."

"What makes you think I'd want my child to get what I got?"

Papa flinched like she'd slapped him. He stepped back with his mouth slack and tears welling in his eyes.

"Lu?"

Mama came up beside me. Her words had scraped her face clean. She stood inside them with her silence and her silence filled the whole room.

Why can't he just love me? Without taking it back, without hiding his eyes, without walking away when I need him to stay and hold my head and tell me that he doesn't love anyone in the world as much as he loves me and never could and never will stop loving me or making me more important than anything including his next breath. Who in the world is ever going to love me like that?

Questions with no answers.

The apartment that we shared was so much smaller than the space between us. There was no room.

He left.

*   *   *

THE NEWS CAME ON July 3. Everybody was talking it. Word spread along the street corners and in the barbershops and from kitchen doorways. Men and women clustered in the trolleys and subway tunnels, desperate for information.

On my way home from the factory, as the trolley passed by 115th Street, I saw an old woman from the before time, a slave woman, with her white hair standing up in alarm, her dress open and her back exposed. Dark as coal, but still the raised edges erupted like scales from her skin, harder, more pronounced than her spine, too easy to see. Not a flowering tree like you hear so many poets talk it. She had a thick and woolly bush, hacked off, lopsided, sprouting up from the back of her dress. Her flesh looked dull and burned. So the way those scars glowed could only be unnatural. Unnatural in the way that the hate that put them there was unnatural. She was crazy. Women ran beside her, trying to cover her up. But she wouldn't let them. She turned and swept toward the trolley, pointing at the driver and baring her teeth.

"Look!" she shouted. "Look what they do to us! Look what they do to us still! Don't you turn away! White man! White man! I'm calling to you. Look this way. *See me!*"

The paper that Tuesday morning read: JULY 3, 1917—THE WORST RACE RIOTS IN U.S. HISTORY SWEEP ACROSS EAST ST. LOUIS.

It was everywhere. The newspapers conjured up vivid descriptions of the massacre. Those with people in St. Louis and access to a telephone got the news firsthand.

It started at the Aluminum Ore plant. And at Swift and the other packinghouses in National City. Management shutting out the complaining whites and the union organizers. Bringing in Negroes to haul manure and slaughter hogs. The blood didn't seem to bother *them*. Tensions had been building for months. Small incidents, here, there, unreported for the most part. But then on Sunday a gang of whites in a two-tone Ford drove up Market Street and started firing pistols into Negro homes along Market and Seventeenth Street. Then down to Bond and Tenth. By the time the police arrived at Bond Street, a brigade of more than two hundred black men, armed and ready, came marching to meet them. The Negroes opened fire, killing one officer and wounding another, who wasn't expected to live. The city exploded.

Monday morning, a mob formed at the Labor Temple and marched toward Broadway, picking our people off, one by one, where they found them. Women, children, it didn't matter. Streetcars were stopped and the Negroes dragged off to be beaten and shot in front of crowds of cheering whites. Fires blazed up across the length of the South Side. All along Third Street, from Brady to Railroad, Negro homes were torched. They lit fires in the back so when the families tried to escape through the front door, the men waiting outside could pick each person off, one by one, as they ran out. A newspaper report coming out of the city said, "The Negroes are being shot like rabbits and strung up to telephone poles."

By midnight the South End was painted with flames that shot so high into the air that the Pittsburgh Lake seemed to be roiling with fire reflected off its surface.

The papers reported that thirty, possibly forty people had died. But we knew that hundreds of souls had been lost. Exactly how many wasn't clear, but our people saw the bodies hanging from telegraph poles and light posts, ears missing, pants down, skin eaten by flames until limbs began to untangle from the brittle sinew and drop off. They saw the bodies piled high like winter logs in the alleys. They saw it, so we saw it, too.

I found Mama that evening with her best friend Mrs. Tillson at Bernice's, a beauty shop where Bernice kept a phone in the back room. Mrs. Tillson was beside herself. She, along with fifteen or so others, lined the walls, praying on phone calls from people in Illinois. Eventually, around nine, her sister Riley phoned. Riley was all right, but their brother was still missing. And she'd seen with her own eyes, two little girls about eight years old being carried back into their burning home and tossed inside by grown white men. Then the men nailed boards over the doors and windows and watched the house burn. She'd seen many other things that couldn't be said yet. Maybe not ever. This was bad enough: Negro women being held down by mobs of men and even by white prostitutes, beaten, cut, opened up everywhere. Strung up like men, with no clothes, their bodies stripped of flesh. But there were other things that couldn't be said. This was enough.

I left the others at Bernice's and dragged myself home. Enraged, terrified, trembling, I trudged up Mott Avenue. What could I do?

I walked into the house and went straight into Mama's room. Her mirror hung on the wall over her bureau. I looked hard at my face. My straight nose. My slanted eyes. Thin, bow lips that so many had remarked on and cherished. I didn't look like a Negro. Yet I was. I looked more white than anything else, although I could never be.

I had to do something.

The next evening on the way home from the factory, a young Colored man held out a piece of paper to me. "Marcus Garvey Speaks on the St. Louis Riots!" the page proclaimed. When I got home, I told Mama in a loud voice, loud enough for Papa to hear, that Reverend Bishop wanted me to accompany some singers at a ceremony for the souls lost in the riot. I'd say yes if she didn't mind. He kept reading his paper and never looked up, so that meant it would be all right.

That Sunday evening at seven o'clock, I showed up at Kingdom Hall. The meeting room was jammed. A young man in overalls in the second-to-last row saw me and waved me over. "Seat, miss?"

"Yes, thank you, sir."

Not two minutes later, Marcus Garvey strode onto the platform dressed in full regalia. His plumed cap waved like a reed above his head and the medals on his jacket gleamed in the dim light. At the sight of him, the crowd leapt to its feet. I jumped up as well, trying to see something more than arms and necks and bushy heads. Garvey let the shouting continue for another minute before quieting the crowd with a hand.

"The East St. Louis Riot, or rather massacre, of Monday the second, will go down in history as one of the bloodiest outrages against mankind for which any class of people could be held guilty."

"Hear hear!"

"Speak!"

"This is no time for fine words," he roared, "but a time to lift one's voice against the savagery of a people who claim to be the dispensers of democracy!"

The crowd whistled and applauded. Garvey's deep, rumbling voice spread out across the room, overpowering it. It mixed into the heat, the smell of packed bodies, and transfigured the men's faces. His voice thickened and descended on us like thunderclouds, his round, plum-colored cheeks quivering with indignation.

"I do not know," he told us sadly, "what special meaning the people who slaughtered the Negroes of East St. Louis have for democracy, of which they are the custodians, but I do know that it has no literal meaning for me as used and applied by these same lawless people.

"America has no satisfaction to give 12 million of her own citizens except the satisfaction of a farcical inquiry that will end where it began—over the brutal murder of men, women and children for no other reason than that they are black people seeking an industrial chance in a country that they have labored three hundred years to make great!"

The crowd shot to its feet again, fists pumping, chanting for justice and redemption. The words were indistinguishable. Tongue and lips could not carry this voice forward. The sound came from way down deep inside, in the blood.

"A reign of terror prevails!" Garvey pounded the podium, sweat pouring from under his cap. "Negro faces were seen at frames of windows and when they saw what happened to those who flew from the burning structures, they dropped back into the fire rather than tempt a similar fate.

"The mob and entire white populace of East St. Louis had a Roman holiday. They feasted on the blood of the Negro. White people are taking advantage of black men today because black men all over the world are disunited!"

At the close of the speech, I shouted and cheered like all the others, applauding until I bruised my own hands. Men and women wept together without shame, and I was one of them. We called his voice back, called for him to lead us. But Garvey didn't wait. He stared for a moment out over the symphony of Colored faces and then vanished with a stern nod and a flourish of his hand.

That was it.

People filed out slowly, in spite of the heat, in spite of the hour. They were waiting for something. Some direction, a call into action. I felt it too. I needed to do something. The need simmered inside me, underneath my skin. It made my breathing heavy and labored. Agitated. It felt like I was giving birth again. But to what, I couldn't tell. I walked uptown toward my trolley stop in silence, surrounded by clumps of hungry men and women, their heads hung low in thought or lifted way up, looking like prayer.

"You know, in the *Evening Mail*, they had an article about a woman from the South Side who actually said she fell down on her knees and praised God when the riot started."

The young man who had given up his seat for me fell into step beside me.

"Really? Why?"

"She said that it was the first time in her life that she'd seen Negroes stand up and act like men," he said. "She knew they were going to die, most of them. That she might probably die too. But that it was worth it. She could die happy. She'd never been happy in her life until that moment."

He wiped his hand over his sparse, scraggly little mustache. *This young boy*, I thought. *I bet he brushes those three mustache hairs every day.*

I smiled and said, "I understand her."

"My name's Coleman," he said.

"May."

We stopped at the corner just as my trolley came into sight off of Seventh.

"May, would you be willing to die for the Movement? Like the woman in South End?"

He is young, I thought.

"I think that's the wrong question, Coleman," I answered softly. "I think the real question must be, am I willing to live for it? To do something. The answer to that question is yes. I just don't know what."

Coleman bit his lip and stared at me.

"How old are you?" he asked.

"I just turned twenty-one. How old are you?"

"I'm nineteen," he said proudly. "In three months."

I laughed in his face, and he was just young enough not to take offense. The trolley pulled up and the crowd shuffled toward the doors.

"Say, the NAACP is organizing a rally in a couple of weeks on the Saturday. Headed down Fifth Avenue. You going?"

I hadn't even heard about it, but as soon as he said it, I answered, "Of course. Will you be there?"

He nodded. "I'll find you."

Almost as soon as Coleman turned away, I forgot about him. So many other things rattled around in my head. Specifically, I heard a voice that sounded very much like my mother's. Over and over again, this voice said to me, *So what are you going to do, May? What are you going to do?*

I had no answer. I didn't even know what the question meant, truly. But it was there. Eating me. Wrestling with me. Making me know that my life was about to change. There was no backing away from it and no way to quiet the voice now that it was awake. I itched. I couldn't sit still. It felt almost like love in the way that it took my breath and distracted me. But the voice expanded within me so much wider than that. Sudden and insistent. It wanted my life.

My God. Then take it. Just tell me what to do.

There was no answer right then, but the very next night I heard a knock at my door.

I opened the door, still smelling like sweat and grease and ink, with blue smudges across my face and my hair hanging all around my head in an undone cloud.

It was Lila. Lila, her little boy and Carmen Jackson. They stood in the hallway, smiling. Little Tyler hid behind his mother with a pinky finger up his nose. Lila and I fell into each other's arms, screaming, and she kissed my cheeks even though her lips turned slightly blue. Carmen and I shook hands. Then Lila lifted Tyler into my arms and I started to cry. Lila and Carmen thought I was crying because I missed them when really it was Tyler and the way he wrapped his little arms around my neck and kissed his Auntie May. So sweet.

Lila couldn't have been more beautiful. Her belly was pushing out again, and she was so happy. She kissed and kissed Tyler's pudgy hand even though he'd had his finger in his nose. Mothers just don't care about those things, I decided. I offered them tea so that I'd have a reason to run into the kitchen and compose myself, wipe the sweat from my forehead and my neck. I came back with a plate of sweet biscuits and oatmeal cookies to go along with the tea.

"What are you doing here?"

"We missed you, May," Carmen said. "You disappeared."

I'd dropped out. I worked at a factory tying ribbons. No one from our old crew would be seen with me now. But the politeness had to be said. Otherwise she'd have to explain where she'd been, too. So I followed along and pretended that it was all my fault. How careless of me.

"May, Carmen was telling me the most interesting thing the other day. Go ahead. Tell her, Carm."

"Well—"

"Carmen is starting at Columbia University in the fall. At Teacher's College. Isn't that great?"

I kept smiling. There had to be a reason for this. Lila was loyal to me. She loved me. My sister. She wouldn't come all this way, so late in the evening, tugging Carmen and a baby at her side, just to break my heart. There had to be more.

"Anyway," she continued, "Carmen just found out that there's another entrance exam coming up."

"Yes," Carmen interrupted. "You can take the exam in three weeks. If you pass it, they'll place you for fall."

Mama had something to do with this. I could smell it.

"But I dropped out," I reminded them. "I don't even have a diploma."

"Just take the test, May," Lila pleaded. "Get in and worry about that later. I'll go with you if you want."

"Oh, I don't know. I don't think so . . ."

"Please. Just try."

My heart suddenly felt heavy in my chest. Hungry and open. Sore. It couldn't be possible. After so much, after all I'd done, could it really be possible?

"Well, maybe I'll stop by," I whispered. "I guess."

Tyler hid his head in his mother's lap and Carmen turned her face away as Lila and I cried, holding hands across the table.

THE ENTRANCE EXAM was held on the same Saturday morning as the march. Needless to say, I was the first one finished. The proctor tried to give my sheets back, but I wouldn't take them.

"Yes," I told him. "I'm sure I'm done."

From Low Memorial Library, I ran past the chapel and out onto Amsterdam Avenue, crowded with Saturday shoppers. I flew down to 116th Street, dodging pushcarts and pedestrians and carriages, still breathing in time with the voice in my head. The voice hadn't gone away since that night outside the hall. If anything, it'd gotten louder, more persistent. It demanded things of me that I had no idea how to give.

Fifth Avenue. I got there just as the children were passing. Six, seven, eight years old, all dressed in white, marching with wide hand-painted banners that read: "Mother, Do Lynchers Go to Heaven?" and "God says: Thou Shalt Not Kill!" I pictured my son in a little white Easter suit, looking up at me, walking by my side, and wondered how I'd allowed myself to get comfortable marking time rather than living.

The women passed next, thousands of them, also dressed in white. Like me. Everyone marched, fixed into their silence, the only sound the beating of muffled drums in the background. I ran off the curb and fell into step with the women. One woman handed me her end of a pole that held up a banner, which said, "Mr. President, Why Not Make America Safe For Democracy?" She then went to go hand out pamphlets to the whites who'd gathered along the sidewalk to watch.

The farther we got downtown, the more the crowd thickened. Some pointing, some in tears, some laughing. In silence, we met their gazes. Silence until there was no place else to walk, until we'd reached our destination outside city hall.

That was it. The end.

The people slowly dispersed. Seeing them walk away, heads bowed, faces tight, made me sick. What had we accomplished? What had we changed? So many people, tens of thousands it seemed, all hemmed in, all trying to move in different directions. None of us going anywhere. I wanted to scream. I needed to breathe. Just breathe. Why was that so hard?

Someone grabbed my shoulder. I looked up and saw Coleman standing there.

In the middle of all those people, he'd actually found me. Surrounded by thousands of bodies, the faces blurred together and stamped with resignation (or fear or sadness or anger) he'd spotted me. It didn't seem possible. But there he was. Coleman smiled at first, but after he really looked at my face, he grabbed my elbow and led me away. With him shielding me, the crowd parted.

"Tell me where you live," he said. "I'll take you there."

At that moment, I didn't know.

Chapter 11

T he letter came two weeks after I took the exam.
My hands shook so bad that at first I couldn't even open the envelope. If Columbia wouldn't take me, I was stuck. After I took the test, Mama and I kind of went into an education frenzy—looking up schools, weighing far-fetched possibilities. We kicked around the idea of applying to Julliard, but then found out it was too late. The only other place that interested me was far away at Fountainebleau, where my hero, Walter Damrosch, headed the American School of Music. But when the application came, the blank above the very first question asserted, I am a White American and I apply for admission to this school. Since I couldn't check off that space, no matter what I looked like, I threw the papers in the garbage before Mama got home. Columbia was my only chance. I was starving, and the rest of the world seemed so small.

The paper wouldn't give. I passed the envelope to Mama. Her

hands were shaking too, but she didn't have any problem ripping through that seal.

"On behalf of Columbia University's Teachers College, we are pleased to . . . *Oh God! Oh my God! May!* You're in, baby! They want you!"

"I . . . I . . . I . . . Mama that's impossible . . . I don't have a . . ."

"Look!"

She shoved the letter in my face. And, yes, it was an acceptance addressed to Miss May Edward Chinn. I'd scored so high on the entrance exam that they were accepting me as a full-time music student—even with no high school diploma.

Me. They wanted me.

I got in.

A warm, floaty haze rose through my body and up through the top of my head. Mama threw her arms around me and we cried but I was only partly there. The rest of me watched from a great height, wrapped in a wholeness, a fullness that I don't think I'd ever felt before.

But then Papa looked up from his book and said, "She ain't goin' nowhere."

Just like that, the feeling inside me disappeared.

"William! How could you—"

Papa slammed his book on the floor hard enough to crack the spine.

"Goddammit! Would you get out of your pipe dream for a minute! What that girl gonna do with a college degree? Huh? Who's gonna hire her unless she pass? If she ain't willing to pass, all she's gonna be in four years is a lonely Colored wench with a piece of paper in her fist. And she's sure as hell gonna be lonely. Don't no man want to marry someone got more education than them. Even those college-educated boys don't want that. Can't have two men trying to run the same house.

"Lulu, please." Papa lowered his voice and walked over to Mama. He held her softly by her shoulders. "I know you don't believe it anymore, but I only want what's best for the child. She needs a man that can give her some protection. A place in this world. We don't have to tell nobody about what happened before. That's between us. Family. As long as nobody knows, the girl can still make a good match."

My father was ashamed of me. Still. But I couldn't blame him. I was ashamed of myself. It didn't feel like that smallness, that tightness in the center of my chest would ever go away. It had become part of me, like a fingerprint.

Mama took his hands and squeezed them. Just as softly, she said, "She's going."

The table went over first, dishes crashing. He pounded my piano until I threw myself over the keys. Hesitating for only a second, Papa spun around and snatched a picture from the wall beside me. It was a framed portrait of a house on a hilltop, one that he loved because he said it reminded him of Fleetwood. He bashed the canvas through a lamp then sent the picture and the lamp flying against the door. Spitting and sweating, with bloody hands leaving tracks across my mother's things, he raged through the apartment. Then he stopped. Just like that, he stopped and turned to face me.

"How much that school cost?"

"Two hu-hundred dollars."

"A year?"

"N-no. For each . . . semester . . ."

"Two hundred?" he repeated. Papa smiled and then wiped his face, leaving a blood smear across his cheek. He still didn't realize that he'd hurt himself breaking things.

"Two hundred dollars." He started laughing. "Two hundred dollars!"

Then Papa walked right up to Mama. Right up so that they

were toe to toe, each one staring the other down without so much as blinking. Prizefighters, bloody and hot.

"Where you gon' get two hundred dollars in three weeks, Lulu?"

My mouth fell. I hadn't even considered tuition. I never even thought it was possible for me to get in. Trying to raise two hundred dollars in three weeks was as good as trying to walk to the moon. That was nearly a full two months' salary for the average Colored man. My job at the factory paid less than half that, no matter how backbreaking the labor was. I had exactly seventeen dollars in savings.

My stomach contracted. Again. And again. I lurched into the kitchen, slipping through spilled coffee and tea and kerosene oil from the broken lamp. I barely made it to the sink before throwing up all over the supper dishes. The metal sink was cool and wet. I rested my head against the rim and then slid down to the floor, huddled next to the lead pipe, too empty and disappointed to cry anymore.

"Get up, May." Mama's voice sounded easy almost. "Come here, daughter."

I shook my head. I couldn't move. Didn't feel like it. It was too hard.

"Come here."

Her voice hadn't risen. It never did. But there was no more discussion left in it. She wasn't giving me the choice. I edged back into the room and looked at her.

Mama righted the table, motioning Papa closer with her finger.

He walked toward her, smug, smoldering, near tears himself, and stood there with his hands on his hips, daring her to say something more.

But she didn't.

Instead, Mama opened the buttons on the front of her blouse.

One by one. Slowly. Methodically. Making sure that Papa's eyes stayed on her hand, on her intention. Third button. Fourth button. Fifth. Little round imitation pearls popping open. From inside, tucked into her underclothes, she drew a worn leather pouch. The two of us stepped closer.

It simply wasn't possible.

Mama reached inside her pouch and pulled out a wad of money. Papa and I both cried out at the same time. Two high-pitched yelps, his from shock, mine from awe.

Slowly, still so slow, she unfolded the thick wad of notes. All twenties. She peeled each bill off the roll with a deliberate, dramatic flick of the wrist and plunked it against the crooked wooden table. One, two, three, four, five, six, seven, eight, nine, ten.

Then she looked at Papa, square in the face—and did it again.

Four hundred dollars.

Putting the rest of her money back into her pouch, back into her underclothes, Mama walked over to me and placed the bills into my hands. Up until that moment in my life, I don't think I'd ever touched a twenty-dollar bill.

"This is for you, Sweetness. Don't you never, *never* step foot in that factory again. Let them keep the rest of they money. You don't need it. That's not who you are. Now, you go down to that school tomorrow and you tell them that you are Miss May Edward Chinn. And you are there to complete your education."

TWO WEEKS LATER, a black man turned up dead behind our building. He'd been stabbed in the heart and bludgeoned with a mallet that the killer didn't even bother to take with him when he left.

That was all my mother needed to hear. She had the perfect excuse.

The first day of school was also moving day. Again. We left the Bronx and moved to 138th Street and 7th Avenue, right in the middle of Harlem, within walking distance of Teachers College.

Coleman helped Mama pack and load our things. Papa wasn't home. When I got out of class and walked up to our new place, they were already waiting, grinning, having some good conversation on the front stoop over lemonade and cookies. As the sun began to drop, Coleman excused himself and asked if I'd walk him to the corner. I turned to ask Mama if it was all right, but she was already through the door, on her way upstairs.

Harlem was hot. Ripe. Children dashed through the street, dodging trucks and mule carts, the boys bare-chested and barefoot, the girls with their plaits unraveled and standing straight up off their heads. Overhead, two sax players duked it out, legs hanging from fourth-floor windows on opposite sides of the street. Jazz wars on every corner. Everything was music here. Syncopated rhythm. I wanted to enjoy it, but I wasn't comfortable with the idea of being fast.

"I'm leaving day after tomorrow, May," Coleman said.

"I know. Where you headed?"

"South Carolina, I think. But I don't think we'll be there too long. Hope not anyway. They ain't got much use for nigger soldiers down there. They need us, but they ain't got no use for us."

"My father says being a soldier is a death sentence—one way or another. Says shouldn't any Colored man fight for a country that will just as soon kill him as look at him. He wanted to fight more than anything when he was younger. But now, with all that he's seen, especially lately . . ." I shook my head and watched two little girls at the corner feeding sugar lumps to the vegetable man's crotchety old yellow horse.

"Can't say I don't know how your father feels," Coleman admitted. "The way some of those recruiters look at you, you wonder if you was standing next to a German with a grenade in his hand and the pin pulled out, which one they'd shoot first. But I can't think on that stuff. All I got to know is that me going over there is going to make everything different when I get back here. We stand up, do our bit, they gon' have to allow us our place. There's no way they can't. It's not possible."

He shrugged and brushed his fingers against my hand. "Anyway, I came up here to join the Fifteenth, and that's what I'm doin' regardless. But that's not what I want to ask about. What I wanted to ask was, could I write you? My family's in South Carolina so I'm hoping to get to see them when we go. But from overseas, well, it's gonna be hard writing with them. I'm the only one that can read. Anything I write, they got to take it to the penny man first. And that drunk old cloaker say just about anything if he think he can get some more cash off you. But that's not the point. What I'm tryin' to say—"

"Yes, Coleman." I laughed. "I'll write to you. I'll answer every letter you send."

"Promise?"

"Promise."

The boy kissed my cheek and skipped—and when I say skipped, I mean skipped—down Seventh Avenue.

I watched him until he merged with the crowd and got lost. A young boy at war.

I turned back up the block and went inside. There was already work to do.

AT COLUMBIA, I was the litmus test.

From the first day, in my public health class, when Dr. Broadhurst called my name and said, "Chinn? Oh! *You're* Chinn, my dear? Why, I must say I'd never have guessed you to be Oriental. Now that I look I can see it around the eyes, though."

And I said (more loudly than necessary), "Oh no, ma'am. I'm not Oriental. I'm a Negro."

The other students in the class (sixteen white males and one white female) shifted and dropped their eyes. Dr. Broadhurst, however, met my gaze evenly. She smiled at me and then, without missing a beat, she said, "Excuse me, Miss Chinn. My mistake. Well . . . welcome. I'm very glad you're here."

After that, people all across the campus knew who I was. The few dark-skinned students spoke much more freely to me, knowing I wouldn't draw back or hiss things like *dirty nigger* under my breath for the benefit of the whites around us. You could count the number of visible Negroes on the sprawling Columbia campus. But there were others, a whole class of others, who'd chosen to stay invisible.

Those were the ones who simply allowed people to assume they were white without ever correcting them (Carmen included). They sailed gracefully across the campus, smiling, blending, making excuses, I suppose, about why none of their new friends could come home to meet their families. These were the ones who watched me suspiciously. I frightened them. When our eyes met, they'd look quickly away and I'd know not to act like I recognized them unless I met them around the neighborhood.

The ones who were race conscious, stubborn, would walk right up to me and shake my hand or kiss my cheek out on the quad or in the library where everyone could see.

See, they were saying, *I'm not white. I'm Colored, like she is.*

Only a couple did that.

To be seen with May Chinn or not to be seen with May Chinn? A question that could literally determine one's future. Columbia, the land of my dreams, suddenly became a very, very lonely place.

To make matters worse, I was flunking out of my major. Already. And school had barely even gotten started.

A balding, hawk-nosed German named Dr. Strauss taught my first music class, something called Tone Thinking. Twelve young white men and me. As the head of the music department, Dr. Strauss made it absolutely clear to me, and the rest of the class, what he thought about having me waste his valuable time.

"Young woman," he said on the first day, "I shall give you the opportunity to sign out of this class now so you can pick up something else for your credits."

"No, sir," I said politely. "I believe I'm in the right place."

Strauss's face went blank and still. A red heat crept up his neck and across his cheeks.

"Stay if you insist," he said calmly. "But let's be clear. I know who you are. I know what you are capable and not capable of."

"Excuse me, sir—"

"And it is simply not within the scope of your people to understand what I am trying to impart."

If he'd slapped me, it would have been easier. There was nowhere for me to go, no way to get any smaller in my seat.

"It is simple truth that no person of . . . syncopated origin can hope to entertain the genius of Bach, of Beethoven," he determined. "You will just never get it."

The class continued and, from that moment forward, I became invisible to Dr. Strauss. When he asked a question, if I were the only one to raise my hand, he'd answer it himself. When he brought each student up to play, he conveniently forgot to call my name. Every evening, I went home in tears.

If it'd just been one class, no problem. But Strauss was the head of the department. I had to take at least five more courses with him to get my degree. Even if I were willing to be tortured for the next four years, he clearly wasn't willing to give me the chance. We both needed a way out.

One afternoon, Dr. Strauss called on a young blond man named Kenneth to come to the front of the room and play. Kenneth stood, bowed, and said, "I'd like to give my turn to Miss Chinn, sir. Thank you, sir." Then he sat back down.

Mutiny. Strauss turned to another young man, named David. "You. Come up."

David stood and said, "Excuse me, sir. But I'd like to give my turn to Miss Chinn. Thank you, sir."

Strauss was apoplectic. I was confused.

By the time the fifth student had said the same thing, I figured out that they were closing ranks against the professor for reasons of their own. There'd be retribution, of course (mainly against me). But regardless, I got to play that day.

After class, I rushed home, dying to tell Mama what happened. But when I got to the house, no one was there. Mama had left a note on the table that said, "Gone to Bernice's. Stop by. Signed, your mother."

Bernice, the beautician, had also moved her shop to Harlem. New and pink and just a block from Striver's Row, Bernice's House of Beautification had quickly become the place to be seen. Mama didn't care about any of that. She would just nose on through quietly, taking up some time, having a cool drink with an old friend.

"Miss May!" Bernice called as I burst through the door. She stood over the sink in the back of the shop, with her hands massaging pink suds into a young girl's scalp.

"Evening, ma'am." I grinned. "How are you, please?"

"Fine, sugar, just lovely. Can't find no reason to complain as long as God stays good. Your mama ran out to Larry's shop at the corner. Be back shortly. In the meantime, let me introduce you around." She took her hands out of the child's head and wiped them on her salmon-colored apron. Then she walked over to a gorgeous dark brown woman sitting in the corner with her legs crossed, reading a magazine.

"A'Lelia? A'Lelia, honey? May, come on over here. A'Lelia, this is the child I told you 'bout some time back. Lulu's baby girl. May—come here girl! May, this is Miss A'Lelia Walker. 'Course you heard of her mama, Madame C. J. Walker."

Wrapped in a silver turban and a matching silk dress, Miss Walker looked like a shimmering moon. Except she was so long and tall. So certain. She stretched her hand out and I took it carefully, not really sure of what to do with such regality. So I bowed low from my waist, like a gentleman. Miss Walker's face lit up, and she laughed, loud, also like a man. Laughed for all she was worth.

"Oh my goodness! Isn't she just the berries? Love me a child that's got good sense," she told Miss Bernice. When she turned back to me, her eyes lit up my face. How odd, how wonderful to see a brown woman fill up her skin like that. She made my heart race. "So, May, Miss Bernice tells me you play the piano like nobody's business. You can get on those keys and really do it twice in the same place!"

I blushed hot red and she laughed again.

"So is this true? Or is Bernice over here just bull-skating?"

"I . . . I play some, yes, ma'am."

"Oh, she just embarrassed now," Miss Bernice piped up. "Got herself a scholarship to Columbia University, playing that classical music."

"Really?" Miss Walker leaned forward, suddenly very interested. "Say, little Miss May, would you be interested in coming to play for me at my home? I throw parties every now and again. Small affairs but I think you'd like it. The right sort of people always seem to gravitate to my place. I think you might be just the person to help me entertain them. What do you think?"

"I would love that, ma'am."

"A'Lelia, child. Call me Miss A'Lelia, please. And speaking of the right sort—this is exactly who I was waiting for."

As she said that, a young, somewhat pudgy dark-skinned boy strolled through the door. He couldn't have been more than fourteen or fifteen. But he was all dressed up—jacket, tie, waistcoat, with the gold chain from his pocket watch glittering ostentatiously against the heavy brown of his suit.

"Come here, love," A'Lelia called him. "There's someone I want you to meet. Miss May Chinn, this is my good friend Mr. Countee Cullen."

"It is my pleasure, Miss Chinn."

He bowed, took my hand, and made as if to kiss it. But then he stopped just short and released me with a scrunched smile.

I giggled. What a dickty little fellow. But there was something about him, something soft that I decided to like anyway. He seemed like a good boy.

"Countee, I want you to run this letter over to your father, hear? See that he gets it right away. It's important. Matter of fact, take May here along with you. Introduce her to your people. She needs to know them. We're going to be seeing a lot more of her now."

"Yes, ma'am," he said, and then held the shop door open for me to follow. I gave Bernice a hug and a kiss and shook Miss Walker's hand, then raced out the door behind him.

Miss Walker's hands, her voice, and her presence struck me like lightning. I felt wide and open, spacious like her smile. If she wanted me to go with this little boy, I'd go and know that only good could come of it. We fell into the foot traffic headed down Eighth and had walked a good while before Countee turned to me, with his wide, triangle nose downcast, and said, "So exactly what do you do, May?"

He had a high voice, babylike. But his words carried weight, a certain studied calm that held true with the softness of his eyes and his body. It was womanly, rather than childish.

"I'm in school right now. Columbia."

"Oh, I'm thinking about Columbia. Either Columbia, Harvard or New York University. I've got some time yet, of course." He dropped his head, almost embarrassed. "I'm only in the ninth grade."

"Well it's good to know what you want. How else will you ever get it?"

Countee shook his head. "It's a long time between now and then."

"Not really. Not nearly so long as you might think. The thing to remember between now and then is that you can have anything you want—no matter what anyone else says. No matter who thinks they can stop you. The only thing that you need to know is exactly what it is that you want and that it's already yours."

I told him the things that I'd come to hear my mother tell me. In return, he graced me with a true smile. Small and uncertain, but real. The smile spread across his puppy-dog cheeks so that his nose stretched out a bit wider and his eyes narrowed with happiness.

We walked a while in silence. Then Countee whispered, "Want to see something?" He pulled a tiny square from the breast pocket of his suit. The page was old and obviously well loved. I unfolded it carefully, so as not to rip through the worn creases. Inside, I found:

I am for sleeping and forgetting
All that has gone before;

I am for lying still and letting
Who will beat at my door;
I would my life's cold sun were setting
To rise for me no more.

In my mind, a picture of my child flashed and then was gone. I understood this boy.

Refolding the page, I looped my arm through his and pressed the square back into his palm. I couldn't find the words, but I didn't need to. He understood as well.

The only thing that you need to know is exactly what it is that you want. And that it's already yours.

What a liar. That's not all I needed to know. It couldn't be. If that were true, I wouldn't be losing everything. Everything that my mother had literally given over her life for. Everything that had kept me from losing my mind since that woman walked out of the attic cradling my son in her arms.

Without my music, who would I be?

Strauss was flunking me out.

Midsemester exams had just passed and I'd done exceedingly well in everything—except tone thinking. We'd had to play for him, one by one, in the empty room while he sat in the corner, fingertips brushing softly to make a steeple, obscured in the dark. There was a light sitting next to him, but he refused to turn it on. He liked it better not being seen.

I'd played my music lushly. Excavating that man from the space all around me, seeing nothing but the notes in front of me. It was the only way for me to get through the test. I made Dr. Strauss unreal. Better for him to be a ridge of shadow. Nothing more. By the time I finished, I was sweating and close to tears.

I curtsied in his general direction without looking at him, then walked from the room.

The next Monday when grades were posted, I found that I'd gotten a "D."

20. October 1917

Dear May Chinn,

   Hello there. How are you doing? This is Coleman on this end. I just thought about your pretty smile and decided to drop you a note. How are your parents? And how is school? I know that you are really showing those fays what a good Harlem girl can do! (smile) South Carolina is just the way I left it. Although the good folks of Spartanburg seem to have taken nigger hating to new heights (excuse my language). Klan is big time down here. They burned a scarecrow wearing army digs on a cross just off the base. There's been some other incidents, too. It's scary. And the officers make us train using sticks for guns. So we don't even have nothing to fight back with, if the need arises. The only good news is I don't think we'll be here too long. Oh man! France will look like the pearly gates of Heaven (not literally, I hope) compared to Spartanburg. We certainly won't be missed down here. Some cracker overheard Jim Europe say we was going to join the Rainbow Division in France and this fay turns around and says, "Why would you do that? Black's not one of the colors of the rainbow." I'm trying hard not to let it get to me, but it does sometimes just the same. I just keep trying to remind myself of why I'm here. We have to be here. We've got to make this work.

   Anyway, I think I've bored you enough for now. Hope you're not sorry you said you'd write! 'Cause I'm going to hold you to it! I'll have better, happier news next time. Promise. Tell your folks I send my love. I miss you too.

                                             Your friend,
                                             Coleman Fortlow

Dr. Broadhurst called me into her office when public health class ended one morning shortly after midterms. She closed the

door quietly behind her and sat on the edge of her desk while I settled into a chair.

"May," she said, "let me ask you a personal question. You're a
music major. Why did you choose to take a public health class?"

"Honestly, ma'am?"

"Yes, of course."

"I just needed the extra point to make up the twenty-one points
on my schedule."

Dr. Broadhurst threw her head back, laughing, and clapped
her hands together.

"I should have guessed it was something like that. Isn't that always the way?" She shook her head. "I'm sorry. I don't mean to
confuse you. It's just that some of the other professors and I have
been talking a bit about you. May, I don't know if you realize it or
not, but to be bluntly honest, Dr. Strauss intends to fail you in his
course. I won't go into the details about what he said, but he's
made it clear that under no circumstances will you get a degree
within his department. Normally, such things wouldn't be discussed with a student. But some of the other teachers and I have
taken a special interest in this. We've been trying for weeks to figure out what to do about 'The May Chinn Problem.' "

Dr. Broadhurst chuckled again. Then she got quiet for a long
moment, as if she were wondering whether to proceed.

"The only reason that we've been keeping track of this, May, is
because we all agree that you have extraordinary potential. That
paper that you wrote on sewage disposal for my class is one of the
finest that I've read in years. You've got a gift for assessment that I
don't think I've ever seen before. If you have any sort of interest in
the field, I'd like to offer you a spot in the science department.
Considering Strauss's intentions, I think it would be in your best
interest. Because as you know, if you fail your major, you can't stay

in Teachers College at all. None of us want to see that happen, dear."

"Oh. Well. Thank you for the offer, ma'am," I mumbled. "I'll think about it."

I was stunned. She'd only told me what I already knew. But to hear it come out of her mouth, to have it confirmed, bluntly told all the ways it wasn't possible to dream . . .

What do you call a Colored concert pianist?

A dishwoman. A factory worker. A maid.

A dreamer.

A fool.

"May?" Dr. Broadhurst called as I swung the door open and stepped into the chilly hallway. "When can I expect to hear from you?"

"End of the week, ma'am. I'll be by to see you."

"Good. I'll be waiting."

Gabriel popped into my mind as I walked out the door, even though I rarely thought of him anymore. I saw his face, young and warm, bent over a beaker, smiling. Would he be proud of me? Right behind that, I thought of my son. Nearly a year and a half. He'd be walking by now. Speaking strings of words that I hadn't taught him. What in this world could make that a viable sacrifice? Looking back, I wondered which choices I ever really made for myself.

Other people's opinions and ideas and desires and hates and needs clashed inside my head. Waves of demands rolled and receded. I hurried outside so I could be alone and think. At least for a minute. Sinking down into the tall, thick grass behind the Russell building, I looked like any other young woman taking in the crisp autumn air between classes. No one could tell.

I needed to get clear. But the only thing that came up for me when I tried to still my mind was: *These white people are going to kill me. Oh my dear. I can see that now.*

I mean, what went through their heads? Was it all a game to them? Let's see how many ways we can find to drive this one over the edge. You strangle this dream over here, and we'll implant a new one over there. Plus a new identity to go with it. See? It all makes sense.

Faces swirled in my mind. Arrogant, indifferent, bursting with love and longing, tilted in kindness. Why did everyone want so much from me? What was it that they saw? I'd been palmed and pawed and corrected so much that my own face wasn't even familiar to me anymore. Only my scars, which never changed.

I didn't know what else to do or how to stop those stupid, meddling voices. I slumped on the lawn with the grass rubbing my legs under my skirt, cold and damp. It felt nasty, but at least it was real. It anchored me.

Everything was about to change, and somehow I not only had to be all right with that, but make the changes mine. What else could I do? I took a deep breath and surrendered it. All of it. All of the fear and the doubt and the nagging disbelief. Gave it all over.

"This is going to work out," I said aloud. "No matter what the end result looks like. It'll be right. It has to be. There is simply no other choice."

Over and over I said this. I refused to move until I finally began to relax inside those words. My legs cramped. The wind blew harder. I stayed. Breathing, getting quiet and still, I sat there for a very long time, releasing things that no longer served me, deciding which new things did. After a while, a sense of peace bloomed inside my chest. Then, and only then, did I stand up and start the long walk home.

People tell me all the time that I'm brave. Courageous. A teacher of miracles.

But can those things really be true if you don't know that you have a choice?

4. January 1918

Dear May,

How are you? Sorry to hear about your classes. But maybe this is a blessing in disguise, even though I know it doesn't feel that way now. I just know that God meant for you to do good things. Big things. Maybe they just aren't the things that you thought they'd be. I don't know.

France is different than anything I ever expected. I never knew white people could be so nice, so good-natured. Most of them don't care one bit that we're Colored, only that we're Americans. Only that we're here to bring freedom and democracy. The training is the hardest thing I've ever experienced in my life so far. They put us right to it as soon as we stepped off the boat. My bayonet has become my best friend, another arm. I don't know how you feel about that, but it's just how it is for now. We're to be going off to the front soon, I've heard. We have to be ready. I'll make sure to write you before I go. Please write to me. I'd very much appreciate having something to take with me on the road (smile). All the best to you.

Your good friend,
Coleman Fortlow

Chapter 12

HARLEM, NEW YORK—1918

Music raged up and down the streets like the war was going on over here. Everywhere, everywhere jazz took over. Piercing swirls of sound, uncontrolled, spontaneous, cropped up in every tavern, coffee shop, rent party and nightclub in Harlem. Braying sounds, like rough voices, rushed in all night long through my open window. Eating the noise like food, I leaned out the bedroom window for hours on nights when I claimed to be studying, emptying the whole of myself into the street below.

My father spoke to me about this once, shortly after Christmas. He hadn't spoken to me directly for more than six months.

He and Mama were discussing the food rationing in Germany one morning. The Allies might not have to beat the Krauts in a fair fight, he told her. They might all starve to death before then. Mama sucked her teeth and reminded him that, German or not, they were still human beings, children of God. Papa grunted and belched. So much for children of God.

"More coffee before you go, William?"

"No thank you, Mother. I'm late enough as it is. Be home early tonight."

He opened the door, but before he stepped outside, he turned back to me and said, "And May? Don't you ever, *ever* pass the open door of one of those cabarets. You do, and they'll drag you inside and make a bar girl out of you. I mean it. I find out that you even walk in front of one of those places when they got their doors open to the street, you'll have to deal with me. You understand?"

Stunned, Mama and I both nodded at the same time.

My father had to be the oddest man I ever met.

So picture me, scuttling down Jungle Alley, early in the morning, late at night, clutching my books to my chest and zigzagging from one side of the street to the other. The Catagonia Club. The Bucket of Blood. Brownie's Basement. Avoiding all of them, each one open at all odd hours. It didn't even matter if I crossed the street. I could still see inside. Could still watch the women as they pealed off laughter like the men peeled bills off their fold; could still hear clarinets wailing, rubbing up against the saxophones (much like the women) and feel the rumbling piano sounds inside my own fingertips, making me sick to my stomach with longing.

But it seemed best to shut all that out. I had other things to do now.

I'd switched my major to science.

And instead of teaching piano to the little boys and girls from St. Phillips for extra money, I got a job working in a pathology lab, preparing blood specimens and cultures as a student assistant for Dr. Broadhurst.

Oftentimes, I was all alone in the lab, until ten or eleven at night, trying to find in the strange clusters of cells and tissues some of the magic that I found in a cluster of notes in my head.

But you know what? It made sense to me, the order of the

body. I found that I could sense lapses in the structure and function in the tissue samples in the same way that I could find the unnecessary notes in a phrase and slice them out, whether I was supposed to or not.

Of course, I wasn't supposed to be doing that with the tissue samples either. Merely prepare them for diagnosis by the real doctors. But I had to do something more to occupy my mind. If I didn't, I started hearing things, sliding scales that took my breath and made me shaky. It was like my lover had left without telling me where he'd gone or if he'd ever be back. And I, for lack of knowing, had let him go.

One evening, at the start of my shift, Dr. Broadhurst walked in with a beautiful young woman trailing behind her. The girl looked somewhat like me. But she was shorter, haughty and butter-colored, like my son, whereas my skin tended toward pale cream. Her hair had been chopped into the wavy bob that was the absolute rage. She tossed her head like a colt and stuck her hand on her hip.

"Eslanda Goode," she said, without waiting for Dr. Broadhurst to make the introduction. Walking by the doctor, she shot out her other hand and grabbed mine in a vigorous shake. "Pleasure to meet you, May."

Dr. B. smirked. "Well, now that I've done that, I'll leave you two to your own devices. May, be a dear and show Essie around the lab."

As soon as Dr. B. closed the door, this Essie woman turned to me and said, "Don't trouble yourself, kid. I've done this all before, you know. All I need to know is where she keeps her equipment. That sort of thing. So you're the famous May Chinn. Not bad. Not what I expected (what happened to your face?), but not bad. So what do you think of Broadhurst? What's in her bag? She's got two of us down here working together. Kind of odd, don't you think?

Seems like she's into collecting jaspers, doesn't it? But she's not a bad old girl. Hey, want a smoke?"

Eslanda Goode.

Somehow, along the course of things, this rude, brilliant scythe of a girl became another new best friend.

8. April 1918

Dear May,

It'll be night here soon. They'll be coming again tonight. No matter what we do to them, they never stop coming. But then again, neither do we. I wanted to write to you beforehand. Wanted to let you know that when I stop and think about things, when I think about my life, about who I think I am, I see your face instead of my own now. I think that's because you're easier for me to recognize. The sky is so gray today it's hard to tell the hour. Makes it easy to lose track of time. Next thing you know, it's night. You know, they call us the Fifteenth Heavy Foot now. I like that name. The Boche know who we are. They can hear us coming. Feel us. The Heavy Foot. I don't know how many days it's been. A couple of months on the front now I think. No break. The Boche call us French Moroccans. At first we thought it was German foolishness. Now we know it's because only the French claim us.

May, I think I was wrong.

Yours,
Coleman

"Say, Lil' Bit, you done over there?"

"Not quite, Essie."

"What the hell. 'Not quite' sounds close enough to me. What do you say we get out of here? There's some jaspers meeting over at the Oriental. I don't want to miss it. Bud Fisher is up from Brown. He and Jean and some others are going to be reading some of their poetry. I think your little friend Countee is coming, too."

"Really?"

"Uh-huh." Essie was already up and at the door with her camel hair coat halfway over her shoulder. "Well?"

She cleared the hallway and was already at the stairs before I could say, "Do you really think we should?"

We headed uptown and rounded the corner onto 136th Street. The Oriental occupied the entire house in a three-story Victorian with carpeted floors and linen-covered tables. Just as we walked through the doors, a loud whoop went up in the back corner of the otherwise empty room. Essie headed straight for it.

"*Ridicule! N'attendez aucune reconnaissance de ces blancs,*" cried a long, leggy yellow boy.

"*Oui. C'est exactement ce que j'attends d'eux!*" answered the woman he was yelling at. She answered coolly, smoothing her wavy hair behind her ears and looking off over his head, as if she expected something far more interesting to come along at any moment.

"Gwendolyn, *je*—"

"This is exactly what I've been talking about," Bud said to Essie and me, as we strolled up. "Listen to these dickties. Here they are—a pack of Negroes, in Harlem, *at night,* curled up in the darkest corner of the room—and yet all they can do is play white and bright. *S'il vous plaît!*"

"Ha!" snorted a very dark young man named Claude. "All that from a voluntary Negro like Bud Fisher. How do you like that?"

Gwendolyn turned and beamed broadly at Claude. "McKay." She sighed. "You'd be heaven on earth if you weren't so irascibly bitter and jaded. But then again, perhaps that's precisely your charm. *Ne me quitte pas . . .*"

Alain, Bud, Countee, and the handful of others at the table all laughed. Claude crossed his legs and faced the wall, pouting. The discussion continued without him, but only for the moment. The others needed Claude, his acid wit, his anger. He, through some great play on words or intentions, had become a leader in their midst. Claude would never have claimed that of himself, because he openly disdained what he called "the talented tenth hypocrisies." But his brilliance, his obvious genius kept others enthralled, even as he figuratively (and once literally) spit on their shoes. In another moment or two, someone would begin to massage his back gently with a comment about the war or the "Movement," and he would turn his face back toward the circle.

"How rude of us," Bud said. "We haven't offered Essie and May any seats. Here, May, you can sit next to me. How about a drink?"

"Careful, May," Alain called. "If he buys you anything, make sure he's got his hands in his own pockets and not yours when the bill comes!"

Bud, who was always notoriously broke, took the joke with a sly smile.

"Say," Essie said. "Who's up next?"

"That would be Jean," said Gwendolyn. "He's been hiding in the corner all night."

"As if that hunky-hunk could ever hide *anywhere*," Essie said in a mock whisper.

Jean ducked his head, which just made the others laugh more. When we'd all quieted a bit, he finally stood, tall and broad-shouldered, and pushed his hair back out of his face. Like my papa's, Jean's face held nearly nothing of his race in it. But Jean was far more handsome than even my father, ruddy and healthy and strong. He looked more like a football star than an aspiring writer. But a writer is exactly what he was. Among so many other things.

Standing in front of us in the only patch of good light filtering down from the silk lantern overhead, he shifted his feet and waited for us all to finish getting quiet. When he saw that every eye lay fastened on him, he cleared his throat and began.

> "In time, although the sun is setting on
> A song-lit race of slaves, it has not set;
> Though late, O soil, it is not too late yet
> To catch thy plaintive soul, leaving, soon gone,
> Leaving, to catch thy plaintive soul soon gone.

> "O Negro slaves, dark purple ripened plums,
> Squeezed, and bursting in the pine-wood air,
> Passing, before they strip the old tree bare
> One plum was saved for me, one seed becomes . . ."

No one moved. In the silence, I could see Jean beginning to get embarrassed.

"I . . . I'm thinking of writing a book," he said, and then shuffled his page between his fingers a bit more before sitting down.

"The sun is setting on a song-lit race of slaves . . ." Alain mulled this over, softly mouthing the words, as if he could taste them. "Do you really believe that, Toomer?"

"I believe," Jean said quietly, "that I am either the very newest race of man or the very oldest. Either way, I am what the world must become if we're going to survive. All of us here at this table are the same, in some way or another. Even the dark ones among us." He glanced quickly at Claude and Countee. Countee turned his face away, but Claude didn't even notice. Instead, he stared down at his feet, looking pained, almost betrayed.

"Nordics would never accept such a proposal," Countee said to the table. "It could never happen."

"Who the hell cares what *they* accept?" Jean shot back. "Don't you understand? *They are us.* There is no separation. What we accept, they must be compelled to act upon."

"So, say we accept our part as equals in this supposedly democratic society," Gwendolyn interjected. "Say we accept our place as legitimate sons and daughters, however despised and despising the parent may be. What then? Who births this magic that compels them to act? Where and when do they do their part?"

"It happens here, when we stop speaking it and start believing it," Jean said.

"Then we shall never live to see the day," said Claude miserably. Everyone turned to stare at his hunched-over back, still contracted in the corner. "Then we shall die around this table, doing just what we're doing right now."

Abraham, the hulking black Jew who ran the place, had long since closed the kitchen. The coffee was cold and the cigarettes had burnt out, too. After a while, the silence got to us all. Bud stood up and stretched.

It was almost time to go home.

18. May 1918

Dear May,

I can't stop shaking. Even now, I can barely hold the pen upright. I want to talk to you. Can I? I don't know if I can find the words. Even if I do, would you be able to hear them? I don't know what to do. May, tell me what to do. Tell me why I'm here. Tell me what you see when you see my face in your mind. What do you remember?

They came again last night. I was on patrol duty with Henry and Needham and two others. Henry and Needham said they'd stay up. We could sleep. I hadn't slept in nearly fifty hours, I think. I passed out right there in the dugout, without even unstrapping my pack. When I woke up, they were already on us. A raiding party of maybe two dozen men. By the time I got my eyes open good, Henry and Needham had already killed about half of them.

They had blood all over them, all on their faces, like lampblack. Somehow that came up clear to me, even in the dark. Blood and pieces of bone and hair. Only it was me covered in those things and I was throwing grenades right along with them, except I didn't even remember waking up. But there I was. I was doing it too. Henry was yelling, "Turn out the guard! Turn out the guard!" Flinging grenades like baseballs. I saw him shoot down one Boche and then flip the gun around and crush another one's head with the butt of the rifle. The man's head actually split, May. Like fruit, straight down the center past the cleft of his nose. I was so busy watching that that I didn't even see two come from behind me. They jumped on me and started choking me but Henry was there again with his bolo knife. One throat he slit. In the same sweep, he shoved the knife straight through the crown of the other man's head. Before the man could hit the ground, Henry had pulled a grenade off his body and tossed it at the other Germans, even as they were running away. I think only two or three got away. They left everything behind, guns, wire cutters, grenades, everything. By the time the reinforcements came, Henry and Needham were sitting alongside a pile of offal, singing and laughing. The other two fellows were still unconscious, knocked out by the first grenade blast. Needham had been wounded too many times to count. He was covered from head to toe in his own blood, but he still laughed right along with Henry. I just knew he was going to die right there in front of me, laughing. They wanted me to laugh and sing with them too, but I couldn't.

I can't sleep anymore, May. I dream now and I never used to before. I shake a lot too. But I can't let any of the others see that. Henry's a hero now. I'm trying as hard as I can to be like him. But really I would rather just come home. When I think about your face now, it gets hard for me to breathe. Can I come see you when I get home? Please say yes.

With Love,
Coleman

PS—Do me a favor. Burn this letter after you read it. I just wanted you to know.

Coleman's letters shook me. I found myself talking to him at odd hours of the day, telling him about the price of collards at the market or how Mr. Williams's goat got out of their gate and wandered down Lenox Avenue. They finally found him (the goat, not Mr. Williams) across 132nd Street, trying to sneak past the ticket taker at the Lafayette Theater. I hoped that these were things he wanted to know.

Right or wrong, Coleman had made a choice. He believed in something enough to offer his life for it. Me—my friends and I— we talked, we read, we argued and marched, but what did any of that really mean?

"Those kinds of thoughts are foolish, May," Essie said one evening in the lab. "You do what you can, just like the rest of us. You do a whole lot more than ninety-nine percent of these darkies. Just let it go."

"You're probably right, but I can't let it go. I feel like I'm stuck. What's all this about, Essie? All of it? Us being here in this school? In this lab? They let us in, they hand us slides and specimens all day long to make us think we're doing something. But can we diagnose? Can we have even one creative thought on our own without stepping over some kind of invisible line? No."

"My God. Now you sound exactly like Jean and Wallace. Is this where you pull another long-winded speech out of your 'I don't know if I can teach' bag? If it is, I'm going outside for a break."

"Essie—"

"You know, May, if you feel that strongly about it, you never should have left music. Damn their department. The sun, the moon and Jesus Christ do not bow down to Columbia University. Unfortunately, that's water under the bridge at this point."

"So what do I do now?"

"First of all, quit whining. It's not constructive. If you really don't want to teach, just do something else. There's plenty of ways to help the Movement. You don't see me sitting around complaining all day, do you?"

"What else?"

"Long-term or short?"

"Long-term."

"Well, for starters, change your focus. Stay in science if it makes you happy, but pick some other aspect. Maybe you could become a pathologist. Or even a doctor, like me."

A doctor.

Essie always made me smile. She had such wonderful, grand notions inside her. I reminded her that, for a Colored woman, becoming a doctor was only slightly more impossible than becoming a concert pianist.

"Wrong again, Lil' Bit," she said. "I'm doing it. And why not? It's time to make a change in this city. Do a new thing."

"Well, what can I do short-term?" I asked.

She leaned back in her chair and chewed the eraser off her pencil.

"How about this?" she said. "My cousin Randolph is organizing a USO benefit for the soldiers at Fort Dix in Jersey. Why don't you help out with that? You could perform for them. That would be something."

I contacted Randolph the very next morning on the telephone from Miss Bernice's shop. He said he'd heard of me and happily invited me to perform that weekend. That gave me someplace to start.

By nine in the morning on Saturday, I was seated at a piano practicing in a huge, drafty auditorium. In a couple of hours, the place would be packed with more than one thousand men. I'd decided to mix some classical tunes like Opus 25 with more popular songs like "Over There." I'd just finished warming up and walked offstage into the wings when I felt someone ease up behind me.

"Pardon me, Miss Chinn. I'm afraid my accompanist hasn't arrived yet. And I understand that you are a marvelous accompanist. Would you do me the honor of accompanying me this afternoon?"

That voice.

I turned around and found myself at eye level with a golden Phi Beta Kappa key and an All-American Football emblem. The pendants dangled from a watch chain strung across the barrel chest of a young man in a dark blue three-piece suit. We'd never met before, but like everyone else, I knew exactly who he was.

"Of course, Paul," I said. "I'd love to."

I looked right up into his face and thought, *He must be the most beautiful man I've ever seen.* Seal brown skin. Wide nose. Hefty, cushioned lips. And gums like blackberries. He had the softest eyes in the world. The young man beamed at me, a broad, full rich smile that seemed to take in everything in the room, including my heart.

Paul Robeson.

He handed me his sheet music, then held his giant arm out for me to grab. "Shall we get started then? You know, I really appreciate this, May. I can call you May, can't I? I've heard so much about you around town. It's good to finally meet you in person."

My mouth fell open. Imagine, Paul Robeson telling *me* that he was glad we finally met! Incredible.

The concert passed in a haze. The best way I can describe Paul's voice is to say that it filled you to hear it. It curled up around you, a rumble or a purr, depending on his mood. What secrets in that voice! I played Negro spirituals in public for the very first time. White and black soldiers alike sat rapt, unable to move their eyes from Paul as he towered above them from the stage. He commanded the room effortlessly, left people floating in the wide gulf of space that he created with his presence.

And I played. I played to cradle his voice, to lift it above the notes, making a crest of sound that his words could ride over, above language and thought. Each time I rose, he rose to meet me, widening his reach.

When the concert was over, Paul pulled me to the side and said, "That was amazing. The way you play is . . . well . . . remarkable. I don't really know what to say. I've got another program to do at the end of the week. Would you be interested?"

That's how I became Paul Robeson's accompanist.

We spent the rest of the summer shuttling between New Brunswick, Asbury Park, Newark, Central Park West, Greenwich Village, Fifth Avenue, Hartford and too many other places to remember. We practiced on my piano at home, always when Papa wasn't there. Mama fed us cookies, sandwiches, homemade bread— whatever she could whip up. Anything that she made, Paul gratefully inhaled. Paul ate so much that some nights, when Papa came home, there was no dinner left for him. Mama blamed the chintzy markets. She blamed the economy (a dollar just didn't stretch like it used to). She blamed her own forgetfulness. She blamed everything but me and my friend.

Usually, my mother left me alone when I practiced. But when Paul was there, she sat quietly in the corner listening, enraptured by his voice. The only time she interrupted was when I chastised Paul for not wanting to work the low parts of the songs. His voice may have been a gift from God, but it could still stand to be honed into a more disciplined shape, just like everything else. Every time I drummed my fingers along the piano keys and said, "*Now, Paul!*" Mama made frowny faces at me and offered him more cookies. Undermining me all the way.

When Paul and I played for white people, we always prepared a program comprised almost exclusively of spirituals. And more often than not, by the end of the set Paul had brought the entire room, men and women alike, to tears.

"You touched places in me," they'd say, "that I never knew existed before. Brought life to feelings that I thought were long dead. God Bless you, sir. God bless you, miss."

When we played for other Negroes, however, quite often they would pull me aside, somewhat embarrassed, and make suggestions.

"Do you think you might persuade Mr. Robeson to do some more contemporary selections? I, uh, hate to bring it up, but, well, you see, we'll be having Caucasian guests at this affair as well. Very prominent people, you understand. And you know how *they* are. They'll think that's all we know how to play. I've never cared for those songs anyway. They bring the race down. Put us back on the level of the slave people. It's time to move on. That's what I think. Anyway, thank you so much, dear. I knew you'd understand."

I did understand. Quite well. Paul did too. Although part of his greatness was that he never let it show.

We traveled once to perform at an afternoon banquet in Asbury Park. The railroad car was stifling, the windows streaked with fog and sweat. Paul didn't seem to notice. He sat with his back against the slippery window, his cap pulled way down over his eyes, singing "Oh Danny Boy" in a rumbling, theatrical whisper. Still, his voice carried through the whole car and I could see people craning their necks around the seats trying to get a glimpse of where that sound could be coming from.

He laughed at something going on in his head and then, because he didn't seem compelled to share, I said, "Well?"

"Nothing. Nothing at all. I was just thinking. Wondering if you realize that Bud Fisher is madly in love with you."

"Of course. Me and every other girl between Lenox and Fifth."

"May, don't be so jaded. You break his heart every time he sees you. Somehow you just won't give him the time of day. Not that I'm pressing his case, you understand. Personally, I think you could do much better."

"Is that so? And who do you have in mind for me?"

He plucked his cap up so I could see his eyes and gave me a wicked grin.

"Me, of course."

I watched the yellow and green pastures outside the window slip by. The train slowed, bringing the willows and the elms into focus. The heat had bleached and softened the leaves on the trees until they looked spongy, as supple as felt. When the train picked up speed, they blurred together again, like the feather strokes of a watercolor.

"You can't ignore me forever. I'm serious, you know."

"I know that, Paul. You're serious about me, about Frankie Quiett, about Gerry Neale—"

"Frankie's a pal. Great girl. But it's nothing long-term. Now Gerry—Gerry broke my heart. But a man's got to get over a broken heart sometime."

He fingered the frayed edge of his jacket and grinned even wider.

That man was nothing but a hobo and a scamp. My scalp itched with sweat. The lump in my throat made it impossible to speak. He loved it.

"You're something special, May. I can't quite explain it. But you could drive a man out of his mind. There's a softness in you, a gentleness. Then again, you're hard as nails. You keep a man on his feet. And there's nothing phony about you. I like that."

He slid his hand across the nape of my neck and played with the sweat collecting in pearls at my hairline. Then he leaned in and put his lips against my ear.

"Our stop, beautiful. Come on, I'll buy you an ice-cream cone on the way to the place."

Paul bought me not only ice cream, but cotton candy, a fountain soda, a steak lunch, lace cuffs to put on my sleeves and a lace collar for my good blue silk blouse. By the time we got to the house for the banquet, he was broke. But we were having such a good time that neither of us realized it until we'd finished the concert and been dropped off by the hostess's chauffeur back at the train station.

"Say, May. Do you happen to have an extra three dollars?"

"For what?"

"Our tickets."

"*Paul!*"

"I'm sorry, sweetheart. I must have gotten carried away."

He pulled off his cap and ran his fingers through his woolly hair. Again, that smile. Tapping his scuffed shoe against the curb like a little boy who's been up to no good all day long. I made him turn around so I could open my blouse and pull out the emergency money that Mama gave me every time I went somewhere with Paul. She knew how he was, too.

"Mama gave me two dollars. Shoot! That's only enough for one ticket. What are we going to do?"

Back to the house we trekked, as the sun started to dip, to beg the woman who'd commissioned us, Mrs. Lewis, for carfare.

"Of course, my poor dears! As a matter of fact, let me hand you your payment checks now too. You should have said something. My goodness! You little urchins, you!"

Paul towered over this plump, blond-haired woman by at least a foot. But he made no move, showed no displeasure at being called an urchin. He kept smiling.

Mrs. Lewis gave us our carfare, checks and a little something extra. Paul promptly spent this "extra" on dinner at a Hungarian restaurant next door to the station because he said he couldn't possibly exist after having heard the word "goulash" and not know what such a thing would taste like.

We missed our train home.

6. January 1919

Dearest May,

I'm coming home soon. With all my heart, I thank God for sparing me long enough to look into your eyes at least one more time. Your letters held me together. No matter what, I will always be grateful to you. You saved my life.

Love you always,

Coleman

Coleman sent me a Valentine. A box of French chocolates wrapped in brown paper. Bitter truffles that tasted like coffee. Papa loved them but wouldn't eat any more after Mama told him they were mine, a gift in the mail.

They arrived two days before Valentine's Day, the day that the SS *La France* pulled into port in New York.

Five days later, more than a million people lined the sidewalks, waiting in the cold to see the Harlem Hellfighters come marching up Fifth Avenue. Black and white, they crowded together in shop doorways, leaned out of windows and clustered on street corners. Little brown boys shinnied up lampposts and into the icy crotches of maple trees, angling for the best views. They wore brown, peaked hats, tiny replicas of the ones that the fighting men wore, and waved American flags. It seemed like almost everyone had a flag that day. Proud and forgiving, we laid claim to this country too, just like everyone else, as we cheered and waited to see our men marching home.

I stood at 110th Street and Fifth Avenue, at the edge of the park. The cobblestones chilled my feet right through my shoes and my fingertips turned numb. I huddled on the corner, caught directly in the crosswinds, searching the street for my first glimpse. I couldn't explain how I felt, why my stomach had been loose and jittery for days. Or how I could lose myself in thought for hours and then feel ashamed of myself for falling behind in everything and having no excuse for it at all. Always claiming to be so busy, and yet so far behind in work that never seemed to get done. I found myself slipping into Mama's room when no one else was home, staring in her mirror and touching the scars on my face. They'd lightened some over the years, but I still saw the railroad track across my jaw. Sometimes it made me uncomfortable looking people in the eye because I knew they were seeing parts of me that had never healed well. Strange things to be thinking on at a time of such celebration.

I stood there, absently rubbing my fingers against the side of my face, waiting for the music to start. And it came. Finally. A booming heavy drumbeat coming through Bojangles Robinson. I guessed it was him, because the procession was still blocks away when the music started to swell. I'd never heard him in person, but Coleman had described the sound in his letters, called it a heartbeat. Then I heard the horns, ripping into each other, mounting and then molding the phrases.

By the time they reached my corner, the thunder of the drums and the marching men had the crowd screaming, ready to swoon. The young men flipped their caps into the air and spun the women around. The old men sat on curbs and cried. These soldiers were exalted! They had triumphed at every turn. A glorious Jim Europe led the way, high-stepping with his band. I jumped up and down, clutching on to a woman I'd never met before, both of us crying and waving and screaming.

As they hit the edge of the park, Europe strutted on into a raucous rendition of "Here Comes My Daddy Now!" and that seemed to be the cue. The men broke formation and ran through the streets. They pulled women out of the crowd and twirled them, cakewalking, turkey-strutting, trucking. In their khaki pants, high brown boots, jackets and sharp peaked caps they looked every bit the fierce black warriors that the whole world now knew them to be. I'd never seen a more beautiful sight. Look at what they'd done!

I fought my way through the mass of people up to the corner of 115th Street and Lenox, right where I wrote Coleman I'd be. The crowd jammed the street to the point that Lenox Avenue began to look like any other Shout or Jump, where people packed an apartment so tight that to move from one side of the room to the next became an issue that required thought and strategy. People got to grinding at those parties, doing slow, hot-tempered drags because there wasn't room to do anything else.

I turned up the block toward Seventh Avenue, searching and anxious. Perhaps I'd missed him.

Just then, a pair of arms wrapped around my waist and took the breath out of my lungs. Gently, Coleman turned me around to face him. He took off his cap and the first thing I saw was how tender and red his ears were, and how short his hair had been cut. *My boy*, I thought. But they'd taken away the boy and left this person standing in front of me whose hands seemed as wide and as rough as the ocean he'd just crossed. I didn't recognize him. He had a thick, shining mustache now and sleepy-looking eyes. Earthen skin, smooth everywhere that I could see—face, neck and hands. This man towered over me. Glowing with cold, he stared into my eyes like he'd never seen me before, like my face was another expanse that he needed to cross.

"Hello, May," he said.

Coleman's voice was husky, velvety along edges that had been so sharp when he left.

I loved him already.

Chapter 13

Coleman and I never spoke about it or made a formal decision. Our coming together was just something that was understood. Coleman didn't talk much anymore. Not at all like the questioning boy that I'd met more than two years before. The man that came home stayed silent much of the time. Thoughtful, watchful. But that didn't bother me. I understood why. I even started to get kind of warm and comfortable in his silences. They suited me.

It took some time, but by summer, Coleman found a job as a porter for the Long Island Railroad. He hated the uniform, dark blue and shabby. It was a letdown after he'd been so used to the richness of his army uniform. But his army uniform had been packed away in a box that sat at the bottom of my wardrobe. He never even asked to see it.

As terrible as it sounds, I was relieved. Negro soldiers were being killed regularly. The uniform, rather than protecting a veteran man, seemed to make him a target in many places. So many lynchings of these uniformed men. Sharp-creased trousers cut away at the crotch, for souvenirs. Burning the khaki to black until it flaked like paper from stiff and contorted bodies. Those beautiful boys rocking away in the pines, hands bound in front of them with their own Sam Browne, army-issue belts.

I was glad when Coleman put down his uniform and became another inconspicuous brown face. Right or wrong didn't matter to me when it came to him and it was something that he never talked about anymore. All I needed was for him to live and keep trying.

And he did. He began to adjust, although I know the effort cost him. I could see it when he came to pick me up from Columbia in his work clothes and got thoroughly ignored by everyone, including the other Negro students. I could see it in the strain on his face when he came with me to parties. It cost him to stay pleasant with most of my friends.

"You don't like my friends, do you?" I asked one evening, as we strolled up 136th Street to Streeter's Chinese Restaurant. Jean Toomer was going away, down to Washington, D.C., and possibly farther south after that. So we were having a party at Streeter's to see him off.

Coleman walked quietly for maybe half a block. Then he said, "They sure do spend an awful lot of time gum-beating and bookooing. How do any of them ever get anything done with all that time they waste talking? Seems to me like they use a lot of big words to say nothin'."

He had a point.

Inside Streeter's, our people packed the yellow-painted booths, murmuring quietly as they poured over copies of *The New York Age*. The place smelled stale, like a mix of chow mein and eggs and cigarette smoke. But no one paid any attention to the food sitting in front of them. Everyone had their heads down, scanning the paper. Not quite the party I'd expected.

Jean saw Coleman and I walk in and pushed over to make room for us in his booth. He pressed down on his mustache and then rubbed his eyes before sliding a copy of the *Age* across the table in front of me.

Another riot. This one in Washington, DC. Where Jean was heading to the very next day. How many did this make so far this year? Even just this summer? Chicago, Omaha, Nebraska, Knoxville. There were so many others that I just didn't have the heart to recall. The papers vividly detailed the deaths, dozens of them, re-creating each hanging, the stench of the burnings, the rapes and the marauding (although the white papers often attributed the marauding to the Negroes and the former actions, a regrettable response to the menacing reality of The Black Presence). I couldn't take any more. I was full. I pushed the newspaper back toward Jean. Coleman hadn't so much as glanced at it.

"You know why they're doing this, don't you?" Jean asked no one in particular.

"Because," Alain said, "that is the precise nature of the psycho-social parasite that's feeding off this country's blood . . ."

"No! No, Goddammit, no!" Jean slammed his fist onto the table, shaking all the heavy trays and platters. "It's because the people are waking up. They're seeing the capitalist ruse for what it is. They're understanding that their lives and liberties have been stolen by the corporate monopolies. The fays aren't getting it factually yet, though. That's the problem. They're feeling the squeeze, the pressure, you know, that sick feeling that Negroes have been living with in this country for two or three hundred years. But they're not getting the truth of it. So they feel like the only thing they can do is blame the Negro. But the Negro isn't the one who's taking the food out of their mouths. It's these corporate raiders. The monopolies."

"So that's an excuse to string a man from a lamppost?" Countee muttered.

"That's nothing," said Gwendolyn. "Did you hear about the woman outside Waco? Nine months pregnant and they hung her from an elm tree. Then they cut the baby out of her stomach with a hunting knife and stomped it to death."

Gwen's chin began to quiver. Her eyes filled and she dropped her head into the crook of her arm, crying softly. None of us could do anything to comfort her. "Why?" she asked. "Why do they do these things?"

"Because they can," said Bud.

"They rape and murder defenseless women because they can?" Essie screamed.

"They can't very well rape the men before they murder them, can they?" Jean shot back.

"Of course they can."

Everyone looked at Coleman and then at me.

"I'm going to be sick." Gwendolyn coughed into her napkin and jumped up, stumbling toward the bathroom. Essie followed close at her side. Countee got sick too, shortly after Gwen, but he was a young man and so he blamed it on the noodles and made the waitress take his back.

I turned my attention to the red-painted lanterns strung in rows above the table. None of us wanted to look directly at the others. It was too hard. I thought back to the day after Coleman came home. I was elated, talking all through breakfast about the parade, the smell of the people and the frigid air, how strong the men seemed, so full of hope and promise. Mama smiled and encouraged me with questions. What did this one or that one look like? Did I see that man Jim Europe? What did they play? Papa stayed silent until he'd finished his fried eggs and sipped the last of his coffee. Then he folded his paper in half, stood, and dropped it down over the food on my plate. He pointed to the lead paragraph at the top of the editorial page in the *Saturday Evening Post*. Then he fit his bowler hat snugly over his ears, turned, and left. I looked at Mama and then down at the article, which described the parade shortly and went on to say, "Hereafter, 'nigger' will merely be another way of spelling the word American."

I never mentioned the parade again to my parents or anyone else. I didn't join in with any of the discussions when people talked about it for weeks afterward. I just didn't know what to say.

That seemed to be my problem in general those days.

The tables stayed silent after that until the food had gotten cold and clumped with grease and the waitress began to get impatient. Eventually Gwendolyn came limping back with Essie holding her loosely by the arm.

By the time Paul bounded through the door, we'd all given up on any idea of a good time.

"Hello there!" He strode in waving at us. The heat from the pavement clung to his body and wafted ahead of him through the cluttered space.

"What's got you all looking so down?" Paul leaned over and kissed my forehead before taking Coleman's hand in a crushing grip.

"Nothing new, Paul," I said.

"Maybe that's the problem." Jean sighed.

"Jean Toomer, Paul Robeson. Jean's the one who's leaving tomorrow. This is his party."

"What old cloaker's trying to call this funeral a party? Whoever he is, he need to be ashamed and oughta be shot. If this is a party,

I want to know what kind? A slumber party? 'Cause that looks like the only thing I could do around here—collar a nod. So what's a Negro got to do to liven things up?"

People started smiling then, chuckling here and there.

By the time Coleman and I left an hour later, Paul was in the center of the group leading them in a rousing chorus of "Oh, Danny Boy." Everything, absolutely everything about that man was a miracle.

Coleman and I walked slowly through the dark.

"What's wrong, May?" he asked. "You're awfully quiet tonight. Is it what those birds was talking about before? You still down about that?"

"In a way. I guess I just feel so helpless. I feel like the world is racing ahead without me. I want to do something that matters, you know? Something that affects other people's lives. But I don't ever feel like what I can do is worth anything. So I graduate in two years. What then? Harlem gets one more science teacher. It just doesn't seem right to me. It doesn't seem fair."

"First of all, May, don't down talk yourself. You are doing things. Real big things. I've never met anyone like you before. Things that seem impossible for other people, you just walk right through them like don't none of that stuff even exist for you. A Colored woman as a science teacher. I don't know about you, May, but I call that doing something."

I opened my mouth to tell him about Essie's suggestion. Even though I hadn't admitted it to anyone else, the idea had been shifting around in my brain since she said it.

A doctor.

"What is it, sweetie?"

I smiled and squeezed his hand. Coleman had such a beautiful soul.

"Nothing. Just . . . thank you for saying those things, Coleman.
I appreciate it."

He kissed my fingertips. "Well, since you don't seem convinced, let me ask you this. What would you like to do? If you
could do anything in the world, what would it be?"

Standing on the bottom stair of my stoop, Coleman held me as
I began to cry softly into his chest. He kissed my forehead over and
over, but he never asked me why I was crying.

"DR. B.?"

She took off her glasses and looked up toward the door.

"Yes, May? What can I do for you?"

"I have a question, ma'am. I was just wondering . . . well . . . do
you know of any other hospitals or programs where I could pick
up some shifts in their labs?"

"Do you mean full-time?"

"Yes, ma'am."

Dr. Broadhurst rested her chin on the bridge of her joined
hands.

"That's an awful lot of work, May. You're already overloaded
as it is."

"I know," I said. "But . . ."

Dr. B. waited. Someone came and rapped on her door, but she
made no move to answer. Her eyes never left my face. She looked
at me almost like my mother would, like she had all the time in the
world.

"Well, honestly, we need the money, Dr. B. I won't be able to
finish the program without it."

Mama just couldn't make it alone anymore. She'd exhausted
nearly every penny of her savings, working three, sometimes four

jobs during the week. Quite often I'd find her kneeling in the dark in our cramped sitting room, adding bluing to a tub of someone's laundry. I'd tell her to, please, at least turn on a light, but she wouldn't do it.

"Why? No need to wake you all."

Then, as the sun came up, she'd be out the door, on her way to a house on Fifth Avenue or the Grand Concourse or Crotona Park. After a full day's work, she'd change uniforms and go serve at dinner parties. The serving wasn't steady work, but she went whenever she got called for, sometimes two or three evenings a week. At night, when I got home from work, she somehow (I never had the heart to ask how she did it) had dinner waiting. And she'd be right back where she was before, in the sitting room, mending gowns and trousers, or stringing the beads back onto the willowy silk of a purse.

Even still, with all of that plus my money, it was never enough.

Mama's one close friend, Mrs. Tillson, lived in the apartment directly across the air shaft. I'd hear them whispering, chuckling to each other for a few moments each day, always on the way somewhere else. Mrs. Tillson had no people. Her son and husband had both been killed some years back. Her sister had moved from St. Louis back to the Deep South to a place, the old lady said, where they'd never see her living face again. So she enjoyed Mama's daily talk about Papa and me, got involved in us, and never failed to give loud, often funny and generally useless advice. Since Mama never took this advice, Mrs. Tillson knew to yell loud enough for us to catch it firsthand. Somebody was going to hear her out, regardless.

Every time tuition came due and we didn't have enough, Mama would tap on the metal door of the air shaft, then lift it and wait. The old woman didn't have to be asked anymore. She'd look at Mama's face, and tell her, "Be back directly, Lu." When she finally came shuffling back, she'd reach across the air shaft and press her only possession of any value, a pear-shaped diamond wedding ring, into the palm of Mama's hand.

"I'm obliged." And then Mama would throw her wrap around her shoulders and hustle down to Palmer's Pawn Shop on Eighth. She always came back with enough to pay the balance for the semester, whatever the balance happened to be that term. Sometimes more, sometimes less. Everyone who went into Palmer's knew to leave Mrs. Tillson's ring alone. It took some time, but Mama always came up with enough to get the old lady's ring out of hock. The one time some passing-through man tried to buy the ring for his woman, Palmer chased them both out of the store. When the man came back, loud-mouthing, Palmer chased him away again, this time with his iron-handled broomstick and two of his broad-backed cousins.

Everyone did their part to get me through school. From the women who signed their children up for piano lessons they didn't want or need to the men who lost good money to Papa at card games and dice. These men would always wink at me when I passed and ask, "Now did your Papa lay that fiver on you like I told him, Lil' Bit? Make sure he don't hold out now, you hear?"

They didn't know about the difficulties between me and Papa, or else I'm sure they'd have found another way.

"I've got the experience," I told Dr. B. "I've worked at Presbyterian and for you . . ."

"It's not that, May. I know you're qualified. I daresay you're one of the best students I ever had. But you've only got one more semester after this one. I'm not sure how you'd be able to work full-time and complete your requirements."

"I don't know yet either, but at least I'll still be in school to try."

Dr. B. couldn't argue with that. "They're looking for someone at Flower Hospital," she said. "I'll get a name and set up an appointment for you."

This is how I became a clinical pathological technician in bacteriology and serology under a woman named Dr. Haven Emerson. I'm not sure if Dr. Emerson took me on so quickly because of my references or because, as she said, I was the only other woman besides the cleaning ladies and nurses that she'd seen working at Flower for more than four years.

So for the last six months of college, I worked in the hospital from 8:00 AM to 5:30 PM and attended classes at night. Dr. Emerson was a fine physician to work for. Not warm or at all personally concerned like Dr. B., but rigorous and efficient. From her I learned to be painstakingly accurate, sensitive to the slightest disturbances in my tissues samples and serums. She, in turn, judged my work fairly and never once made reference to my color.

One evening, about two months after I started working there, Dr. Emerson called me into her office before I left.

"Sit down, May. I want to ask you something."

"Yes?"

"Would you be interested in going to medical school here? We have a wonderful program. It's a homeopathic school and as long as you agree to teach our clinical pathology students, I can guarantee you a full, four-year scholarship."

She shocked me speechless.

"Well?"

"Well . . . I . . . don't know what to say. May I have some time to think it over? Talk to my mother and Dr. Broadhurst?"

"Of course. Just let me know by the end of the semester."

When I told Mama what Dr. Emerson suggested, she took her hands out of the sink and flopped down on a chair at the table.

"A doctor, Ladybug? You want to do that?"

"Yes, Mama. I don't know why, but I think I can do this. I know I can."

"How many more years that mean?"

"Six."

"But then, after them six years, you'd be a regular doctor? Same as Broadhurst and the rest?"

"Yes, ma'am."

Her eyes wandered across the yellow kitchen, skimming the hills of pots and plates piled high on the cupboard, past the covered-over bathtub with its rusted claws, out the window. We couldn't see the river from there, but at this time of night, when the streets were still and empty, we could smell it.

"You do whatever it takes, May," she said softly. "I'm right here. I'm backing you up. You do whatever it takes, you understand?"

"Yes, ma'am."

So I talked to Dr. Broadhurst the very next morning on the telephone from Bernice's before work.

"Well, if that's what you're interested in, I think you ought to fill out applications for some allopathic schools, not homeopathic. Natural cures are out. Everything's about drugs, hormones and metals now. It's a bit late now. You're pushing it. But if you're serious, I'll get on it right away. Is this really what you want, May?"

You could be a doctor, May. Like me.

I'd laughed when Essie said that. But as I stood with the telephone receiver cradled against my cheek, sweating, shaking, I wondered if I hadn't been headed to this place from that very instant.

"Yes, Dr. B.," I said. "I want this more than anything."

IN APRIL, I GOT a letter of interest from New York University. But if I wanted to go to Bellevue, the NYU medical school, I'd have to interview first. A man named Childress conducted my interview. The acceptance that I needed hinged on his say-so.

I wore my good blue dress that day, with Essie's white calfskin gloves and cloche hat. Mama pinned my hair back at the nape of my neck just the way Dr. Broadhurst wore hers.

"Chinn!" he yelled through the door.

I got up, cracked the door open, and peeked my head inside.

"You called me, sir?"

"Come in. Sit."

I did as I was told. This squat, bald, red-cheeked old man proceeded to rifle through my paperwork for another ten minutes without even looking at me again.

"Says here that you changed majors from music."

"Yes, sir."

"Why?"

"Oh, well, I just thought that . . . I'd be better able to serve my . . . comm . . . city . . . in another field. I still play piano though."

"Where?" Dr. Childress asked, uninterested. He kept his head buried in my files.

"When I have time, I usually play with Paul Robeson—"

"Paul Robeson!" His head shot up. "Are you serious? You know Paul Robeson? Personally? My God, why didn't you say so! That man is a genius. An absolute genius. The biggest credit to your race since Frederick Douglass. My God!"

For the next forty-five minutes, Dr. Childress raved about the genius, the daring, the artistry of one Paul Robeson. How he was an old Rutgers man himself, had even played football for a time. But nothing like that Robeson. Athlete, orator, scholar, singer, actor and now lawyer. My God! Was there anything that Robeson boy couldn't do? Paul Robeson's voice was the music of the spheres. A national treasure.

I glanced above his head at the clock and almost cried. My

time was up, and this man hadn't said a single word about me or my application.

"Well, I must say, Miss Chinn, I've enjoyed this interview." He stood up, smiling, and came around the desk. With one hand out to shake my hand and the other already on my shoulder, he started to usher me out. "Been a pleasure meeting you."

"*But sir . . .*"

"What is it, young lady?"

"I just . . . well . . . well what about my application, sir?"

He looked startled for a moment. "Oh, yes! There was a point to this meeting, now wasn't there? Well, I'll tell you this, Miss Chinn. What we look for at Bellevue, above all, is character. You obviously have the right kind of character. I can tell that by the company you keep. So I'm going to recommend that your application be approved. Now don't be mistaken, young lady. This is no small task. You'll be the first Negro woman ever to attempt to complete this program. But if you're up to try, there'll be a space for you."

Chapter 14

On the way home, I thought of all the ways to tell Mama and Papa. I thought about what Coleman would say. Whether he'd be supportive and what I'd do if he wasn't. Could I give him up? I didn't think so. His presence made me understand in my gut what Papa'd been talking about all these years. I didn't necessarily agree yet, but something new in me understood.

When I walked through the door, I found Mama pacing, one hand on her head and the other knotted up in a fist pressed against her stomach.

"Well?" she asked. "What happened?"

"I'm in. New York University accepted me. I start training at Bellevue in the fall! What do you think of that?"

"Say that again, May."

"They want me, Mama. NYU Medical School. They said yes."

"Even though you Colored?"

"It doesn't matter."

"They still said yes?"

"Yes!"

"My baby's gonna be a medical doctor?"

"Yes, Mama, yes!"

Her shoulders started to shake, and I thought she was crying. But then she lifted her head and I saw her wide-open mouth with all her teeth showing, way down to the back. We spun around in circles, laughing, singing, leaping up and down like girls until we fell exhausted onto the sofa. Then we laughed some more. Mama gathered me up in her arms and sang to me with her laughter. Sweet and high, like notes on Papa's violin.

Speaking of my father, we decided not to tell him right away. It felt so nice, saving this good feeling for just the two of us, and there was no telling what that man might do to spoil it. It seemed a much better deal to tell Coleman first and then figure the rest out from there.

That Saturday night, Coleman convinced me to go with him to Happy Rhone's. Happy's was a plush "millionaire's club" up by Lenox and 143rd. The kind of place my father made me swear on my life that I'd never step foot in. Happy's motif was one of integration and gracious coexistence, all black and white. We sat on overstuffed black sofas, two glasses of contraband gin in front of us on the tiny square table draped in white linen. A brown-skinned waiter in a two-button white dinner jacket with a satin collar and a white bow tie appeared in front of us, offering to refresh our glasses. Before I could decline, Coleman nodded and slapped down two crisp dollar bills. The waiter beamed and filled the glasses to the absolute rim, too high for me to raise mine without sloshing gin all over my fingers.

"You having a good time, Lil' Bit?" Coleman asked.

Just then, the piano up at the front of the room began to rumble. Out of habit, my ears strained to identify the chords, but there was something about this rhythm that was too lush and unpredictable for me to grasp it immediately.

Coleman pointed to the musician, a large, sandy-colored young man with surprised eyebrows and an impish smile.

"Do you know who that is?"

"No. Who is he?"

"That's Fats Waller. Just wait. You're gonna love this, baby. This bird is something else."

Fats burst out into a rich, deep, shouting melody that instantly swept the house up into its rhythm.

> *Say up in Harlem at a table for two*
> *There were four of us,*
> *Me, your big feet and you*
> *From your ankles up, I'd say you sure look sweet*
> *From there down there's just too much feet*
> *Yes, your feet's too big*
> *Don't want cha, 'cause ya feet's too big*
> *Mad at ya, 'cause ya feet's too big*
> *I hate ya, 'cause ya feet's too big*
> *My goodness!*

And when he shouted *My goodness!* the man seemed genuinely shocked, even menaced, by the magnitude of this poor soul's extremities. The audience screamed its approval.

"Sing it!" they shouted.

"Play it again, you dirty no-gooder!"

"That's right, man! Tell her 'bout herself!"

Women jumped up, and grabbed their guys by the arm, rushing to the checkered tile dance floor. As the floor quickly filled, Fats mugged at the dancers, rolling his eyes, making up juicier lyrics right there on the spot, eager to please.

Oh your pedal extremities are colossal, he told this imaginary beast of a woman. The crowd howled.

> *To me you look just like a fossil*
> *Oh I've never heard of such walkin', mercy*
> *Your pedal extremities really are obnoxious—*

The piano roared to a crescendo and then snapped off as he held his hands suspended in the air above the keys. Mugging the moment for all it was worth, he grinned and told the audience in a rumbling, sarcastic baritone:

One never knows, do one?

We danced until the club closed. I'd never danced like that before in my life. Swept up in the rhythm, Coleman spun me in circles. He grabbed me by my waist and hoisted me in the air and I wasn't once afraid of falling. Other women flew even higher, up over their partners' heads, showing long stretches of silk stocking or, sometimes, scandalously, a glimpse of bare behind. On and on, until the music faded and the waiters began to heave the chairs on top of the pretty, linen-covered tables.

We stumbled outside, laughing, making up silly new dance steps. The breeze fanning in from the river cooled and dried the sweat from my face. Coleman steered me that way, east, toward the oil black Harlem.

"Come on," he said. "I want to see the moon in the water tonight."

I should have gone straight home, but I let him take me the other way. I would've gone just about anywhere with him in that moment.

"So did you have a good time, baby?"

"Yes. I think that might have been the most fun I've ever had in my life."

As we reached the water's edge, I reached up and kissed him. "Thank you."

"I know a better way you can thank me." Coleman reached into the inside pocket of his jacket, pulled out a small velvet box. Inside was a thin gold band.

"Marry me, May. I love you and I want you to be my wife. Will you say yes?"

His eyes filled with tears, and he didn't bother to brush them away. He stood there, naked, staring into my face. I knew he was showing me something very important. And I accepted it. I trusted him because he'd trusted me.

"Yes," I said. "I'd love to marry you."

Coleman closed his eyes and pressed my head into his chest.

"Baby," he murmured. "My sweet girl."

And he kissed me again.

WHEN I BROUGHT Coleman home to tell my parents, I thought for a moment that Mama might cry. But she didn't. Papa cried. And then he spoke to me for the first time in nearly four years.

He said, "Congratulations, Ladybug. This man right here seems like a fine, hardworking young man. I hope you'll be happy. I give you my blessing."

See, Papa, I wanted to tell him. *See, I didn't have to choose.*

But I was enjoying his voice and his arms wrapped around me way too much to ruin it with petty reminders.

I rushed to school the next day to tell Essie.

Essie gave a typical response. I found her at her microscope, reading the batting statistics for the National League team in New York.

"Since when do you care so much about baseball?" I asked, hopping up onto the desk beside her.

"I wouldn't give a good goddamn if every baseball team on the planet fell into a black hole and died," she said.

"So?"

"Paul loves baseball. He hasn't been coming around so much lately—"

"And so you thought maybe you'd impress him and invite him out to a game."

"Gee, May, you're smarter than you oftentimes look."

"So who's winning?"

Essie gave me a withering look, lip curled up and everything. Then she shrugged and said, "I'm pretty sure New York is going up against New York for the World Series this year. I think the NL will take it, don't you?"

Paul and Essie had been going steady for nearly two years. They'd only met briefly at Jean's going-away party. But shortly afterward, a football injury put Paul in the hospital for months with a hole in his leg the size of a baseball. Of course, when word got out, Essie just happened to find herself on duty in the same ward.

Eslanda had a tongue like a cook's knife and was given to all sorts of affectations. But if there's one thing that was true of her, she loved her man. She'd found her husband, whether he knew it or not.

"Es, guess what?"

"Just tell me, Lil' Bit. I'm not in the mood."

"Coleman asked me to marry him!"

Essie stared at me for a long while before turning to her paper. "Congratulations," she said. "What about school?"

"I'm still going. Coleman wouldn't do anything to stop me."

"Hmph. You don't sound too sure about that."

I wasn't. I hoped, but I didn't really know. Men could be so funny. When we'd finally told Papa, he hadn't said anything at all. Mama came out of the kitchen, stood in front of him, and said,

"Your daughter got into New York University Medical School, William. She's going to be a doctor. *A doctor.* First Colored woman to graduate medical school in this city. What do you think of that?"

He never looked up from his paper. "What do her husband think of that?"

Mama wiped her eyes and straightened the wrinkled apron over her gray skirt.

"If the boy love her and want her to be happy, he'll be happy. He claim to be such a race man. He'll be happy."

Papa sucked his teeth and glanced over at me.

"Don't mess up a good thing over a pipe dream," he said. "Don't you be foolish."

That was the extent of the congratulations we got. What if Coleman responded the same way? I made myself believe that he'd never make me choose between the two of us—me or him. I trusted in the fact that he loved me because of who I was and what I wanted to do, not in spite of it. But how did I know?

I finally got to see him two days later. We'd made plans to meet in Central Park by the lake. I waited for him beside the tall, blond grass at the water's edge, watching the geese and ducklings glide through the pond. Someone's cream-colored cocker spaniel kept rushing the banks, making a game out of harassing the birds since he couldn't actually reach them. They fluttered their wings and arched their necks each time he pounced, but the movement seemed to be aimed more at teasing the poor little dog than trying to escape him.

"Lil' Bit! There you are!"

Coleman trotted up to me. He kissed me on the forehead and scooted up behind me, wrapping his arm across my shoulders. With his nose buried in my hair, he breathed me in.

"I feel like I haven't seen you in forever."

"It's only been three days." I laughed.

"Well, then, that was the longest three days ever lasted."

Coleman rocked me and stroked my hair.

"Baby, I have to tell you something."

"Me first, Lil' Bit. I've got good news. I finally heard back from my folks down in Carolina. I told them about us."

"Really? What'd they say?"

"My mama said it was the best news she's ever had. All my folks can't wait to meet you. I sent them a photo of you with the letter, and they showed it to everyone in town. The entire town is talking about you now. Can't nobody believe that you're with me. Mama wanted me to make sure you're Colored. She said she couldn't even tell from the picture. But she's beside herself cause her grandbabies are gonna be so pretty with such fine hair."

He laughed. "Seems like she forgot just how nappy my hair really is, like I ain't got nothing to do with it. Shoot. Hate to see her get disappointed. My folks want me to come home and visit for a few weeks before we get married. If that's all right with you."

"Why wouldn't it be?"

"Well, you know. Most women wouldn't want their man going off for two or three weeks without them."

"You need to be with your family. You go on and have a good time."

He hugged me and kissed my left ear and then the right one.

"I knew you'd understand. Later on this year, after the wedding, we'll get some more money up and we'll go down to meet my folks together. Would you like that? My mama won't feel right until she sees you in person."

"I'd love that, Coleman. I'm really looking forward to it. Will you be back in time for graduation?"

"I'll make sure I am. You know I wouldn't miss that, Lil' Bit. You worked too hard. We got to celebrate the fact that you out of school and movin' on with your life. That's a big thing."

Then we started talking on the trip, his cousins Boo and Red-field, his mama's chicken and dumplings and her dirty rice and just how long he'd have to work when he got back in order to move us into the new place he found. With all that talk, Coleman forgot that I wanted to tell him something, too. Plans had to be made, tickets bought, clothes mended (would I mind?). So many things to consider.

I thought about reminding him but in his excitement, I lost my nerve. Later, when he got back, there'd be time. I'd make sure of it.

COLEMAN LEFT AND finals ended. Nothing for me to do until graduation. I spent most of my time in the lab daydreaming, and letting Dr. B. and Essie do mostly all of my work. Sometimes my dreams were good and bright. In those dreams, I had a kind, supportive husband, my son (through some unnamed miracle) had been returned to me, and I had a booming medical practice. My mother didn't have to work anymore, and my father loved me. Most of the time, I allowed myself the pleasure of living inside these good dreams in which I was always warm and well fed.

Sometimes I had other dreams, though. Dreams where Coleman cursed me and called me a fool or, worse yet, refused to even look at me at all. My father, in these dreams, disappeared. He left Mama and me alone, thinking up places he might have gone and reasons to call him back, but never being quite able to reach him. I never saw my son again either, in spite of Mama's promises to talk with the Robinsons. These dreams kept me awake some nights. I woke up to them most mornings. During the day, however, I managed to shake them off and actually see what it was that I wanted to see. Most of the time, I really did believe in my own happiness.

Essie told Paul about my medical school acceptance and he was overjoyed. He sent word through her that he was leaving me a ticket to his new show, *Shuffle Along*, to celebrate. After the show we'd all hang out just like old times.

I took the Seventh Avenue subway downtown to Forty-second Street and walked back up to the Cort Theatre on Forty-eighth Street. When I got to the Cort, lines of excited patrons were already queuing up outside the doors. Police had to cordon off the block and turn Forty-eighth Street into a one-way thoroughfare to accommodate the massive, anxious crowds. *Shuffle Along* was beyond merely being a hit. It had become a craze.

Inside the lavish theater, ushers in crisp red jackets with gold braids across the shoulders escorted us to our seats. A freckled white boy took my ticket and led me to a prime orchestra seat. "Enjoy the show, ma'am," he said before hustling back up the aisle.

I sat between a heavyset white man and a young white woman wearing a red turban and gold slave bangles on her wrists. I heard the young woman turn to her companion and say, "Tell me, Rachel, do you know what the show is about?"

Her friend sighed, and said, "Does it matter? This show is simply *de rigueur* for anyone wishing to be *au courant*. Yes?"

The girl nodded demurely and I turned my head so that they wouldn't see me laughing.

The lights went down and when they came back up, I found myself transported to another world. The singers belted out a string of infectious tunes that had the entire audience going wild. "Bandanna Days." "I'm Just Wild About Harry." "Gypsy Blues." On and on they went, barely seeming to come up for air before spinning off onto the next song and dance number. Paul, one of the Four Harmony Kings, came out in his straw hat, overalls and cane, and sang a number called "Old Black Joe" that literally stopped the show in the second act.

When the play ended, I kept dancing. All the way out the doors and up to the Oriental, I danced and I sang. The songs repeated themselves over and over in my brain while I played a mysterious piano that appeared out of the chair backs on the trolley and manifested sideways along the grooves in the lamppost trunks. All around me and inside me there was so much music.

It took me so long to get to the Oriental, that by the time I walked through the doors, everyone was already there. Paul spotted me and yelled, "Hey, everybody, she's here! She's here! Hey! Listen up, you roughnecks. Be quiet, now. For anyone here who doesn't know her—and at this point I don't know who that could be—but just in case anyone doesn't know her yet, we're here tonight to celebrate—"

"Anything!" cried the beautiful Adelaide Hall.

"Quiet, hussy! Don't interrupt me! As I was saying, we're here to celebrate one of my very best friends, Miss May Edward Chinn. She's just gotten accepted into medical school, at New York University, no less. May is currently on her way to being the first Negro woman to become a doctor in this city. Now what do you all think of that?"

The entire group applauded me then, genuinely supportive and impressed.

"Thank you so much, everyone. Paul, I couldn't have done it without you. Literally. Remind me to tell you the whole story later."

Paul smiled gamely. "Sure. I love to hear any story where I get to be the hero."

After the performers took turns hugging me, the topic of conversation quickly turned back to the show.

"Wow," said Paul. "Eubie and Noble sure gave those fays some ragtime-itis."

One of the chorus girls, a pretty brown named Josephine, leaned over Paul's shoulder with a crooked smile. "That's the truth. I sure never thought the fays would flock to it like this. Paul, remember how terrified they were over 'Love Will Find a Way'?"

And Paul told this story about the composers and how afraid they were of the audience's reaction to a love song about Negroes. They were so scared that while Eubie Blake played the piano in the orchestra opening night, his partners Noble Sissle, Flournoy Miller and Aubrey Lyles, secretly put their things together and were waiting by the stage door, ready to make their escape into the alley if the theater erupted into violence.

"God forbid Florence had to kiss anybody." Josephine laughed. "They'd have called out the National Guard!"

Countee and I stretched across each other laughing so hard I got a cramp in my side. Just then, someone tapped me on my shoulder.

"Bud! Good to see you!"

Bud hugged me close and kissed both of my cheeks.

"I wouldn't have missed this party for the world, Lil' Bit."

"Bud Fisher wouldn't miss *any* party for the world," said Paul.

"Ha-ha-ha, my friend. You're hilarious. But unfortunately I'm not dealing with you right now. I'm speaking to Miss Mayflower."

A pretty, lemon-colored boy with thick wavy hair cleared his throat from behind Bud.

"Oh! Excuse me," Bud said. "I'm being rude. May, I want you to meet someone. This is my friend Langston Hughes. Jessie Fauset introduced us to him a minute ago and, let me tell you, this boy is brilliant. Absolutely brilliant. Already been published in *Crisis*. What was the name of that poem again?"

" 'The Negro—"

"—Speaks of Rivers.' That was it. Unbelievable. And look at him. He's only about twelve years old—"

"Actually, I'm almost twen—"

"So anyway, Langston's starting at Columbia in the fall. I thought it'd be good for you two to meet. Maybe you can get him up to speed."

"It's wonderful to meet you, May. I've heard so much about you." Langston's eyes lit up as he grinned at me. He was so warm and gentle. I loved him on the spot.

"It's a pleasure," I said. "Really. Please, sit down with us."

When Countee didn't scoot over, I glanced at him. There he sat, staring full on into Langston's face with his mouth hanging slightly open. Bud discreetly looked the other way, suddenly interested in saying hello to people way across the room. But I watched for a minute or two, until it became too uncomfortable.

"So," said Langston. "Uh . . . hmmm. So."

Countee snapped awake. Flaming with embarrassment, he scooted over. Now and then, his eyes darted toward Langston's face but never caught his gaze directly after that.

"Bye, May!" Josephine called from near the door. "Congratulations!"

"Bye-bye!" I yelled back. "Thank you!"

"Wasn't that one of the chorus girls?" Langston asked.

"Yes, that was Josephine Baker."

"Yeah! I noticed her. Pretty little brown." He leaned over and said in a low voice, "I'm surprised they let her in the chorus at all, what with all the light brights in there."

"She's wonderful though. Funny."

"Sure," Bud said. "But her nose is too big. And she's too skinny for my taste."

"Really!" Paul laughed. "I didn't know that any girl could be too anything for your taste!"

"Don't listen to him, May." Bud brushed Paul's voice off his sleeve like a fly. "He's just beating his gums again."

By the time I left, it was practically time for the sun to come up. If I couldn't sneak into the house before Papa woke up, I might as well not go home again at all.

Creeping through the door with my shoes off, I felt my way through the dark to my bedroom. Barely breathing, I slid the door open just enough to squeeze my body through. It creaked, and I held still, waiting to hear a noise come out of my parents' bedroom. When nothing happened, I gently shut the door behind me.

While undressing, I noticed an envelope lying on top of my covers. I couldn't read it in the dark and didn't dare turn on the light, so I left it by my bedside. I'd read it when I woke up. It had to be from Coleman. He was supposed to be coming home in another week or so. And it couldn't be too soon for me. There were too many things that could happen to a young Colored man down South. I wouldn't feel safe again until he was home, back where he belonged.

June 10, 1921

Dear May,

Hello. You don't know me, but I'm Coleman's mother, Mrs. Ida Fortlow. Coleman has told me so much about you that I feel like I know you already. He said what a beautiful, smart girl you are, and I believe that for my son to have loved you so much, all of those things must be true.

May, I sincerely regret to inform you that Coleman passed away last Saturday morning in a swimming accident. It was no one's fault. He got dragged into the river past where it was safe. As you can imagine, the family is broken-hearted. I only find the strength to write this letter to you because, as his wife-to-be, you are family too and should be told as soon as possible. The funeral is being held down here in the morning. By the time you receive this letter, it will be too late for you to attend. But if you would like to come visit with us and see the grave at any time, just say so. As I said, as far as we are all concerned, you were already family and we love you dearly. I will go for now, but will write again if anything else comes up. Please take good care of yourself and your family, especially your mother. Coleman told us all what a good woman she is. May the Lord Jesus bless you all your days. Please find it in your heart to pray for us here. I truly don't know what will happen to me with my only boy gone. But God will provide. He must. Believing that is all that I have left. I love you dearly, daughter.

*With love from
Coleman's mother,
Mrs. Ida Fortlow*

And just like that, it was over.

PART THREE

Chapter 15

I've known rivers:
I've known rivers ancient as the world and older than the
    flow of human blood through human veins.
My soul has grown deep like the rivers.

Love is the only thing in the world that matters. There's so much love, so much brightness here that sometimes the radiance of it hurts my heart. I try to relax and stretch into it, to make myself a big enough container to hold even a sliver of it, but I never quite know if I've made it or not. I need to love. But it can be so frightening to spread your nakedness at someone's feet, to let them watch you do it, never knowing if you'll see the truth and recognition of love in the eyes staring back at you. Not even when they're your own. You open your heart knowing that there is no such thing as possession of another soul, knowing that surrender, change, is the only working order of the world and that somewhere, somehow, deep inside, that knowingness must be good. You love until the blood of it congeals in the marrow of your bones and, even deeper still, *into the places of breath and being that have no physical home, but that quicken the form, these gated walls of effect, regardless. This is where I live.*

This is where I lost him.

Too much death. Too much sadness inside me, spiraling up, getting congested all in my lungs so I can't breathe. The suddenness of the pain like a burn on the flesh that sizzles and peels the skin with it when the brand is removed. That's how it is inside me. Neat flesh, intact skin that's smooth and clean and then suddenly it's just not that way anymore and there's nothing you can do to take it back. No return. "I love you" lies meaningless and empty in your throat, swallowed up by circumstance. How does one live with that? (Which itself is a question that implies that you will live with it. Forever.) What I really want to know is how to not have to live with it anymore. How to set it free. How to not hate myself for living when he couldn't. How to stop wishing that I could give myself over instead and counting up all the things that, between the two of us, gave him more to live for. I need to know how to love us both again.

LONG AND BROAD, I dreamt of Coleman for many nights after, as a tree with no branches, tall as a river, the width of twenty men touching fingertips in a circle. Cut by hands I could not see, I barely had time to tumble out of the way before the tree cracked and pitched forward, sliding endlessly down the steep slope of a mountainside. Waves of mud snatched me up, and I rode through the avalanche of upturned earth that crashed down the mountain in its wake.

But this dream was only one of the ways his face came to me. So many others began filtering in. Smelling, touching and tasting all of the stubborn parts of my mind. Opening up wide to memory. And it seemed like suddenly I remembered everything. His sweet, heavy-lidded eyes. The soft mouth beneath. Heavy hands, skin like the rutted earth in my dream, palms like the dust that covered the ground in the beginning, before the fall.

Coleman had a way of nodding encouragement to all those who passed, whether he knew them or not. But only when I finally understood I'd never see him again did I begin to locate the sweetness of appreciation. And that was something I had no way of living with. Why did these tools of love seem more real to me all of a sudden, simply because death had touched him in places and ways that I could never? I had no excuse.

For nearly a year I lived this way, with the days blending almost seamlessly one into the next. They meant very little to me one way or the other.

Friends paid their condolences and then quickly got back to the business of their lives, not wholly sure of what to do with a death like his. Coleman wasn't a victim of a lynching or rabid police or cancer or even a stabbing. Just an accident. Taken away from me by a rocky current. Snagged on a log, bobbing two feet, maybe less, from the surface while the air slowly drained from his lungs. What was there to rally around in a case like that?

Papa stopped speaking to me again after Coleman died, as if his death were somehow my fault. This time, though, I craved the silence. At times I felt like if he never said another word to me again, the only thing I'd have to tell him on his deathbed would be thank you. Mama got quiet too. For months. But her quiet was different. It wasn't full of regret and fear and shame and pity. I could live with her silence because it was spacious, gentle. Only occasionally did it get a little bit sad.

By the third month, I'd pared my way through the thickest skin of mourning. There weren't so many nights that I'd wake up to find Coleman standing at the foot of my bed, looking crisp in his army uniform, smiling. On those nights, he'd reach through the dark to touch me, clasping my hand hard, so that when I sat straight up in my bed and lit my lamp, I could still feel the imprint of his fingers in the center of my palm. By the end of the third month, things like that didn't happen as often. I could see again, and I could smile.

Right around that time, Dr. Broadhurst started calling on us at home. Mama and I always greeted her politely, offering fragrant ginger tea and a light snack. We discussed polite news and light gossip until it was time for her to go. I thought she'd soon give up, but week after week, she kept coming back until eventually I agreed to go back to work at the pathology lab.

When I'd deferred school for a year, no one said a word to me about it. They called themselves respecting my grief. I appreciated it, even though it seemed like there was so much more to it than that. Still, each of them had their own way of letting me know that they thought I needed to start making some decisions. After so many months of solitude, I guess I thought so, too. So I went back to work. A few more months after that it struck me one day (sitting alone at work, scribbling notes over cold coffee) that I was very lonely. I tried to strike up some of my old friendships but people had been disappearing. Jean had taken to Buddhism, Carl Sandburg and the Deep South, where he began, as he put it, "striving for a fusion analogous to the fact of racial intermingling."

Fine.

Claude published a book of poems called *Harlem Shadows* to rave reviews and instantly became the darling of the liberal literary world. But then, disgusted with Harlem and its Negro elite, with the white people who encouraged them and, actually, the United States as a whole, he stormed off to Russia. Paul and Adelaide left too, both in the process of becoming sensations over in Europe. Essie stayed around, but as the new wife of Paul Robeson, she kept her plate brimming with all the engagements and responsibilities that she thought the wife of Paul Robeson should have. Successful and radiant, fame had scattered almost all of my friends to the four winds. Apparently, carrying the weight of the race had suddenly come into vogue.

"It's very hard, demanding work, you know," Langston said one lazy afternoon, doing his best Alain Locke impersonation. "Chasing down the meaning and import of negritude within the confines of Western society can't help but keep a jasper on his toes."

I laughed and said, "Well, I'm certainly glad you stayed around."

We stood at the rim of Turtle Pond in Central Park, gazing up at the jagged stone castle hanging over the bluff.

"I'll always be around for you, May. No matter what."

Strolling away from the pond, we headed east toward Fifth Avenue. The breeze smelled fresh and wet like snow. By now it was deep into February. Both of us had wrapped up tight in long wool coats and scarves, being rushed along by the rough, flickering Manhattan wind. Snow would have been so much better. It never felt as cold when the sky just went ahead and let loose with some snow.

"When are you going back to school?" he asked.

"Next September, I guess. What about you? Are things any better at Columbia?"

"Not really." Langston shrugged. "I don't think I'm going to last there much longer. Which doesn't particularly bother me. I was only in it for my old man. When I leave, it's going to bother him something wicked, though. I think it'll kill him if I actually become a writer."

"The only way to live your life is for you," I said.

Langston stopped in the middle of the path and held me loosely around my shoulders. As we stood there, it finally began to snow.

"Remember you said that."

My eyes burned, but I found that I couldn't cry any more. In my body I felt the shock of recognition when he kissed me softly, and said, "Even though you still don't have answers, you must at least have resolve. You know that."

The blocked-up tears started my nose running. When Langston heard me sniffling, he reached into his coat pocket and offered me his handkerchief. I wiped my nose and handed it back to him, but he said, "Keep it. I don't need to know you that well."

We held hands all the way out of the park, laughing, watching the tree branches get heavier with drifting snow. Ice everywhere. Underfoot, in the naked eaves of the trees, shivering on Langston's skinny mustache. We skidded across the cobblestones, pretending that our imaginations were ice skates and that the world really was this free-form thing with no edges, flowing in drifts, unwrapped and open in front of us in so many sparkling shades of white. I picked an icicle off the hanging edge of a holly bush, popped it in my mouth, and sucked it. It tasted so good.

BY FALL, I'D STARTED at Bellevue, and Langston had dropped out of Columbia. He went to work, first as a delivery boy and then as a picker on a vegetable farm on Staten Island. Countee thought it was romantic, said he had a good mind to leave school and do just what Langston had done—take control of his own life like a man should. Because they really were men now, weren't they? It sounded good, but we all knew that Countee would finish out this last year of high school and head off to NYU just like his father wanted him to. He was nothing if not an exemplary and loving son.

Bellevue wasn't what I'd feared or expected. No one hissed or spit at me or made obscene comments. No teachers tried to flunk me out of class. On the contrary, no one quite knew what to make of me. I became the invisible woman on campus. Everywhere I went I got ignored, unless my presence somehow became absolutely unavoidable.

For example, when a group of Negro migrant workers were brought into the TB ward, I got called to examine them because it was thought that I could better classify their "characteristics." One by one, I had to denote their skin color (ivory, tan, light brown, medium brown, dark, black) and their hair texture (straight, wavy, curly, frizzly, woolly) and then, on the back of the form, their symptoms.

In the operating theater, I always sat in the seventh tier, at the very top, surrounded by close to three hundred other students—almost all of them white men in dark brown or black suits and bow ties. In the entire class, all but nine of us (five white women, three black men and me) fit that bill. Those of us who didn't each had to contend with our differentness in our own ways. We made do however we could. I allowed myself to be the invisible woman and I never openly contradicted anything I was told.

When the doctors informed us that the reason Negroes living in the slums of New York had a higher rate of infection and death from TB was because they simply had a higher natural affinity for disease, I never raised my hand. I didn't look away when we examined Negro cadavers and the attending physician pointed out how, anatomically, the Negro musculature wasn't fit for sports or refined movement. Negro bodies had been built and conditioned for heavy labor and that was why they gravitated toward backbreaking menial work. And although Negroes were known to be immoral and predisposed to venereal disease at substantially higher rates than whites, they couldn't contract syphilis of the brain. Not enough blood flowed to the Negro brain to carry the disease.

"This," said our teacher, "is one of the ways that God, in His provident wisdom, has provided for the protection of this unfortunate race."

Of course, the downside of this "protection" was that the Negro brain was also not fitted for thinking on any type of high, abstract level either.

That began my tenure at Bellevue. For the next four years, I would attend classes from nine in the morning to four in the afternoon. Then from five o'clock to eleven at night, I worked in various labs across the city as a pathologist. In four years of living on that schedule, I never missed a day. I studied in the morning before class, at night until I fell asleep, sometimes sitting up at the kitchen table, and on the weekends.

Langston and Countee and sometimes even Paul tried to drag me out on the weekends. If I could keep my eyes open, I went. There was too much going on all over Harlem for me to not be a part of it.

The Savoy, the Nest, Small's, Connie's Inn—we made the rounds everywhere. One Saturday night a group of us headed east on Fifth to a place called Edmond's. Bud led me, Langston, Countee, Paul and some woman that none of us would talk to (who Paul claimed was just a family friend) across 130th Street. We headed down a short flight of brownstone stairs and squeezed into a narrow, peeling hallway that opened out into a dingy basement lair. Two-seater tables stood stacked along the wall, practically on top of each other. A dense cloud of blue-gray smoke wavered in the air like bay fog. Because Paul was with us, a group of men hopped up to give us their seats. Paul clapped each one of them on the back and ordered them a 50¢ bottle of gin, which they happily guzzled standing in the far corner. He ordered another bottle for us. Since I didn't drink, I asked for water and spent my time trying to hear snatches of conversation over the din and making thumb tracks in X's across the sticky tabletop.

"Thought I might find you monkey chasers here."

We all looked up to find a tall, stunning man in fitted leather pants and a brown bomber jacket standing with his hands on his hips in front of us. Paul stood up and grabbed the man in a tight vise. Whoever this fellow was, he was as tall as Paul and had shoulders just as broad. Not an easy feat.

"Everyone," Paul yelled. "I want you all to meet my man Fauntleroy Julian."

Paul went around the table with his introductions, but not one of us said a word. We sat there, like bug-a-boos, staring wide-eyed at the one and only Black Flying Eagle. Of the handful of Negro pilots in the country, the Eagle was known to be the most daring and infamous of them all. When Paul pointed at me, Fauntleroy swept my hand up in his, bent low at the waist, and kissed my palm. He left his lips there an extra second, letting his mustache tickle the pads of my fingers. Then, without lifting his head, he raised his eyes and winked. Curling lashes, copper skin and a peaked, childish nose. Dimples and a bow mouth almost like a woman's. That smile.

I snatched my hand back and looked toward the stage. He laughed but I pretended I didn't hear him. He was still laughing when a tall, haughty young woman with deep brown skin and a bored-looking set to her mouth sauntered out and stood there. This crowd, which hadn't once gotten quiet all night, immediately began to settle.

"Who's that?" I asked.

"Ethel Waters," Langston said. "Now that woman is righteous."

"Yes." Countee nodded. "Her voice is so different than all the others. They all seem to have this raspy, kind of growling tone. What would you call it?"

"Chronic laryngitis," Bud said. "They get it from playing in noisy, gut-bucket dives like this."

Ethel opened her mouth and song poured out until even Bud set his drink down and put his hand over his lips.

Mmm, did you ever love, when they didn't love you?
You know there wasn't satisfaction, didn't care what in the world you do . . .

She looked off into space, above our heads, like she couldn't be bothered. Like her real self was already off, somewhere miles and miles away. Ethel sang three more songs that way and then walked back off the tiny stage as disenchanted as when she entered. We sat there waiting an entire night to see if she'd come back, but she never did.

Outside, we all said our good-byes at the corner, wrapping up tight against the wind.

"Just a minute, young lady." Fauntleroy strode up beside me. "There's no way I'm letting you walk all the way home by yourself this late at night."

He smiled and held his arm out, then smiled even wider when I didn't take it. I can't lie. The man made me nervous. I found myself walking with my hand cupped around my jaw, covering my scars.

"So I hear you're a doctor."

"I'm in medical school, yes."

"I think that's incredible. Really. A magnificent accomplishment." He grinned at me. "I'd love to take you out sometime and have you tell me about it."

Coleman's face flashed in front of me. I hadn't been out with a man in nearly a year and a half. No one since the accident.

"I don't think so."

"Excuse me?"

"I said I don't think that would be a good idea."

Fauntleroy considered that for a minute with his two fingers pressed against his bottom lip.

"I see. And what do I have to do to get you to change your mind?"

"Oh, well, I don't think—"

"Say, do you like to fly?"

"Fly?"

"Sure. You know, like in airplanes."

"I've never been in an airplane."

"Perfect. Next Saturday you and I are going up."

"Now wait a minute—"

"Oh, come on, May. You know you'd love it. Gliding along in an open cockpit. So high above everything else in the world. Going faster than you've ever gone before in your life, or ever will again. Well, unless you get to know me in a whole different way. But we won't talk about that yet."

Something in my chest began to stir. The warm feeling of it flowed out and down my arms, all the way to my fingertips. Tingling and suddenly short of breath, I peeked at him from the corner of my eye. His beauty was full, like the moon. I could see plainly where it had gotten him in trouble. I could see why in each place that he went, women followed his every move, transfixed. What I didn't understand was why he wanted me to be one of them. Especially since I never could be.

But to fly. To be free like that, even for a minute, untouchable, unstoppable, weightless. To be able to look down and see the world not as a maze of streets and byways, but as a whole, the beginning, middle, and end laid out in front of you, the way God sees. That, I could do.

"If I went with you," I said, "it wouldn't be a date. If you'd be willing to take me up in your airplane as a friend, just one friend to another, I'd be willing to try that."

Fauntleroy put his arm around me.

"Whatever it takes, that's what I'll do."

So the next Saturday morning, I set aside my homework and waited downstairs on the stoop until Fauntleroy pulled up at the curb in a shining, brand-new black Nash. Out to Jersey we drove, windows open wide in spite of the cold, listening to him sing. Fauntleroy had no voice to speak of, but his joy at hearing himself was contagious. Soon we were both laughing and singing, red-nosed, heading across the bridge and southwest to Teterboro.

He sauntered into the airport like a celebrity and everyone, from the controllers to the mechanics to the other pilots, treated him accordingly. These white men actually tipped their caps and said, "Morning, Mr. Julian," as we passed. His pride became a growing, reaching thing, unfurling in great tendrils as he got to see himself again through my eyes. His head tilted up and his stride got a bit longer.

After fitting me in a thick leather cap and goggles, Fauntleroy took my hand and led me out onto the tarmac. But the closer we go to the airplane, the harder my heart began to pound. About twenty yards away, I stopped.

"Roy, I'm not sure if I want to do this anymore."

"There's nothing to be nervous about Lil' Bit. No need to scrunch your face up like that."

"No, I'm serious. Something doesn't feel right to me."

"I know you're scared, but flying is like anything else. You feel the fear and step out anyway."

I thought about that. Roy could see that he'd gained an edge, so he pressed it.

"Listen, it's time for you to try a new thing. You have to become what you've never been before in order to do what you've never done before."

That made sense to me. I walked the rest of the way to the plane without holding Roy's hand, a little in front of him in fact, and climbed in.

Roy strapped me in and then jumped up front. I closed my eyes and breathed deep until I heard the engine began to whir. When I looked up, the propellers were spinning full force, the blades moving so fast that they looked solid, like silver plates. We taxied down the runway, knocking about, rocking with every dip and lump in the road. I clutched the inside of the cockpit until my fingers turned red and then white.

step anyway

Bit by bit, we picked up speed. I watched the trees on the sidelines begin to blur, the grass, the gravel, the Tarmac turning soft and fluid as the plane gained momentum. Then I felt it. The nose pitched up and the wheels left the ground and my heart rose inside my throat. I could feel it pounding inside my temples and my fingertips and all the way down to my groin. I wanted to go home. I wanted to cry. But I also wanted to open my eyes and see.

It took seconds to clear the treetops. We rose gently, and the entire world below me looked gray and blue and brown and white with frost. No boundaries, no borders. No separation of the things I'd always assumed to be innately, inexorably distinct. I understood, all at once, like a picture in my mind, the power of created thought. Congealed thoughts erected walls where God had placed none. Dissolve the thought, dissolve the wall.

My heart began to pound again. My heart began to break, but for new reasons.

We lifted higher and higher, heading east. I saw roads snaking under me, brown and wilted marshland and then a hazy line of blue. We passed through a pillow of low-hanging clouds and, like a child eating snowflakes, I opened my mouth for a taste. Dipping lower, we made a left turn so sharp that it felt like the plane would flip. I screamed and Fauntleroy looked over his shoulder at me, grinning. I don't know if he could hear me scream or if he just assumed that I had, but either way, he seemed pleased with himself.

Directly beneath us lay the southern tip of Manhattan. I recognized what used to be the bloody fields, caves and alleys of Five Points. By now it'd been sanitized into a regular run-of-the-mill slum. Nothing remarkable. The heads taken off the spikes and the ghosts beaten into sullen exile. Farther up, on the ocean side of the island, we passed the Bowery and then the crumbling-down tenements of the Lower East Side. I thought for a minute that I recognized the building where I used to live as a baby, but we cut by too quick for me to be sure.

We climbed again, moving deeper into the white cap of sky. It got thinner, milkier, the higher we flew. The air tasted so crisp this high up. I felt the salt of it settle on my tongue, floating in from the sea. It froze every part of my body left uncovered, whipping my cheeks and chin until the lower half of my face got completely numb. But I barely noticed. There was too, too much to see.

In Harlem, the people knew Roy's red-striped airplane. At one point, I think he called back for me to "hold on" and then dived between the buildings on 138th Street. He went in at a tilt so low I could see into the fourth-floor windows. I screamed and laughed and craned my head over the side, watching the people below holler up as they waved their caps in the air in salute. So much freedom in this, like the curve and the speed of the plane was somehow mine. Like it was OK to love this freedom and to need it because I could have it now and nothing could stop me.

By the time we landed in Teterboro, I'd grown larger than my body, too big for words or even ideas. By the time Roy's airplane taxied to a halt, I'd settled comfortably into a place that didn't even have thoughts attached to it. A place of being where suddenly everything was possible.

Roy drove me home in silence. I knew then that he really did like me because he held his tongue and respected the opening that he helped to create. And I knew I liked him too because any man free enough to live in that letting-go place, to call forth a home there and invite somebody else into it, had to be touched by God. No matter how many times he looked at himself in the mirror every day.

I suppose that was why it shocked him when we pulled up in front of my place and he asked if he could see me again, and I said no.

I kissed his face and those fantastic lips because I didn't know any other way of releasing what I had in my heart. "Let me remember this for exactly what it is," I told him. And then I stepped out of the car and headed upstairs.

Roy let me go, but he didn't give up. I think he just loved the challenge of a woman saying no. It may have been something that he'd never heard before. Whatever the case, it made him happy.

The very next weekend, as I sat at the kitchen table over my books, I heard an airplane directly over us. Mama and I both ran to the kitchen window. Every head on the block was peeking out of the windows, watching this plane cut capers on top of us. The red-striped plane climbed at such a steep angle that it almost looked like it was standing straight up in the air. Out over the river, it leveled off and turned. Smaller than a child's toy, it circled back. Just in front of our building, from the back passenger seat, Roy leapt out into open space.

People screamed on the street as they saw his body do a somersault and then plunge straight down toward the earth. At the last possible moment, a parachute shot up and then ballooned around him. Roy wafted slowly down, arms stretched out wide.

Across the parachute, in bold red letters, it read:

May, will you please go out with me?—Roy.

In his bright red suit and helmet, the parachute melting all around him and across his shoulders like a magician's cape, he landed softly in the center of the Williams's goat farm. Then he bowed with a flourish in the direction of our kitchen window, cut the strings from his parachute and sauntered off, brushing the dust from his shoulders and knees.

People talked it for months. Everywhere I went women eyed me with envy, amusement or just plain awe. The men stared, not daring to speak.

I became a Harlem celebrity, thank you very much.

Even so, the next time Roy came to call, I still had to tell him no. Hearing the word *no* again (and again) confused him. He didn't understand that he'd already given me what I wanted. And because of that, Roy had more of me than he really desired or ever expected to receive. Being with him, standing by while he loved all his women and his women loved him, could only diminish his gift to me. I wouldn't let that happen. So Roy went the way of all the others and eventually forgave me enough to be my friend.

Chapter 16

"I'm off, kiddo."

"I still can't believe you're going. You're so brave."

"No. Just dumb. And stubborn. And kind of tired too, I guess."

That June, Langston signed up as a seaman and set sail on the *West Hesseltine,* a trading steamship headed across the Atlantic to the west coast of Africa.

We celebrated his leaving by finding Duke at the Savoy, all set up in his white suit, gleaming hair and razor-sharp mustache. Duke snatched up a little rag called "Rainy Nights" and rode it to its edge, filling in the lonely spaces between the notes with a striding Charleston beat. It was all but obvious that the leader of his five-man band, an older guy named Elmer Snowden, could barely keep up with this pianist of his. Every eye stayed fastened on Duke Ellington.

I ordered a drink that night, a watered down gin, because I didn't think I had the heart to be sober if Countee started to cry.

He slumped over, his stomach poking out like a heavy beach ball beneath his suit coat, nursing a fountain soda. Langston smiled extra bright and tugged my ear.

"Girl, you sure are dogging it tonight!"

"Liar. This dress is older than dust on a mountaintop. But thanks anyway."

Countee had on the new suit, not I. But I would've been an awful heel to mention it. Instead, I asked him, "Will you write to us?"

"Every chance I get. But only if you promise to put your books away long enough to answer."

I promised I would, and when Duke finished his set, Langston drained the last of his drink, stood, and kissed my cheek. Then he turned to Countee with a shy smile, dragging him up by the arm to be hugged.

"Well." He sighed.

And that was it. We walked outside into the night air, as hot as daytime and balmy like that too. Langston walked one way without looking back at us, Countee and I the other.

So much love poured out of that dark-eyed boy, through his slumped shoulders and his empty hands. I hated to see unhappy lovers. It put me in the mind of Coleman and Peter and my mother when she was young. Happiness in love is often short-lived, but unhappy love, especially in a dark-eyed boy, somehow seems so endless.

"He'll be back in no time," I offered.

"I don't think it matters," Countee mumbled. And then he did cry.

April 15, 1924

Dear Langston,

Well, another school year is almost over. Just two more to go. I pray every day for the strength to make it through. It's hard, sometimes, to look up and find that another year has passed. I miss you. I miss the colors in your life. Color helps me to get through. When will you be home?

Love you always,
May

May 20, 1924

Dear May,

I'll be back before you know it. Not quite sure when. I jumped ship a minute ago and here I am now in gay Par-ee! (Just so you know, you can reach me at Le Grand Duc in Montmartre. I work in the kitchen there. Full address on the outside of the envelope. Whatever you do, don't, I repeat and underline, don't write the ship again.) Lost my passport in Genoa recently. Talk about getting stranded in diddy-wah-diddy! That was a tight spot. But actually, I got a swell poem out of it. Josephine says hi, by the way, and love to Paul. How is Countee? He hasn't written to me lately. Is he sore? I miss you too, Lil' Bit. Stay strong. You'll get to the mountaintop. I promise. There's no way you can't. But you have to believe it. You understand? I love you. Write more shortly.

Sincerely, this hunky-hunky you call . . .
Langston

November 12, 1924

Dear Langston,

My God! That last poem you sent me left me in chills. You have words spilling out of you like daybreak. Your poems make me want to play music again. How do you do it? How can you understand so much about life and love and purpose and human beings in such a short time? There's so much I could learn from you. Sometimes I just feel like I'm floundering. Seeking, but getting further and further away from the goal. Things are going exceedingly well at Bellevue, at least as far as grades go. But I still feel like a ghost there. The others make jokes about Aubrey Maynard (the only other Negro left).

They call him the Gold Dust Twin. But at least they see him. Ack! I'm sick of complaining. It won't happen again. Promise! More later. My love to you always . . .

May

A gauzy, blue and red striped airmail envelope arrived shortly after Christmas. On the outside, across the bottom, it said *on my way . . . see you soon . . .* On the inside I found the torn end of a brown paper bag folded in a square. No greeting attached. Just truth.

We as individuals, we as a people, must learn how to see ourselves. To see and accept as God sees and accepts. To nurture the genius and the far truths. To understand, to forgive. To become fully and truly who we are (fully aware and truly grateful). We must. Because the world can't live without us.

JLH

PS—Stop seeking! Know that what you're looking for, you're looking with.

Our scores came back from our exams. I came in third out of a class of 303. So much for the limited cranial capacity of the Negro. Mama was so proud she bought me a big silver locket with my initials engraved on the front. I carried that slip of brown paper pressed flat inside the locket, against my chest. Every so often I touched spirals engraved on the silver beneath my clothes. I decided to let the world open up around me. I began to let it be OK.

Mama and I went out that weekend and we celebrated.

*   *   *

SO MUCH GOLD ON a Saturday afternoon in April. Gold clouds, golden green buds on the trees. Fire on the river, as the steamships pushed away from their moorings.

Tan men and brown men tossed heavy ropes braided as tight as their muscles and climbed the white, peaked sails of the smaller boats. Ropes as thick as my thigh held the boats in place. When the current pulled them away from the pier, these ropes stretched and made explosive cracking noises, like breaking trees. Hawkers along the pier sold fish fresh from the Sound because the river no longer would yield what the people wanted to eat. I walked up the Hudson feeling fitful, like I hadn't slept or eaten in days. Anxious. Walking the hard way from the water, through the park and down the tower stairs carved into the rock face of the cliff in Morningside. Up Eighth Avenue to 137th Street I walked, waiting for something to happen.

On the stoop of the boardinghouse at 267 West 137th Street, Langston sat reading the *Amsterdam News.*

"Hey, kiddo!"

"Hey yourself, young man."

He bounced down the stairs and rushed into my arms, kissing and kissing me.

"How was Europe?"

"Too many Nordics in too close a proximity. How's Harlem?"

"Too many Negroes trying to get in too close a proximity to the Nordics," a woman's voice answered.

We looked up at the young woman tilting in the open doorway. She had her hands folded across her chest. A crumpled black felt hat with a large purple feather shooting out of the back leaned across her face. It hid her eyes. The woman swaggered down the stairs in a tight gray skirt that rode her thighs with every step.

"Most Colored folk I know run as far and fast in the opposite direction as they can," Langston said. "What Negroes are you talking about?"

"The niggerati, of course."

Rather than take off her hat, the young woman twisted her head up at a taunting angle, to make her eyes partially visible.

"That's Zora's new name for us," Langston explained. "Any of us that fancy ourselves part of the Negro literati circle. May, this is Zora Hurston. Zora, May."

"Charmed," she said, and pumped my hand. "Welcome to Niggerati Manor. We all up in Thurman's room tryin' to figure out what kind of hijinks we can get up to tonight. Countee just rang and said he can't make it."

"Oh no! Now what?"

"Oh no, my foot! One monkey don't stop no show. So how 'bout it? If you two done bookooin' and swappin' spit, we can head on inside and get our digs together. What you think?"

But Zora was already halfway up the stairs.

"Does it matter?" I asked.

"Not particularly. It's good to realize these things right off the bat with her. That way don't nobody misunderstand or get their feelings hurt."

Inside the corner room on the second floor, our group lounged around in a lopsided circle. People hung off the edges of the bed and the apple crate/nightstand next to it and spilled over onto the splintering floor. A lamp, a small desk, and a plywood bureau were the only other pieces of furniture in the room. Every available corner, every surface with a flat top was stacked nearly to the ceiling with books.

"Move over, Thurman." Langston nudged a gangly brown fellow out of the way. "This is Wallace, May. He's our host. He's also the managing editor of *The Messenger.*"

"Oh! Wonderful. He's the one who bought your first stories.

Nice to meet you, Wallace. It must have felt so good to get your hands on a writer like Langston."

"Are you kidding?" Wallace muttered. "His work is terrible. Choppy and uninspired. Plain as day-old bread. The best thing I can say about it is that it was better than the other crap I got. That's the only reason I took it."

"Oh Lord," said Zora, "pass the bottle."

"If I'd had the choice though . . ."

Langston shrugged. "Don't worry, May. I don't take offense."

"Yeah," said Bud Fisher. "Wallace doesn't mean it. He's just too much of a genius for his own good. He hates anything that he hasn't written himself."

"That's not true," said Wallace. "I hate my writing too."

"He's a great writer," Langston insisted.

"Lies! Proust is great. Melville and Tolstoy are great. I am sometimes adequate."

Langston smiled amiably like Wallace hadn't spoken and stage-whispered in my ear, "Wallace really is an honest-to-God genius, though. He's read everything. He can read eleven lines at a time. He's gone through every single book in here, and tons more. Not only that, but he can discuss them all at length and find something horribly wrong with each of them. Even the stuff he loves."

"He's a strange bird," Aaron Douglas agreed, nudging the apple crate up onto its two back edges.

"Me"—Langston sighed—"I have no critical mind at all. Either I like a thing or I don't."

"Wait a minute. Go back. How am I strange?" Wallace wanted to know.

"Ha! He's kidding, right?"

"How long can the list be?"

"Can we all get in on this action?"

"First off, you're a walking hyperbole," offered Gwen Bennett.

"An intellectual superlative that got cooked in the oven a little too long," said Bruce Nugent.

"You drink too much and then threaten to throw yourself out of windows at people's parties," Gwen added. "Why do you think Jessie Fauset won't have you back?"

"Hmph," said Zora. "I guess we can add crybaby to the list too."

"There's not one of you that couldn't get up and go home right now," Wallace sulked.

Zora sucked her teeth and cut her eyes. "Then don't ask."

"Think about it," Langston said. "Nothing about you makes sense, really. You like to drink gin but don't like to drink gin."

"Who's callin' this pot liquor you got in here gin? There oughta be a law . . ."

"Zora—" Wallace warned.

"You like being a Negro," Langston continued, "but feel it's a handicap."

Wallace slapped his forehead and groaned. "Well isn't it?"

"You adore bohemianism but think its wrong to be a bo-hemian."

"They talk too much and don't know nearly enough to warrant the expended energy. They waste too much time."

"*You* love to waste time. But wasting time makes you feel guilty. (Stop me or I'll go on for days. No? OK.) Another thing—you loathe crowds but hate being alone."

"Then again," said Wallace, "I could learn. That being alone thing, I mean . . ."

"The funniest thing of all is that you almost always feel bad, but don't write poetry. My God!" cried Langston. "If I could feel as bad as you all the time, I'd come up with the greatest books of poetry ever written!"

"Not if the niggerati got to you first."

"*Zora!*" Wallace's face turned dark and juicy like a grape. "I have one single solitary nerve left and you're treading it."

"So!" Zora stood and threw her hands on her hips. "What you intend to do about it? Besides nothing."

She eyed the rest of the room and flexed her right arm. "Shoot! That boy know he don' want me to get up and straighten out this African soup bone. If I got to do that, somethin' bound to fall."

We all keeled over laughing. Even Wallace smirked. She had us.

"Ya'll heard me. I say, if a man don't fall when I hit him, I got to go 'round and see what's propping him up! You Russians know what I'm talkin' bout."

"Russian?" I asked. "What's a Russian?"

She rolled her eyes. "A Russian. You know. Them trashy rascals from way down in 'Bam that be 'rushin' to get up north."

Langston wiped his eyes and said, "Zora, you just about the only Russian in this room."

Zora's jaw dropped. "Now that's a slew-foot, resurrection lie if I ever heard one! Don't you never let me hear you repeat such scandalous nonsense again. I do and you gon' see some trouble like you ain't never seen before. I tell you, I'm already fittin' to sweep out hell and burn up the broom! And that's hot!"

By the time they'd emptied the bottle (and the next one), it was time for me to go home. The others never went anywhere that night. They slept, for the most part, on Wallace's creaky floor.

I walked the two blocks in the pearl-blue darkness, still laughing. Climbed the stairs and laughed a little less on each landing, trying to get myself together in case Papa was home.

At the door, I cleared my throat and straightened my face. But before I could turn the handle, the door swung open and Mama pushed me back out into the hallway.

"We got company, baby. I wanted to tell you before you came inside."

My mother was vibrating. I don't know how else to explain it. Her skin, her eyes had a light that hadn't been there before. A subtleness, a density. It frightened me.

"Who is it?"

She held my face tight between her two hands.

"Mr. Robinson and the boy. They came to see you."

I fell. My legs just gave out. I nearly hit my head on the floor next to Mama's feet. She hoisted me up and over to the stairwell. Clinging to each other, we sat with our backs to the door and the very thing that I'd prayed for every morning for more than six years.

I couldn't go in. I couldn't even move. I sat there, shaking and trying to take deep breaths so I wouldn't throw up. Mama eased my head onto her shoulder.

"You can do this," she whispered.

"What are they doing here?"

"I've been trying to get Mr. Robinson to stick to his word ever since they took the child. He was willing, but the wife . . . It just took this long. May? Don't you want to see him? He's beautiful."

"Oh God. Why now?"

"The truth? Because of Paul."

"*What?* What does Paul have to do with it?"

"I stop by the Robinsons' shop every so often. Just to make sure they don't forget. Well, Tuesday I was on my way in there when Paul comes running up to me outside they door, hugging me and carrying on. Mrs. Robinson like to break her neck getting outside to meet him. Then she finds out he's a friend of yours and that you know DuBois and the Johnsons and those types. Finishing medical school, too. Suddenly you got a lot more appealing to her. Worth something. Offered to have her husband bring the child by first chance. Said she was gonna tell him he was coming to visit his godmother May. So that's who you have to be now, you understand? Can you do that?"

"Yes."

"Can you do it?"

"Yes."

"You sure?"

"Yes."

I stood. Mama had to hold my arm, but I stood and we walked inside.

I think I closed my eyes. Because one second I was alone and the next he filled up the entire space. There was nowhere, not even in my imagination, that he didn't occupy with his with his wide, green eyes.

My son had green eyes. Green eyes and honey-colored skin. His hair swept back in curling waves off his forehead, which was moist and glowing. My child was hot. Why hadn't anyone else noticed that?

"Mama, open a window please. It's stuffy."

He smiled and quickly hid his dimples behind his hands.

"What do you say?" asked Mr. Robinson.

Phillip scooted to the edge of the sofa and hopped down. He walked over to me and put his hand out.

"Pleased to meet you, ma'am."

Words. Words on my skin. Pictures filling my mind—as always without the right thoughts to complete them. Being so big, so full in the moment that I began to disappear. I knew I was supposed to say something. The man stood beside me, stone-faced. I could feel him worrying. Hoping he hadn't made a mistake. But it didn't matter. Nothing mattered to me but my son's smile. Nothing mattered to me but my child's smell, like cornstarch powder and soap. Placing the pale green, ocean-water color of his eyes into the loom at the base of my throat so I could speak of him in cross patterns in the days to come—that mattered to me.

"Hello," I finally said. "Hello."

"How are you today?" he asked, checking his father's eyes.

Mr. Robinson nodded and the child puffed up. He was doing well.

"I'm fine, thank you. And how are you this evening?"

Phillip blushed and pulled his chin way down into his chest. "I'm fine, ma'am," he whispered. Checked again for his father.

"My goodness. You have got to be the most beautiful little boy I've ever seen. I would very much like to be your friend, Phillip. Would you like that?"

Phillip giggled. For the first time in nearly three years, I thought of Gabriel and thanked God for how wide, how beautiful he was. He was so much more than he ever even knew himself to be. I had the proof of that standing in front of me.

"I'm already your friend." He laughed.

My knees gave out and I had to pretend that I was trying to kneel. I opened my arms.

"Phillip, would you mind giving your godmother a hug?"

He swung his arms in a wide arc first before grinning and jumping into my arms.

That was the first hug I'd ever had in my life.

GRADUATION TIME CAME. After four years of being silent and invisible, I got to stretch. The yearbook claimed only to have had five women in the class of 1926, but even that couldn't hurt me. I made it.

Itchy in black and finally free, Mama and I held hands in the subway all the way downtown. Itchy and hot and open to the possibility and the nature of dreams, that was how I walked in front of all those solemn white faces. Speakers came and went, and I paid no mind. The sun gleamed too brightly for me to notice much of anything outside of its light and the sky and the trees playing in a rich maze of sunshine.

Everyone on Lenox Avenue wanted to come to the graduation ceremony. No one came. (No one except Phillip and Mr. Robinson. They stood in the back and waved to me as I passed. That moment, by itself, made the four years worthwhile.)

The people didn't come because they didn't feel comfortable or welcome. They'd celebrate with me later, uptown at home. I missed my friends, but not even that could give me pause.

I was about to start my medical internship at Harlem Hospital. They'd never accepted any Negroes. This was the first class in which there would be three of us, myself and two young men. I'd come so far. And now I only had two more years to go. What would happen after that, I had no idea. But I didn't need to know. I needed only to step out one day at a time.

Chapter 17

I guess the right word for it is *loomed*. I'd never seen a building actually loom before. I'd read it, but it always seemed a bit silly to me. A little overdramatic. However, when I looked up at this place, the gleaming red bricks and the wide, closed windows seemed to grow taller. They got heavier. The building arched. It leaned. It *loomed* over me. For nearly nine years I lived two blocks away from it, had passed this place nearly every day. But it had never taken such a bold interest in me before. I'd walked on about my business, relatively unmolested by Harlem Hospital. However, now that I'd won an internship there, things were different. The relationship had changed.

After standing across the street for nearly a half hour, I decided that if I didn't give it the attention it was looking for, it couldn't menace me this way. It was just a building, for God's sake. A regular old place like Bellevue, like Teachers College. I couldn't let it take any meaning it wanted. If I did, I wouldn't make it for two years. So I stood there, between two parked Fords, and glared right back at the building until the windows became just windows again, not eyes, and not teeth. The bricks were still red, yes, but they didn't glow and stretch and hover. Just a building.

The only way a Negro woman had ever gotten inside Harlem Hospital was if she'd been shot, stabbed, beaten or poisoned. I think one or two may have been cleaners, but even those jobs were reserved for the Irish and German women who trekked over from Riverside and farther north up in the Bronx.

I was the first. The only.

Our class of nineteen had only two other Negroes. Aubrey Maynard had gotten in and another man by the name of Louis Wilson. Louis refused to speak to me. He avoided looking at me altogether if he could help it. After the first four months, when I won the right to ride in the ambulance like all the other doctors, I overheard him yelling at Aubrey in the interns' quarters.

"This is ridiculous. What kind of woman goes riding through the streets at all hours of the night? How's that going to make us look?"

"May's a good doctor," Aubrey said.

"I don't know anything about that. All I know is that she's an embarrassment. And did you hear? They're thinking about putting her in charge of the Negro unit of the Speedwell clinic in the spring."

"I heard."

"If they do that, I don't know that I'll be able to stay here."

"Now you're just bull-skating, Louis. You'd never leave. You're lucky to be here and you know it."

A locker door slammed. "I don't see any white man being tied to some woman's apron strings."

"The appointment might not go through anyway. Fields is trying to block it."

"What if he can't? Are we supposed to just sit here and take it? I don't know about you, but I'm with Dr. Fields. There has to be a way to get her out."

I moved from in front of the door. The men changed, ate and slept in this room when they came on duty. The hospital had no facilities for women. To accommodate me, they'd cleared out a storage closet next to the emergency room and put a cot and a small metal desk back there. All night long, I heard the ambulances come and go—bells and frightened voices at the back door. I headed back that way, toward my room, to get into my uniform. Ready to ride for the next forty-eight hours.

I thought about Louis as I changed. He was very dark. Darker than Maynard even. I wondered if that had anything to do with why he hated me. He'd enter a room and one of the white interns would call out, "Hey look, fellas! There's a fly in my milk." And everyone would laugh. It was nothing compared to what they did to me, but it could be enough to make a man sensitive.

Louis had such a cold, superior manner. It reminded me of these two men that I'd met the summer before at a dinner party. Carl Van Vechten, a very famous white literary critic, invited me and my friend Jessie Fauset over to his home. We walked in and found Carl, his wife and four other white guests seated on the floor on a sumptuous Persian carpet staring with rapt attention up into the faces of two African diplomats. These men were dressed in fine tuxedos and spoke rich, perfect English. They were both very, very black. Clearly, they loved the attention being paid to them by their adoring white hosts. Jessie and I introduced ourselves and sat in the best Victorian chairs directly opposite them, since they weren't already in use. When the evening came to an end, Mrs. Van Vechten asked the gentlemen to see us home in a cab. They readily agreed, even though they'd barely spoken to us all night. No sooner had we gotten in the cab then one of them looked directly into my face and said, "You know, we'd never marry anyone like you two. You're mongrels."

Neither of us even drew breath. That man, with his shining

black skin and wide lips and narrow eyes, literally knocked the wind out of my body. I felt like he'd slapped me. Jessie's mouth just hung. Well, you know, we hadn't asked for anything. We'd barely spoken. And yet we were mongrels. When I finally got my breath, I asked, "Well then who would you marry?"

The man smiled confidently and told me, "We'd marry the daughter of the most important delegate—Caucasian delegate— that we could. It doesn't matter if she has blond hair and blue eyes, but she must be Caucasian."

I banged on the partition behind us. "Stop the cab!"

The driver pulled over at Ninety-seventh Street and Central Park West. The street was dark as pitch and deserted but Jessie had already jumped from the cab and was holding the door for me. Before I stepped out, I turned to the men and said, "It's quite possible, then, that if we're mongrels your children will be mongrels too."

That shocked them. Obviously, they hadn't thought that far. I slammed the door and let them think on it a little more as Jessie and I grabbed hands in the dark and started walking the forty blocks home.

Every time I saw Louis's face, I saw those two Africans. He looked at me the same way, without ever really seeing me. He couldn't seem to forgive the mistake of my presence, even though if it wasn't for me, he wouldn't be interning at Harlem Hospital in the first place.

New York City hospitals refused Negro interns until I petitioned the state during my last year at Bellevue and threatened to sue for entry based on unlawful exclusionary practices. Mama and I hadn't a dime for a lawyer or the slightest idea of how to start, but that's what we said. Apparently they'd been under considerable pressure for some time. Our petition happened to be the chink that burst the dam. Harlem Hospital agreed to open its doors to Colored interns that year. I still read the acceptance letter every night before going to sleep.

```
Dr. May Edward Chinn
145 West 138th Street,
New York

Dear Sir:
     I beg to inform you that the Trustees at their
meeting on May 18, 1926, on the recommendation of
the Medical Board of Harlem Hospital appointed you
Interne, Harlem Hospital for two years from July 1,
1926, Medical Service.

                              Very truly yours,
                                 Martin E. Dyer
                     Secretary, Board of Trustees
```

That was it. The extent of recognition. But it was enough. Our doctors still couldn't practice in any of the city hospitals but at least now there was one that we could be trained in.

Still, that didn't seem to impress Louis enough to get him to be nice to me. I expected it from the whites, but when that kind of rank animosity came from him, it made me weary all the way to my heart. Unfortunately, it was something that, over the years, I learned to get used to.

By the end of my shift, I'd delivered two babies (one in an alleyway), stitched up six superficial knife wounds, amputated a forearm and transported three bodies to the city morgue.

I was tired.

The cold hugged against me, rubbing around under my skirt and grazing my legs like a cat. Even that could barely keep me awake. Five thirty in the morning. Time to tuck the moon behind the river and let it rest. How come everyone else got to rest but me?

I climbed the stairs to our apartment slowly, putting my bag down and resting on every landing. Halfway up the stairs on the fourth floor, I stepped into a dull shaft of light filtering down on me from the open door of our apartment. It didn't make sense. Voices floated down on me too. A man's heavy voice and then Papa's voice going, "Uh-huh. Uh-huh. I see." Maybe that's what did it. The voices coming from my home.

My eyes snapped open. I ran up the last few stairs and threw open the door. Papa stood in the kitchen doorway with his hand over his mouth, stroking his mustache. He glanced at me and held my eyes.

All at once I was five years old and certain that I would disappear if my mother left the room and didn't come back for me.

Dr. Jackson knelt beside Mama, who lay on the sofa with her eyes closed and her white cotton blouse open to her navel. Her long, blue work skirt trailed over the side, draping the floor.

When did she get so old? I thought.

With closed eyes and still hands, Mama looked worn down to nothing. Like the color had been washed out of her skin. The stillness dulled the shine in her face to clay, gray and cracked with wrinkles. And when had her hair turned so gray, too? When she was awake and alive, it looked coated in silver.

I actually felt the blood draining from my face. My body got very cold, very numb and ready. I'd been trained. I knew what to do in these situations.

"What happened?"

"May, it's all right. Don't look that way. Your mother is just resting now."

The doctor stood up and walked toward me, motioning both Papa and me to the kitchen table.

"How many jobs does your mother work?" he asked.

"Two. Sometimes three," Papa said.

"Or four."

Dr. Jackson tugged at his beard and pushed his glasses up on his nose.

"She has to stop," he said. "May, your mother collapsed this morning. If your father hadn't found her so quickly, it could've been much worse."

Papa dropped his eyes. Saturday morning, and he didn't have to work. Why would he be up unless he hadn't been to sleep? He came in and found her, sprawled out in a pool of soapy water, a washtub full of linens pitched over on its side.

"What's wrong with her?" I asked.

"Her heart. It's weak. Too much stress on it. She's had a mild heart attack. She's been under a lot of strain lately, hasn't she?"

I nodded. Like my father, I couldn't meet his eyes.

Dr. Jackson cleared his throat. "It has to stop. Otherwise her condition will only get worse. There's not much more I can do. Get her to take it easy. I know both of you have tough schedules, but maybe there's a neighbor or a relative that can stop in and check on her, help her out with the housework, that kind of thing."

He stood up, reaching for his bag and his wool overcoat.

"I'll check back tomorrow to see how she's doing."

I gave him that week's grocery money and the next week's money too. He tipped his bowler hat and bowed before he left.

That Thursday, Mama was up and out to work by 6:30.

"Missed four days already and I'm late today. What more you want?"

I cried. I yelled. She kept getting ready. I trampled things, like Papa would do. That didn't work either. Desperate, terrified, I threatened to leave school. That got her attention. Mama turned around and fixed her eyes on me. The look she gave me made me take a step back.

"No you won't," she said. Then she turned her back and left.

Eventually, we compromised. Mama agreed to only work two jobs, and then only until I graduated. I agreed to find some other way to pay my expenses. I brought the arrangement up like I had ideas and plans in the works. But the only thing I really knew was that I loved her more than life and I was afraid.

I DOZED IN THE cab of the ambulance under the Seventh Avenue El. Even in my sleep, I argued with Mama, thinking up more ways to convince her. In the dream, she looked over at Coleman and shook her head. "You talk to her. I give up," she told him.

The rumble of an incoming train vibrated the seat and woke me up. As it passed over our heads, the ambulance shook with the weight and the speed of it. The last train of the night.

Without any warning, the train screeched to a grinding stop halfway inside the station, nearly a block and a half away. Even in the dark, I could see the rear end of the train poking out, beyond the covered station platform.

Something had happened farther down the block, around the station. This late at night, a crowd was forming. The stairway got busy; people rushed out of Cheney's Bar and Small's Paradise on the northwest corner. Everyone going up the stairs, no one coming down. That's what it looked like anyway. From so far away, in the dark, I couldn't tell. The only clear thing was the noise and the bodies milling around.

Robert and Andrew saw it now too. They both tensed and leaned forward. Andrew put his hand on the ignition key.

A young man came running toward us, his arms and legs pumping frantically. At the corner, he darted out into the street, around the driver's side of the ambulance, and banged on the window. He was talking before Andrew could get it rolled down.

"—just fell. He's under there."

"Whoa, whoa. Slow down, boy. What happened?"

"My friend slipped and fell in front of the train. There's police up there but no doctor. They went to get a doctor but he needs help now."

"Step back," I told the boy. Andrew pulled out and gunned it down to the station.

I jumped out and pushed my way through the crowd, with Robert and Andrew close behind. A grim-faced police officer stood at the top of the stairs, blocking onlookers.

"Officer O'Rourke," I yelled. "It's me. Let me through."

The officer squinted, but couldn't see good. He held up his baton and cracked the man in front of him in the ribs with the tip. "You! Move out my way! You're not made of glass. May? Is that you?"

"Yes, it's me."

"Come on, then." He waved me up.

Behind us, the bells of a fire truck shrieked as it barreled around the corner and stopped next to the ambulance under the El. People made way for the firemen. They didn't have to push.

At the edge of the platform, four police officers clustered together, speaking low and gesturing toward the tracks. Four more firemen bounded past me and went straight up to the officers. I recognized the four officers and two of the firemen. All eight of them ignored me.

"Officer Scallon," I called. "What happened here?"

One by one, they looked over at me and then looked away.

"I say, what happened?"

"Aw, May, what're you doing here? This is no place for you."

"Apparently that's not true because I'm here. Now what's going on please?"

"We got a man pinned under the train," said Officer Finn. "Don't know how bad he's hurt yet. We're trying to figure on the best way to get him out."

"Well, we can't move the train," said a stout officer named Mike Molloy.

"That's quick, Molloy," said Scallon. "Now tell us what we can do."

"Do you know if he's just pinned or did the train actually hit him?" one of the firemen asked. "If he got hit, he could be dead already. Anybody heard anything?"

"Well," I said, "what we should do—"

"No, I haven't heard anything a'tall. Have you, Finn?"

"Nothing."

"Well I think—"

"Somebody's going to have to climb down there, you know."

They all nodded.

"All right," Scallon said. "Who's gonna go?"

"I am."

The men turned in my direction. Officer Scallon threw up his hands.

"Aw, blast it, May! You're not climbing under any train. Not on my beat. Do you know how far it is if you fall?"

"Doesn't matter. I won't fall."

"It's at least a two-story drop, May," Finn informed me.

"Two stories. You hear that? Not one. But two. How am I supposed to go back and tell my captain that I got Dr. May killed on the subway platform? You wanna make me look bad? Jesus Lord. If I didn't know better I'd say you did this on purpose just to make my life harder."

"I'm going, and I'll let you men know what to do when I reach him."

Between two cars, I lowered myself down onto one of the wooden railroad ties.

"I need light!" I yelled. "And kill the engine!"

After the engine sputtered out, I heard him in front of me, not more than five yards. The man was awake, whimpering and trying to call for help. I crawled toward him, using one hand to balance myself on the track and clutching my medical bag with the other.

The wheels were warm and grimy black. All the smoke and steam and grit trapped under the belly of the train made it near impossible to breathe. But he wasn't too far. Splinters and nails slanting up from the ties tugged at my skirt, ripping it, slicing my knees, piercing my palms.

Right in front of me, a leg stuck out from behind a wheel. On the other side, closest to the platform base, a young man waved an arm. I heard him say "here" and "please," but that's all he could get out.

"Don't worry, sweetheart. You're going to be fine, OK?"

A young Puerto Rican boy, probably about eighteen. The train wheel had partially severed his leg at the thigh.

"Light! I need some light down here!"

Someone lowered two lanterns into the space where they heard my voice coming from. I grabbed them and set them down next to us. The boy's eyes began to close.

"Come on, sweetheart. Don't do that. Stay with me. Talk to me. Tell me your name."

"Freddy," he said. His mouth was bloody too and he winced, so I didn't ask him anything else.

Feddy's thigh had been deeply slashed and I noted both venus and arterial bleeding. But, miraculously, the train came to a complete stop before it took his whole leg off. That meant that this boy was supposed to keep his leg. I just had to figure out how to make that happen. I took a scalpel from my bag and dug it into my skirt, ripping out a long section from the seam on the side (Mama would be able to patch that later). Carefully, I slid the material under his leg and tied it on top to hold the blood back. With clamps I quieted down the bleeding and, inch by inch, my own foot braced against the wheel, slid him from beneath it.

"I need two men down here right now!"

Scallon and one of the firemen came shinnying down between the cars in front of us, and together we eased Freddy into the crawl space at the platform base.

"Get the engineer to back this train up. Now!"

Once the train had reversed about twenty feet, the other officers jumped down and, on my count, lifted Freddy onto the platform, where Andrew and Robert waited with the litter. The three of us hustled him down the stairs and off to Harlem.

When I knew that Freddy was stabilized, and they wouldn't remove his leg, I left for home. I was too stiff to bend my knees properly, too tired to see straight. But there were very few times that I could remember being happier. Wait till Mama heard about this! That boy was alive because of me. And even though I had to fight them, those white men listened when I spoke. We worked together. I did something. How many people can ever say that? That night, I did something that made my life worth living. It helped me see myself differently. Like new.

And then I tripped.

PAPA CAME OUT OF surgery about ten that morning. They kept him in the hospital for observation because he didn't seem to be doing too well. Dr. Crump told me that they'd caught the appendix just as it ruptured and not after so they were pretty confident that if he wanted to live, he would.

Dr. Crump, one of the head surgeons at Harlem, had insisted on doing the surgery himself. Unlike Fields, Dr. Crump enjoyed my presence and took special care to look out for me. His family had been abolitionists during the war, and he considered himself a vocal, progressive-minded liberal. So he was very solicitous of the Negro in general, and of me in particular.

When someone wrapped a miscarried fetus into the blanket on my cot, Dr. Crump made sure Fields followed up to catch whoever was playing "practical jokes," as they called it. They never caught them, so no one got expelled, but I appreciated the effort. Another time, when all of my tools mysteriously disappeared from my medical bag, Dr. Crump replaced everything that I needed at his own expense. He was a sprightly older white man, short and wiry, with white hair and a freckled nose. His family was also god-awful rich. He worked at the hospital not because he needed the money but because he loved medicine. Dr. Crump loved others who loved medicine like he did. He looked at me for my skill, not my color. I do believe he saved my father's life that morning.

"Go home, May," he said, once the surgery was done. "You have to work later, don't you? Go get some rest while you can."

But I couldn't rest. At least not comfortably. Even after collapsing into bed exhausted, I paced the hospital floor in my dreams. It felt like I'd barely closed my eyes before I had to get up again. I took a scalding hot bath, did stretching exercises to soothe my sore muscles and thanked God that I only had a twelve-hour shift coming up.

"MAY! WAIT UP!"

Zora dodged between two trucks as she darted across the street. "Look at 'cha, you dirty no-gooder. Trying to get away from me. You know you heard me calling you."

"I'm sorry, Zora. I swear I didn't. My mind is just a million miles away."

"Where you going?"

I didn't know, and I didn't have the energy for simple answers.

"Where are you off to?" I asked.

"Downtown to lunch with some Negrotarians. I think Van

Vechten is going to put me in touch with funds to get me to Florida this spring. And not a minute too soon! It's cold as a witch's tit up here. New York in the winter just ain't got 'em."

She shivered for confirmation and wrapped her purple-striped muffler around her neck again.

"Speaking of money—you got any, May?"

"No. Sorry, dear. I'm flat broke today."

"Doggone it! I got to haul hiney and ain't got a nickel to scratch with. How am I supposed to get on the train?"

But before she could really get on a roll, something else grabbed her attention.

"Say, say, say, fella! Come here a minute."

Zora left me and rushed over to a tall, coal-black man in a pea-coat who'd been walking in the opposite direction.

"My word, you got a big noggin." She circled the man and whistled as she examined the dimensions of his head. "That's quite an impressive cranium, brother. You wouldn't mind if I took a second of your time and measured it, now would you?"

Zora pulled an instrument from her cache that I can only describe as a mixture of a crossbow and a scoundrel's snap brim hat. The man promptly took off his own hat and let his head get measured. She was in school, she explained, and her professor (Franz Boas the anthropologist—have you heard of him?) needed her to collect important information on her people. A little to the left, please, and chin down.

Only Zora could walk up to the average Harlemite and not only *not* get cursed out for suggesting a head measurement, but get a hat tip and a "thank you kindly, miss" to boot as she left.

When she finished with the man, we fell back into step headed up Lenox.

"Zora, can I ask you a question?"

"If you can't prove it, I didn't do it."

"Seriously. How are things going for you at Barnard?"

"Couldn't be better. Why?"

"Well . . . do you ever feel like you don't belong? Do the others ever give you trouble because you're Colored?"

Zora's eyes softened. "First of all, I belong everywhere I am. That's obvious. Otherwise, I wouldn't be there. I figure it this way—I didn't get into Barnard by accident. That being the case, I'm not gonna let anybody try to play me close. Especially not when the bottom line is that all they want to be is me anyway. They wish they had my nerve. They won't admit it. Not in so many words. But a cat is still a cat, whether it's got long hair or short. So, no, I don't get no trouble. In fact, you just aren't anybody on campus at Barnard unless you've had lunch with Zora Neale. And I keep my calendar selective, if you know what I mean."

As we got to the subway stairs, a blind beggar called out from where he sat on a milk crate outside the station.

"Pardon me. Spare a nickel for an old man? Could you spare a nickel, please?"

The old guy had filmy, gray eyes. He'd wrapped himself up in a tan-colored blanket, the same shade as his skin. He rattled the coin in his tin cup and held it out.

Zora put her hand over her heart and smiled.

"God is good," she said.

Then she walked right up in front of the old man. The beggar felt her presence and raised his cup higher.

"A nickel for the poor?"

"Tell you what." Zora dug inside his little tin cup and grabbed the one coin that was already in there. "I need this nickel worse than you do today. But if you lend it to me for the subway now, I'll give it back later. Promise."

Moving over to the stairs she turned around and yelled back to me, "By the way, you busy Saturday? No? Good. Come on over in the morning 'bout nine. Come to the new place on Sixty-sixth Street and the park. I need help moving in. You're swell, May. I appreciate it. Okey-doke. See you then!"

To the beggar, she called, "Thanks, mister!" and was gone.

SATURDAY MORNING I showed up in front of a leaning yellow brownstone right across the street from Central Park. Zora was already waiting.

"I'm coming down," she yelled out the window before I could ring up.

Zora appeared with her hair tied up in a polka-dot kerchief and a pair of denim overalls on. Her face gleamed, bright and pale in the morning sun.

"Come on up!"

Wedging a dictionary in the front door so it wouldn't lock, she led me up the stairs to the second floor.

"This one."

Her voice echoed off the wooden floors, the whitewashed walls, and then jumped high, toward the ceiling. I could see the entire apartment from the doorway. The sitting room windows overlooked the park on the right side. The kitchen (a counter, a coal stove, a sink and an icebox) was on the left. At the back of the sitting room, one doorway led into an alcove, which I assumed to be the bedroom, and another led to the washroom. Except for two suitcases and a pile of hatboxes, the entire place was empty.

"Zora? What exactly am I supposed to be moving?"

"We'll see when it gets here," she said, and settled down to wait.

An hour later, nothing had gotten there. We sat on the floor next to the coughing radiator underneath the bay window playing two-man whist.

"Zora, I've got books to—"

"Relax, oh ye of little faith. It'll be here."

"*What* will be here?"

She looked at me like I'd spoken Greek. "My stuff. What do you think I called you over here for?"

"Well, where's all this stuff?"

"Good question. Folk sure are slow today."

"*What folk,* Zora?"

Finally, she explained her missing stuff. Zora's idea of furnishing her apartment was to tell everyone she knew that she was moving into her new place on Saturday. Unbelievably, this new place had not a stitch of furniture to put in it. The people, of course, would then take that information and do the right thing. She couldn't understand where they might be, though. The day was a-wasting.

I couldn't have been more disgusted. A whole long morning gone. I'd trekked all the way downtown (two subway trains and a six block walk) and for what? To play cards and listen to her radiator grumble.

"Where you going?" she cried.

"Home to get some work done." I kissed her cheek and shoved my work gloves and my kerchief down into my bag. "Call me when the room doesn't echo anymore."

I yanked open the front door. A young blond woman in a straw cloche and a camel hair coat fell into the room, her hand still clutching the knob.

"Helen!" Zora crowed. "How good of you to come see me."

"Well, I heard you say that you were moving in today and I thought you might need a few things."

My mouth fell.

"Isn't that typical! Always thinking of the other guy. I can't believe you. You know, I think I'm going to have to have lunch with you one day. Helen, this is my friend Dr. May Chinn. May's helping me move in today. Aren't you, May?"

They both beamed at me.

"Of course," I mumbled. "That's what I'm here for."

Dumbfounded, I set my bag back down and went out into the hallway to retrieve "Zora's things."

Helen from anthropology class brought dishes and linens. Margaret from sociology had her driver carry up a study desk and matching oak chair. Professor Boas sent over a brass bed (that just so happened to perfectly fit the linens Helen left) with a letter of love and good wishes for his "dusky daughter." Fannie Hurst sent, with her warmest regards, a brand-new chenille sofa. Brian, who knew Zora through mutual friends and hoped to, at some point, get better acquainted, brought a small dining table from his father's showroom. It wasn't top-of-the-line, but it would last till kingdom come.

By the time I left that night, the apartment was full. Cozy even. Sofa, end tables, lamps, pots, pans, bureau, towels, an imitation Oriental rug, even paintings for the walls—she had everything.

"Doggone!" Zora scratched her head. "Didn't nobody bring me any forks and knives. What's goin' on in the world? I can't eat with my hands."

I hugged her close. "Don't worry, Zora. It'll come."

That made my friend laugh. She laughed till her throat got dry and creaky.

"Now you learning, Lil' Bit," she said.

Not really, but saying it felt right inside my skin. And because I need always to act on my gratitude, I came back the next day before work with three bags of groceries, most of it from my own icebox, and a shoe box full of utensils.

"Oh, you're here!" she exclaimed, like she'd expected me.

"Of course. Where else would I be?"

Zora put the silverware away and asked me to stay for her housewarming party.

"I told everyone it would be a hand-chicken dinner, since I didn't have any forks. So let's us just put these utensils in the back of the drawer. I mean, it would be such a shame to disappoint the people, after they get here expecting to get good and greasy. 'Cause, girl, you know I aim to please."

SPRING CAME BACK. I took the first Saturday in April off, the whole day, to attend my friend Countee's wedding. It was the biggest social event that Harlem had ever seen. More than three thousand people showed up to watch Countee marry W. E. B. DuBois's only daughter, Yolanda. Crowds formed more than a block from the church, everyone dressed to the nines and hoping for a way to get inside to see the ceremony.

"May!"

Paul came charging toward me, vibrant and glowing. He scooped me up and tossed me in the air like a baby.

"Put that woman down."

Essie limped up beside us. She smiled, but her face was puffy and sallow. As always, the woman set the standard in a gorgeous navy blue-and-ecru satin dress. The skirt of it fell in delicate pleats straight down to her ankles. She wore a matching alpaca cape tossed over one shoulder and a navy blue slouch hat that all but hid her eyes. I would've sold my last ten years of life for an outfit like that. But underneath the clothes, Essie's body bulged and sagged, weighing heavily against the fine cloth.

"You look good, Es," I said, staring at the dress.

"Liar. The bags under my eyes are big enough to pack a full suitcase. But the baby's fine, Paul's fine, and I'm getting better. What more can I ask? How are you?"

"Very well. I'm finishing my internship—"

"In three months," she said.

Essie's face got very still, almost soft. Her eyes circled for a moment, two restless brown sparrows, then lit on something in the distance, way off in front of us. "Paul's starring in *Porgy* now. Have you seen it? If you haven't, you better hurry. He's getting ready to head to London to do *Show Boat*."

As we strolled toward the church, Paul tried to fill the awkward silence.

"The new baby's amazing, May. You should see him. Who ever thought something so tiny could be so much fun? Speaking of kids, I wonder if Yolanda and Countee are planning to have any."

Essie snorted. "I wouldn't take bets."

With Paul leading the way, we trundled through the crowd into the church. Everyone made way for him. In the pew in the front row, W. E. B. DuBois and his family sat staring straight ahead, like royalty.

"Sir!" Paul grabbed Papa DuBois in a firm embrace.

He shook hands with Paul and Essie, then kissed both my hands and my good cheek.

"My beauty," he said. "So good to see real friends here. I'm honored. How is your father?"

"Fine, sir. He sends his warmest regards, and he wanted me to tell you that no matter what, he's here for you faithfully."

Papa DuBois sagged a bit. His posture never stooped. His shoulders stayed firm. But inside his skin, in a place not connected to bone or blood, he left off from himself. That hurt my heart. I called him home.

"Papa, you must be proud. I'm proud for you. Look at this. Look how much you mean to all these people."

"Yes." He glanced around but never met anyone's eyes. "There's much to be proud of. There's truth here. A future. Isn't there?"

"Yes," I said. "And it's all because of you."

He kissed me again. "You must sit up here. With us. You're family, too."

Paul, Essie and I got settled and looked around. James Weldon Johnson sat beside us, Alain Locke behind.

"Look, Essie," I said. "There's Jessie Fauset with Gwendolyn Bennett."

Essie rolled her eyes, unimpressed. "Ever since Jessie's book *Plum Bun* came out, she thinks the sun rises and sets on her own behind."

Paul read his program.

"Look. Is that Claude McKay back there?"

"Where?" she cried. "I sure hope that black monkey chaser isn't here. Why ruin a perfectly good affair with his nigger hijinks? But did you hear? *Home to Harlem* is a best seller. Can you believe that darkey has the first best seller by a Negro author? Typical."

"Zora!" Paul called out, raising his arm above the crowd. "Move over, Es. Let's make room for Zora."

"You know," Essie said, "I like that woman less and less every time I see her."

So many friends milled about in the crowd, some of whom I hadn't seen in years. Nella Larson, Bud Fisher, Aaron Douglas, Duke Ellington, A. Phillip Randolph, Wallace Thurman, Fauntleroy. I even halfway looked for Jean Toomer to show up, but I knew he wouldn't be there. When *Cane* got published a few years back, white literary critics called him the greatest Negro writer ever born and the genius of the Renaissance. That made him very angry and he refused to be a Negro ever again. I knew there was no way he'd show up at an event full of thousands of dark faces. But I missed him anyway. After a while, I stopped calling out the names of people when I saw them so I wouldn't have to hear

Essie's commentary. I allowed myself the pleasure of enjoying them in silence.

The ceremony was stunning. Langston ushered and Countee's best friend, a handsome young schoolteacher named Harold Jackman, was the best man. The newlyweds drove off, auspiciously somber-faced and dignified, in a gilded carriage drawn by six white horses. All of Harlem stopped to watch them pass.

By the time we'd finished mingling and socializing, by the time I'd said all of my good-byes and made all of my promises to keep in touch, it was already dark. I strolled home, full of faces and music and stories to tell Mama. She woke up long enough to hear it all and ask me if I was happy. Then she yawned into her closed fist and went back to sleep.

I LOOKED AT A strand of my hair in the lamplight, the bottom split in many shafts like the end of a bug's leg. I'd put on some weight, too. Soft and round in the center. The men liked it, smiled a bit extra when I passed, but it made me tired.

I worked too hard. Needed to take better care of myself. But, funny thing, the harder the work got, the more I became compelled to navigate my way through it.

It was almost over. I'd be done at Harlem in another month or so, finally on my own. It felt good, even though I had no idea what that meant or how I'd survive. The others, Louis included, took bets on how long I'd last in Harlem by myself. Sometimes they asked me if I wanted in on the pool.

Time to go. I put away the letter I was reading.

May, have you heard? There's scandal afoot! Countee's circus of a wedding isn't but two months past and already he's hightailed it to Paris with Harold

*Jackman. The best man! Scandal, I say, scandal! The W. E. B. DuBoises
and the Frederick Cullenses are understandably horrified. And of course, their
detractors are syndicating the news all across Harlem. Darkies can be so
tiring . . . Kisses to you.*

Yours,

Essie.

Too bad. But there wasn't time to worry on that now. I had a
house call to make before I could sign out for the weekend.

I picked up my bag and headed out the back entrance, just as
the ambulance cruised in with another patient. Walking down
Lenox, I cut across 131st Street in front of the Lafayette Theater
and waited there for the streetlight to turn. I purposely didn't cross
onto Seventh until I'd passed Connie's Inn, which still didn't allow
Negroes.

The sun shaded the low brick buildings with gold and amber
inlays. The trees lining the street had sprouted buds, like puckered
lips, tight and cool and green. Women simmered food in great pots
in the rooms above my head. I could smell it clear. Colored women
cooked good on evenings like this. Their attention was generous,
slow and easy and full. They poured love into their food and left
the windows open. I strolled to my appointment, soaking it in,
smelling trees and collard greens and, from somewhere above, a
whiff of lavender perfume.

I walked up to the third floor and knocked on the door. Nothing. I knew Mr. Daniels had to be in there. He had no way to leave
by himself. I started banging. Still no answer. I banged on that
door so loud that Mr. Raimes, the super, came running up to see
what was going on. When he saw me standing there, he hustled
back downstairs for the spare key.

The old man unlocked the door and pushed it open. Mr.
Daniels was waiting.

Naked, he hung by a belt from an exposed pipe beside the radiator, next to the window. Mr. Daniels's legs had been amputated at the knees during the war. So he couldn't reach the light fixture in the ceiling. You could tell that he tried by the scuffmarks all around the molding. His dead body looked like he was just sitting on the floor against the wall, except that his behind was suspended about four inches off the ground. Purple and stiff, his skin had already begun to simmer and deteriorate in patches.

All I could think was that this man was only Coleman's age, the age he would have been had he lived. They knew each other in the war. The Fifteenth Heavy Foot.

Mr. Daniels's open eyes bulged and leaked, like he was dead and yet he still couldn't stop crying.

A slip of paper lay beside the body. Mr. Raimes kicked it with his foot until it was far enough away. Then, with his hat covering his nose, he scooped it up.

"For you," he said, handing it off.

> *Dear Dr. May,*
>
> *I'm sorry. Thank you for all you've done. It's not your fault. If it wasn't for you, it would have been sooner. God bless you. Find my family, if you can. Tell them it wasn't hard.*
>
> *With deepest love and gratitude,*
> *Edward Daniels*

"Come on out," I told Mr. Raimes. "Close the door. I'll have someone come 'round for the body within the hour."

MR. DANIELS'S EYES stayed on my mind. That's why, when I walked into my room behind the emergency ward, I didn't see it right away. My thoughts had wandered, years back, looking for new outcomes.

The smell hit me first.

A skinned raccoon, oozing and raw, lay on top of my desk, legs in the air, its eyes and tongue and front paws missing.

I didn't vomit or scream. The fetus had been worse. The dark gray genitals sliced from a vagrant's cadaver and left inside my bag had been worse. But I stumbled back out of the room and slammed the door shut behind me, retching. Three or four of the other interns just happened to be passing by.

"Did you do this? Did you?"

"Do what? What are you talking about?"

Some voices around the corner snickered and then a heavy metal door crashed shut. I ran behind the sounds, through the staircase, up to the top floor, and all the way down. The stairs were empty. They were gone.

I crouched on the bottom step, chest pressed against my knees for the longest time. Then I went looking for one of the cleaning ladies. I waited more than an hour until a Colored woman came on duty because I was too ashamed to ask any of the white cleaners to help. The woman, Dot, helped me wrap the raccoon in canvas and dump it outside. Then she came back with me, and together we scoured the room. As I cleaned, I stayed mindful of every thought that boiled up inside me. The searing, bloody thoughts had to be released. I refused to hate them, to become as small as they kept trying to crush me. But it was so, so hard. Every time I felt a scream welling up in my throat, I said out loud, "two months," and closed my eyes and put my head down until I could breathe.

The next week, I found Dr. Crump waiting for me in my room when I signed back on duty.

"Rotten thing they did to you, May. You all right?"

"I'm fine, sir."

"There's just a few weeks left until Boards. You going to make it?"

No one else had asked me that question. Ever. I could've cried.

"Yes, sir."

Dr. Crump smiled. "Good. Then I have something for you."

He handed me a slip of paper with the name and address for a Dr. Ronald Williams at 44 Edgecombe Avenue.

"You won't be able to get an appointment at any hospital after graduation, of course. This man is the head doctor at the Edgecombe Sanitarium. Seven Negro doctors practice there, and I have word that there's an open office for an eighth. It's not really like having institutional support, but it's better than being all on your own. Go see him."

I didn't know what to say. He'd offered the help I needed before I could ask. That told me, more than anything, that I had to be doing the right thing. And if that were the case, then everything else would work out as well. Somehow.

THEY HELD A commencement service for the graduating interns six weeks later.

Mama went. I slept through it. It was the first good sleep I'd had in two years.

Chapter 18

Mama's graduation gift to me was a shiny brass shingle with my name on it:

DR. MAY EDWARD CHINN, MD.

We hung it outside my new office on the parlor floor of the Edgecombe Sanitarium.

I'd showed up at Williams's door the day after Dr. Crump gave me the lead, my curriculum vitae in one hand and a letter of introduction in the other. Dr. Williams glanced at my resume and put the letter in his vest pocket, unopened. He looked me over, asked if it was true that I knew Paul Robeson and W. E. B. DuBois, and agreed to take me in on the spot. He even offered me the office space and the two-bedroom apartment above it for only a hundred dollars a month. I grabbed it, although it seemed too good to be true.

The sanitarium was actually two brownstones connected on the fourth floor by a glass-and-brick walkway. Overnight patients slept in the southern wing of the fourth floor next to the operating room. On the parlor floor, I had a long waiting room that overlooked the park. The small, square room behind that became my office. Somehow I managed to cram an examining table, a glass supply cabinet, a waist-high filing cabinet, and a mahogany desk (graduation present sent by Paul) in there. To slide out from behind the desk, I had to scrunch down and turn sideways. I immediately converted the storage closet between the waiting room and the office into a mini–pathology lab so I could do my own blood typing and tissue analysis. That was it.

I did it. Mama and I did it. We made it.

Dr. May Edward Chinn, MD.

On my first day, the other doctors came over to my office to introduce themselves. The thing that impressed me the most about them was their sameness, a lack of definition that made me feel like I was shaking hands with the same man over and over again. They were sepia men, not one of them darker than a soft slice of toast. I could see the pride that they took in that fact. Each had wavy hair standing up off his face and parted down the side with a slick barber's cut. Their fingers felt hard like piano keys when they squeezed my hand, but not at all welcoming. Their hands made me nervous.

In order to differentiate between them, I had to keep track of the small things. Dr. Rayburn had a cleft nose, wide in the center with narrow nostrils, which gave him a strong resemblance to the devil. Dr. Woodbine clicked his false teeth together whenever he wasn't talking. They sounded like porcelain castanets. Dr. Randolph started every sentence with "er-rer" (as in: "Er-rer, this is, er-rer, exactly what I, uh, was talking about. Er-rer."). Dr. Murray stared.

I didn't mind Dr. Murray though. He wasn't threatening, and at least he saw something when he looked into my face. He responded genuinely to my hello and actually showed his teeth as he smiled. I hoped he'd be my friend.

"It's a good thing you're here, May," said Dr. Williams. "You're exactly what we needed."

"Thank you so much, Dr. Williams. I appreciate your kindness, and I want you to know that you won't regret placing your trust in me."

"Just make sure, young lady, that you don't leave the building after eight-thirty at night," said Dr. Woodbine.

"Uh, excuse me, sir?"

"You heard what I said," the old man snapped. He turned his back to me, toward the window.

"What he means, May," said Dr. Williams "is that New York State law requires that someone be on duty at all times if there are patients here overnight in the south wing. And there usually are. Since you live in the building now, that person would be you."

My hands started shaking. I balled them into fists and crossed my arms to hide them in my armpits. But I still kept shaking, little tremors that rolled like waves from my hands, up my arms, through my ribs and out to the rest of my body.

It made sense. Dr. Williams's quick acceptance. His inability to look me in the eye without grimacing slightly. Dr. Murray moved away and stared out the window too.

"I'm the resident."

Williams patted my shoulder. "I wouldn't put it that way. It wouldn't be a helpful way to look at things. And we all just want this to work out. Don't you, May?"

"What did you do before?" I asked.

"We took turns. But that's not necessary anymore now that you're here. Besides, that kind of schedule was a strain. Too much time from our families. You don't have a family. So I'm sure you agree that this is the fairest way."

The word *no* jumped up in my body, a little metal knot twisting between my ribs.

It got bigger, hotter, uglier, the longer I stood there. I refused to let these men chain me to my dream. It wouldn't happen. There had to be another way. But I couldn't actually say no to them. Where else would I go? What would they think of me? What would Dr. Crump think?

"I'll do the best I can," I murmured. "Excuse me, gentlemen. I need to get ready."

And I made a big show of straightening my spotless waiting room, opening the shades, moving a pile of paperwork as I prepared to start the day.

All of this, even though I had no patients.

FOUR DAYS LATER, I still hadn't had a single patient.

I'd discovered one of the reasons why the day before. By seven that morning, it was already sweating hot. I figured I'd run up St. Nicholas to catch the iceman on his route. As I stepped out the door and started down the stairs, I overheard Dr. Rayburn, one of the older fellows, telling a patient of mine from Harlem, "She's not in, Mrs. Fontaine. Probably she overslept again. Bring your son down to my office, why don't you."

"I'm not too sure about that sir—no offense to you. But Dr. May is his doctor."

"My dear!" he exclaimed. "What in the world can a woman do for you that a male doctor can't do better?"

And he led her by the hand into his office on the ground floor.

I watched his door shut, feeling like an utter fool and so ashamed.

After that morning, I took to waiting in one of the chairs by the window. By the following Tuesday, I finally got my first patient. A good-looking pregnant woman in a pink cotton tubular dress and a wide-brimmed straw hat waddled up the stairs.

"You Dr. May?" she asked when I opened the door for her.

"I most certainly am. And you are?"

"Anabelle Lincoln. Dr. Lincoln's wife?"

Dr. Lincoln had the southwest office on the third floor. I forced myself to keep smiling. So I wasn't good enough for their patients, but I was good enough to treat their wives and children—who, of course, got treated for free as a matter of professional courtesy. Doctor's rules.

That summer, my only steady patients were the other doctors' families. Two pregnant wives, one sister with a broken leg, a grandmother's failing kidney, a toddler with a marble lodged in his ear and old Mrs. Woodbine's cat Nipsey (who was just the same as family and he'd been feeling poorly for quite some time. Would I mind? Just a quick peek). Mama kept one of her jobs and I think she took to sneaking in some laundry on the side, when she thought Papa and I weren't paying attention.

Every so often, Dr. Murray knocked on my door.

"Just checking up on you, May. Everything all right?"

"Fine, Steven. Thank you."

He'd wave and disappear back downstairs to his office. One afternoon, when it was too muggy to go outside for lunch, he came in carrying a greasy, brown paper sack.

"Hungry?" he asked.

The smell of fried whiting and potatoes wafted in with him. My stomach growled loud enough to echo off the walls.

"I'll take that as a yes."

"I'd love to," I said. "But I haven't got an extra chair in here."

"Let's go out to the waiting room."

"Oh, I don't know if that's a good idea. How would it look if a patient came in?"

Steven cocked his head to the side and raised an eyebrow. To his credit, he didn't try to pretend that I'd given a worthwhile excuse. He called me out like he should have. There hadn't been a patient in my office in a day and a half.

"Well, I guess if we eat fast, it'll be fine."

We sat in front of the open window, swatting flies over sandwiches made from thick slabs of wheat bread stuffed with three cornmeal-coated filets each and slathered in hot sauce. Steven made sure that the fried potatoes were also smothered in salt, pepper and hot sauce.

"Bet you didn't think I knew how to make good food like this."

I nearly choked on a fish bone. "You cooked this yourself?"

"I bet you thought all I ate was salmon croquette and watercress."

"It crossed my mind."

"No, ma'am." He laughed. "My family's from Charlotte. Just regular folk. And my mother was the independent sort, too. After we got a certain age, she said if we wanted to eat, we'd better figure out how to move around the kitchen."

He popped a tailfin in his mouth and licked his fingers.

"Well, I think it's about that time. Thank you for your company, ma'am. It's been delightful. I wonder if we could do this again?"

That was how Steven and I first started talking. Little by little, he filled me in on the workings of the sanitarium. But all of his advice more or less amounted to this: Stay out of their way. I followed that advice as best I could during the day and filled out applications for the city hospitals at night, even though I knew they didn't hire Negroes. Steven ran interference and tried to keep the others from snatching my patients.

Eventually, people did begin to trickle in. Mostly old patients from Harlem Hospital who'd tracked me down. There was quite a mix in my little office. Italian, Irish, West Indian, Polish, Puerto Rican, Chinese, even a tribe of Mohawk Indians—they all came to me. I never discriminated against anyone and, perhaps more important, I never turned down a patient just because they didn't have the money to pay. I couldn't. That wasn't what I'd come this far to do.

Late one evening, when a few months had passed and it was already chilly again, a young woman walked in. She looked around, then back at me, and then out into the hallway again.

When she couldn't find anyone else, she peeked back inside and said, "Excuse me, ma'am. I'm looking for Dr. Chinn."

"I'm the doctor."

"Oh," said the dark young woman. "Oh."

"There's seven other doctors in the building if you like."

"No, ma'am. I'm sorry. I wasn't expectin' you, that's all. I got a friend who told me to come to Dr. Chinn. She said you were real good. And nice."

"What do you need, dear?"

The girl unbuttoned her shirt and pulled it back from her shoulders. At the base of her neck, right on top of her spine, sat an egg-sized abscess filled with blood.

She turned back to me and dropped her eyes. "I ain't got no money. My friend didn't either, but she said you treated her anyway. Thought maybe if you could take care of this, I could work it off somehow."

Her voice got low, and I wondered what "work it off" meant to her.

"What's your name, baby?"

"Henriette."

"How old are you, Henriette?"

"Seventeen, ma'am."

"Do you mind if I ask what happened to you?"

She didn't answer, so I said, "Never mind," and led her into the back.

Henriette's neck and shoulders all around the abscess were purple with bruises. I cleaned the area and talked her down from the pain every time I touched her. Reaching up to the top shelf in my cabinet, I pulled down a large brown jar and unscrewed the lid. With a pair of sterilized tongs, I gripped the leech inside, lifted it out and placed it on the girl's neck. She cried as the thing latched onto her and began siphoning her blood.

Once she'd been cleaned up and bandaged, I asked again, "Who did that?"

"Boss at my agency. Brung me and a bunch of other girls up from different places down South. He said there was good work up here."

"Where do you live?"

"At Red Rose Home. LaValle hires us out in the day, and we stay there at night. But it's . . . it's not what he promised. One of the other girls is pregnant. She ain't doing well."

I couldn't ignore the hint.

That's how I became the physician for the Red Rose Home for Girls. The place was a three-story brick building just off the river supposedly where young working girls could get decent rooms in a respectable boardinghouse.

The next evening, Henriette and I snuck in through a loose plank in a boarded-up airshaft at the back of the building that opened onto a rear staircase. She led me down the narrow concrete stairs to the basement door. The girls had learned how to pick the shabby lock on this back door so when someone needed to, she could sneak out after dusk. When Henriette opened the door at the bottom, the stench gagged me. The dim, concrete room reeked of urine, feces, packed bodies and the unmistakable tang of unhealthy flesh, open wounds left raw and festering. As my eyes adjusted to the darkness, I made out more than thirty pallets, crammed together and lined up in rows on the floor. Some of the girls were already asleep, passed out in exhaustion wherever they found room, some sleeping sitting up against the wall. The basement was smaller than the apartment that I shared with my parents. It had no kitchen or toilet. I lit the lamps we brought and got to work.

By the time I'd gotten through every girl, it was dawn and I'd found six cases of TB, three cases of dysentery, two more pregnancies (all from this LaValle character, I assumed), and a broken rib. Two girls had the telltale sores of syphilis and I gave them my address and told them to come to me, at night, for medication and a referral. All the girls had bruises and quite a few were missing teeth. None of them were more than twenty-two years old. The youngest was thirteen.

This man LaValle had three partners, I learned. The four men lured all the girls up to New York, just as Henriette said, with promises to their families of honest work. When they got them here, they hired them out during the day, for all sorts of things. Then they picked the girls up and locked them in the basement all night until it was time for work again in the morning. The girls couldn't leave "the agency" until they'd paid the men back for transportation, room, board and expenses. These, of course, were very expensive things.

What I saw were children who'd been frightened and beaten into submission. It seemed as though they could've escaped if they wanted to. But they had nowhere to go and were too terrified to try. Though I'd never been involved with this kind of operation before, I'd heard of them. A combination of urban sharecropping and slavery here in the twentieth century.

I treated my patients, all night, all day in my thoughts, and again all night, mumbling to myself over unlikely schemes and plans. In my office, if there was a lull between appointments, I slept on the examining table.

"Be careful," Steven told me. "People who get mixed up in things like that come up missing. The police don't even get involved. May, you can't change the world all by yourself."

"That's not what I'm trying to do. But I can't pretend not to see what's in front of me. That's not who my mother raised me to be."

"Let's call the police," he offered.

"What are the police going to do for a bunch of Colored girls? They may roust the man, hassle him for a minute, but then what? They probably already know about him."

"What do you want to do then?"

"I'm not sure," I admitted. "I think I should find somewhere to take them. Maybe if they know there's somewhere safe to go, they'll be more open to leaving."

"What if Williams or one of the others finds out you've been sneaking out?" Steven said. "What if one of the patients here needs attention and there's no one on duty? You could lose your license, May. They could shut us down."

That made me stop and think. What if a patient rang for help in the middle of the night and no one came? I'd be to blame for that. We had only three inpatients, but they were still my responsibility. Steven was right about that.

I stayed away from Red Rose for nearly a week.

When I returned (and I had to return), I found out that one of the TB girls had died the Sunday before sometime just before dawn. A sixteen-year-old from Winterville, North Carolina, named Ellen. She'd been left lying on her pallet all day and the next night, until LaValle could find someone to take the body away, they said. By the time I came back, Ellen's pallet was already filled.

Two weeks later, Henriette came up missing. The other girls said that she'd been called upstairs two nights before and never came back.

I tracked her down. After two days of telephone calls, I got word that a body fitting her description had been found bobbing at the foot of the lighthouse in the swirling Hellgate waters off Welfare Island. It was still being held on the island, in the morgue at the Blackwell Penitentiary.

I canceled three appointments so I could make the trip out there the next afternoon. It was her. Apparently she'd been hit or kicked hard enough in the chest to crack a rib, which stabbed her straight through the lung. She'd choked on her own blood. The doctor was shipping her body out, with eight inmates from the prison who'd also recently died, to be buried in Potter's Field.

I had no money to offer for a proper burial, and no information on her family to even alert them. So I said my good-byes and headed across the water on the ferry.

Back at the sanitarium, Williams was waiting for me.

"Chinn. I need your notes from last night on Sadie Dempsey. She's got to go back into surgery. Probably in the morning."

I froze. Everything Steven said about being stripped of my license came tumbling back into my head. Why hadn't I listened? He told me, but I ignored him. So stubborn. So caught up in things that I couldn't fix. Just like he said. Williams stood there, glaring, waiting for me to hang myself.

How many years had we worked for this?

"What notes, sir?"

"I don't have time for this, Dr. Chinn. You're the one who knows what happened. I'm still trying to find out. I need to know what you did for Mrs. Dempsey's leg last night. She said she had pain in the same location where I found the blood clots, and she said the doctor on duty last night took care of her. So where is her chart?"

"The doctor on duty?"

Dr. Williams removed his glasses and squeezed the bridge of his nose.

"Doctor, I'm not going to ask you again."

"I'm sorry, sir. I'm just off today. Can you give me a minute? I'll . . . I'll come down to your office with the report."

He flung the door open and disappeared down the hall. As soon as his door slammed, I ran to Steven's office.

"Come in. I was just finishing up." He pulled a yellow folder out of his desk. "Here's your report. I initialed it for you, so read it carefully before you hand it back to Williams."

"You've been staying here every night that I'm gone?"

Steven shrugged. "You're a good doctor. If I'm honest, I'd say you're better than any of us. You just don't think. When I look at you, that's the only flaw I can see. But you know what? Sometimes I wish I could be more like that."

"No you don't," I said. "You're wise to be as you are."

A man like Steven Murray would never find himself trolling the muddy waters of Hellgate looking for reasons in the river. He wouldn't risk everything he'd worked more than ten years to earn without explanation, without a plan.

"Thank you, though. For everything. But you were right. I won't be going back."

Upstairs, I knocked on Dr. Williams's door and then slid the report underneath. Before I could get back down the stairs, he opened the door and said, "Dr. Chinn, I'm scheduling Mrs. Dempsey for another surgery tomorrow afternoon. I need you to take one of my house calls for me."

"But Doctor, I have patients scheduled in the afternoon."

"Move them," he said.

I paid one of the neighbor boys a dime to run and tell my appointments to come early in the morning. For them, I opened my office at seven instead of eight thirty. That left my afternoon free. I caught a trolley uptown to 190th Street and walked swiftly west, toward the gray river, to the outskirts of Ft. Tryon Park. In front of me stood a four-story Victorian house. Verging on the edge of collapse, the bleached, ramshackle house looked more like a mansion. I walked up the path, lined on both sides with spidery rosebushes, the branches weathered and forked like veins. Towering dogwood and cypress trees shaded me from the November wind. I pressed a bell at the door, and somewhere off inside the house, a large, guttural gong sounded. The door swung open and a middle-aged Negro woman in a black habit ushered me into the foyer.

"Good afternoon," she said. Her dark face gleamed. "I'm Sister Bernadine. You must be the nurse."

"Dr. Chinn," I said, and reached for her hand.

The woman squealed and clapped her arms around me in delight. "Wonderful! A doctor. God is good, isn't He? He always puts the right people together. Welcome. This order is called the Handmaidens for Mary. This is our home."

"A Catholic order of Negro nuns? I've never heard of such a thing."

"And I've never seen a Negro woman doctor before, so I think we're even."

Sister Bernadine laughed and squeezed my shoulders, and I hoped all the other nuns were like her. She showed me through the house, a gift from a wealthy white benefactor (see, God has Negrotarians, too, I heard Zora say). The vaulted ceilings arched easily twenty feet over my head in the first floor sitting rooms and the main dining room. Little white cherubs molded in corners and on banisters and windowsills watched us pass. The rooms were sparsely furnished with wooden benches and chairs and, occasionally, a rough, obviously hand-woven rug to cover the cool stone floors. A likeness of Jesus withering on the cross hung prominently in every room.

"This place is absolutely incredible. How many nuns are in your order?"

"Our group is small," said Sister Bernadine. "As you can imagine, not many Negro women are attracted to the nunnery. There are about twenty-five of us, nearly half of whom have come down with something terribly nasty."

I left my questions, along with the churning feeling in my stomach, and let her lead me into the solarium. Three walls of the room were windows, the middle panel a stained-glass image of Jesus crying tears of blood on the cross. Outside, Ft. Tryon Park shaded the house in branching shadows. Just beyond that, one could make out the lazy sway of the Hudson.

I set up shop and Sister Bernadine led the other nuns in one at a time. The last sister to come in that evening didn't have a cough or the flu like the others. She looked like Henriette to me, bruised and shaken. This woman was lighter than most of the others, so the marks on her chest and back and neck stood out like handprints. I gave her salve and pain tablets, but there wasn't much more I could do. She nodded to me and left without a word.

"What happened to her?" I asked Sister Bernadine.

"She's new. From a convent in Maryland. From what I gather one of the priests did that. Their Mother Superior sent her with a letter of introduction and asked us to take her in. That's all."

"Do you often take in people in trouble like that?"

"We haven't in the past."

"Would you?"

Sister Bernadine thought for a moment. "Yes, I would," she

said slowly. "I believe that's what our Lord Jesus would command us to do in His name. Care for the weak and the afflicted. Otherwise, what are we here for? Don't you agree?"

"Of course."

The things happening in my mind seemed almost too good to be true. I didn't speak on it though. It was too soon, too fragile a hope. But I locked it away inside my chest, in a place where it could take root.

WE MOVED THE GIRLS at night. Steven and I in a borrowed truck with hoods over the headlamps.

Only twelve of the girls trusted me enough to creep out that night and wait, hiding in the mud along the riverbank until they heard our signal. The others were too frightened to leave.

"The devil you know is better than the devil you don't," one of them had said.

It hurt my heart to go without them. Hurt me more to know the empty pallets would be filled again before the end of the week. But at least the girls who stayed didn't tell.

The truck coasted to a stop on Harlem River Drive, a block or so from Red Rose. Steven whistled for them, a robin's call over the edge of the embankment. But then a light flicked on in the second floor of the building. I tapped Steven's shoulder and pointed as someone's shadow passed over the window and stood there. Steven whistled again and the movement along the bank froze. It looked, from where we sat in the dark, like the window opened and a man's head peeked out searching first west, then east, out over the water. I grabbed Steven's hand and we slouched down in the cab of the truck as far as we could.

"It's all right, May. He can't see us from where he is. He's too far."

But we didn't move until the man shut the window and disappeared back inside the room. Again, Steven called. Seconds later we heard them scraping up the rise, hoisting themselves and each other toward the road. As soon as we saw movement, we jumped from the cab and ran over, plucking the girls from the water's edge.

None of them carried anything. They didn't even ask where we were going. They just huddled together in the back, faces pressed down against the wind, arms linked.

Steven looked at me and kissed my hand. Then he started the truck and drove north, alongside the choppy Harlem River. At 145th Street, we turned left, to the west, just as the sun started to rise.

Sister Bernadine answered the door immediately when I rang. She led us upstairs to the third floor, where four empty rooms waited. Clean nightclothes lay folded on each bed and the bedcovers had even been turned down.

"Baths first," said Sister Bernadine. "Then bread and tea if you want it. Get a few more hours' sleep, and when you wake up we'll all get to know each other a bit better. We'll take it from there."

The girls held on to one another tight, and the three pregnant ones began to cry.

Once the girls had gotten settled, Sister Bernadine walked Steven and me out. Frost glazed over the rose branches and crunched beneath our feet. The sun made soft, red shadows to cloak the brittle edges of the thorns. In front of us, the stuttering cypress bowed slightly as the sun leaned on its crown, making more shadows. A perfect morning.

Steven took my hand again and squeezed.

"Don't look so sad, May," Steven said. "You did all you could."

"Some is better than none, I guess."

We got back downtown just in time to open our offices.

Chapter 19

A little at a time, my love shifted from the past to the present. Eventually, it opened up into the moment. *Now* became real, maybe for the first time in my life, as an eternity of insight and revelation in which nothing else existed and nothing had an end. I looked into mirrors and saw myself clearly for the first time since I was a child; my heart began to remake that child, a fat-faced little girl who didn't see herself as separate at all. Imagine that.

My mother noticed and began reading her Bible again. She pointed out promises, like where it says, *I will give you back the years that the locusts have eaten,* and then asked, "What you think?"

She picked out parts in Song of Solomon, and said, "You remember this, Ladybug? How 'bout this?"

My father softened somewhat, but still wouldn't speak. It didn't bother me much though. I became content in ways that, finally, he couldn't touch.

Winter came again. So much to do.

"Do you really need to go out in the morning?" Steven asked one night when we were alone. "It's Saturday. Take the day off. Let's do something together."

The rollaway bed we lay in barely fit the two of us. Steven bought it because I couldn't afford to, and we propped it against the wall in my waiting room at night. Since I couldn't leave the building, he had to come to me. It was so warm between us, even with only a sliver of space and the mattress springs sticking me in the ribs. We got to laughing when the bed buckled and folded and one of us went tumbling over the edge. How sweet to be held at night in the winter and to be at peace.

"Let's do something in the afternoon. I'll be back by twelve."

He buried his nose in the nape of my neck. "I don't like you going over there. It's too dangerous."

"It's no worse than anywhere else I've been. And I'm not going at night."

"So what? The last time you got held up over there was in the middle of the afternoon, too. What happens if the next one decides to pull the trigger?"

"Then you'll have to pick up my rounds."

Steven turned his back to me and upset the bed.

"That's not funny."

"What? My joke? Or you falling out of the bed again."

"May, please." Steven pulled himself up and rolled over toward me, grabbing my waist. "What are you looking for over there?"

"They need me."

Steven saw their eyes the same as I did. But he didn't see inside their eyes the way I did. In the shantytown along the river, under the 135th Street Bridge and the 145th Street Bridge, the people were being eaten alive. It kept me awake at night to not be able to figure out the cause.

The TB made sense. Once a week, I'd make the rounds and

then phone the morgue at Harlem to tell them how many bodies needed collecting and where. The cold. The wind and chill rolling off the water. The open sewer running down the center of the shantytown. Not only did TB make sense, it was inevitable. The only thing that may have been a bit surprising was the fact that the epidemic hadn't spread to the outside streets. But there was something else. Something that left people wasted, cracked open with sores that stained and crusted over their clothes. Something that left them too weak to move. Some coughed blood from their lungs. Others leaked blood from anuses and, sometimes, spontaneous fissures in the skin. Still others just wasted away. It seemed like cancer, but I hadn't found a way to be sure. No other doctor wanted any part of it. Not only was there no possibility of payment, but even walking into the shantytown quite often meant having to fight your way out. Addicts held codeine powder and cocaine as the same thing, which, essentially, it is.

"I need you, May. Stay with me."

"I'm not going anywhere."

"Are you sure? Sometimes I don't know."

I kissed his eyelids and the bridge of his nose. Then I licked the corners of his mouth until they turned up in a smile.

"I'm not going anywhere."

"Will you marry me then?"

I can't say that I hadn't been expecting it. But still, to hear the words. How many ghosts floated into the room with us when he said that? Gabriel. Coleman. My son. My father. It got real crowded all of a sudden.

"Steven—"

"Don't put me off anymore. Do you love me or not?"

"You know I do but—"

"There are no buts. If you love me, if you want to be with me, there shouldn't be a problem. We're both grown people. We have no business sneaking around like this."

It sounded simple enough. More than simple, it sounded right. Like I could finally let go and rest. I didn't have to miss anybody anymore. I could stay with him and make every moment new. Immediate. Open. How would it feel never to have to be alone again?

"Steven, I would like to marry you."

"But?"

"No. No buts. I think that's my answer. I think I'd like to marry you."

Steven wrapped himself around me, hands tangled in my hair, legs swathed around my hips, and kissed me. I fell asleep to the sound of his promises.

He didn't even fight me in the morning when I got up and got dressed to go to the river.

I PASSED A ROW of huts, cardboard-covered and strapped together with twine. Some of the huts had plywood walls with corrugated tin for the roofs. But that was very, very rare. Such costly building material was hard to come by. Icy mud cracked under my feet as I hopped and zigzagged through the rows, trying to avoid the puddles of slush.

"Mornin', Dr. May. Mornin'."

From all corners, people called out to me. Men knotted around the rag-and-newspaper fire shooting from the belly of a steel drum shouted my name. The women waved from doorways. Children wrapped in blanket squares tagged along beside me and offered to carry my bag.

"How you doin' today, ma'am? Got any candy?"

I had no business giving the children candy. Some of them had rickets and were losing teeth when they weren't supposed to. Others had teeth worn down to the nub by a variety of diseases or just plain old lack of care. I reached into my pocket and pulled out a wad of peppermint balls anyway. They so rarely got a treat.

Down the lane, I came to a shack where the plywood walls had been tied together by rounds of frayed rope. Unfolded boxes weighted at the ends by stones made the roof.

"Mr. Wilson? It's Dr. May."

"Mornin', Lil' Bit."

I pushed the weathered tarp out of the way and stepped inside. The old man lay on his side with a pile of soggy, flattened boxes between him and the ground.

"Brought you a new blanket, sir. That other one looks kind of ratty."

"I'll keep it though, and add the one that you brought on top."

"How you been holding up?"

"Not so good, Lil' Bit. Not so good a'tall. I ran out of them pain tablets you gave me. My stomach been cuttin' the fool ever since."

Mr. Wilson had wasted to somewhere around eighty or ninety pounds. His wrist was the size of my three fingers held together. I'd grown up with this old man. He'd worked with Papa down at Gorham's until his wife quit him a few years back and he took to drinking. When Papa took a new job as a bank watchman downtown, we all fell out of touch. I'd found him out here a few weeks before, while making my rounds.

"Tell you what, sir. I'm coming back Monday early morning. I want to get you in my office so I can look you over properly. OK?"

"Don't see what good it'll do. But if you think it's best, I'll come."

I finished up with him and my other patients just in time to get back to the sanitarium by noon, as promised.

Steven met me at the door with a kiss.

"Afternoon, Mrs. Murray."

"Afternoon, Steven. How are you?"

"Walking on air. I telephoned my parents. They're dying to meet you. I thought maybe we could take a trip down South in another month or two. When it starts to warm up. What do you think? And we're also going to have to figure out what to tell Williams and the rest. They're not going to take this very well. I think—"

"Did the postman come by?"

He'd been hanging up my coat when he stopped and frowned.

"Yes. He stopped by about an hour ago."

I ran into my office and closed the door.

Squeezing behind my desk, I sat down in front of the stack of bills that had my name on them. Mama was still paying most of the rent. Steven gave me money (and patients) discreetly whenever he could. But still, I didn't know how the rent on the office and my other expenses were going to get paid come the end of the month. It made my stomach queasy every time I looked at the letters and invoices and IOUs that kept on piling up. I worked as hard as I could. It didn't make sense that everything I had was going out and nothing coming in.

At the bottom of the stack I found what I'd been looking for. A response to my request for placement on staff at Memorial Hospital. City hospitals still didn't allow Colored doctors to practice within their walls. But I figured it had to be like everything else so far. You just pressed on until they changed their minds. Eventually, they'd have to open their doors. Most people were still very skeptical of me. Some, especially men, especially male doctors, got downright hostile. It was taking much too long to build a steady, *paying* clientele. My practice wouldn't last if something didn't change. But I couldn't figure out what I was doing wrong.

It withered my pride to admit that, after ten years of medical school, after giving up my entire life for this, some days I didn't have money to eat. Mama always tried to keep something on hand. But when she didn't (or couldn't) I'd tell her, "That's fine. I ate in the office downstairs. You go on to sleep."

Pride and fear really are the same thing.

Sometimes patients who didn't have money to pay brought me casseroles or chicken dinners, peas and rice. I was grateful.

December 10, 1930

Dear Dr. Chinn,

On behalf of the Board of Trustees at Memorial Hospital, we regret to inform you . . .

I tore the letter in half and threw it away. Seconds later, I fished it out of the trash and put it in my folder with all the others.

Steven knocked on the door.

"You all right, baby?"

I wiped my face, squeezed back out from behind the desk, and opened the door.

"I'm fine. So what do you want to do this afternoon?"

"Memorial said no too, didn't they?"

"I've got other letters out. Something will happen. It has to."

"Let's go out. Let's forget about all this work stuff, just for a little while. I want to celebrate."

That sounded good to me.

Steven treated me to a fine steak lunch and then we went iceskating in Central Park. Every time he fell backward, I dodged him, so he couldn't drag me down too.

"See." He pouted. "You're being a disloyal wife already."

"If that's what you want to call it. All I know is I don't take well to having an icy behind."

For spite he wrestled me down to the ice and lay on top of me until I laughed myself hoarse.

MONDAY MORNING, I borrowed a pushcart from Mr. Feinman, the greengrocer, and headed back across town to pick up Mr. Wilson. The wheels rattled and spun and got wedged in the mud about every ten feet. Men left their fires and their talk and their early-morning drinking to come help me down the path and back up, with Mr. Wilson tucked into the cart like a gray-faced old baby in a carriage. He even had his bottle.

A fine river mist coated us in silver. It made icy wishbones in the folds and creases of my coat. Our progress was slow going, but eventually we made it all the way back to the west side. By the time we got to the office, I was sweating against the wind. Steven came out and carried Mr. Wilson upstairs for me and then left me alone with my patient.

Two hours later, I'd finished my examination. I was convinced. The old man had cancer. I couldn't prove it, but I felt it in my gut. He'd wasted to where his bones were brittle, his limbs all but useless. He couldn't eat anything because his stomach lining had, for all intents and purposes, rotted away. What was there left for him to do but drink?

I called Memorial. I called Syndham. I called Wadsworth. No one would take him. Finally, I called Flower and begged my old mentor, Dr. Emerson, to get Mr. Wilson an appointment.

"Come over now," she said. "I'll make sure he gets in."

Steven took on my patients in addition to his own so that I could leave with Mr. Wilson. He gave me cabfare both ways and all the money that he collected when I got back.

When the lab results came back five days later, it confirmed what my instincts had told me. Stomach cancer.

"How long do you think he has?" I asked the technician over the phone.

"I'm surprised he's not dead already."

I hung up thinking about the implications. How many of my patients were dying because no one had ever taken the time to diagnose them properly?

"What did he say?" Steven asked that evening.

"Exactly what I knew he'd say. Do you know what this means?"

"If you're right, that means there's an epidemic here, and something needs to be done."

"But how do I prove that when I can't even make a proper diagnosis? I can't very well walk into Memorial with a patient and say, 'you know, I feel like this person has cancer. Check it out.' "

"Why not?"

"Do you think they'd listen to me?" I asked.

"If they don't listen, you stay at them until you make them listen. That's what you've always done. What's different now?"

He had a point. The next Saturday, I got up early and walked across town to the river to take Mr. Wilson some more pain pills. That's all the comfort I could offer. Maybe I couldn't save his life, but at least he wouldn't die in a surfeit of agony.

I hadn't made it to his shack when someone screamed out, "Dr. May! Over here!"

A skinny Italian boy named Martelle, who lived in the shacks just like the Negroes, came running at me. He dragged me across the street and into an alley between two tenements.

"Look, Dr. May!"

My eyes followed his pointing finger about halfway down the row. Two bare feet stuck out from between the spilled trash cans. Martelle picked up a handful of stones and threw them at the rats scuttling through the trash and over the person's legs. I grabbed a rusted pipe and beat the ground, trying to scare them away. The rats scampered off to the side, not too far though. One fat brown one that was nearly as big as a cat stood on its hind legs and bared its teeth. Martelle threw another stone and hit it square in the face. The rat squealed, shook itself, and charged us.

I stumbled back out of the alley, tripped, and went down hard on the ground. Just as the rat got close enough to strike, Martelle grabbed a broken brick and slammed it down, smashing its skull. The body spun in circles, oozing blood onto the filthy pavement, jerking and twitching and making hissing noises as it died. I couldn't look at it. I had to step over it to get to the person inside the alley, but I couldn't bring myself to look. The other rats scattered as we rushed forward. When we got close enough, I saw that the feet belonged to a young, semiconscious Puerto Rican woman. She was in labor.

We dragged the woman out of the alley and Martelle flagged down a passing truck. The driver was a young Negro boy about Martelle's age, but big and burly. He scooped the woman up, put her in the back of his truck, and covered her in burlap sacking. I jumped in the cab, but when I turned to look for Martelle, he'd already gone.

The boy drove us to the sanitarium and carried the woman upstairs to my office. On the way up, I banged on Steven's door.

"I need you!"

When the boy left, I stripped the woman down and began to clean her wounds. She couldn't have been in the alley for too long. The rats had only chewed small holes in her legs and along her side, dangerously close to her stomach. But it could have been much worse. If Martelle had come by an hour later, it would've been another story.

Steven came and helped me get her cleaned up. He held her head over the side of the table when she started vomiting and put smelling salts under her nose to revive her enough so that she could push. The baby's head crowned before I could get her legs apart and up. The woman's eyes kept fluttering open and then closing back. But in spite of everything, she did push when she had to. The baby's head popped out. Then the rest of her body slid right into my arms, almost easy. I slapped the baby's behind. Nothing. Her pale, slick body lay still except for some slight tremors.

Like a fish, the baby started jerking and almost slipped out of my grasp. Her body floundered and shook. Her little chest began to heave and her head jolted forward. Everything trembled in different pulses, different rhythms, the convulsions growing stronger and stronger. Then her eyes popped open, rolled back in her head, and her entire body went stiff. I didn't know what to do. I'd never seen anything like it.

"Wrap her up," Steven yelled. "She's going to hurt herself."

I grabbed a blanket from the shelf and swaddled the baby, pressing her arms and legs tight against her body so she couldn't injure herself. I laid the child on her side with my finger in her mouth, draining some kind of filmy vomit as it came up.

The mother began speaking in Spanish but we couldn't understand her. When the baby stopped moving, she cried.

"She's not dead," I told the woman. But she only cried harder.

I sent for Dr. Crump, who came immediately but didn't have any better ideas than we did. The baby lapsed into a coma. The woman was going through withdrawal from something— trembling and convulsing like the baby, vomiting and, at the same time, leaking diarrhea. I kept looking her over for some clue. She had needle marks all over her arms and thighs. I took blood samples and ran some tests to see if she had a blood disease. The tests came back negative.

There was only one other thing I could think of to do.

The sun was about to set. I had to hurry. I wrapped up tight in

Steven's hat and long men's coat, which was so much warmer than my own, and walked back over to the river.

I saw Martelle and a short black boy scrounging some newspaper and cardboard for a fire, so I started there.

"Thank you for what you did earlier, Martelle. You saved that woman's life."

The boy seemed embarrassed in front of his friend and shrugged me off.

"I have a question for you boys. Will you tell me the truth if I ask you?"

They looked at each other first and then up at me. "Yes, ma'am," said the black boy.

"The woman that we found had holes all over her arms and legs. Needle marks. Bruises. She had to be doing something to herself to get those markings. But I don't know what. You boys know anything? Anything new out that could do that?"

The boys considered me a moment. Then the black boy said, "Must've been shooting smack. That's the only thing to leave holes in you."

"Smack?"

"Yeah," Martelle said. "It's like coke, but worse. After you get hooked, if you stop taking it, you go crazy and die or something."

"Thanks. I appreciate your help."

The boys nodded and went back to their foraging and I walked away wondering about cocaine derivatives and possible antidotes that might mitigate the side effects.

"Mr. Wilson?" I called at the door of his shack. He didn't answer.

"I brought your medicine, sir."

Peeking inside, I saw a mound curled up, cushioned in mud and shadow. No noise. No breathing. None of his presence left there. Not even the telltale smell of spilled wine. He was already dead.

I put the pills back in my pocket and walked out. The body would have to wait until Monday for collection. The city morgue wouldn't send a truck for a John Doe on Sunday. Too short-staffed. Too many other things to do.

I remembered Mr. Wilson from before. Tall and loud and wiry. He had a crush on Mama. Back then, his wife used to laugh a lot and rub his head. She'd tell him if he wasn't careful, she'd let my mother have him.

"Lord have mercy, woman. You know I don't want nobody but you," he'd say.

"Won't nobody else take you," she'd say, and kiss the bald spot on the top of his head.

How did things get to be a certain way? At what moment did change become change, irreversible and complete?

I was so deep in thought that I didn't hear the two men coming up behind me until one of them latched on to the neck of my coat and dragged me down to the ground.

Chapter 20

Steven's face was the first thing I saw when I opened my eyes. It frightened me.

"What happened to you?" I whispered.

That made him laugh. And then cry.

Two men, he told me, had punched and kicked me unconscious. They'd tried to drag me into an alley, but the people came, a swarming crowd of them, with sticks and bottles and hammers and drove them off. They got my medical bag but, thank God, that was all.

As he spoke, it seemed like the pain in my body began to recognize itself through his telling. When he told me two ribs had been fractured, my right side welled and throbbed. Only after he said that my eye had been blackened and swollen shut did I realize how dark and fuzzy the room seemed.

The room. I was in the recovery room at the sanitarium. The addicted woman slept in the bed next to me. Her baby, still as a little doll, lay in a basinet on the other side. I appreciated the irony, but luckily I didn't have to think about it for too long. I fell right back to sleep.

When I woke again the next day, Dr. Williams was taking my temperature.

"Good morning, Doctor," he said. "How are you?"

"Better."

I tried to sit up, but his hand gently pushed me back down.

"Later. When you have more strength. Believe me, I won't let you rest a moment longer than necessary. We have a lot to discuss."

I turned my head toward the door, looking for Steven. He wasn't there. And neither was my patient.

"What happened to the woman and the baby?"

"What woman? Mrs. Broderick?"

"No. The woman from the alley and her baby."

"Oh. I had the ambulance service come and take her to the charity hospital. They took the baby too."

"What do you mean they took the baby? What's going to happen to her?"

"If it lives, I imagine it'll be placed in an orphanage. That woman you dragged in here was in no condition to care for an infant."

"Dr. Williams, she was my patient, not yours."

"Dr. Chinn, this is my sanitarium. And if you don't like the way I run it, you can leave. Now, you may enjoy catering to bums and addicts, but that's not the kind of establishment I run, and it's going to stop. Or else you're going to find somewhere else to practice."

The old man walked over to the next bed to check on another woman. He never looked back or acknowledged that I was still there, still staring at his back, dizzy with frustration and pain.

As soon as I could walk, I dragged myself downstairs and started packing.

"So you're leaving?" Steven materialized in my office doorway, like he'd been waiting.

"How'd you know I was here?"

"I heard you thumping down the stairs. You're hard to miss. You haven't answered my question."

"Yes. It's been time for me to go. It looks like now I don't have much choice."

"I figured you'd say that. Where are you going?"

"I have no idea."

Steven sat on the edge of my desk, fiddling with my stethoscope.

"You know," he said, "I passed by an office on 125th Street day before yesterday. It's available. Two offices, a waiting room, lots of storage space and an extra room for your lab. Right off Seventh. It's a great location. We'll make a killing there—no pun intended. But if we do this, you're going to have to promise to start charging at least half of your patients. What do you think?"

At first I didn't think I'd heard him right.

"An office of our own? Are you sure?"

"Would I ask you if I wasn't?"

"Do you really think we could do it?"

"You can do anything," he said and kissed me softly.

Three weeks later, Steven and I moved into our new office.

We hung our shingles outside the shining mahogany door. His on one side, mine on the other.

THEY KEPT ON COMING. Every week brought more. Now that I knew what it was, in some ways it just got worse. Old women, young children, men who cried in my arms at the thought of leaving families behind. After a while, I could walk into an apartment and feel it. Cancer has a spirit. A vibration all its own. When I walked into a house where cancer was present, I felt the energy get dense and shadowy inside my body. My stomach got jittery and loose, almost like a caffeine high. And, when a patient was too far gone, when I'd only be able medicate and console, I'd feel the shadows blocking the doors and the windows. Shutters drawn on a house already in mourning.

There was one young girl that I thought I could save, a fifteen-year-old girl named Liberty. Her mother, Miss Julie, had brought her in the month before, screaming and cussing that her daughter was pregnant. Not only was she pregnant, but she had the gall to lie about it, too. To tell a bald-faced lie when she could plainly see the child's stomach growing bigger by the day.

Liberty said she liked school and she liked to read and she had a boyfriend, but she'd only let him hold her hand. She couldn't be pregnant.

The girl was telling the truth. I knew that before I'd even so much as taken her temperature. I could feel the growing shadows inside her, feeding on her. But I pretended like I didn't know and made an appointment for her at Memorial. Much to their surprise, I showed up at the hospital the next day and went in with them.

"I'm Miss Towns's physician," I told the other doctor. "Would it be all right if I stay and watch the procedure?"

"I don't see why not," the doctor said. And so I got my very first lesson on how to do a biopsy.

When the results came back, I put on my doctor's face and told the child and her mother that she had a tumor, not a baby, growing in her womb. By the grace of God, the tests showed that the tumor was benign. If we removed it, she'd probably be OK. Miss

Julie's face froze like a stone mask. She asked if we could schedule the surgery for the next week. The sooner the better. I hugged her very gently and whispered in her ear, "You didn't know. It's all right. You didn't know."

Slowly, very slowly, the mask cracked. She broke down in my arms. And I held them both, mother on one side, daughter on the other, for hours, until neither one had any more tears left.

STEVEN ASSISTED ME IN this operation. Because only minor operations were done in the office and all major operations at the patient's house, we showed up at Miss Julie's apartment two days before to prepare. She lived in a two-room, cold-water flat on the northwest corner of 125th Street and Eighth Avenue, right above the Borden's Milk sign. We brought our surgical lamps and batteries, because from 125th Street and above, the flats only had direct current. Most people made do with kerosene lamps.

A downtown train rumbled by as we set up the lights, and the power of it shook the whole room. Steven shot me a look. He knew what I was thinking. "Don't worry. It'll be all right. If a train comes by, just stop. Hold still until it passes."

Miss Julie lit the coal stove for me and I wrapped our dressings in brown newspaper. I put the package on a cookie sheet and left it to bake in the oven. By the time it was done, the dressings would be sterilized.

"Remember, don't open the paper at all, under any circumstances."

"Yes, ma'am."

"Where's Liberty?"

"Sick in bed. She hasn't been up and about much this week. I think she's in some kind of pain."

I walked over to the bedroom and knocked on the door.

"Come in, please."

The little room smelled rank and coppery. The odor surprised me. Miss Julie kept such a clean house.

"What's wrong, Liberty? Your mother said you've been weak. Not feeling well."

What a pretty little brown girl. She had wide eyes and shrunken cheeks, her hair falling out of its bun. I wouldn't have guessed her to be more than eleven. She still wore short dresses.

Liberty hid her eyes behind her hand. "I been bleeding, ma'am."

She pulled a paper sack from beneath the bed, and showed me a mound of blood-soaked rags stuffed inside.

"I been washing them every day but I can't do it fast enough."

"You tell your mother?"

She shook her head.

"Don't worry. I'll explain it."

I told Miss Julie that because of the tumor, her daughter had been losing large amounts of blood and I had her come back to the office with us so I could type her blood. My feeling was that Liberty would need a blood transfusion before this was all done. Luckily, her mother turned out to be a match.

On the day of the operation, I boiled our instruments in Miss Julie's washboiler while Steven set weights on the ironing board to keep it steady. That was our theater. We laid plywood across the bathtub to make a second operating table. Miss Julie would be our floating nurse until the time came if and when I needed to do a transfusion. I'd have to gauge it once I got inside.

Steven lifted Liberty up onto the ironing board and administered the anesthesia.

The first train came thundering by just as I made my initial incision. But I did like Steven said and held still. So still I didn't even breathe.

The tumor was the size of a hefty grapefruit. Miss Julie began to pray as it came out. After removing it, I stored the bloody gray mass in an oversized preserves jar on the chair next to me. I'd study it later.

"Miss Julie? I'm going to need you soon. Get ready."

Once the incision was sewn shut and Liberty had been bandaged, Miss Julie lay across the bathtub near her daughter. I inserted a syringe into her artery that was attached to a Y-shaped tube covered in paraffin. The other side went into Liberty's vein. In the center of the tube was a ground glass stopcock. I controlled the flow of blood by turning the knob of the stopcock, like a kitchen faucet. After a few minutes, I turned the knob until the flow stopped completely.

"That's enough, I think."

"How much time has it been?" Steven asked.

"I don't know. But it's enough."

We removed the syringes and left the two of them resting while we cleaned up and prepared to go. I even washed the dishes in the slop sink, swept the floor, and heated some food for them while Steven transferred Liberty back into her bed.

It was very late by then and I was tired, so Steven did most of the loading and carrying. On the way back to the office, he kissed my forehead and said, "We make an excellent team. Don't you think?"

"I do."

"You know, May, I love working with you. Once we get married, it'll be even better. Things will change, of course. Not that I'll ask you to stop working," he said quickly. "But I do think we should try to make more time for each other outside the office.

And speaking of getting married, you still haven't answered my question."

"Steven, I don't know when would be a good time. There's always so many things coming up at the last minute."

That wasn't the right thing to say. I'd made that excuse far too many times. His face crumpled in anger and disappointment.

"May, it's been more than two years now. I can't even get a date out of you."

"Soon," I promised. "Soon."

Steven pulled up to the curb outside our office. He got out, slammed his door, and then yanked open the rear door.

"That's what you always say. If you really don't want to marry me, then just—"

"It's not that."

"I'm not your father. I'm not any of your old beaus. I'm no one but me. But that doesn't seem good enough for you."

He dragged the lamp from the backseat and lugged it toward the door without looking back.

IT WAS A BEAUTIFUL, sunny Wednesday morning. By eleven, the streets were full. Men stood around everywhere—under the El, in the middle of the road, resting on car hoods and fire hydrants, catching some shade under the blue striped awning of the C&G Food Market on Lenox. They lounged in the doorway of Daniel's Bar and Grill, pushing up their caps and biting on the ends of cigars that they never smoked. Others walked through the street pulling empty wooden carts, looking for things to fill them. More than half of the men in Harlem were unemployed. And they weren't even calling it a depression yet. The world suddenly seemed full, teeming with broad-chested men looking for something to do till nightfall.

I walked from the office all the way up to 138th Street, right off Striver's Row. Just a moment alone to think. Steven wasn't speaking to me. Again.

The only thing he'd say when I cornered him was, "It's been four years now, May. How long am I supposed to wait?"

Honestly, I had no real reason. The thought of losing him made my chest hurt and my legs weak. But it seemed like I just couldn't do right by him. What hadn't the man done for me? He believed in me when others told me to my face that all I was good for was delivering babies and that I should leave the real medicine to men who could handle it. When all the hospitals kept slamming their doors in my face, he showed me another path that I could walk and still keep my dignity. Our practice had grown while so many others, including the Edgecombe doctors, were barely making it. Some had closed altogether. But the people came to us because they believed in us. They trusted us. They trusted me. Patients from all over New York and even as far as New Jersey and Brooklyn County came to see me. I didn't even have to go to them unless I wanted to. Steven had shown me the way to make that possible.

Even Mama had asked me the other day, "When that boy comin' to drag you down the aisle? It's been an awful long time, Ladybug. Pretty soon you gon' be so old the only wedding gifts you'll get will be matching canes and false teeth."

I owed Steven my mother's health. Because the practice was growing, I could finally afford to pay most of the bills. Mama, for the first time in her life, got to stay at home. The timing couldn't have been more perfect. Or necessary. Her heart had gotten weaker. She had less and less energy to do even the simplest things. Finally, at the age of fifty-three, my mother got to rest.

I rang the doorbell of a stately town house at the corner of Eighth. A young, pale-skinned man with a long, hooked nose and his tie hanging loose opened the door.

"Oh. You must be Dr. Chinn."

"Yes, I am." I moved to enter the house, but the young man didn't budge.

"Beautiful day," he said.

"Yes it is."

"Did you walk or drive your car?"

"I walked."

"You left your car on a perfect riding day like this?"

I knew what he was getting at. I'd had this conversation many times before.

"I don't have a car, sir."

"Oh," he said. He looked me up and down. "I see."

"Where's the patient, please?"

"This way. I guess."

Up at the top of the stairs, in a tiny room on the third floor, I found my patient laid out on a bare mattress in his underwear. Someone opened the window as far as it could go, but the little room was stifling. The old man on the sweat-soaked bed mumbled and turned his face to the wall.

"What's the problem?"

"Don't you know?" the other man quipped. "You're the doctor."

"I mean why did you call me? What are his symptoms?"

"He's having stomach problems. Really bad pains that come and go. Sometimes his arms and legs get hard and he can't even walk or clean up after himself."

"Is this the first time anything like this has happened?"

"No. He used to get sick a lot. Same symptoms. But that was a long time ago. Maybe ten or fifteen years. We thought he'd gotten better for good, but then last year he started having fits, throwing up, getting screaming headaches. That kind of thing."

"What's his name?"

"Richard Glass. He's my uncle."

I put my fingers on the old man's cheek and gently turned his face to me. When his watery gray eyes met mine, he began to shake.

"Don't be afraid, Mr. Glass. I'm Dr. Chinn. I'm here to help you."

Parenchyatous Syphilis, including Tabes and Paresis . . .

"I'm telling you, doctors. This is a case of a Negro with syphilis of the brain."

. . . occurs ten to twenty years after the initial infection.

"No. It is not impossible. Sir."

While Negroes are known to be generally immoral and tend to contract venereal diseases, including syphilis, at a much higher rate than Caucasians . . .

"I don't care what the textbooks says. Look at this man . . ."

. . . they are incapable of contracting syphilis of the brain. The Negro brain, being smaller and underdeveloped, does not have sufficient blood flowing through it to effectively carry the virus.

It took three doctors from Columbia, four from Bellevue, three from Harlem Hospital (including Dr. Crump, thank God) and three from Memorial to review my findings. Then it took them weeks to agree with my outcome.

But I was right. They had to change the textbooks, the means of diagnosis. I personally petitioned the city to build more clinics in Harlem. The syphilis rate was nine times that of any other part of the city. Not surprisingly, the mental ward at the Charity Hospital stayed disproportionately full. Now they knew that what they'd been calling the inevitable breakdown of the undersized Negro brain was, in many cases, untreated venereal disease. I was sure things would change now that they knew the truth. (My assumption turned out to be completely wrong, of course. The city refused every one of my petitions. At the time, however, I was hopeful. Certain and proud.)

"We should celebrate," I told Steven. "Let's go on vacation. I'll drive."

"You don't have a car."

"I know. I've decided to buy one."

"Good," he said. "Otherwise people will think you're either too cheap or too poor to afford one. No one wants a poor doctor. They wonder what happened to all his patients."

I went out and bought a brand-new, dark gray convertible Nash. My first luxury item ever.

We decided to go to Saratoga Springs. But the day before we left, one of Steven's patients had a relapse and needed emergency surgery.

"I think I'll go ahead, if you don't mind. I really need the break."

"That's a good idea," Steven said. "Telephone me when you get there and let me know that everything's all right."

When I started out early that Saturday morning, the sky was bright, soft and turquoise. The hills and the green-and-gold fields that rolled past made me feel like I was flying again. My heart soared.

The sleepy little town of Saratoga Springs had drifting fields, farms, and imposing Victorian houses that seemed like museums. I slept late three days in a row, not stirring until way after nine, and had coffee and crullers delivered to my room. Whether to have an afternoon of horseback riding or take in a motion picture at the town's only theater were the biggest decisions I made that week.

But then by the fourth day, the sky got heavier, thicker and sticky. Blue filtered into an angry-looking mass of dense gray clouds, the underbellies near black. The clouds roiled like the flames of a broiler. People boarded up their windows, brought the animals in from the fields, and locked them away. When the winds and the rains came, they whipped roofs off their foundations, up-rooted trees and telephone poles, smashed through bridges and overturned automobiles.

For three days after the storm ended, I couldn't get word to my mother. Eventually I got through to the phone in our office.

"Stay where you are," Steven said. "Your mother said that if I should hear from you, I'm to get the address of the place and come get you. The roads are too dangerous for you to drive by yourself."

The next morning, I was packed and sitting on my suitcase in the foyer of the inn when Steven pulled up in his Cadillac. He grabbed me and crushed me to him, kissing my hair, kissing my lips, examining me from had to toe.

Driving slow, we circled out of town, winding around fallen trees and gutted houses. At one point, Steven got out of the car and helped a group of men haul on ox carcass from the middle of the road. The countryside that had been so peaceful and pristine when I drove up had shed its insides. We passed animals and people, bloated from the river and the rain. We helped everywhere we could, but most of what we saw was burying work. After a while, I didn't want to see any more. I went to sleep.

When I woke up we were riding by the

WELCOME TO CONNECTICUT!

sign at the border. I shot up in the seat.

"Steven, where are we going?"

"I love you, May and I'm going to marry you. Right now."

"That's not possible. There's things we have to do first. Papers—"

"Not here. All you have to do is be willing to sign your name on the marriage license. We'll go to the same place that Paul took Essie. Remember? You told me about it yourself. They got married in one day."

"I can't marry you right now. My mother's not here."

"Then we'll have a second wedding and invite everyone to that."

"But what about my practice?"

"I never asked you to stop working. I wouldn't do that."

The sun was setting. It would be dark soon. Too dark to find my way home on my own. I panicked. I started to cry.

"Steven you take me home right now. I mean it."

He pulled the car to the side of the road and cut the engine.

"Look at me, May. Do you love me? At all?"

"Of course I do."

"But not enough to marry me."

"Love has nothing to do with it."

His spirit withdrew. Right then, at that moment. I felt it. Steven turned his face from me and looked out over the flattened hills of wheat.

"Wrong answer."

He took me home.

MAMA HAD DR. CRUMP waiting at the house when I came lumbering through the door. She threw her arms around me and hugged me and kissed me and spun me around, searching for anything that could possibly be wrong.

"Dr. Crump need to look you over, honey. Just in case. I'll be in the next room if you need anything, hear?"

When the door clicked shut, I hugged the doctor and told him, "I'm fine. You can go now."

"I could. But your mother would never forgive me."

He examined me thoroughly, noting every detail and asking questions. He treated me the way I treated my patients.

"So, how's Dr. Murray?"

I cupped my hand over my cheek. "Fine."

"He's a lucky man, I must say. You're quite the catch."

"No. That's not true."

Dr. Crump pulled my hand away from my face and stared at me.

"You're beautiful."

Then he went back to work. He examined me in silence until it was time to go.

"Perfect bill of health." He snapped his bag shut. At the door Dr. Crump turned to me and said, as if he'd just thought of it, "You know, May, I can take care of those scars if you want me to. There are some amazing new advances in reconstructive surgery that are coming out. If you like, I can work on you. When I'm done, your face will be like brand-new."

"Oh, no, sir. I don't even think about it anymore. I'm afraid I'd be a waste of your time."

"Well," he said, "the offer stands if you change your mind."

I thanked him and closed the door.

THE NEXT MORNING I went in to work. Steven had movers, some of the men from the avenue, loading his equipment onto a truck.

"I'm going," he said. "I'm not leaving you. I love you and I made a promise. But I think it's best that we have space between us. I've left some names inside of people you might contact to share the space. I'll pay my half of the rent until you find someone."

Then he walked away and left the movers to haul the rest of his

things on their own. I went into my office and sat down behind my
desk for the longest time. Somehow I missed the note sitting right
in front of me until the entire day had passed and I got up to go.
Inside the envelope was a card with a painting of a white rose on
the front. I opened the card. It was dated August 23, 1933, two
days before I left for Saratoga Springs, just before his patient
called. I'd missed it even then.

> *I live to let you know that you are loved beyond your imagination.*
>
> *Steven*

I closed the card and went home.

GOOD TO HIS WORD, Steven still came to see me as often as he
could. But his new practice had grown and so had mine. The
times between visits got longer and longer as our schedules got
busier. Now, other doctors all over Harlem, and even many white
doctors downtown, sent me their patients' tissue samples if they
suspected cancer. I'd do a biopsy and then pass the samples along
to Memorial if I detected signs of cancer. Memorial was the only
place at that time doing research on early cancer detection. I baf-
fled their doctors. They couldn't figure out how I diagnosed so
many cases. They still wouldn't give me privileges, but they called
on me whenever a case had them stumped or someone needed a
hand with work that could be done off premises.

Eventually, we got so busy that if I saw Steven twice a month,
it seemed like a rare gift.

One evening I was at home going over a stack of client files
when someone knocked at my door. A pretty young woman about
my height and build but a few shades darker stood in front of me,
twisting a silk handkerchief in her hands. She had an open, clean

face. Wide eyes and a lovely bow mouth without lipstick. Her straightened hair hung in fresh-pressed curls against her collar.

"Good evening. May I help you?"

The way she searched my face looked almost hungry. Ashamed. But then the woman swallowed and raised her chin.

"Are you May Chinn, ma'am?"

"Yes I am."

"My name is Lucille Brewer, ma'am. I'm a friend of Dr. Steven Murray."

My heart softened and sunk a bit. The room seemed to get warmer the longer she stood there, with tears in her eyes, staring in my face.

What did I expect? I'd done it to myself. I created this. It wasn't right to play the victim now.

"You're beautiful," I said.

Lucille took a deep, shuddering breath and smiled. "Not as beautiful as you. That seems to be my problem. I don't know how else to say this, so I'm just going to come right out with it. I love Steven, Miss Chinn."

"Call me May."

"Uh . . . OK. All right. I'm in love with Steven, May. And I need to be honest with you. I've never been in love like this before. He's wonderful and handsome and kind and gentle and successful and loyal . . ."

"I know, Lucille."

She laughed a little. "Sorry. I'm nervous. What I'm trying to say is that I want to be with him so much that I left my husband for him. But he won't marry me. He won't even so much as call me his woman 'cause he's promised to you. You two never broke off your engagement. So, I guess what I'm standing here asking is will you release him from his promise? Please. Otherwise, I don't know what I'll do."

This woman deserved to be happy. She knew enough to ask for what she wanted and, more importantly, to expect to get it. I could learn so much from her.

"You're a very lucky woman. I hope you'll be happy together."

IT WAS TIME TO let go. How long had it taken me to realize that? Long enough to lose Steven. My best friend. Long enough to find myself alone, no man, no children, very few close friends. It had taken me most of my life. I'd been so busy looking for answers in other people, studying their stories and expecting those stories to answers the questions about my life. I'd been so terrified of being confined to a small space that I'd created an even smaller one. For most of my life, I'd been so many different things to so many different people. But what was I to myself? That is what I needed to find out.

I scheduled my surgery with Dr. Crump for the day of Steven's wedding.

Everyone told me how beautiful the wedding was. Lucille got pregnant weeks afterward. When the pregnancy was confirmed, they came and asked me if I would be the godmother. I gladly accepted.

After six weeks, Dr. Crump announced me completely healed. It took another three days for me to get up the courage to look in a mirror. When I did, I found new, smooth skin, soft and clear. It didn't seem possible. I had a perfect face. It was so new, so crazy and unbelievable that I caught myself almost missing my scars. They were safe. Familiar. But they didn't belong to the woman I'd become.

It was time to let go. And I was proud of myself because I did.

Chapter 21

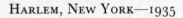

By the time the riot happened, Harlem had already been decimated. Cocaine. Wine and gin. Jobless men. Hopeless women. Disease. Soup lines that snatched the people's pride. Self worth for a full belly can never be a fair trade. The people had so many enemies.

Late one afternoon, the enemy took on form.

A young boy swiped something off the counter at the five-and-dime and tried to walk out of the store with it. The white sales clerk caught him, grabbed the child by the collar, and started slapping him around. Two other sales clerks joined in. The boy tried to escape through the front door but the clerks were on him too fast.

People saw what was happening and began to grumble. The grumbling got louder, sharper. By the time word reached Seventh Avenue, the boy had been beaten within an inch of his life. By the time it reached Lenox he was "probably dead," and when it'd circled back around the neighborhood to Eighth, everyone knew that the boy had been murdered in the street like a dog. The seething, frustrated rage, which had been brewing for so long over so many things, finally erupted.

Hundreds of people poured into the streets, screaming and chanting and cursing, throwing bricks through windows. The police fled. They barricaded themselves inside their precincts and called for the riot squad. That's when the looting started.

Trapped inside my office by the fires and the bullets, I could hear the people rampaging through the streets all night long.

By morning, my home had been devastated. Glass, broken furniture, trampled food, and unconscious men littered the streets. The smoke from the fires that had raged all night clogged the air like low-hanging mist. No business had been spared—department stores, clothing, furniture and jewelry stores, meat markets and bakeries. The owners, black and white, sat weeping in the burned-out husks.

The boy, I heard, had been found safely in his parents' apartment three blocks away. He'd escaped through the crowd, ran back into the store and out the rear door.

The world seemed unnaturally quiet that morning. Hatred spent, but nothing given over in return. I headed up the center of Seventh Avenue, sleepwalking, dead inside, warmed by stray fires, watching light play inside the smoke wafting from gutted homes.

Not that long ago, we were all so hopeful, ready to give our lives, our breath and blood for the Movement. And what had it come to? Besides an end.

Mama had slept in a chair by the door. I kissed her forehead to wake her.

"I'm safe. I love you."

Still half asleep, she nodded and staggered over to the couch and fell right back to sleep.

"Ladybug? That you?"

Tricks, I thought. *More tricks.* But then he called again.

I rushed into the room. The man had to be desperate for him to call out my name directly. "Papa! You all right?"

"Yeah. I'm fine. Fine as I'm gonna get till I'm dead, anyway. Just worried about you when you didn't come home. Your mother stayed up all night."

I stood in the bedroom doorway, dumbfounded. He couldn't have confused me more if he'd waved his arms and parted the Harlem River. How many years? My father had just said more consecutive words to me than he had in ten years.

"Come sit by me." Papa patted the edge of the bed. "I saw the fires last night. Heard all that mess goin' on down there."

He sighed. "Nothin's like it used to be. I'm an old man. Is it too much to ask for somethin' familiar?"

"No, sir."

"May, you're a smart girl. Just about the smartest girl I ever even heard of. It amazes me sometimes that you came from me. I hardly believe it. I been wanting to ask you something for some time now but I suppose I never had the nerve. But I realize now that if I don't ask, I may never. So come here."

Papa touched my cheek, the one where I'd had my scars, and then pulled me close and kissed me there. Just like he used to. He reached behind him and grimaced from the effort.

"What you need? I got it."

"No, girl. Sit back down. I can do it myself."

From beneath his pillow, my father slipped a worn, leather-bound copy of the Bible into my hands. He laughed.

"Don't look so shocked. Man about to die, he gets interested. I don't say that I agree with a lot of it, but I figure to at least be able to argue some of the main points with God if I have to. Now look here, girl. I want to ask you about this."

He pointed to a section of Matthew. I followed his bony finger and read:

By your faith, you will be healed.

"Read this over for me. Don't answer nothing now. I want you to think on it. Get back to me, Lil' Bit. We'll talk later."

We never did, though. Every time I tried to bring the subject back up, he shooed me away. I wanted for him to be impressed with me. I wanted to have a clear, helpful answer that could ease his transition and take back the years that we'd both wasted. But he acted like I was crazy. He'd shrug his skinny shoulders at my mother. "Lu, what this girl talkin' about now?"

That was OK, though. For the rest of the summer and into the fall, we did other things.

I left work early one afternoon and took my father to his favorite place from the old days: Ye Olde Barber Shop on 133d between Lenox and Fifth. It was a tiny shop where the old men swapped stories and told big, purple lies they all claimed to be able to prove. Wedged between an abandoned lot and a Laundromat, the place smelled of age and lather and cigar smoke. I sat outside on the step sipping a Coca-Cola while my papa and his cronies dished up the past as something worthwhile and fat and ripe.

After, we strolled over to Fifth and turned left. Between 133d and 134th, there was a place called Peace Shine where my papa got a shoeshine for 3¢ and some good conversation to go along with it. Again, I waited outside and let the men do their business. But I'd made sure to stick a couple of dollars in his pocket so he'd be able to pay for everything himself. On the way home, we passed the office where the government gave out food rations. The food line stretched almost the length of the whole avenue. Here in Harlem, like so many other parts of the country, soldiers with automatic weapons watched carefully as the food line crept forward.

They kept the peace and made sure that people got out of the line safely with their food. We walked in silence until we'd passed that.

The rest of that afternoon went wonderfully. By the end of it, we loved each other again. Neither of us said sorry, nor did we mention our past. We simply let it go. A modest, but a lasting peace.

Six months later, he died.

BACK TO WORK.

Now it was just Mama and me. She's all I had left. We played cards in the evening, went for walks by the water on the weekends. But never too far. She got tired so quickly. Nothing like the Lulu I'd known.

One afternoon, as we walked down Broadway, I caught a glimpse of a woman in a shop window. *Who's that woman?* I thought. *Oh my dear! She's lovely.* I walked a little closer, trying not to be conspicuous. She seemed so familiar. I had to know her. It wasn't until I got very near that I realized that I was looking at my own reflection in a shop mirror, which faced out the window and into the street.

"She's beautiful, isn't she?" Mama said, and kept walking ahead.

I stood there, staring, until the shopkeeper came out and asked if I was feeling good.

"I'm fine," I said. "I really am." And I hustled after my mother.

IN THE SUMMER OF 1942, Mama died. I came home from work one evening and found her in bed looking so peaceful and free. She hadn't needed me to tell her to go. She already knew.

There comes a point in grief where the feeling is so sharp, so acute that you can't even feel it. Where tears are an insult. People told me how strong I was. They told their daughters, "Look at Dr. May. You're going to be like her when you get big."

They didn't know.

At the funeral, it seemed like half of Harlem showed up to pay their respects to my mother. With a deep and sudden burst of regret, I realized that that's pretty much all most people knew of Lulu Chinn. She was Dr. May's mother.

Had my mother ever wanted anything for her life that didn't revolve around me? Had I ever asked her?

After the funeral, I moved.

Being in that old apartment, with her ghost sitting next to me, walking through the kitchen, asleep in the chair by the door, nearly drove me out of my mind. I missed her so much I thought I'd die. I couldn't sleep. I stopped eating. Some mornings I'd be so distracted that I'd forget to bathe and then I'd be embarrassed all day in the office, having to be in such close proximity to other people.

It had to stop. Something had to change. That's why I decided to move. I couldn't walk around, all alone, jumping in my skin every time the floor creaked or the neighbor's cat crawled across the fire escape through my window and rubbed against my leg. There were no other footsteps in that house and it was slowly driving me crazy. Crushing, mind-numbing questions kept popping up in the silence. How many chances had I been given to love? How often had I thrown them away? I'd been so desperate for approval for so long that I didn't know how to accept it when it came. If I grew old all alone, I had no one to blame but myself.

I rented an apartment and an office on the ground floor of the high-rise at 409 Edgecombe overlooking the Polo Grounds. Everyone from the DuBoises to the Aaron Douglases to the Walter Whites lived there. It was the most exclusive address in Harlem.

I could afford it now.

* * *

"COME WITH ME TO Alabama, May."

Dr. Crump sat in a shining leather chair in my new office.

"What's in Alabama?"

"Every year I sponsor a program called National Negro Health Week in Tuskegee. About fifty of us doctors from the North go down South to treat patients, hold seminars, share knowledge and that kind of thing. If you think you've had it tough up here, imagine what the Negro doctors in Alabama have to deal with. Most of them aren't recognized. They don't have degrees and they certainly don't have privileges. They just help people. Now you can help them. What do you think?"

"Do you think people will show up to hear what I have to say?"

Dr. Crump sighed. "Are you coming? I think the change of pace is very needed for you right now, wouldn't you say?"

I had to agree. I could feel myself slowly unraveling inside my skin. Something needed to change.

Three weeks later, my bags were packed and I was ready to leave for Penn Station. I opened the front door, set my suitcase in the hall, and dug in my purse for my keys. The telephone rang. I almost didn't answer it. But then I ran to the back inside just in time to reach the exchange.

"Hello?"

"Hello? Dr. Chinn? This is Dr. Maitland at Memorial. I just wanted to give you an update on your, patient, Mr. Jackson."

"Yes?"

"The lab results came back, and you were right. He has a malignant tumor. As his physician, we're recommending that you tell him to come into the hospital immediately."

I shouldn't have picked up the phone. Now this was going to be weighing on my mind all week long.

"Thank you, Doctor. I appreciate the call. I'll be in touch."

"Hold the line for a moment, Dr. Chinn."

"Actually, I was just on my way out the door—"

"This will only take a moment. There's someone here who wants to speak with you."

The phone rustled for a moment, changing hands, then a woman's husky voice picked up and said, "Hello? Is this May Chinn?"

"Yes it is. Who's speaking?"

"My name is Dr. Elsie L'esperance. I've been looking for you, Doctor. Your number is hard to come by around here. You'd think that wouldn't be the case with all the work you've done through this hospital."

"What can I do for you, Doctor?"

"Actually, I have an offer for you. I've started a clinic called the Strang Clinic. We specialize in early cancer detection, and I was looking for you to offer you a position as a clinician. We're affiliated with Memorial and the New York Infirmary. I hope this is something you're interested in."

My first thought was, *Wait till I tell Mama!* That's all I wanted. Nothing else was more important to me in that moment than to tell my mother what we'd done. I told Dr. L'esperance that I was definitely interested and as soon as I returned from Alabama I'd call her office for an appointment. As I hung up the phone, a wave of emotion hit me so hard it made my stomach cramp. I ran into the washroom and vomited in the sink.

Suddenly, I was so sick I could barely stand, but it wasn't sadness or loss. It wasn't fear. It wasn't even anger.

There was an energy, a radiance shooting through me, and I don't think I was at all equipped to handle it. It made me light-headed. It felt like my body could never expand to fit what was unfolding in my soul. I had so much inside me. All of it was me, good and bad. My life, my choices, my experiences. And I discovered all at once, as I leaned against the edge of the tub with my knees pressed into the floor, that no matter what it looked like, it was all good.

I was all right.

I was better than all right. I was worthy.

That thought sent chills through me. And, ironically, it had nothing to do with the phone call. The knowing inside me had preceded the phone call. But I hadn't recognized it as a knowing, a realization, until I'd set the earpiece back in the cradle. In an instant, it became so clear that I hadn't been offered anything that I didn't already have. And I could never be.

It had nothing to do with my patients or my new office. It had nothing to do with the plaques and degrees and citations and awards. It had nothing to do with the people who loved me. It had nothing to do with those who despised me. It had nothing to do with the lives that I'd saved or the people who'd died in my arms. It had nothing to do with being poor. It had nothing to do with my son. It had nothing to do with death. It didn't even have anything to do with my life.

I saw myself in that instant, unscarred and whole. Perfect, whole, and complete. I understood, for the first time maybe, that my *beingness* was worthy. The actions and the circumstances of my life didn't matter. It had everything to do with the intrinsic truth of who I was.

I am worthy.

Over and over, I created my mantra as a trinity of faith.

I am worthy.

Everything else just fell away.

DR. CRUMP LEASED A special train for the trip. It had heavy black wool curtains that had to be drawn as soon as we crossed the

Delaware state line. Black doctors and white doctors traveling together in the same car on the same train. Unheard of. Potentially deadly. But we were doing it.

Each time we stopped to pick up a doctor who wanted to attend the conference, the engineer was instructed to stop the train at the sidings outside the town. In the pitch darkness, the doctor would be ushered on board. The train engine would begin to hum again immediately and we'd speed off.

One time the train stopped outside a station at a place where there was no doctor waiting. Dr. Crump rushed to the front of the train. Even though I shouldn't have, I lifted the curtain.

Outside, a sheriff's car blocked the way of the train. A posse of others stood with him, some on horseback, others carrying torches and rifles. About sixty, maybe seventy white men in all. Everyone got still. We knew what would happen if they boarded the train. Many of us, especially the Negroes among us, wouldn't make it home.

Somehow I wasn't afraid. Those men couldn't harm me. I knew that even if they didn't.

We heard quick footsteps rushing toward us from the cabin ahead. One of the Colored men grabbed me, and then hands were all over me pushing me to the back of the car, behind the crowd, out of sight, covered by a wall of protecting bodies.

"We're moving. Everybody stay down."

"Dr. Crump, what happened?"

I heard the doctor laugh.

"The sheriff and the good townspeople heard rumors about what might be on board this train. So they came out to see for themselves. I stopped them."

"How?" someone asked.

"I told them the reason the train never stopped in a town was because it was contaminated. We had fifty men and one woman

inside, all of them infected with smallpox. I said they were welcome to step aboard and see. They, however, graciously declined."

Later on, people laughed. At the moment, the entire car
watched Dr. Crump silently, kind of in awe, I think.

WE ARRIVED IN TUSKEGEE in the early hours of the morning.
Negro farmers with horses and buggies, oxcarts and even a couple
of trucks met us at the railroad track sidings and whisked us onto
the safety of the campus.

When I awoke in the morning and walked out onto the quad-
rangle to join the other doctors, I saw the most stunning thing.

The entire hill leading up to the campus was filled with stretch-
ers. Thousands of people had come during the night, some, I was
told, from as far away as Georgia. They came in the dark, in carts,
on horseback, in cars and in rumbling trucks for the lame. They
rode and walked through the dark, even though the darkness
could be so hostile there. They risked all that they had because
they wanted to be healed.

I saw this and turned my head up to the sky and laughed. I
laughed with everything in my soul.

It had taken me so long to understand. How many years had I
searched so desperately for what was already mine? I looked
around at all the people who'd come so far because they believed
more than anything in wholeness. Some had come hoping that I
could perform a miracle of healing for them. But as I looked out
into the sea of faces, I understood that to perform a miracle meant
nothing. What mattered was having the courage to be the miracle.

How many years had it taken me to have the courage to really
live, to accept and embrace that one truth?

Love ran so deep within me that it became something new,
something much more than a feeling. In every face, every mo-

ment, every tear of gratitude, I expanded into a space of love in which all things existed as center and circumference, parts of me so integrated that they ceased to be aware of themselves. And yet they were always aware.

Who was it that said that when you surrender to life, it will roll in ecstasy at your feet? That's what it felt like in my soul. Like I could surrender and be whole.

Hope and surrender and clarity had merged within me into a love that answered me before I'd even spoken. Love had given me life. It rained down from above me and bubbled up from within. Finally, finally, on the cresting slope of a hillside at dawn, it became me.

Those people didn't need my help at all.

By your faith you are healed.

It was the most beautiful thing I'd ever seen.

Dr. May Edward Chinn went on to become one of the leading early cancer detection specialists in the country. She established a thriving practice and worked exclusively in Harlem, seeing it through almost all of its phases in the twentieth century. By the time Dr. May made her transition in the 1980s she'd delivered thousands of babies and saved countless lives.

Though the list of her awards, honors, citations and appointments would go on for pages, she never spoke of those things. Only of her patients. Her families.

"Oh, I had quite a time with that family." She'd laugh and then get lost in remembering. So often, Dr. May got called on to find jobs for the unemployed or homes for the homeless. She counseled marriages and reconciled parents with their children. All over New York City and all across the nation, her name is remembered.

The doctor lived quietly and alone, in the projects on LaSalle Avenue for all the later years of her life. Surrounded by her mother's antique furniture and her memories, Dr. May settled into retirement in the late 1970s. Her eyes had begun to fail, and the city had changed. Better to leave the job to the young people who'd come behind her.

Dr. May brought joy to all who knew her. She inspired faith in those who followed the paths that she first laid bare.

In these times, in this world that we've inherited, we sorely need more truth-tellers like her. Dr. May has my love and gratitude forever.

Kuwana Haulsey
September 11, 2003
Los Angeles

ACKNOWLEDGMENTS

This life is such an immense blessing. There are no words, written or spoken, that can begin to describe its beauty. I am so grateful to the Spirit that is alive inside of me, because it allows me to know that there is nothing else that could ever be as perfect, wondrous, beautiful or important as . . . right now. I embrace this moment, and all that it brings, as the perfect gift of God that it is.

To my family, I am so grateful for your love and support. These have been some interesting times. Your faith in me not only remains unwavering, but has grown stronger—no matter what I seem to get into.

Mommy, in creating Lulu, I had so much to pull from. I know that everyone thinks their mom is the greatest, but that's because they haven't met you!

Michael Harris—I love you with my whole soul. More than that, I appreciate you and all that you've brought into my life.

Rev. Dr. Michael Beckwith (oh wait, I mean Michael *Bernard* Beckwith) and my Agape family—you are such an incredible light. Your presence has helped transform this strange place called LA into my home.

I would love to list every person who helped bring this book to life. But there are too many people to possibly name. Know that even though I only name a few now, each and every one of you are in my thoughts and my prayers. To: Jacki Simone Elliott, Maya Azucena, Parvwattie Ragunandan (and my boys!), David Rotman—RSL and MFG, Mama Michelle Kemba Posey, Tanisha Hopson, Elena Eaton, Alexia Robinson and all of my fellow superstars at Alexia Robinson Studios, Mary Oyaya and beautiful Eshe—your love keeps me going. I am absolutely indebted to Deborrah Hyde for her medical expertise and her gracious heart and Pierre Peyrot for his off-the-hook language skills! Eileen Cope, you're the best agent ever!

During the last five years of Dr. Chinn's life, George Davis used painstaking research and hundreds of hours of interviews with Dr. Chinn to help her form the suppressed strands of memory into a coherent story. There were also a number of wonderful books that I was able to use to round out the research that went into creating this project. This list includes, but is not limited to: *The Portable Harlem Renaissance Reader,* edited by David Levering Lewis; *Their Eyes Were Watching God,* by Zora Neale Hurston; *Cane,* by Jean Toomer; *The Collected Poems of Langston Hughes,* edited by Arnold Rampersad; *Paul Robeson: A Biography* by Martin Duberman; *The Timetables of History* (new third revised edition) by Bernard Grun; and *Jazz: From Its Origins to the Present* by Lewis Porter and Michael Ullman.

I am so grateful for the invaluable contribution made by each one of you. God bless you all.

ANGEL OF HARLEM

Kuwana Haulsey

A Reader's Guide

READING GROUP QUESTIONS AND
TOPICS FOR DISCUSSION

1. May Chinn's father is adamantly opposed to her becoming a doctor, and he makes his opinion very clear to her. What about his race identity might have motivated him to feel this way about May?

2. In today's world, May might have been looked upon as interesting or special due to her mixed-race parentage, but in her time, her skin color was a source of confusion and shame. What specific problems did her race cause her internally, and how might these things be different or the same today?

3. Fanny is an instrumental part of May's father's life. How did learning about her change May's opinion of her father? Or did it?

4. Getting May a good education comes across as the driving force in Lulu's—her mother's—life. Is it surprising that Lulu was so dedicated to her daughter? Why or why not? Do you feel your mother had a similar driving desire for your life?

5. Many people influence May to change the course of her life. Consider the differences between Lulu's, Coleman's, Lila's, and Steven's inspiration for May to make choices.

6. Is there anything about May's talent for music that helps her in her studies to become a doctor?

7. How did May Chinn's decision regarding her baby affect her personal happiness? What sort of happiness did May look for in her life? Would you have made the same choice? Why?

8. Kuwana Haulsey makes Harlem come alive, almost as though it were another character in the book. How does place figure in May's story? Can you imagine this story having taken place in another city?

9. What is the difference between May's relationship to the musical world and her relationship to the medical world?

10. Ultimately, Dr. May Chinn becomes a pioneer in the cancer field, beating all odds. Choose three obstacles that May faced in order to achieve this, and discuss how she overcame them, and how we might translate these into tools for our lives today.

Read on for a look at

THE *Red Moon*

Kuwana Haulsey

Available in paperback from One World
an imprint of the
Random House Publishing Group

CHAPTER *One*

· · · ·   · · · · · ·   · · · · · ·   · · ·

SAMBURU, KENYA

THE MOON WAS RED on the night my mother died.

Fat, fairly bursting, as I remember, it rode so low in the sky that it grazed the backs of the leopards who hissed and spat and cursed it for interrupting the hunt. It caressed the thorny tips of the acacia trees, bending them, seeming to crush them with light.

Close to six years have passed since that night, and when I think on it, the moon is always the brightest image. I remember quite clearly my breath catching in a painful bubble in my chest as I stumbled out of the compound just after dark and looked toward the sky. For the rest, I must dig back far and dig hard, past the heavy sounds of weeping and swells of humiliated rage. The memories and images hide, season after season, deep inside the soul of my marrow.

But the moon is what I was speaking of. I had never before noticed it so red. It seemed to me to be crying blood. Perhaps this is how and when my fixation with my mother's blood began—on the night she died. To me, then, the red moon is death.

That night, I sat outside the manyatta as my father's other wives prayed in my mother's hut. I remember the manyatta as it was before my mother's passing as a world of singing women hidden away from all the rest of the world behind a fence. The thick, circular fence had been constructed from thorny branches of the acacia trees that dot the hills and groves of the highlands and that reached much higher than my short head. We kept our animals close in bomas opposite the low-roofed, bark-colored huts. Sometimes, late in the night, we even brought some of our sheep babies and our goats next to us in the huts, at arm's reach. That way, no lions could creep up on them as we slept, slipping through the fence and disappearing into the brush with their jaws full before any of us had even opened one eye. Outside that fence lay a vacuum of dead space, sulking and creeping like the leopards, immense and terrifying.

That night, I watched as the clouds began rolling in slowly from the south. Soon I could not tell where the earth ended and the horizon began. It all merged together, confusing me, lying to me. But for once, I convinced myself not to be afraid of the leopard's darkness. I sat down, closed my aching eyes, and invited the dark inside.

The hours passed, and when I opened my eyes, I found that the wind had pushed the clouds behind me out over the valley's edge. Once again, I saw the stars. They glittered violently against a rich indigo sky, bathing the plains and bushes, the distant forest and smoky mountains, in a pearly, cascading shower of secrets and light. When I breathed, the night sky breathed with me, soothing me, molding the white warmth of starlight like a clay cast against my skin. I settled into the night shadows with thorns pressing angrily at my back and waited.

My mother's co-wives and I had known since the passing of my Father that my mother, Nima, was also marked to die. Still, I prayed and watched and hoped that she would spare herself for my sake.

We all knew it wouldn't be long, and I wondered whether the prayers of the three other women's hearts were actually for Nima or if they were frightened of what her death would mean for them. She was the last wife and, therefore, according to tradition, deserving of little or nothing. And yet she, the outcast, had been the wife of my Father's heart and an unprecedented prize. They, the respected ones, had gotten the remnants. There was no sense of propriety or traditional justice in my Father's heart regarding this matter. There was only a love that, at times, even I couldn't understand. I knew only that my parents' devotion made me conspicuous, a target for the other women's children, my older sisters and brother, who were outraged in a way that their mothers could never express. And so no matter how I tried or coaxed or begged, their hearts refused to open to me. After a long while, even their mothers relented (Nangai and Nkaina, at least) and began loving Nima as well as they loved and treasured their own hearts. But my sisters and brother nursed a hate so old that they couldn't even remember it firsthand.

To the hut of my Father's first wife, Kedua, they would run, and she would stoke the withering flame in their minds. She would invoke the image of her dead sons, of all the dead children, until they were so real that even I, as I hid listening in the smoky shadows of her entranceway, could feel them breathing and gurgling in my ear. Kedua always mangled the story to make their deaths all the fault of my mother. Even after I was old enough and I learned the truth, the sound of those tiny ghosts rising from the past and flying up out of Kedua's mouth terrified me so that I always ran and hid under my mother's sleeping hutch. I covered myself in Father's brown-and-black bull skins (thinking that no ghost would consider looking for a little girl tucked away under the skin of a bull) and prayed to my dead brothers and sisters not to kill me. For in Kedua's stories, that was always the right and justified end.

By the time Nangai and Nkaina began bringing my younger brother and sisters into the world, I was already in school. So while these young ones never hated me, we were never particularly close, as I was often gone for months at a time. As hard as I try, I cannot remember a time when I did not feel alone. When I was not different. It was Nima who protected me, Nima who gave me worth. Nima who stopped my fear. And I hid behind her skirt or wrapped myself up tight in her lesso like an infant, so I could always feel her warmth. Her voice singing softly in the pale half-light just before dawn was the balm that soothed my spirit, even when we were far apart. But now Nima lay dying.

"Ngai inchunye ana nkerai naji Nima ichero marou lino lomelok lemeylo likatingaui." *God give this daughter called Nima the healing power that only you can give to people.*

Over and over they chanted the same inane request, until it began to sound like the bleating of a dying goat inside my head and I wanted to cry out loud but I couldn't. Perhaps that is not even what they said, only what I remember. Anything is possible. I make no claims to accuracy. I can only report my heart, which is flawed. But I do know that I passed nearly the entire night sitting outside that thick thorn fence, which had been built by the hands of my father's sons so long ago and which separated me from the huts and the animals and the people that were my world.

Sitting alone, shivering in the dark dust, I refused to dwell on these things. Instead, I stripped the thoughts from my mind as completely as possible and concentrated on things that I could see or feel and understand, like the night sky and the cold. Especially the cold. I wrapped my ragged brown lesso around my shoulders as tightly as I could. But it was cheap and thin, with holes the size of silver shillings forming all along the edges, and no match for the night air. The wind leapt and danced, numbing my bare feet and covering me in dirt and nettles. It bit into my thighs, climbing higher, growing stronger in the dark, and carrying with it the sharp odor of sickness that wafted out of the smoke hole in my mother's tiny hut. The smell, mingling with the stale scent of goat meat and cloves, merged again with thin trails of smoke and hollow voices, drifting up then spreading out, catching the cold night by its throat.

If only I could speak.

The chanting got quieter, and I could tell that my mothers were tired of waiting. This death was long in coming. I hated them then, stupidly and without consequence, because I was too much of a coward to do anything about it. I didn't understand them or myself. I only knew that they planned to give my mother over to Lowaru Nyiro. He knew and was waiting close by and laughing at me.

Soon after the moon reached its apex, I saw him. He ran, crouched low to the ground, with hungry, powerful strides, his sleek, rippling body weaving in and out of the moon shadows across the plain. He stopped dangerously close (as though he was taunting me), lingering between two stubby cactuses directly ahead. With his head cocked to one side and his jaw slack, it seemed as if he was tasting the air.

"Not this night, Lowaru Nyiro," I whispered and let the wind carry my thought rather than my voice on its back. "Not this night. We have yet time."

The beast, sensing my thought, sent back his own.

No, I have time, he told the wind as he rolled out his long tongue and yawned and stretched insolently.

No hurry. I'll wait. Plenty of time . . .

Then, suddenly, he bolted, disappearing into the blackness of the brush. But I could still feel his gleeful eyes as he stalked, hiding behind the night. And somehow I knew that his thoughts were of feeding.

ABOUT THE AUTHOR

KUWANA HAULSEY is the author of *The Red Moon*, which was a 2002 finalist for the Zora Neale Hurston/Richard Wright Legacy Award for Debut Fiction. Born and raised in New York City, she graduated with a bachelor's degree in journalism from Rutgers University magna cum laude and Phi Beta Kappa. Haulsey has led seminars for the PEN/Faulkner Foundation in Washington, D.C., and at Rutgers University. She has also taught writing at UCLA and Agape International. She is an actress and currently lives in Los Angeles. Visit her website at www.kuwanahaulsey.com.